Cath[illegible] Doug Taylor series.
Field [illegible] Doug Taylor series.
Guar[illegible] DI Doug Taylor series.
The [illegible] of John Pye's service with Staffordshire police.
The Vampire of The Villas is a short story and is the author's own true account of the death of a man who believed in vampires.

Some events as outlined in 'Endnotes' are factual.
Cover design by Mark O'Leary

Dedication

In Memory of Ossie Dennis

A knight of the road.

Thanks folks, couldn't have done it without you

Gladys Pye

Charles Rae

Nick Tucker

Kevin McNulty

Mark O'Leary

Guardian
Of
Lies

John Pye

ONE

Wednesday 13th March 1991

KIM HARDING looked down from her rain speckled bedroom window as the funeral cortege rolled to a stop at the kerbside. Blinking away the tears she turned to the mirror for one last check on her appearance. Of course the emotions would well up but she didn't want to spoil her make up at this early stage.

Doug Taylor bowed his head as he stepped from the landing through the tiny doorway. His tight-lipped smile was added to a raised-eyebrows expression. He'd made the two hundred mile journey from his home in the Midlands to Kim's apartment in Tedham, near to Exeter the day before. His career as a detective inspector with Staffordshire Police was now on hold for ten days – a last minute leave application. This was a difficult time for Kim. She was going to need his support.

A hint of crisp white shirt cuff peeked from the sleeve of Taylor's dark suit as he fiddled with a cufflink. 'Okay?' he asked quietly. 'The hearse and funeral cars are here.'

oOo

Thirteen Years Earlier

Tuesday May 9th 1978, Porton Down, Near Salisbury

A milky film sealed the woman's eyes into her dead face. The glistening twinkle of life had been exchanged for a fixed and unseeing stare. A blue plastic tarpaulin separated her hideously contorted corpse from the bare concrete.

A large tent had helped to hide the scene from prying eyes overnight. It covered both the body and the car from which the two men had struggled to extract her. The arrival of another bright May morning allowed the powerful lights inside the tent to be switched off, but failed to lessen the horror.

Night time guard duty on the gates to Britain's Chemical Defence HQ was normally boring but such a description could never fit this stint. The three soldiers had watched transfixed as the two silhouetted figures went about their work through the small hours. The eventual sunrise ended the ghoulish shadow theatre.

'Keep your fucking mouths SHUT,' said the Sergeant in his usual no nonsense style. The order came as the soldiers' tour of duty ended. It followed on from a Captain's stern reminder of their obligations under the Official Secrets Act. The threat of a jail term reinforced the words.

Inside the tent the two men continued their work at a glacial and meticulous pace. Each new step was only taken after complete agreement. It was as though their very lives depended upon every move they made. They knew better than anyone that this was indeed the case.

Crooked and grasping, the body's posture mimicked a scene from a horror movie. The arms pointed skywards, locked out rigidly as though seeking salvation. Wrists remained cranked back at a ninety degree angle, fingers and thumbs still gripped a steering wheel, no longer present. Mrs Eleanor Thornberry had retained her final in-life posture with the macabre accuracy of a Pompeii body cast. A typical road accident victim could never embrace that concluding moment of death long enough for rigor mortis to freeze frame the actual end in this manner. Gravity would make the body sag, loosening the grip of the fingers causing the arms to drop. Other outside interferences would normally have played a part. The poor woman would have been pulled from the vehicle and laid flat whilst attempts at resuscitation were tried. That hunched partial sitting position would have been lost long before rigor set in. But this was no road accident and the deceased was not worthy of the pity implied by the phrase "poor woman".

Attempts at resuscitation were never a consideration. The checking for a pulse and lifting of the eyelids would have been akin to a death sentence for any would-be Good Samaritan. The two men knew with complete certainty that she was dead. They also knew that even in death she would remain the most dangerous human being on the planet for a considerable time.

The younger man was forty-three and highly qualified. His scientific training had incorporated work on human corpses and so he was familiar with the condition of rigor mortis. Microbiology though, was his particular discipline. His professional concerns were with the manner in which the woman had died and the actual ingredient which had killed her.

His colleague, at fifty-seven was senior to him and infinitely more experienced in everything to do with death. Andrew Prestwich was a pathologist. The initial awful scene on view to the men through the car's windows had stopped them in their tracks. Their joint knowledge of the substance with which the woman worked amplified their fears many times over. The precautionary eight hours before opening the driver's door had allowed the body to become set in its ways. It also permitted the two experts to calculate the levels of toxicity remaining within the vehicle. The car's windows were closed and so the lethal cargo remained inside. Thornberry's BMW 323i was almost brand new but no car is completely airtight.

So extreme was the hazard that the high-tech, orange coloured protective outfits the men wore were necessary even before that initial door opening. The nuclear, biological and chemical (NBC) suits complete with helmets and filtered breathing cocooned the men inside their own environments. A probe forced in through the car's rubber window seal still showed lethal levels even after many hours.

The urine stained driver's seat and vomit coated windscreen evidenced the horror of the woman's last thirty seconds. Her car had not even made it from the staff car park within Porton Down's Microbiological Research Establishment. It had come to rest at low speed against an on-site lamppost with its wheels churning at the tarmac until the engine stalled.

Thornberry died within that one minute following contact with the lethal toxin which still swirled invisibly inside the car. Her safety belt kept her fastened into the seat whilst muscle contraction maintained her grip onto the steering wheel. The convulsive fit initiating this was triggered by contact with the world's most deadly substance – the nerve agent, VX.

An airtight body bag lay nearby, one of several kept in stock in case of such an unlikely event. Its design and production was an undertaking which the microbiologist had directed along with his normal duties. The largest size available though, did not cater for the woman's awkward final pose.

The hours the two experts had already spent on site meant that they were well overdue for toilet breaks, rest and refreshment. The timeout would also allow for some necessary contact with the outside world and for compliance with important bureaucratic and legal requirements. In-suit showers and further naked showers would be completed before this could be started.

The police and Coroner needed to be informed and under normal circumstances would be invited onto the campus to take over the enquiry. But these were NOT normal circumstances.

oOo

Kim Harding glanced through the landing window as she started down the stairs. The overcast sky darkened by the minute as a depressing drizzle of rain dragged the mood unyieldingly into the predictable setting for a funeral

oOo

The colour drained from Wiltshire Coroner, Harold Winton's face as he listened to the pathologist's account. After giving a 'no-interruptions' instruction to his secretary he unlocked his safe and withdrew a box file. Its lid bore a label: *Porton Down – Special Orders.*

The involvement of the police on this case would be all but non-existent, save for a person to person conversation between Winton and the Chief Constable. The backing given to Winton for these extraordinary powers came in the shape of several high powered signatories to a document kept within the box file. The Home Secretary's name topped that list.

Acting upon Prestwich's telephone testimony Winton made his decision. He removed his half-moon spectacles to give them an extra polish as he accepted the inevitable. 'Thank you Andrew,' he said replacing the glasses. He cleared his throat as though preparing for a speech. 'I agree with all your findings and declare that the death be treated as CODE ZERO. Only personnel acting with your permission can play any part in the investigation. On the grounds of public health only those people specified by you can have access to the death scene and exhibits.'

The identification of Mrs Thornberry, her time, date and certification of death, would all be supplied by Prestwich and corroborated by his colleague. The cause of death again, would be provided by Prestwich, who had the required status of being a Home Office approved Pathologist. His findings would be limited to the results of subsequent tests made upon samples taken at the scene.

Prestwich's post-mortem examination would be only as thorough as he deemed was safe to carry out. A full, normal, post-mortem was unthinkable due to the deadly concentrations retained within the lungs and body fluids. There would be no cutting and slicing on a mortuary slab. No weighing and close examining of internal organs. No opening of the cranial vault with the small circular saw that pathologists use. His findings would be drawn entirely from the circumstances and the test results taken on site. The risk of death to other parties was extremely high. Winton needed no lectures on these matters; he'd considered such an event on the day he took up office as Her Majesty's Coroner with jurisdiction over Porton Down.

Prestwich would issue a death certificate and Winton would make an order for immediate on-site cremation as soon as he received the paperwork.

Thornberry's senior status within the Government operated Microbiological Research Establishment was a fact well known to both the pathologist and the microbiologist. They were team members with her. They were friends and like minds, or so they had thought. She was a microbiologist herself, specialising in a British military project christened "Purple Possum".

The Rainbow Codes system from which Purple Possum had been so named was a scheme used to disguise the highly sensitive nature of certain research ventures. Although discontinued years before, a handful of the more insidious government defence undertakings continued to be known in-house by these colour code nicknames.

Purple Possum sounded like an agreeably acceptable alternative to the spine chillingly more accurate Venomous Agent X or VX. It was also the most insidious of the 140 stratagems encompassed by the Rainbow Codes that Britain would ever enter into. Its production in Britain ceased in 1969 following the UK's signing up to *The Biological and Toxin Weapons Convention*. That agreement allowed for the manufacture of only tiny amounts of such potions. Even these could only be used for necessary scientific research and defensive measures.

Thornberry's work on Purple Possum had centred upon antidotes to the toxin and to the efficiency of NBC suits and storage vessels. There had even been a degree of testing of its effects upon living animals. In keeping with the strict international constraints though, only minute quantities of VX could legally be produced by her for all of these trials. At least that should have been the case!

TWO

PEOPLE'S PERCEPTION is often that police officers are impervious to emotions. The daily dealings with death and trauma and the injection of spontaneous black humour evidences the notion. This is a myth; the black humour is nothing more than a defence mechanism. The relatives and friends at the funeral though, would expect Kim Harding to be her usual calm, collected, in-charge self. She had after all been a detective for some time now with several years at the sharp end of policing behind her. All of that mattered for nothing. This would be one of the hardest days of her life.

oOo

Dr Thornberry's work sheets and day diary confirmed her stated intention to drive down to a subsidiary government laboratory in North East London. The pleasant sounding address, 61 Colindale Avenue London NW9, suggested nothing other than perhaps a desirable London family home. It was in fact the HQ of CAMR (The Centre for Applied Microbiology and Research).

From here she headed some parallel research and made regular visits. Her workload was spread between the two establishments and with apartments both in Salisbury and London she juggled her lengthy days a little more comfortably.

She often legitimately signed out certain items of laboratory paraphernalia from Porton's stores for use by fellow scientists at the London lab. The movement of chemicals in this fashion was forbidden but the delivery of harmless equipment was acceptable. On the afternoon before her death she signed out: *Two plastic flask trays, forty aluminium flasks and two new NBC suits.*

The documentation appeared in order and the reason given simply read: *Required by CAMR Colindale.* It was not a comprehensive explanation but adequate under normal circumstances.

An hour and a half passed before the scientists clambered into a set of brand new NBC suits and awkwardly trudged back to the tent. The risk of contamination was so high that the usual safety protocols, stringent as they were, had been intensified for this particular affair.

Normally the suits would be used up to ten times before destruction. A powerful shower treatment would take place after every laboratory procedure. A large tear-off patch across the shoulders declared the number of uses from 1 to 10. The removal of the final patch number revealed the wording:

EXPIRED DO NOT USE – INCINERATE.

The suits were proven to be good for up to fifty re-uses, but policy dictated no more than ten in normal circumstances. The dangers associated to this incident dictated even more caution. The first suits had already crackled to destruction in a high temperature incinerator.

Prestwich's solution to the problem of the contorted body was born out of necessity and his idea bypassed the usual scientific approach. He forced Thornberry's arms down to waist level with the pressure delivered by his right boot. The resulting sickening *snap* came as the humeral head of the upper arm bone dislocated from its snug fit in the glenoid socket of the scapula. The upward bent knees and sitting position of the pelvis received equally nauseating brute force. This unorthodox procedure allowed the corpse to be installed into the bag.

The heavy duty plastic zipper delivered a slow purring rasp as it drew along its full length. An additional precaution of applying a bead of builder's silicon sealant gave a belt and braces afterthought. The bright orange body bag did not portray the sombre, respectful tone given by the black everyday model. Words of warning in thick black lettering endorsed the gravity of the situation:

HAZARDOUS MATERIAL – DANGER OF DEATH. DO NOT OPEN.

Thornberry's corpse, now safely sheathed no longer presented an immediate threat but residues left within the car seemed likely to remain extremely dangerous. An onsite torching may even be a consideration for safe disposal of the almost new car.

Prestwich and his colleague first needed to discover how the woman became contaminated. This was important both for the continuing work at the facility and for the benefit of the subsequent in-camera (held in private) Coroner's inquest.

The results of the initial tests bewildered the microbiologist. These had been taken with the body still enclosed in the car. The readings for VX were not only positive but off the scale, hundreds if not thousands of times higher than expected. The man shook his head as he checked and rechecked the latest test results. 'This is incredible,' he muttered from inside his helmet. 'It's only slightly down from when we first opened the car door.'

The two men kept the secret of the high readings between themselves during their mid-operation break. They needed to establish some facts on the issue before divulging anything.

They were now back in complete isolation from the outside world, even though nothing more than the tent's thin fabric formed that barrier. It was then that they opened the car's boot and discovered the terrifying enormity of the situation.

oOo

Kim stopped in the hallway and turned to the mirror to check her appearance again. It was a delaying tactic. Her blurred view through the front door's opaque glass showed the black outline of the hearse parked on the road. She needed a few more seconds.

oOo

The four bespoke Porton Down plastic crates lay stacked, two side by side with another two on top. Twenty equally bespoke aluminium screw top flasks stood upright in each crate making eighty flasks in total. A briefcase sized, locked, metal document container with Thornberry's name Dymo-taped to the lid lay on top of the crates. The consignment looked similar to many delivered by Thornberry to the London satellite laboratory. The puzzle which sprang into the minds of the two scientists though, was that there should only have been TWO crates of flasks.

The two top crates did not require much muscle power to remove. They comprised of nothing more than plastic, foam rubber, aluminium and air. But when the younger scientist gripped the side handles of one of the lower crates a different story was clear. Prestwich knew from his colleague's stance and interaction with the crate that this was far from a repeat performance. The way his arms jerked down showed his unpreparedness for the heavy weight. The two men looked at each other, their horrified expressions visible through the visors as the dreadful realisation came. Another twenty, sloshing, liquid filled flasks also filled the last crate.

If what they thought could possibly be true and the flasks did all contain VX an appalling scenario existed. One pinhead sized droplet onto the skin would kill a man in seconds. There was enough here, in individual doses, to kill millions of people. Again the two men took advantage of their currently isolated situation to consider their next actions. The microbiologist lifted out one of the flasks and delicately removed the screw cap. A brief check with the electronic probe followed this and once again the meter's needle flicked off the scale.

If it had been possible for the microbiologist to have scratched his head he would have done so. 'These flasks are all tightly sealed, so how the hell has she been contaminated?' he said. 'If it had happened whilst she was putting the crates into the boot she wouldn't have made it as far as the driving seat. She would have been writhing in agony on the concrete before even opening the driver's door.'

Prestwich's helmeted head nodded in agreement. 'Well she did make it to the driver's seat. She also fastened her seat belt, pushed in the keys, started the car and engaged first gear.'

'Yes,' his colleague answered. 'But she managed no more than thirty yards before the car came to rest against the lamppost. By that time she was dead or as good as.' His visor misted over as he gave a long sigh of frustration and then came to a part conclusion. 'So it must have been vapour rather than skin contact and that fits with the huge readings.'

The car boot discovery prompted a closer look inside the vehicle. On the rear seat lay two folded, vacuum packed, NBC suits complete with cumbersome built-in over-boots and respirators. These were part of Thornberry's legitimate consignment. The ZERO shoulder patches proving their unused condition was clear to see.

The younger man lifted both packs upwards against the seat rest with his gauntleted hand. His puzzled expression showed that he'd seen something else. The thick black crepe soles of two more boots attached to another complete suit also lay on the seat. This one was not packaged. It was not new. The peel-off sticker across the shoulder showed the words:

EXPIRED DO NOT USE – INCINERATE.

Both men looked at each other with worry showing on their faces. Their vision now focussed onto the sole of one of the boots and the glistening oily film which oozed from the rubber.

oOo

Kim linked arms with Taylor as they stepped through the front door – overcoats and gloves against the cold damp morning. A slow intake of that cold air joined forces with a slight but determined raise of the head. The phrase "chin-up" was apt.

A jumble of thoughts passed through Kim's mind as she took the few steps towards the gleaming black limousine parked behind the hearse. She gripped harder at Taylor's arm as she caught sight of the polished beech wood coffin in which her father Geoffrey Fry now lay. Recollections of her childhood swamped her; so much humour, generosity and kindness; all that good advice and help. Geoff Fry had been everything that a dad should be and more. The death of his wife, Kim's mum, twenty-five years earlier from cancer had been a blow. It made his duties as a parent harder… There were always puzzles though.

THREE

December 1990 Barrow-in-Furness, Cumbria

AT NINETEEN years of age and a mere ten stones and four pounds Dennis Huddlestone was ideally suited to his current job. His employers, Daniels' Air Ducting of Barrow-in-Furness, Cumbria, on England's north-west coast had specialised in their trade for over forty years. With the ever increasing importance of air conditioning, hospitals and factories had created a profitable and regular trade base for the firm.

One of Daniels' most lucrative contracts since 1970 had been the Vickers Shipbuilding and Engineering firm (VSEL). Its factory, close to the town of Barrow was responsible for the building of nuclear powered Polaris submarines for the Royal Navy. From 1986 the factory also saw keels laid down and work commence on the new giant nuclear deterrent subs of the future – Trident.

Huddlestone's occasional visits to VSEL excited him. This was only his third but he'd been happy to alter his rostered day off to take up the opportunity. The security requirements were extreme and Huddlestone proudly sported his photograph ID tag clipped onto his overalls. He, his workmate and even all their tools had undergone stringent searching and scanning before entry onto the site.

Their view of the shop floor deep below the concrete access apron where they stood was spectacular. It would get even better as they commenced their climb up to the top of the five stages of scaffolding erected for this job. The sight of the partially completed submarine, Vengeance, became more extensive as each upwards step was taken.

With a rolled up copy of the duct plans gripped between his teeth, Huddlestone's colleague, George tramped up the ladder behind the young man. George showed casual disinterest in the myriad figures swarming around the gargantuan hull. He'd seen it all before. The sound of the heavy machinery, the metallic clangs and bright blue flashes of arc welding machines were not that thought-provoking to him. He'd spent a lifetime working in and around shipbuilding.

Eighteen metres further the pair reached the top platform which gave them access to a rusting louvered metal grating fastened to the aging brickwork. George made easy work of the four equally rusty looking bolts which held the cover in place. The two feet square black opening reverberated a hollow echo back at the men as they peered inside.

The stretch of aluminium ducting led away into the darkness. Its grimy pop-riveted panels still showed traces of silvery reflection against the power of George's torch beam. The duct's route travelled through half a metre of brickwork and then onwards across the huge supporting roof beams of a separate smaller shop floor.

With the plans unfurled George pushed his spectacles up the bridge of his nose and checked out the direction and length of the duct. The paperwork indicated that it turned to the right before reaching an outside wall fifteen metres further on. From here fresh air would be drawn, courtesy of a big, three phase electric fan to flow into the vast submarine workshop.

The men's earlier work proved that the motor was operating but had failed for many years to do its job effectively. Other parts of the ventilation system compensated, but now an additional malfunction elsewhere had forced a proper repair.

Some earlier attempts to fix the problem, almost certainly a blockage, had failed miserably. The huge fan and ducting should have been easily accessed from a metal fire escape type stairway attached to the brickwork outside. A lack of maintenance over the years led to the steps being condemned. The cost of erecting scaffolding up to this towering section of wall and around the decaying staircase would have been astronomical.

Daniels Air Ducting proposed a cheaper, quicker fix. They would send in their secret weapon from the other side to remove the problem. Young Dennis – the secret weapon – had become known at the firm by the rather unkind nickname of "The Crawler".

George's torch light shone along the channel. The men hoped to catch sight of an obstruction or some deformed panelling which might be the problem. The distant silhouettes of a couple of small objects were clearly not the cause. The time had arrived for Dennis to earn his wages by doing that job which no other employee of Daniels' could do. He slotted his wheeled crawling board into the duct and gave a nervous smile as he wriggled off the scaffolding into the hole. He had found from experience that he could move along by lying on his back and using his hands on the top panel to propel himself forward. It was a slow, claustrophobic undertaking and he knew he would have to struggle free from the board when he eventually reached the corner.

Dennis's miner's style helmet lamp reflected back from the top panelling a few inches above his nose as he trundled along. His colleague let out a reel of nylon rope which was attached to the board as Huddleston's size nines retreated further into the gloom. The voice of the other man occasionally chimed out: 'Okay Dennis?'

All went well until the board wedged against something. It was a couple of feet before the right hand turn and Dennis knew he'd have to dismount and turn over anyway. He managed this and then squeezed his wrist around under the front edge of the board to get at the obstruction. He'd recovered some peculiar items during his two years with Daniels at different locations. This would often be stuff left behind by workmen installing the system originally. Various tools, a hat, a packet of Woodbines and even a Tupperware box filled with ancient sandwiches, had been some of Dennis's discoveries.

When his fingers gripped the cylindrical metal object and he sensed its sloshing contents he'd been sure it was an old can of pop. With some difficulty he brought it around and into view allowing his helmet lamp to play onto it. The aluminium canister was sturdy and rigid, nothing like the hairs-breadth thickness of a pop can. Its red screw-cap and grubby pitted surface gave away that it had some age to it. The logo printed on its side showed a black skull and crossbones on a yellow triangle. It registered a little concern in Huddlestone's mind but not enough to interfere with the job in hand. He set it down into the corner of the right hand bend and eased himself forward.

From the plans he now expected to find the motor fitted into the outside wall. He caught some slender glimpses of daylight through the blades of the fan and even the louvres of the metal outside wall grille. But the large mound directly in front blocked the duct almost completely. Whatever it was had become jammed tightly. How such a mass came to be there at all seemed a complete mystery.

Dennis shuffled a little closer. The narrow shaft of bright daylight through what could be seen of the grille only hindered matters. He took hold of part of the obstruction and gave it a tug. It came away in his grip like old rotted cardboard. A cloud of dust hung around the handful as he realised that in another life, years before, it had been clothing. His fingers squeezed a little harder and he became aware of a stick-like centre. He turned his head to shine the helmet lamp onto the handful and in doing its beam moved across the mound.

A wizened, mummified face stared back at him from the brittle remnants of a denim jacket. Dried, black-pea eyes were set deep down inside sunken sockets beneath a mop of dusty dark hair. The stretched open mouth formed a wide "O" filled with angular discoloured teeth and edged with potato-crisp-thin lips. Dennis's horror was so intense that his diaphragm became temporarily paralysed. His desperate gasps for breath resulted in little more than a rhythmic clacking sound. He started a manic backward scramble using the toes of his boots. His dinner-plate eyes widened some more as they stared at the shrivelled human hand with jutting wrist bones which was still clamped in his fist.

It seemed unfeasible that so many memories could be grasped in the moments it took to step inside the funeral car and shuffle for comfort on its leather seats. Kim fixed her eyes onto the back of the driver's headrest as the car started to move slowly forward. More thoughts churned – echoes of laughter from the like-minded banter she shared with her father. The weekend sailing trips out on his small boat. The glum face she'd always pull when he broke the news that he would be working away again. Aunty Doreen's efforts to quickly bring a smile back to her cheeks as they waved him off from the window with her favourite Enid Blyton book tucked under her arm.

FOUR

Wapping, East London January 1991

THE NEWS room of the Daily Herald occupied the second floor of its Wapping, East London headquarters. Reporter Benedict Cappelli's desk was one of many laid out into regimented lines.

Cappelli briefly looked up as he smoothed out a slightly crumpled single sheet of paper. The melee which surrounded him was the norm – the usual daytime battleground. A bustle of bodies mixed with the din of intermingled conversations, impatient shouts and ever ringing telephones. Beneath it all rattled the underlying clatter of fingers on keyboards.

Cappelli bumped forward slightly on his wheeled desk chair as a filing cabinet was roughly shifted from one corner to another. The spotty faced youngster in charge of the load muttered a half-hearted apology before returning to his dream-world ambition of becoming a reporter.

An unknown hand annoyingly ruffled Cappelli's hair from behind. 'Mornin' Benny,' said an equally unidentifiable voice. Cappelli ignored the assault and casually leant back in his seat as a paper airplane inexplicably drifted in from somewhere. An unpleasant smell caused him to exhale and give a disgusted waft of the hand. He looked up in time to catch the raised eyebrows and grin of the culprit – a fellow reporter from three desks down with form for similar offences.

None of this was conducive to prolonged concentration, but it was a way of life to which he was now accustomed. News reporters, features reporters, picture editors, fashion reporters, assistants and many other faces and names all called the half-football pitch sized space their workplace. Goldfish bowl offices surrounded the central area on three sides. Glass panels and doors separated these additional hutches and their occupants from the main scrum. The architect's plan allowed for the best use of the space but also combined a raised editor's office at one end. The one-way glass allowed the current incumbent, Kelvin Stewart, to scrutinise the tenants of the desks and offices without having to lift his backside.

The letter which Cappelli smoothed was in reality little more than a note. It formed part of the large batch of paperwork dug from his drawer in his latest attempt at tidying. Most of the correspondence already re-examined had ended in the wastepaper bin. A vague recall of his first sighting of this particular document now came back and he doubted that its fate would be different.

Although born in the Dales of Yorkshire Cappelli had some roots back in Sicily. The swarthy Roman tinge which loitered within his facial features belied the fact that he spoke not a word of Italian. He was though, fluent in Yorkshire with an accent akin to that of the cricketer Geoffrey Boycott.

His employment at the Herald as a staff reporter started eighteen months before and followed on from his two and a half years as a freelance journalist. His newspaper beginnings lay back in his teenage years in the offices of the Yorkshire Post. The eventual title "Reporter" brought with it several good stories. These included a corrupt planning official, a senior police officer's double life as a bigamist, a sex scandal at a children's home and a few more besides. It all added some extra nous to his reputation.

His successes had fuelled his urge to move down to *The Smoke* where he believed it was all happening for freelance journalists. Sadly his thoughts that he had *arrived* gradually ground to a halt. The monthly payment on his Stepney flat and the leap in the overall cost of living from Yorkshire to London took the edge off everything. The funds to pay up-front money for information disappeared, as did his wife.

With no contacts and no new leads his independent future looked bleak. His application for a staff reporter's job with the Herald was submitted with crossed-fingers. The charity of editor Kelvin Stewart undoubtedly played a big part in his appointment. Stewart recognised Cappelli's style and drew a comparison with his own world of twenty years before. But Stewart showed some caution and issued warnings – Cappelli was a known risk taker.

Following a successful stint at the newspaper's Bristol office and some work in the south of England Cappelli had settled into the routine of Wapping. He'd investigated and written up a number of high profile stories, but still searched for the real cracker. Throughout the early months of 1990 he centred his attention on a story connecting disc jockeys and TV presenters with under age sex scandals. It proved to be a nightmare. He met a brick wall whenever the cooperation of the authorities was needed.

From late June and through July he put the case on the back burner and earned his corn with another story holding the national interest. Two veterinary surgeons had been targeted by the militant arm of the Animal Liberation Front. Bombs were attached to their private vehicles and sheer luck intervened to prevent a loss of life. The explosions came days apart. One attack happened at the Wiltshire home of a vet based at the Chemical Defence Establishment at Porton Down and the other was on a Bristol housing estate. A small child in a pushchair was seriously injured in the Bristol incident. The resulting outrage of the public kept the story alive.

Cappelli published several articles on the case with appeals to the public hoping that this might lead to the criminals responsible. It led to phone calls and a few letters. Cappelli passed the more interesting ones on to the police. The usual crank calls and correspondence also came in. Some of these attempted to get a foot in the door by using the bombing case as a soap box for their own gripe. Several appeared to be attempts to get free cash for un-newsworthy or even fictitious stories.

The letter in front of Cappelli seemed to fit one or the other of these criteria. It had lain in his desk drawer since June – a full six months. Originally he'd discounted it and his opinion had not changed. 'More shit,' he murmured. The writer clearly had no information on the particular ALF case at all. Cappelli decided to consign the sheet to the bin with the other garbage, but then found himself reading through it one more time:

Dear Mr Cappelli

I have read about the little baby in Bristol and the Animal Liberation people trying to kill the woman who worked at Porton Down. Some strange things happened there – I should know. I would be happy to talk to you about this.

Edward Olivant (Corp – retired British Army).

The investigative journalist inside Cappelli stirred as he began to reconsider the letter. Porton Down's reputation for newsworthy stories went back decades and it was no secret what had gone on there. It was accepted though, that Britain no longer produced chemical and biological weapons. The possibility of other countries using such weapons however, justified Porton Down's existence and maintained the need for their expertise.

Cappelli sat back in his chair attempting to put things into perspective. The in-tray on his desk evidenced his mountain of current stories. Whatever Mr Olivant thought he knew was almost certainly old news by now. If there ever had been anything newsworthy, it must have been bled dry long ago. His eyes took in the Salisbury address and telephone number written in the top right hand corner. The sight of his overfull in-tray generated a shake of the head as he tried to dispel that glimmer of curiosity stirring inside him. He hovered the letter over the waste bin for a moment. Could it even be remotely possible that a phone call to Mr Olivant and a ninety mile journey to Salisbury would be worth the effort?

oOo

Kim remained silent as the funeral cortege made slow progress through Tedham village. She took a deep breath as the church steeple came into view above the trees. Taylor's broad hand pressed down onto her own. She sensed the caring tight-

lipped smile he'd made even though her unblinking eyes remained straight ahead. His idea to drop his own car off earlier that morning at the church was another considerate gesture. He understood that she'd want a little extra time after the ceremony and wouldn't want to keep the driver hanging around.

oOo

Edward Olivant's emaciated frame barely depressed the Dralon cushioning of his two seater sofa. The fifty-two years old former soldier was unwell and weighed in, by Cappelli's estimate, at perhaps seven and a half stones. His now scrawny neck sat inside a crisply ironed and clean shirt collar which had become several sizes too large in recent times.

A photograph sat propped upon an occasional table. It showed a fit, robust and grinning Olivant in a British Army uniform. The stripes of a Corporal were visible on one arm whilst the other linked in firmly with the attractive woman at his side.

The mug of tea which Cappelli now sipped had been delivered to him ten minutes earlier by that same woman. Mrs Olivant had gained twenty years since that photograph. She had also fared a great deal better in the manner of physical fitness and future prospects than her spouse.

The brief phone conversation between Cappelli and Olivant had prompted an immediate journey to Salisbury.

The still proud Olivant searched for dignity with an apology as he released a blood flecked gobbet from his mouth into a handkerchief. 'Sorry,' his voice pronounced with a back of the throat rattle indicating that there would soon be a repeat. 'Good job you came when you did… doctor's only given me another few months at most. I'd forgotten the letter, thought I wasn't going to hear from you.'

Cappelli remained quiet as Olivant delivered an introduction to his story. Clinking dishes in the kitchen created the only other noise as Mrs Olivant went about her chores.

'Why now Ted?' Cappelli said – first name terms had been quickly agreed upon. 'You realise that the Official Secrets Act still applies to you even after all these years?'

Olivant's collar remained stationary as the neck within shifted position along with his two slow head nods. 'Of course,' he said. 'The fact is though, no matter what the doctors say, my illness was brought on by the voluntary tests I put in for at Porton Down. Most of us did them. We were young and invincible. Or so we thought.' Another discreet wipe of the mouth followed before he continued. 'Wrong there weren't we! We got paid a few quid along with a week's leave. Several of my mates who did the tests have died or have poor health.'

Olivant paused as he reached for the face mask of a small oxygen cylinder which stood upright close to his arm rest. There was a hissing sound as he fiddled with a valve and sucked in for a moment. Colour quickly returned to his pallid cheeks. 'I'm not bothered by the Official Secrets Act. They can't prosecute dead men. I've not asked you here to harp on about my illness or what caused it. I am bitter mind you, but it's all water under the bridge now. A lot of other people have tried and failed. No... other things happened at Porton Down and were all neatly brushed under the carpet. Some of those things you might find interesting enough to make a story from. I won't be around long enough to see it happen though.'

Olivant swivelled to glance at the kitchen door and adopted a listening pose – head to one side, eyes at an acute angle, ensuring his wife would not overhear. The muted tones of Jimmy Young on a transistor radio dismissed his worries. 'So maybe your editor could see his way through to looking after the wife if it turns into a story.'

A yellowed newspaper lay on the coffee table between them. Olivant's eyes glanced down at it.

From the earlier telephone conversation Cappelli knew that the newspaper had some relevance to their meeting. The retired soldier struggled forward in his chair and pushed the tattered broadsheet across the polished table top.

Cappelli picked up and clocked the date of the faded edition: Thursday 25th July 1978.

He ran his eyes briefly over the headlines: *Test Tube Mother Has Girl.*

Olivant watched Cappelli's eyes. 'No, not that story. It didn't make the headlines. Take a look at page five.'

Cappelli leafed through and landed on the item.

An archive photograph of Porton Down's front gates with a barrier pole and armed sentries either side sat beneath a headline:

Scientist Dies in Nightmare Government Lab Accident.

A sub heading read:

Secret Inquest details released after questions in Parliament.

The reporter folded over the top half of the paper as he quietly read through the two column account. It was obvious to him that the summary of the inquest proceedings had been strictly censored before publication. It was short on both names and detail.

Olivant let Cappelli take his time, not commenting until he lifted his eyes and sat back into his chair with the newspaper across his lap.

'What you've read…' Olivant said. 'Contains the bits and pieces which can't be denied… The car... the dead scientist… the cause of her death… an accidental contact with the nerve gas she was researching. It doesn't include that she'd been stealing equipment from the site on the pretext of delivering it to another lab. It doesn't include the fact that she'd been purchasing dangerous chemicals illegally. It doesn't mention the inexhaustible supply of cash that she had in two other bank accounts under false names.'

Cappelli sat back upright and shuffled closer to the edge of his seat with every "it doesn't" prefix which Olivant used.

'How come you know all this? he said.

A grin came to Olivant's haggard face. His receding gums showed red against long brown teeth – a consequence of months of strong pain killing drugs and antibiotics. A cough and another use of the handkerchief heralded an insightful laugh. 'You mean with me being a mere Corporal?'

Cappelli gave a nod.

'I was the driver and bag carrier for one of the Captains. He acted as a go-between… MI5 and Special Branch.' Olivant took another look at the kitchen door and lowered his tone. 'A bit of a dickhead. So far up his own arse it was untrue. I worked the switchboard… when it suited… just our department. I often used to listen in. Sometimes he'd leave a few papers around, and some of it made fascinating reading. The woman you see named in the paper… the dead scientist Thornberry… they'd known about her for a while. They'd given her a code name. Rosa… Get it – Thornberry?'

Olivant's cough hawked up more mucus and a slight delay followed before he continued. 'They were ready to arrest her… probably that same day, but she died. They wanted to follow her and find out more. There was something else in the car that worried them. I mean seriously worried them. I didn't get to know what it was, but security got tightened afterwards.

Cappelli gave an involuntary shake of the head at the story. It all seemed incredible and yet Olivant sounded truthful. 'I see that only a few names are mentioned in the story… the Coroner, the dead woman…Thornberry, and the pathologist Andrew Prestwich. No other names are given.'

'That's right. I never knew any of the boffins by name. They'd all got DV high security passes. I'd seen the pathologist before… a regular face, but I only put a name to him after that newspaper story. He must be getting on now, if he's even still alive.'

Cappelli stayed leaning forward throughout this last part of the conversation. He lifted the newspaper from his knees and folded it in half. 'Can I take this?'

FIVE

Wednesday 13th March 1991 (The Present Day)

THE BROAD radial tyres of the hearse and funeral limousines crunched into the gravel of Tedham village churchyard and came to a stop. An umbrella was held up by the driver to protect Kim Harding from the mizzle of rain as she stepped out. A queue of overcoated mourners were still filing in through the church door, thoughtful smiles and respectful nods at the ready.

Less than fifty yards away a burglar's gloved fist thumped down lightly onto a screwdriver handle. The action sent the tool's tip in between the plastic beading and the frame of a window. A firm downward press separated the seal, lifting the beading half an inch from its slot. A sharp upward pull with both hands ripped the beading entirely out.

It was noiseless, as was the relatively easy removal of the remaining three beads. The screwdriver, the only tool needed, again came into play as the burglar pressed it into the crevice where the glass panel met the frame. Nothing other than the bonding effects of harsh weather and strong sunlight now held the panel in place. An insignificant *click* followed the slight pressure of the screwdriver as the panel parted company from the frame. The gloved hands then lifted it free and carefully propped it against the outside brickwork.

The bungalow backed onto woods and so the man's broad daylight approach went unseen. The procedure took less than five minutes – no mess and no noise. Externally glazed units had become a thing of the past as too many burglars had cottoned on.

Inside now, the thief took a careful peek from behind the drawn curtains of the front window. It gave him even more confidence that he would not be interrupted. 'Piece of piss,' was his gruffly spoken comment as he viewed the full car park of the village church almost directly opposite. It looked like a large congregation.

The church service took forty-five minutes. It was customary to spend a little time at the graveside and thankfully the rain had stopped. Typically the two gravediggers would be held back fifteen minutes before they could get on and finish the job. The traditional handful of soil sprinklings usually served as a cue that the time had arrived for the wake. Time for a beer and some pork pie. Time for reminiscences and funny stories.

It normally worked, but two solitary figures remained long after the rest of the mourners had gone. No amount of wristwatch checking or discreet throat clearing produced the hoped for outcome. Another funeral was set to arrive on the car park soon and embarrassment lay on the horizon for the cemetery workers if schedules were thrown out too far.

Kim Harding, attractive, tall and mid-thirties stood pale faced and red eyed in the gloom of the mid-March afternoon. A biting minus two degrees wind chill had followed from the earlier rain. It persistently tugged at the dark shoulder length hair which had been hair-gripped beneath a fashionable black tam. She looked up at Doug Taylor and felt his hand give her own a slow and gentle squeeze. His caring expression succeeded in prompting the preliminary paces back to the church car park. The thuds of shovels of wet earth being sent down into the grave became rhythmic as the couple paused alongside the single remaining vehicle. Taylor dug into a pocket for keys but then stopped and drew Kim toward himself pressing his palms lightly either side of her face.

'You okay?' He questioned as he dabbed a kiss onto her forehead.

She nodded slowly and climbed into the passenger seat.

'Guess this makes me an orphan now,' she said fastening her seat belt. It was an attempt at normality – light-heartedness even. The wrinkled forehead and quivering bottom lip wrecked the endeavour.

'Do you really want to go back to the pub?' Taylor said.

She gave another nod. 'Yes, they'll all be waiting. Anyway, I must do it for Dad… he liked a drink. He'd expect me to be there.' She lifted her eyes as they exited the car park and stared over at the neat bungalow almost directly opposite. It was her father's own home – curtains still drawn as a mark of respect. A slight shake of the head followed as a few more memories flooded back.

Geoff Fry had been fit and well until two years before when he was diagnosed with angina, a heart condition. His illness was not considered of particular concern as long as he kept stress out of his life and ensured that his tablets stayed close by. Kim had found him lying in the lounge. The angina tablets spilled on the carpet suggested that he had been trying to stave off a severe bout. The dislodged telephone handset implied an attempted call for help.

A Crown Court case in London had kept Kim away from home for several days. She'd firstly put the constant engaged tone from the off-the-hook telephone down to a line fault. But after repeated attempts worry set in and hastened her visit. The horror of finding her dad would be hard to get over, despite so many similar tragedies encountered during her career as a police officer.

Taylor kept his eyes on the road ahead as he spoke. 'I feel bad mentioning it right now, but any thoughts on the future yet?'

Kim had doggedly avoided the issue of a transfer from her job as a detective constable with Exeter CID up to Staffordshire to be with Taylor. Her fondness for her dad had been the main sticking point and his heart condition completely halted the idea. Taylor bit down on his lip as his words tailed off. He knew he was premature with the question. Kim's father was hardly buried but the proposal by Staffordshire's Chief Constable to Kim of a transfer with promotion directly to Detective Sergeant was rare in itself. Her courage and initiative on the last two cases she'd worked with Taylor had endeared her to several of the Staffordshire police chiefs, as well as drawing herself and Taylor closer together. Her own immediate boss at Exeter, DI Ken Grainger, gave her a glowing report with the recommendation: "more than up to the job". The deal wouldn't stay on the table forever though.

Taylor had also been offered a job move, a promotion of sorts, albeit not permanent. The suggestion would move him up the ladder half a rung to take on the role of Acting Detective Chief Inspector for the Stafford Division. It was a good stepping stone to the next rank and as a detective post it was something he'd agreed to.

Kim kept her eyes fixed straight ahead as Taylor's question on her own future drilled into her consciousness. 'We'll talk later.' She said as they pulled onto the pub car park.

A sea of sympathetic, smiling faces greeted them as the door to the pub's lounge opened up. Kim did her best to return the smiles and enter into the pleasant conversation. Stories from the past were being related by a group of Geoff Fry's old school chums against the bar. Kim recognised some of the faces. It was good to see them laughing over their antics so many years ago.

Various relatives planted kisses onto Kim's cheek or squeezed her hand as a show of support.

Aunty Doreen and Uncle Tom insisted on an introduction to Taylor. 'So this is Doug then.' Tom said thrusting out a hand. 'Heard a lot about you from Geoff.'

'Nothing bad, I hope.' Taylor responded.

'On the contrary Doug…'

The pleasantries continued as Kim made her way around the room chatting with relatives and catching up. She also got to know some of the people that she'd not met before.

'Lovely chap… your dad,' said one unknown face. The seventy-odd year old shook Kim's hand warmly and added his free hand in a patting motion. It gave the gesture some added tenderness. 'I met him through the pub quizzes…in this very room.' The man's twinkling smile and kind remarks helped lift Kim's spirits. 'Such a clever and humorous fellow. We always won when Geoff turned up.'

Kim passed from one group to the next, shaking more hands and delivering the occasional kiss to the cheek of a relative. She'd made contact with most of the guests before she spotted a wheelchair positioned tightly in against a table. The occupant was eagerly chomping his way through a large plate of buffet food which had been selected for him. Kim puzzled for a few moments over the vaguely familiar features of the elderly gent before recall from her childhood selected a name and title.

Dr Andrew Prestwich delighted in being called "Uncle Andy" by Kim as a young girl. He was a colleague of her father with no proper family connection, but a real friend who Fry held in the highest esteem. Kim's meetings with him as a youngster happened rarely, but often enough for her to remember the pleasant natured chap. Geoff Fry did his best to keep in touch with Prestwich and after retirement paid him the occasional visit at his Salisbury nursing home.

Kim watched the old man from across the room for a few moments. She remembered the distress caused to her dad by his friend's mental decline after dementia started to get a hold on him. "Such a clever man," Fry would often say. "Tragic how this dreadful condition is affecting him. Short term memory failing rapidly".

A lady, no doubt Prestwich's carer, sat in close to him and was trying her best to keep the gent comfortable. Without doubt she knew no one at the gathering and Prestwich's own condition didn't make matters any easier. Kim watched a second longer before strolling over. She doubted if anyone apart from her would know about the old chap.

'Uncle Andy,' Kim said as she got down to her haunches alongside the wheelchair.

Prestwich turned his head, eyes wide as though startled and with remnants of cheese sandwich adhering to his chin. He fixed a stare onto Kim, a furrow of puzzlement entrenching his forehead. The confusion only lasted seconds before the bushy grey eyebrows lifted and the face transformed into a sunshine smile. 'Kimberly?'

'Yes Uncle Andy… not seen you for years. Thanks so much for coming. Such a long way for you to travel.' She applied a kiss to his temple and felt buoyed by the old man's response. *Perhaps his condition wasn't as bad as she'd expected.*

'Oh it's no distance. My, how you've grown. Is your dad with you? I haven't seen him for a few days.'

The carer made a resigned, apologetic smile to Kim as Prestwich resumed his sandwiches, now seemingly oblivious to any conversation.

'Sorry,' the lady whispered in a voice just loud enough for Kim.' She eased out of her chair and the two women stood to one side for a private chat.

She introduced herself, 'Janice Hopkins. I'm a nurse at Salisbury Leigh where Andrew lives now. I hope that hasn't upset you.'

'No Janice, I understand the situation and in a way I knew what to expect, but it caught me off guard a little when he remembered me so quickly.'

'Yes, a lot of his long term memory is still there but as you can see that's not the case with anything recent, although some things stick. He was upset about Mr Fry's death. He insisted on coming to the funeral but then it slipped from his mind within hours. I've reminded him several times what today is about and it seems that he's forgotten again.'

Kim took a chair alongside Prestwich and tried to strike up a conversation. It was surprising how readily his mind could still grasp some of the more pleasant and important incidents even from decades ago. 'Does your dad still have that little boat Kim? He'd often describe the weekends away with you. It sounded great fun.'

Kim played along, and in a way the chat uplifted her. Uncle Andy rattled away as though her dad would appear at any moment. She visualised the way he used to carry two full pint mugs of beer in each hand. That straight-backed bending of the knees he'd perform which allowed him to deliver the consignment down to the table without spillage.

'Geoff always got the first round in,' Prestwich said, as though he'd read her thoughts.

Janice pulled a puzzled face at the seemingly out of context remark. She then made a raised-eyebrows smile at Kim. This was all par for the course with Andrew's condition.

'Sorry I didn't get in touch with your dad recently,' Prestwich said. He leaned forward and patted down onto the back of Kim's hand. 'Very sad news that he'd died Kim.'

Kim looked at Janice surprised at the sudden lucidity. Janice repeated her raised-eyebrow smile. She'd seen it so often.

'Lost my dammed address book you see… well it's gone anyway… a burglary.' Prestwich twisted around to catch Janice's eye.'

Janice gave a nod of confirmation. 'Yes,' she said. 'Andrew's address book has gone missing... all his phone numbers and addresses.'

'Oh that's awful Uncle Andy, I know how I'd be if I lost all my contacts… a real pain to get everything back again.' She looked around to see that Taylor had joined the group and now stood at her shoulder.

Kim introduced Taylor to Prestwich. 'Doug's in the police same as me Uncle Andy.'

Prestwich cocked his head upward to view Taylor and at the same time pressed down onto the armrests of his wheelchair easing up to his feet. Kim looked over at Janice, unsure of the wisdom of this, but Janice gave an approving nod. Prestwich still had some use of his legs.

'Nice to meet you Doug,' he said, extending an open palm to Taylor. 'Do you think you'll catch them? I could do with that address book back… bloody thugs.'

Taylor was at a disadvantage with no prior warning on the man's condition or even his identity. 'We'll do our best sir,' he said, quickly making some sense of the situation and hoping that his response would fit.

Janice explained the story to Taylor whilst Kim kept Prestwich occupied with pleasant chit-chat. 'Yes he's certainly remembered that incident Mr Taylor. A break in at the home a few weeks ago and a few pounds stolen from his room. They did make a bit of a mess as well… drawers out, cupboards opened. The kind of thing you see every day I expect.'

Taylor listened and sympathised at the same time. 'Yes nothing's sacred anymore… old peoples' homes, kids Christmas presents. We've even had churches burgled.'

Janice made a nonchalant expression. 'Thing is I don't think they took his address book. I think he lost it a few days before the break in. I remember because he had us turning the place upside down looking for it. He seems to have decided to blame it on the burglar though.'

It was half past seven when the couple arrived back at Kim's apartment in Tedham. The funeral wake had gone as well as could be expected and a few tales from relatives and neighbours had lifted her spirits, even if only momentarily. It passed through her mind that it had been a rather poor show from her father's old work associates. After thirty-six years as an executive in a branch of the National Health Service and a mere twelve months retirement behind him, the solitary appearance of Andrew Prestwich was dire.

I'm going to take a shower Doug,' Kim said as they entered the lounge. 'Maybe we can talk about my transfer… get yourself a drink'

Taylor kicked off his shoes and poured himself a Laphroaig single malt from Kim's drinks cabinet before settling back in an armchair. He'd managed another one before she'd reappeared – dressing gowned and rosy cheeked.

'You want one?' He asked, lifting the glass.

She shook her head. 'You know I can't stand the stuff, it smells like TCP. I only keep it in for you. No I'm okay. I had a large glass of wine at the pub. Anyway must keep my wits about me… don't want you talking me into anything.'

SIX

THE COLD chill as Kim opened the front door to her father's bungalow the next morning gave the first clue. With the heating on timer the place should have been warm. The steady draught of air sweeping in through the missing window panel in the lounge had defeated the boiler's efforts completely.

'Something's wrong.' She said as she stepped into the hallway with Taylor close behind.

She was soon sitting head in hands on the sofa surrounded by the mess left by the intruder.

A lone detective, a familiar face, arrived on the doorstep within half an hour of Taylor's telephoned report. DC Reg Timson, a close colleague of Kim had also worked with Taylor on a border crossing case nearly five years before.

Timson offered an open right hand to Taylor as he crossed the threshold. 'Inspector… sorry to hear about this,' he said as their warm handshake separated. He turned to Harding. 'Kim, my love… on top of everything else, you must be fed up.' He gave her a hug.

'I can do you a coffee Reg,' Taylor offered. 'I won't be disturbing any evidence, doesn't look as though the bastard's spent much time in the kitchen. Oh, and you know my rules, I'm off duty... it's Doug.'

Timson gave a nod. 'Thanks Doug, coffee's good… black no sugar. SOCO will be here shortly.'

The trio took a stroll around the property. All three were experienced in the subject of burglary, but Timson's local knowledge over several years would provide a sharper edge to this particular crime.

The completely removed double glazing panel sat neatly propped against the brickwork outside along with the plastic beading. 'Seen this MO before… a while back mind you.' Timson paused before adding more. 'Hate to say it… and I'm sure that this has gone through your mind already, but why was the house targeted?'

Kim guessed Timson's theory and agreed. 'Dad's death notice in the paper and the funeral details. The scumbag was screwing the place when we were in the church. He knew he was on safe ground.'

Taylor's expression gave away his accord with the idea. 'Yes, we should have known better, it's a common ruse up north as well. You just don't think about it when it involves yourself.'

Timson gazed around the lounge, taking in the scene: scattered papers, opened drawers and cupboards. He pointed at the row of ornaments on the mantle shelf. 'Couple of Capo Di Monte pieces unless I'm mistaken. A nice piece of Moorcroft and some silverware on the window sill. He's even pushed that to one side to climb in. So why hasn't he taken it?'

Taylor looked at Timson. It made sense; these easy pickings could have been offloaded for cash to an unscrupulous antique dealer within hours. 'If he's good enough to get inside so easily he's no beginner. Look how he's searched all these drawers and cupboards… all this paperwork he's been through.'

A knuckled rap came against the glass of the still ajar front door. A female voice followed. 'Hi WDC Hewitt scenes of crime.'

Kim greeted the young woman in the hallway with a smile. 'Hi Angela, thanks for being so quick.'

Hewitt returned the smile but her forehead showed the sympathy she felt. She placed her bulky bag of equipment down onto the carpet. 'Now let's see if we can find something to identify this toe rag.'

Timson introduced Hewitt to Taylor who was the only unfamiliar face to her. The woman then started her work, taping, fingerprint dusting and photographing.

'Made a damn good search,' she said as the flash of her camera coincided with its clicking shutter. 'Woollen gloves,' she advised as she teased some barely perceptible fibres from one of the window's discarded beadings. She nodded up at the wall hanging painting above the fireplace – askew from its correct position. 'Is there a safe Kim?' she asked.

Kim gave a firm shake of the head. 'No.'

'Certainly seems to have been looking for one,' the woman said as she snapped a couple more photos.

An hour and a half went by before the pair were left to tidy up the mess. Kim busied herself with the strewn paperwork and polished away the SOCO's aluminium fingerprint dust marks. Taylor put his DIY skills to use on the damaged window temporarily restoring it almost to its former state without too much difficulty. Half past five arrived before he came back in through the kitchen door. The quilted body warmer he'd donned for the repair job barely kept out the March chill. His frosty breath still showed as he returned the spray polish and duster into a cupboard.

Kim was seated at the kitchen table with two mugs of coffee at her elbow. She pushed one across as Taylor took the chair opposite. She tapped a biro down onto a piece of notepaper. The intention of making a list of stolen property along with an estimated value was a difficult one for her. She'd cursed herself for not removing the cash from her dad's wallet days ago. She knew there had been sixty pounds in it and had even taken the money out and counted it. For some reason she had pushed it back inside and even returned the wallet to the top of the fridge where Fry habitually kept it. To her, at that time, when the emotions were running high it seemed right. It was his stuff – his money.

It looked as though the sum total amounted to the sixty pounds along with a few knick-knacks. A pair of decent scissors had been taken from a special wooden storage block on a kitchen worktop. She had to think hard before pinpointing the gloves from the hallway. The fact that her dad had been a creature of habit jogged her memory. She'd bought him the brown leather gloves as a Christmas present. They were Aspinal make and expensive. The home for these gloves was a particular hook on the coat-stand behind the front door.

Mr Fry's tweed trilby remained in place on the same hook but the gloves were missing.

The vacant space on the occasional table in the lounge drew her attention to the absence of the electric clock.

'It was mains powered,' Kim said. 'But with a rechargeable battery in case of power cuts.' She pointed to a nearby wall socket and added, 'he had it plugged in there. I think it was a free gift with something, so it can't have been worth that much.'

Timson's earlier suggestion that other stolen items might come to mind during the clearing up process made sense. She'd given the same advice out to many burglary victims as a detective herself. With the boot now on the other foot it wasn't so easy. The bungalow had been a home from home for her over the years. She even lived there for several months while her divorce slowly and painfully moved along. Nevertheless she was damned if she could pinpoint any other missing property at all.

Taylor took a sip at his drink. 'Anything else?'

She shook her head. 'Clock, gloves, scissors and the sixty quid.' Her eyes automatically drifted over to where the wallet lay open in the centre of the table. Its leather looked worn and shiny with age. Flecks of silvery fingerprint dust were now ingrained forever into the stitching.

Taylor picked it up and ran his broad square thumbnail over the edges of the plastic bank cards in a side pocket. 'Burglar never took these and yes I know he'd also need a PIN number. But there's a matching cheque book in here and a signature to copy on the card… weird. Not like any thief I've come across before.'

He pinched the corner of one of the cards between finger and thumb and slid it out – a Barclay's debit card. His brow furrowed with suspicion as he scrutinised the tiny embossed sliver lettering. 'This expires in a couple of weeks, so your old man should have had a new card through by now. He'd get a new PIN number too. They'd come in separate envelopes and be posted by the bank on different days.'

He got to his feet and made towards the hallway.

'What is it?' Kim said.

'Just a thought…'

He was back within a moment, a pile of post in his hand. No thought had been put to who had opened the mail. It had been accepted that Kim's father had done it. It may well have been one of his last acts before he died.

Some circulars along with a couple of utility bills made up the pile. A letter from Mr Fry's old work boss inviting him to a retirement function was another. Taylor pushed these to one side in favour of two particular envelopes. The inside flap of each of these showed the turquoise eagle of Barclay's Bank. The idea that the burglar may have opened some of the envelopes had not been considered.

'Empty,' Taylor said, now in detective mode and treating the envelopes with respect. The burglar's fingerprints might be on them – it was no easy job to open envelopes with gloves on.

He examined the postal dates on the two pieces of mail; they were different. The earlier one bore a franked date stamp of 26th February. It had been carefully opened by slitting along its edge with a paperknife. The second, posted on 5th March had been clumsily ripped open, probably by hand.

'So where are the documents?' Taylor said.

'You're thinking the burglar's got Dad's new debit card and PIN number.'

'Exactly, the first envelope would contain your father's new card. It looks as though *he* opened it. I guess he left it on the hall table to await the new PIN. The PIN came in that second letter several days later and so after you found him. Looking at how the envelope has been torn open the burglar did it. We must get that card stopped by the bank and get these envelopes to Reg Timson for ninhydrin fingerprint tests.'

SEVEN

KIM SPENT a restless night mulling over both the burglary and her potential transfer to Staffordshire Police. She delivered her news on the latter subject in a matter-of-fact way over breakfast. 'I'll be taking that job in Staffordshire; I've roughed out the report. I'll drop it in at the nick for DI Grainger on Monday.'

She had not reckoned with the efficiency of Exeter's branch of Barclay's. A telephone call from the manager quickly altered their planned schedule. Her father's debit card had been stopped and details of the fraudulent transactions had already been established.

Less than an hour later the pair stood together with DI Grainger in Exeter's CID office. They were grouped around the seated figure of Reg Timson, watching and listening as he scrolled a pen down the columns of figures and calculated.

'A total of eight hundred and fifty quid from different cash machines in Exeter, Tedham and Taunton. He's not ventured far afield, so he seems to be a local.' Timson said the words as Kim gritted her teeth with anger.

'He's been withdrawing money like crazy,' Timson added as his finger continued to search through the data. 'Wednesday afternoon… twenty past four… Barclays at Tedham was his first. He looked around at Kim. 'So the theory that he was screwing the bungalow while you were at the funeral holds water.' His finger stopped at the last entry. 'Yes up to the limit on each occasion. He's used several different cash points without much time in between. Odd thing though, he stopped well before the bank cancelled the card. His last withdrawal was twelve minutes past eight. on Thursday evening from Barclays in Bedford Street Exeter. The card wasn't stopped by the bank until nine twenty this morning. The machine hasn't snatched it and so he must still have it.'

Timson rested his chin on his cupped hand. 'Usually in these situations the thief will carry on until the machine gobbles up the card, but there's still a few hundred quid in the account.'

'Can't believe I've been so stupid,' Kim said. 'I should have notified the bank about Dad's death straight away.'

'Don't beat yourself up over it Kim,' Grainger said. 'It's easy looking at the situation as a police officer. I guess it's times like these when we realise how bad it is to be on the receiving end.'

Taylor directed his gaze at Granger. 'I'm still bugged by the fact that he didn't take anything else Ken. It's odd… there was so much nice stuff and he'd got all the time in the world. He's spent ages going through papers. It doesn't add up.'

A uniformed constable appeared at the office doorway, a sealed foolscap envelope in his hand. 'Manager from Barclay's in the town brought this in for you Reg.' He waved the envelope.

Timson stretched out a hand. 'Thanks Tom.' He looked up at Grainger. 'I've been waiting for this. One of the cashpoints has recently had a camera installed. It takes a snapshot of the user. The manager tells me not to hold my breath as it's not that good, but we'll be the judge of that.'

He slit the envelope along its top edge and slid out an eight inch square black and white grainy photograph placing it down centre-desk. The group became silent as they studied the image. It was a man, but hunched over with his face filling the picture. His attempt at stealth by trying to hide his features from nearby shoppers resulted in him unwittingly pressing his face closer to the hidden camera lens. The action also went some way towards creating a distorted shadowy likeness.

Kim, Granger and Timson were the resident cops who could possibly nominate a name from their knowledge of local crooks. It was a difficult test – this picture would not be awarded any photography prizes.

A full minute of silence passed until Timson picked up the photo and held it at arms-length. His eyes narrowed down to surgical incisions before recognition spread across his face. He set the photo back onto the desk, sat back in his chair locking his hands behind his head with interlinked fingers. His long exhalation preceded an assured statement – 'Lenny Fucking Gill… excuse my French Kim.'

Grainger moved in closer, eyes riveted to the picture. 'Bloody hell Timmo you're right – Leonard Alfred Gill, AKA "The Ghost". He's not been heard of in years.'

Grainger turned to Kim, 'Check out intelligence records Kim for his last known address… double check it with the housing department.'

Timson shuffled papers together as he spoke. 'He was on the Burntwood Lane estate last time I paid him a visit… house near the chippie, but that must be four years ago.' Timson swivelled to meet Grainger's eyes. 'Do you want me to get a search warrant as soon as we're happy with the address? I know we don't need one, we'll be nicking him anyway, but just to cover all the bases.'

Granger nodded his agreement and then turned to Taylor to explain. 'Lenny became a bit of a celebrity in the criminal fraternity in his heyday. He was a pain in the arse… could get where water couldn't. One of the newspapers did an article on him following a Crown Court case. We'd had a spate of house burglaries all over the place. Exeter, Taunton… everywhere. He was making fools out of us. We organised a special initiative just to try and get to the bottom of it.' Grainger raised an eyebrow as he turned to face Timson. 'Reg and his old DS ran it and captured the burglar eventually – Lenny Gill. The newspaper decided to turn the screws on us and did a big story concentrating on how good Lenny was at his job. Somehow they came up with the nickname for him: "The Ghost". Lenny disappeared off the radar when he was released from prison; I thought he'd died.'

Twenty-seven Gallway Road lay on Exeter's Burntwood Lane council estate. It proved to be the last known, and according to the housing department, current address of semi-retired burglar and one time Plymouth stevedore – Lenny Gill. His stevedoring career was literally "one time" as he was sacked on his first day for pilfering from his work mates' lockers. Gill had spent a lifetime living from the proceeds of his various crimes with a career covering the entire spectrum of criminal offences. His speciality for house burglary blossomed as he grew older and figured out how to break into peoples' homes with little or no physical effort.

Gill's prison sentences had come along during the early years of his thieving, although there were a few slip ups later in life resulting in small doses of porridge. As burglars go Lenny the Ghost had been good and usually worked alone, thereby reducing the chances of capture. In local criminal circles the word was that Lenny, now almost fifty-six, had decided to hang up his jemmy and gloves for an early retirement. He now lived comfortably on his invalidity benefit, supported by a walking stick, which he did not need, and the proceeds of regular car boot sales. His stock-in-trade consisted entirely of goods acquired under dubious circumstances. This helped provide an additional tax-free income for a few comforts in life; beer, fags and the services of the occasional prostitute. But Lenny made it known that should a good opportunity come along where a skilled thief was required, he was ready and able to spring back into action.

The team arrived at Lenny's in the late afternoon but he was not answering the door. His gleaming Motability Vauxhall Astra stood neatly parked but rather out of place on the rubbish strewn driveway. It seemed a certainty that the old burglar was in but Lenny was a sly one. There would be no twitching curtains to give the game away. He would call their bluff to the end just like he always did. It had cost him a few front doors in his time – they never went away. Taylor and Grainger shook their heads in unison. Police work differed little from one end of the country to the other. Taylor had dealt with many Lenny Gills in his time.

Timson and Harding covered the back door. It was standard procedure regardless of the fact that Lenny was not up to successfully going on his toes.

The decision to include Kim as part of the team had been thought out. Yes, some bosses might have criticised the idea of having the victim of the crime present on a search warrant even though she was a detective herself. But Kim was the one person with a chance of recognising property inside the house which could have been stolen from her father's home. Taylor's inclusion in the raid was also par for the course, and there was no way he was not going to be there anyway.

Grainger's repeated banging on the front door produced a mob of watchers: kids with bikes and sullen-looking youths for the main part. The detective inspector valued his hub caps and had asked a uniformed officer with a marked police car to also attend.

The *shouting through the letterbox* strategy was eventually resorted to by Grainger. 'Come on Lenny, we know you're in there.' This was usually the last action before the *kicking in the door* strategy came into play.

Grainger checked his watch. 'Doubt if he's already in the pub.' He glanced over at Lenny's car. 'I can't see him walking anywhere.' He applied his mouth to the letterbox again. 'Last warning Lenny.'

The front door did not offer much resistance. Taylor supplied the muscle and one hefty nudge from his shoulder did the trick. It would be expected at this stage to be met with a shouted torrent of abuse from the hitherto silent and unseen occupant. But Lenny Gill was, for once, incapable of obscenities. He had been dead for hours.

The closed curtains of the dining room prevented Kim Harding and Timson from suspecting that the assignment was destined to be anything other than run-of-the-mill. Those curtains also successfully concealed the awful circumstances of Lenny's demise. It was not until Taylor pushed open the dining room door and turned back to

Grainger that the fairly standard burglary enquiry shifted up numerous gears. 'Ken, you're going to need SOCO, Forensics, pathologist, the full works, this is murder.'

Taylor was not being hasty with his theory; Lenny Gill was not only dead he was also undeniably a murder victim.

The house telephone started to ring as the group silently peered down at the body. 'Let it ring,' Grainger said. 'Whoever it is will ring back. We need to get our act together.' He turned to the uniformed policewoman standing inside the hall. 'Get onto BT straight away and see if they can fix something up smartish to trace calls.'

Home office pathologist Malcolm Spiller was quickly at the scene and giving a commentary for the benefit of the Dictaphone held by his assistant. 'Hands fastened together at the wrists behind back with silver colour adhesive tape which I believe to be known as Duct Tape. The body is unmoved from its place of finding and is face down on a carpet, head turned towards its left. A large laceration to the throat is evident. The cut can be seen to start near to the left ear. It runs a minimum of six inches and then disappears from sight at a point close to the laryngeal prominence.'

Grainger smiled; he knew that Spiller's medical term referred to the victim's Adam's Apple.

Several pints of blood had leaked from the body and soaked into the carpet forcing Spiller to carefully pick his spot before kneeling down.

Grainger nodded his head in agreement to Spiller's lifted eyebrow expression. This implied to Spiller that he had been granted permission to adjust the position of the body for further examination.

With fingers against the forehead of the corpse Spiller lifted slightly and peered closely at the throat. 'Yes as suspected, the cut runs completely from ear to ear.'

Spiller's commentary continued as he described Lenny's battered face. 'Two cricket-ball sized black eyes, a broken nose and shattered teeth. A heavy beating prior to death, possibly whilst seated in that chair.' Spiller nodded at an overturned wooden dining chair which lay nearby. 'Heavy bloodstaining to the seat of the chair and to the framework. This could be a possible indication that the throat was also cut whilst seated there.'

The pathologist sampled Lenny's thin grey hair between fingers and thumb. Several strands came away with roots still attached. 'Someone may have held him from behind by the hair to allow easy access to the throat.'

'Two people?' Grainger's question had also been on Taylor's mind but this was Grainger's patch and he had to take a back seat. He'd read Grainger's thoughts: *Someone had held Lenny's head back whilst another slit his throat from the front?*

'I'll need to take a closer look at that possibility at the PM,' Spiller said. 'Angle and depth of the cut… left to right or right to left… we'll see.'

Kim quickly recognised her dad's clock. It was sitting in the centre of the living room mantelshelf, its cable untidily draped behind other ornaments and then down to a wall socket. The scissors also turned up inside Gill's cutlery drawer. Much later the missing gloves were discovered by SOCO in the crook's anorak pocket hanging on the bannister post. Apparently he had taken all these items into his own everyday use.

The house phone started up twice more during the search and again Grainger reinforced his orders to ignore the calls until the trace was organised. 'It's sorted now Boss,' the uniformed police woman said after taking a radio call.

'Okay Melanie,' Grainger replied. 'Your job then… you know what to do.' The officer pulled up a chair near to the phone and settled down to wait.

EIGHT

TWO HUNDRED miles away in Wapping, East London, Benedict Cappelli sat impatiently tapping his pen against the woodwork of his desk. He took a sip from the polystyrene mug and shuddered. The office vending machine alleged that the tepid brown liquid was: Coffee, White, with Sugar. It was a claim which appeared to contravene the Trades Descriptions Act.

As the time approached half past six he toyed with the idea of making an early run for Henry's pub down on Dock Street. The open file of papers on his desk stalled the idea; he knew that he should knuckle down and study it. The wad seemed to consist of a mix of photocopied news items and dog-eared journalist's reports, yellowed pages going back years. It was all held together with a star-clip punched through the left hand top corner.

The office was still busy, but the daytime bustle had now gone and there were plenty of empty desks. Cappelli, usually a cool customer whose manipulations nearly always paid off, was actually getting a tad worried. He'd paid out £300 already and hoped at least for some form of update. The best outcome would be a result with the delivery of the goods as agreed against the second part of the payment – £700.

His telephone calls had started on Wednesday evening but as yet none had been answered. He had made a half-hearted attempt at looking through the file but found concentration difficult. He was now beginning to think that his gamble may have turned sour. He was after all, dealing with an unscrupulous, greedy and unreliable man. Paying for someone to commit a burglary was as serious as playing a physical part in the crime itself. He automatically took another sip at the so-called coffee forgetting how dreadful it tasted. Wincing again he pushed the mug to a far corner of his desk to prevent a repeat.

Car headlights from two floors below danced a reflected pattern across the rain drenched window panes as he considered one last call. He punched the numbers into the keypad and his eyes drifted downward as he listened to the ring tone start up. Hope flashed across his face with the sound of an answering voice.

'Hello, who is this calling please?' said the woman.

Cappelli slammed down the receiver, his normally smooth forehead now corrugated into a row of lines. Something was not right. There should be no female at Lenny Gill's house and certainly no one who could string even such a simple sentence together in what came over as intelligible English. He bit down onto his lip as the thought came to mind that the voice sounded like a copper. He'd had enough dealings over the years. They had a certain telephone manner, a special way of delivering a sentence.

'Damn,' Cappelli muttered under his breath. If he was right, he wouldn't get the information or indeed the money back. The whole story may have turned into a dead duck but could it be even worse than that? If Gill had been arrested and went on to spill the beans about being paid to commit the burglary then the police would come looking for *him.* Was there actually any way the police might trace him back from Lenny Gill?

Gill didn't know who he was, but there had been a link between the two men, something from years ago. Would the police be able to join up the dots? Cappelli ground his teeth as he considered the possibilities. From what he knew of Gill he was an Old School criminal and so grassing was not part of his character. There would be nothing to be gained by Gill in telling the police who arranged for the burglary even if he knew who the person was. It would only complicate things even more for him.

Cappelli relaxed a little and then another worry came to mind: *If the woman was a police officer, could they trace the call back to him?* He considered this for a moment and then shook his head. *As long as Gill kept his mouth shut there was no way the police would employ such complex methods for a simple burglary.*

This roller coaster of emotions continued as another less than honest series of actions he had taken gnawed at his conscience. His original meeting with retired soldier Edward Olivant had been straightforward enough. But that 1978 copy of the Telegraph had focussed his attention onto the only possible useful name allowed into the public domain by the Security Services – Pathologist, Andrew Prestwich.

The two weeks he'd spent researching Prestwich had been creditable investigative journalism. All that trawling through British Medical Association records, medical directories, inquest summaries and countless newspaper cuttings had paid off. It had revealed Prestwich's impressive qualifications and career. It had confirmed his engagement at the Microbiological Research Establishment as *the* dedicated Home Office Forensic Pathologist between 1968 and 1986. It had provided details of his additional Cambridge qualifications in the fields of histopathology and neuropathology.

These details gave the reasons why Prestwich had been singled out by Porton Down for retention. It would indeed be handy for a government facility linked with chemical and biological weapons to have their own legal methods of officially sweeping any serious dirt under the carpet.

Cappelli knew that Prestwich's title *Professor Emeritus* meant that he had retired. This was to be expected at the age of seventy-one. But when his enquiries eventually led him to the old chap's address at Salisbury Leigh Nursing Home, it added some disappointment. It indicated that not all was good with his health.

The bigger part of the anti-climax came during a telephone enquiry to the home. The nursing sister's summary had poured cold water on Cappelli's hopes for answers to the puzzle. "Poor Andrew can't remember too much nowadays," she'd said. "Such an intelligent man… distressing to see what dementia has done to him… short term memory almost non-existent."

Cappelli stared down at his desk top and shuddered as the entire dishonest charade which had followed played out in his mind:

"Oh dear," he had bluffed into the telephone. "I do hope Uncle Andrew will remember me. We moved away to Australia when I was eight and I've not seen him since. I promised my parents I'd visit while I was over."

The light hearted, half laugh he added gave some authenticity to his impersonation of Prestwich's missing nephew. The attempt to cover the Yorkshire accent with a laid back Australian drawl seemed successful. The name *Bernard Prestwich* which had been conjured up by the reporter was also swallowed. "Uncle Andy is my Dad's brother."

More pressure was added by *Bernard* with his explanation that his home-bound Melbourne flight was taking off from Heathrow at 21.40 the next evening.

The puzzlement on Professor Prestwich's face as the nephew was shown into the uncle's room was clear. The understanding smile the nurse gave had a tinge of perceptive empathy. If she had uttered anything in response to the pathetic expression it would have been: "Oh bless" – she'd seen it all so many times before. The joy at seeing Uncle Andy after so many years quite overwhelmed "Bernard" and his brave shaking away of the tears caused by Prestwich's lack of recognition could have won Cappelli an Oscar.

State registered Nurse Janice Hopkins had been completely happy to leave the pair to catch up and genuinely hoped that Andrew would soon have a few recollections of young Bernard back in his grasp.

Cappelli's deception was quickly enhanced as soon as the nurse left the room. Black and white family photographs on a chest of drawers were scrutinised and clues gathered from pencil scribbled words on the rear. Names and places were deduced – family holidays, relatives and even the family dog. Within ten minutes a hearty conversation had started. The lines of puzzlement on Andrew Prestwich's face had been replaced with a broad smile.

When Nurse Janice returned with a pot of tea for two and a plate of custard creams Andrew's smile accompanied his head nods. A family holiday in Cornwall was being discussed vividly by the two men.

"And your dog… the little terrier, it pounced on every sand castle as soon as we pulled the bucket off." Cappelli said. "What was his name…Prince wasn't it?"

"Prince… yes indeed. Such a rascal," Prestwich quickly replied.

Janice raised her eyebrows and made a smiling face at Cappelli as she put the tea tray down onto a small central table. "I'll leave you both to it. You're obviously having a good catch up." She gave a wink to Cappelli as she closed the door.

The next part of Cappelli's strategy had been the tricky one. He seemed to have cajoled Prestwich into believing that he was close family. He'd also secured his trust, for the time being at least.

A folded copy of the Times lay on the arm of Prestwich's chair. The fully completed crossword in the old man's shaky blue biro caused Cappelli some astonishment as he instantly accepted that it was a feat of which he was incapable. Clearly there still existed some very high quality intelligence inside Prestwich's head.

Had the professor managed to retain that secretive mind-set which must have been drilled into him? Would he clam up when his old job came into the conversation? Cappelli had to use a softly, softly approach, but he didn't have much time. A second visit would be too risky.

The Scrabble set on the bookshelf looked well used. Cappelli's offer of a game brought a grin to Andrew Prestwich's cheeks. Cappelli's life's work had been in words, but the possibility of a severe drubbing seemed more than likely. He was not wrong.

'I used to play Scrabble with your dad,' Prestwich said. He clicked down a six letter high scoring word which Cappelli felt sure was correct although was unsure of the meaning. The reporter played along, but concentrated his mind more onto his own personal game plan than that of the Scrabble.

Cappelli chose his moment after a twenty minute savaging by the old man. He produced the 1978 copy of the Telegraph from an overcoat pocket and opened it up at the relevant page. 'Dad showed me this. You must have been involved in some interesting things in your profession Uncle.'

Prestwich's eyes twinkled for a second as they ran across the headline:

Scientist Dies in Nightmare Government Lab Accident.

Puzzlement returned as he adjusted his glasses and read through the text of the article. 'Yes interesting times…' The professor thought for a moment and then yawned. 'Bit tired now Bernard, must go to the bathroom and then perhaps a little lie down.' He struggled for a few seconds as quivering wrists pressed down on his chair's arms. 'Give me a pull up young Bernard… legs aren't what they used to be.'

Cappelli eased Prestwich up from his chair and watched downheartedly as the old gent headed for his en-suite.

'Geoff Fry,' Prestwich said half turning towards Cappelli as his hand gripped the door handle.

'Beg pardon Uncle.'

'Geoff Fry, good chap… clever man. A microbiologist you know. He calls to see me once in a while. Good Scrabble player, and like me an expert on anagrams and puzzles. There was only him and me who knew about Eleanor… or Rosa. Call her what you like.'

Cappelli tried to hold his pleasant grin, but this sudden rambling, this unexpected stream of possible connected information quickly warped his expression into one of bewilderment. Had Prestwich actually mentioned the name ROSA? The same code-name that Corporal Olivant used? He listened as the old man gave more.

'Yes, we didn't know who we could trust… so many reds under the bed. A heavy weight to carry around all these years. More for Geoff than me… I mean he still has the file. He knows where all the secrets are and the formula…. "Recipe" he called it. Bloody recipe for disaster I'd call it.'

The old man's face contorted a little as he reached into his decaying grey matter attempting to retrieve more detail from the past. Even the caution and secrecy which for so many years had stopped him from divulging anything had misted over in recent times. His forehead creased with concentration, eyelids flickering with emotion as he cursed himself for not even remembering what he should not talk about. 'Damn, I can't remember… secrets… terrible things… a real life doomsday.'

A flicker of recognition came and a smile curled his mouth back upward again as he managed to recall the banter which used to take place between Fry and himself. 'I wasn't supposed to know where he'd kept it but I worked it out eventually. His secret was safe with me but he was the Guardian.'

Prestwich was laughing as he disappeared into the bathroom. 'Yes, GUARDIAN… my word. A real guardian of lies'

Cappelli shook his head, unsure if the inane ramblings gave anything to go on. His mobile phone was nevertheless in his hand almost before the bathroom door clicked properly shut.

'It's Benedict Cappelli, put me on to Tim Redmond, the Staff Editor, it's urgent.'

There was a short delay before Redmond came on the line. 'Tim, I'm on to something big. I need a meeting with Kelvin Stewart can you fix something for tomorrow. I'm short on time. Can I also give you a name and see if you can earmark somebody to dig out whatever you can find on the guy…. Geoff Fry… probably connected to Porton Down.'

Cappelli finished the call as Prestwich emerged from the bathroom. The old chap set a puzzled stare upon the seated reporter. 'Can I help you?'

'It's Bernard Uncle, we were talking about Geoff Fry. Perhaps I could give Geoff a ring and see when he can come down to you?'

More lines of puzzlement appeared on Prestwich's face. 'Up… up to me, not down,' he said. 'Geoffrey lives near to Exeter.'

'Stupid of me. I'll give him a ring for you tomorrow. Do you have his number?'

Cappelli's fingers were crossed as Prestwich made a frown and then shook his head. The head shaking slowed and then changed to a nod. 'Of course I have… in the drawer.'

Cappelli followed the old man's pointing finger to a cabinet drawer. He pulled it open and looked down at the tidily arranged contents. The blue and white striped A5 sized booklet had its intended use printed boldly on the front: *Address Book*.

He flicked through to the "F" section. The single name of Geoffrey Fry on the page included an address and phone number. It was all that he needed, but the possibility that the book contained other gems of information made the chance too good to miss. After a small pretence at writing the details onto his note pad Cappelli covertly pocketed the book.

A handshake and hug for Uncle Andy along with a beaming smile and a wave for Janice at the reception desk completed the charade and "Bernard" left.

Cappelli landed back in the present with a start and found that he was still sitting at his office desk. There was no escaping from the fact that he was in a mess. Trying to forget his visit to Prestwich would not work. The story, possibly one of the biggest in decades, was lost. Even worse – the police were now at Lenny's house.

Could they connect him to the burglary at Geoff Fry's? Why had he involved Gill? Why had he used criminal methods to get at the facts? Why had he hoodwinked the frail and confused old pathologist and stolen his address book?

He was only allowed a few seconds of self-pity before his desk phone pinged into life startling him into a bolt upright posture. He watched the phone for a few seconds before picking up.

'News…Benedict Cappelli.'

What little colour was left in his cheeks drained as he listened.

Even those swarthy features could not compensate. His Adam's apple rose and fell with the nervous gulp that came as fellow reporter Dave Mardell related the breaking news on an Exeter murder.

Cappelli's sudden silence puzzled Mardell. 'Hello. You still there Benny… hello.'

Cappelli gulped again, struggling to create sufficient saliva to respond. His mouth had dried to the consistency of blotting paper as Mardell repeated the murder victim's name.

'Yes… Leonard Alfred Gill.'

Mardell, a correspondent at the Herald's Bristol office, puzzled at the continuing silence from Cappelli and repeated the name for a third time. 'Are you still with me Benny? Thought for a minute the line had gone dead. Not as bloody dead as Mr Gill mind you.' A half laugh followed the joke. 'My source reckons he'd been tortured… beaten to a pulp and then throat cut from ear to ear, so it's a tasty one. '

'Okay Dave thanks for this... ' Cappelli's pause wasn't for another swallow. He needed to get the necessary train of thought into motion. *Calm down,* the voice inside his head told him. *Think – take control.*

Microseconds went by as the reporter's devious mind battled against the cravings to panic. He needed to assimilate any facts which he could use to his advantage.

Staff Reporter Mardell was a junior. He had been sent from Wapping on a temporary basis to fill the boots of a reporter who'd taken early retirement through illness. His subsequent plunge into the deep end had been unfair on the young chap and a couple of cock-ups had resulted in phone bollockings.

The deep end had quickly deepened for Mardell. Whilst travelling back from another story he became one of the first reporters on the scene of one of Britain's worst ever road accidents – the M4, Hungerford crash.

Cappelli had worked from that same satellite Bristol office for over six months. He knew how things operated out there. He'd dug up some good stories in the South during that time along with a few useful contacts.

He made his decision. 'Look, sorry Dave, as you rightly say this sounds like a tasty one. We'll have to cover it from here from the beginning. You've still got your hands full with the Hungerford crash.' Pausing for a second he then added. 'I have some business in the Exeter direction anyway… so the chances are it'll be me.' Without another word he returned the telephone to its cradle and stared down at the open file on his desk. His left palm slid under the front cover and firmly closed the file with a sweeping single movement. He sat for a moment with the flattened hand resting down onto the cover. The stencilled marker pen name of the subject was legible between his spread fingers: *GEOFFREY FRY.*

Cappelli stood to his feet, picked up the file and headed for the shredder.

NINE

GRAINGER DESPONDENTLY made his way up the steps into Heavitree Road police station just after seven o'clock. He now had a full scale murder investigation on his hands and to that end had commandeered the table tennis room and two adjoining basement offices.

Taylor had wanted to be part of the team, but the etiquette involving two different police forces was not easily circumvented. For once in his career he was relegated to the back seat.

Kim appreciated his offer to carry on with the clearing out of her dad's bungalow and handed over her keys. 'Take my car. All the other keys you'll need are on there. I'll get a lift back in a patrol car as soon as I can.'

Taylor arrived back and started sorting out the ornaments and pictures from the different rooms. Sticking to Kim's guidelines he carefully wrapped and packed things into boxes. It was while he was busy with this that he also came to tidy some of the opened mail now lying on a kitchen unit. This pile of letters had given the clue that money might have been taken from Mr Fry's bank account. He felt uneasy or perhaps nosey might have been a more appropriate word as he singled out what was, without doubt, a personal letter addressed to Mr Fry. He quickly shook off his feelings of guilt and clicked into detective mode as he examined it. The envelope had been carefully slit along the edge, almost certainly by Mr Fry rather than the burglar. The one A4 sheet included the printed Royal Coat of Arms: a rampant lion and rampant unicorn either side of the shield and crown. The title set in bold type read:

Centre for Applied Microbiology and Research (CAMR).

The typed letter had the addition of the handwritten Christian names of both the addressee and the author. The broadly flourished, pale blue fountain-penned ink stood out boldly from the otherwise typed letter giving an impression of importance. A simple inter-departmental address for the CAMR HQ at Colindale, London was pre-printed in the top right hand corner:

> *Dear Geoffrey*
> *Hoping that you are keeping well. A short note to let you know that we have arranged a little retirement soiree for Rosa, who is due to finally rest her typing fingers after 32 years of loyal service.*
> *Rosa's last day will be Monday 4th March 1991 and as the 'bash' has been kept secret from her this will be the date of the event. I do hope you are able to come along and see her off. The celebrations start 3 p.m. in the Colindale office.*
> *R.S.V.P.*
> *Best wishes*
> *Alex*
> *Alexander Tremaine*

At Heavitree Road police station the pressing circumstances temporarily shelved Kim's current on-leave status. Her request for a transfer had become a major issue in view of the events. Grainger's request for her to hold onto the paperwork for the time being was expected. Indeed almost all CID leave had been cancelled. This directive would probably last for a couple of weeks by which time the Murder Incident Room would be properly organised and making headway. Her disappointment showed though when Grainger told her that she would not be working on the murder enquiry.

'Asking for trouble Kim… I hope you understand. I'm thinking of Lenny's involvement in your burglary.' He made a sympathetic face. 'If we get the murderer to court there's the chance of some smart arsed barrister claiming conflict of interest, or alleging tampering with evidence.'

Kim's shake of the head showed her frustration over the decision and gave away a little annoyance. If her transfer was to be put on the back burner then she wanted to be in on this murder enquiry.

'We can't say that the cases are connected Boss. Lenny had plenty of enemies, there must be a chance that someone noticed him flush with cash and thought they'd help themselves.'

'I completely agree Kim, it's doubtful that the cases are connected. None of the cashpoint money or the card has been found in Lenny's house. It looks as though the murderer took all of that, but I have to keep an open mind. I need you in the office… someone will have to hold the fort. You've still things to sort out over your dad's death and so your own leave will be honoured up until when you booked it.' He glanced at his wall chart. 'You've still got a week… back next Monday. A temporary DI is taking over my job and I've recommended that you do a spell of acting DS until we get sorted with this murder.' Grainger raised his eyebrows. 'That will stand you in good stead for your move up North.'

Kim sighed, 'so am I to hang onto my transfer application indefinitely?'

'For the time being Kim until we know where this is all going. How long is Doug staying for?'

'He'd planned to go back next weekend anyway… he starts a new job himself on the Monday.'

Kim arrived back at the bungalow at eight o'clock, an Indian take-away in hand. The uniformed PC made a joke about the smell of curry in his police car before he'd dropped her off. 'Smells like the Tedham Tandoori in here.'

Taylor and Harding discussed the day's events across the kitchen table as they ate and Kim gave and update on the decisions made upon her future.

Taylor mulled over Kim's account of the conversation with her boss. He thought out aloud as he spooned the last morsel of madras sauce onto his plate from the foil container. 'Yes I can see Ken Grainger's point of view. He's going to be busy now and engaged full time on the murder.' Taylor's clumsy attempt slopped a dollop onto the table causing Kim to smile and roll her eyes. The distraction did however build an excuse for Taylor not to look at her as he posed a question. 'Is this likely to change your mind over the transfer?'

His struggle for nonchalance was his own bid at understanding Kim's predicament. He knew she needed to do what was right for her.

She shook her head as she leant forward and wiped away the mess with a piece of kitchen roll. 'What are you like?' She said. 'It's a delay… another delay I know, but as you've said Ken Grainger has a lot on his plate.' She gave another shake of the head. 'Most of yours isn't even on the plate. Now let's eat up and perhaps we can manage another hour before we pack in, there's still a lot to do.'

The hour and some more quickly flew and soon a line of cardboard boxes narrowed the width of the hall down to two feet. The four old suitcases from the loft also came in useful to store some of the items which might be kept. Several bin liners now took up space on the garage floor, their necks tied with string, awaiting carriage to the dump.

The ten o'clock news coming through on Geoff Fry's transistor radio nudged Taylor into the decision that it was time to pack in for the day. He stepped outside the kitchen door and sniffed at the chilly air. The clocks were still not due to go forward for another two weeks and it was already dark. He stared out at the wood that bordered the property and his mind went back to Lenny Gill. He visualised Gill pushing his way through the bushes and clambering over the fence before getting on with the burglary.

Beyond the tar blackness of the slowly shifting branches and twigs two figures were watching. Their eyes followed Taylor's every movement until he disappeared back inside the kitchen.

More thoughts of Gill's hideously slashed throat came to Taylor as he pulled the kitchen door handle sharply upward and turned the key to lock it. His shake of the head went unnoticed by anyone as he pondered the possibility of a connection between the burglary and the murder. It seemed to make no sense at all and perhaps for that reason alone he should have been able to discount it. Maybe it was that reason why he could not.

He looked through into the lounge and smiled at Kim's sudden strength. She sat cross legged on the carpet. One minute she'd been close to tears and now she was getting on with things.

'We'd best be going,' he said. 'It's late now and I don't know about you but I'm whacked.' Kim's jacket and his own body warmer were draped over his arm. He pulled the door from the hallway to the kitchen shut, walked back into the lounge and seated himself on the arm of the sofa. She hadn't heard his suggestion; she was miles away sorting through old family photos and had let out the occasional giggle. Now she was surrounded by an array of small tins and boxes as well as a couple of old Tupperware containers. Keys and coins formed most of the collection. A few pounds worth of current copper coinage filled one tin. *Too much trouble for the burglar to bother with,* Taylor thought.

Another tin overflowed with pre-decimal coinage of all denominations: farthings, threepenny bits, sixpences right up to a few half-crowns. Tin badges filled another box and yet another was taken up with a mixture of foreign currency: French Francs, Lira and other remnants from holidays abroad. Two small Tupperware boxes held keys, and one of these was secured with a firmly fitted lid. Geoff Fry's own careful, distinctive handwriting penned onto a stick on label spelled out the capitalised word *OLD*. Underneath was written: *Why the hell do I keep this rubbish?*

Kim's forehead crinkled with emotion as this reminder of her father's sense of humour flooded back. She blinked back a tear and then giggled turning the emotions into what he had intended.

The other Tupperware box had no lid and its contents of perhaps a dozen keys all looked newer and more in use than the first box. One set, which she recognised as her dad's everyday keys, was on a split ring with a *Charles Clark Garages* leather fob. The stubby ignition key for his Toyota Supra which was parked on the bungalow's drive, formed part of the bunch. The car's future was yet to be decided. The ring also held the property's front and back door keys as well as one for the garage. The remaining unidentified key was a well-engineered sturdy looking instrument but as to what its use was she had no idea.

Kim rose to her feet, jangling the car key bunch at Taylor and made a canny face. 'Not getting caught out again,' she said. 'I'll take Dad's keys back home, in case some toe-rag takes a shine to his car.' She popped the bunch into her handbag.

Taylor smiled and handed her the jacket. 'You seem to be getting sorted now.'

'I think so, although there's still a bit to do, but I'm in the right frame of mind now. I've yet to sell the car; I think I'll ring a local dealer. I don't want the hassle of selling it privately; all things for tomorrow.'

The two figures took the few steps forward from the thick foliage of the wood and stood against the garden fence. They watched Taylor's headlights cut an arc in the darkness as he reversed from the drive onto the road before driving away. The car's engine note was punctuated by gear changes as the sound gradually disappeared into the night.

It was around the same time that Reg Timson finally caught up with the man he'd been looking for. His search had taken him to the Bull's Head and the Burntwood Lane Working Men's Club before he arrived in the bar of the Hollybush.

Donald Dykes sat slouched on a tall stool with his copy of the Racing Times opened onto the bar. The back of his shaven, dome-like head was the only identifying feature for Timson but it was enough. Dykes' roll of neck fat was dissected by several deep lateral lines. It rippled like the bellows of a piano accordion with each slight movement of the dome. A straight pint glass of amber coloured beer stood at his elbow with a creamy foam head three sips down from the rim. Various circles, underlinings and crossings-out were inscribed onto the details of tomorrow's races in Dykes' Racing Times. A small blue biro which had evidently been used for this purpose had no doubt been taken by Dykes from the nearby bookies. He twirled the pen between the fingers of his right hand as he peered studiously down through thick grubby spectacles. Dykes had a problem: *Which horse would be the one to go with the other three outsiders for his Yankee bet and go on to earn him his next million?* The aging thug considered that this was his only problem.

WRONG!

Timson pulled out the stool next to the absorbed punter and shuffled it intrusively close into his personal space.

Dykes set his face with an aggressive leer and slowly turned his head. Yes he was sixty-one, overweight and suffering with arthritis. He was nevertheless over six feet and visually the embodiment of a professional criminal brute. His eyes blinked twice and a frown followed as he lowered his chin for a look over the top of his glasses.

'Not you… what the fuck do you want Timson?'

'Now that's no way to greet an old friend you haven't seen in years.' There was more than a glimmer of sarcasm on Timson's face as he spoke the words.

Donald Dykes was an unpleasant man – the sort of criminal who could only be dealt with successfully by experienced and grizzled detectives, the like of which was Reg Timson. The man had been a life-long mate of Lenny Gill and one of his only confidants. His potential for providing healthy background information on an unhealthy member of society was golden.

Dykes, however, was never likely to play ball and Timson's lone pub confrontation with the old crook soon turned ugly. Timson had been responsible for Dykes' last spell inside – a little matter of a diverted electricity meter in the pantry of his home. It had been running backwards for so long that it seemed that the Electricity Board owed HIM money. Dykes did not like police officers and liked Timson even less than most.

A couple of the pubs on the estate, to the minds of some of the more appeasing police brass, were no-go areas; not in Timson's book though! No matter how many times the bosses warned him, if he fancied a pint these were the places he would visit. One of the benefits being that the beer was good. At least in some of them it was.

Timson had done a bit of homework on Dykes before stepping into his world. If he was going to arrest him he would need an offence more significant than a stolen biro from the bookies. The cunning detective quickly came up with the solution. A check in the summons and warrants box at the police station produced an outstanding arrest warrant in Dykes' name for non-payment of fines.

The conversation between the pair quickly spawned a kicked over barstool, a couple of smashed beer glasses and a handcuffed-behind-the-back Donald Dykes. His ignominious appearance at the front of the pub was witnessed by the usual horde of rowdy onlookers. A police car soon arrived, parking close to the pub's entrance with a rear door held open.

Timson shepherded his prisoner towards the vehicle with the upwards pressure of a single finger held against the overly tightened handcuffs. Dykes' comical up on tip toe gait drew some laughter from the watching yobs. 'You bastard Timson… too fucking tight.'

'Should have come quietly then Donny, I'll slacken them off if you shut up.' Timson reinforced his control with the customary hand pressed down onto the top of Dykes' head to install him into the rear seat.

Evidently Donald Dykes had no knowledge whatsoever of Lenny Gill's demise and as the body had only been found a few hours before, this was to be expected. He leered across the desk inside

Interview Room Number Two at Heavitree Road Police Station. He knew Timson wanted more than just seeing him in court for a non-payment warrant.

'What's your game Timson, what are you after. I never grass on anyone. You should know that by now.'

Timson stuck out his bottom lip and nodded his head slowly and deliberately. 'Indeed I do Donny Boy and I'm forever impressed by the honour that has existed amongst thieves where it concerns Donald Dykes. But your allegiance has always been to the living before.'

'What the fuck are you on about Timson?'

Timson related the tale of Gill's death, holding back on none of the detail. He watched the criminal's aggressive stare and poker face crumple as the realisation set in that this was a whole new ball game. The pressure increased without a word as Timson turned over a ten inch square of stiff glossy photographic paper upon which his hand had rested. He slid the picture in front of Dykes watching the villain's eyes widen with horror as he took in the detail.

The colour print was hardly dry from its express development courtesy of the police photographic studio. It showed the body, now turned onto its back: a head and shoulders view. Cricket ball eyes bulged, tattered lips showed where broken teeth had ripped through flesh. The slashed throat gaped in the manner of the hideously wide curving grin of a circus clown's makeup. Purple staining impregnated the victim's right cheek along with a mottled effect where the carpet's pile had slowly pressed into the flesh. Dykes' eyes enlarged some more as he recognised the green tufted Wilton beneath the corpse – Lenny's back room!

Dykes took one big swallow. 'What do you want to know?'

TEN

TAYLOR made an early start the next morning and by eight o'clock his car was parked on the drive behind Geoff Fry's Toyota. He'd packed most of the bulging refuse bags from the garage onto his rear seats as soon as he'd arrived and managed to squeeze the remainder into the boot. The task took a little longer than expected. His intention to quickly load up and take the stuff to the dump was delayed by the discovery that three of the bags were split open. Too much stuff had been crammed inside and others were not tied securely.

'Women and knots,' he muttered as he finally slammed down the boot lid.

A wristwatch check brought the realisation that he would be back at Kim's later than hoped. His journey across town and down to the council yard would get him mixed up with the Saturday market traffic. He let himself into the bungalow using Kim's own set of keys and picked up the hall telephone. For the sake of convenience the phone had not been disconnected.

Kim picked up within seconds.

'Hi,' Taylor said. 'Slight delay with the loading up, I'm going to get caught in traffic now, so I'll be later picking you up than I thought.'

'No worries, take your time. I'll come down to the bungalow in my own car. I've got dad's set of keys remember, so I can let myself in if you're not back. It might work out better anyway as the estate agent is due this afternoon. You promised Ken Grainger you'd go down to the nick to do your statement over finding Lenny. Two cars will be better.'

'Okay, see you later at the bungalow.' He replaced the receiver and turned to the front door but stopped within two paces. He was looking back down the hallway, confusion spreading across his face as his eyes focussed on the slightly ajar kitchen door.

Kim pulled up the zip on her black leather bomber jacket as she looked from the lounge window of her apartment at the frosty outside world. Her trainers, jeans and floppy necked sweater would be suitable for the day's work ahead. A bit of garden tidying might be on the agenda if the weather stayed dry.

She picked up her car keys from the kitchen table and then rummaged in her handbag, checking for the bungalow keys. Of course they were there and as an afterthought she prised open the split ring of her father's keys with the edge of her thumbnail. A curl of her recently applied red nail polish parted company from the nail. 'Damn,' she grumbled as she squeezed the two split rings together to form one bunch. It made a weighty chunk, but would be appropriate for the time being with less chance of being left behind at the bungalow. There was a metallic *click* as the split ring snapped back into place. She singled out her own car key from the bunch and in doing so focussed on another one. It was that sole key on her dad's ring that she'd not been able to identify. She held it with its tip pointing upwards as the other keys hung down against her palm. The bright March sunlight flashed a reflection along the double sided stainless steel shank with its two rows of intricate, well-engineered cuts. The key had the word SENTRY stamped into its bow along with a serial number.

Nine o'clock had arrived when Kim drove her Fiesta XR2i in behind her father's car. She crept the car forward parking tightly up against the Toyota. Hopefully her careful manoeuvrings would leave enough space for Taylor's car to squeeze in behind when he returned from the dump.

The sun's brightness belied the frosty nip which would hang around for a couple of hours yet. The warmth of the bungalow's interior showed the central heating was doing its job. She shed her bomber jacket and dumped her gloves and keys down onto the kitchen table. Leaning back against a kitchen unit she pressed the fingers of her left hand to her lips contemplating which job to tackle first. A toss-up between cleaning inside or garden tidying were the options. Her eyes drifted over to one kitchen cupboard. The wooden plinth where it sat against the tiled floor was slightly out of line. It was not quite properly fitted. To a less observant person it would have gone unnoticed, but Kim was the extreme opposite to a less observant person. She nudged the toe of her trainer against the plinth. It clicked back firmly into place. She made a satisfied nod, pleased that the simple action had done the trick.

Undecided where to start and after wandering from room to room she landed in the study. It had been the bungalow's third bedroom originally and over the years had evolved into an office. A desk along with box files containing personal papers took up some of the limited space. It was typical household correspondence: car documents, utility bills and insurance policies. The burglar's efforts were clearly apparent as papers still lay strewn around on the desk and carpet.

The wall shelves and a book case also held Mr Fry's extensive book collection. An ancient *Royal Model P* manual typewriter sat on the desk. An assortment of different pens poked out from a china mug. This was the first close look that Kim had taken at this room since the break-in. Drawers and a cupboard still remained open, but to the detective's mind, the search had not been carried out with much diligence or strategy.

She gazed around at the neat rows of first editions which Fry had collected over the years. Nothing hugely valuable but all in nice condition and complete with dust covers. She shook her head at the futility of it all. The stupid burglar hadn't touched the books and yet some would fetch up to fifty pounds. This pleased her, but it nevertheless augmented her opinion on the thief's brainpower.

Memories of her father, his passion for books, his intellect and his humour were everywhere. A boxed game of Scrabble stood on one of the shelves and a set of chess men on their board were positioned on a small table tucked into a corner. A copy of The Telegraph crossword book lay on the edge of the desk. Kim smiled as she flicked through the pages. Geoff Fry's blue biro handwriting filled each solved puzzle. The complete works of Shakespeare were piled against a wall with a card notice in Fry's handwriting: *A good doorstop.* It was another indicator of his humour; he'd never been a Shakespeare fan.

The room was a job she might start when Taylor returned as the emotions were kicking in again. She turned to leave and then something caught her eye. Two books on the shelves were set forward from their comfort zone. They both stood proud from the line of other books by nearly two inches. It seemed doubtful that the burglar had been responsible as he had failed to disturb any of the other books.

She stretched up to press the books back into line but as her fingers reached toward the first one they brushed against something. A sliver of paper tucked between the book's pages poked out from under the bottom edge against the dust cover. She slid the book out and brought it down to eye level. It was a nice condition copy of a book she had never heard of or seen before: *Safe Harbour by Anne Hill.* She pulled a puzzled face. The book seemed to be a romance, certainly not her father's usual genre. Her forehead crinkled with emotion as she saw the cartoon smiley face drawn in fountain pen on the folded paper. It was the trade-mark symbol her dad would put on messages to her. It was as good as his signature. Geoff Fry loved to indulge in puzzles and here was another, but what did it mean?

She put the book down and then reached up for the second out of line one. Her mouth dropped open as she saw the charming dust cover and read the title. She shook her head in astonishment. 'Well I never,' she said to herself. 'So there you are. I thought I'd lost you.' She sat herself down into desk chair to look at the books.

Half an hour went before she heard the front door open.

She met Taylor in the hall and gave his cheek a quick peck as he struggled out of his body warmer. 'Okay?' she asked.

'Yes all done,' Taylor said as he followed her through to the kitchen.

He dragged out a chair and plonked himself down as Kim filled the kettle. Reaching behind he placed the flats of his chilly hands against the radiator. 'Well when I let myself in to use the phone I only thought that we'd had another break in. I was sure we'd pulled all the doors shut and yet this one...' He nodded at the kitchen door. 'Was open a couple of inches… I thought oh no, here we go again.'

Kim's brow furrowed. 'And?' her single word urged him to continue.

'Well I had a real good look around, outside and inside. Everything's fine, so I gather that the door hadn't closed properly in the first place.'

'Thank God for that, I wouldn't want to go through that again. You had a bit of problem loading up the stuff for the dump then?'

'Nothing to write home about, some of the bags had split. I guess there was too much stuff in them and I'll have to give you few lessons in knot tying, some weren't tight enough.'

Kim gave Taylor a stare. 'None of those bags were even close to bursting.' A small grin curled the edges of her mouth with her next sentence. 'And my knot tying skills were honed on dad's boat.'

Taylor sat back as far as the upright chair would allow. 'Well you need to go on a refresher course is all I can say.'

The pair started with a bit of garden tidying whilst the weather looked as though it would stay cooperative.

A neatly built stone and wooden arbour took up one corner of the garden. It had been a reading retreat for Geoff Fry over the years. Taylor started bagging up fallen leaves from where the arbour met the low fence separating the plot from the wood. After a few minutes he stopped and stood puzzling over a patch of flattened earth at the base of the fence. It was the exact spot where it had been surmised that Lenny Gill climbed over. An imprint of one of Lenny's trainers was still visible pressed into the earth where the SOCO had photographed it. Now another footmark, that of a smooth, leather soled shoe, obliterated some of the mark left by Gill.

Kim brushed hair from her forehead with the back of a gardening glove clad hand as she went over to see what Taylor was so interested in.

'Someone's been here since Lenny,' Taylor said. 'Someone's climbed over the fence. They've trekked all the way through the wood to do that.' He looked up from the footmarks to face Kim. 'That kitchen door… those bags in the garage. Do you think it's possible? Has someone else been in? Been looking through those bags… searching again?'

They were soon back in the kitchen sitting opposite each other – two more mugs of coffee and grim expressions. 'I tied those bags firmly,' Kim said. 'No way could they have come undone on their own and to my mind none would have burst open.' She looked down into her drink as she spoke.

Taylor said, 'If someone *has* been in and searched they've used more finesse than Lenny and I'm damned sure I pulled that kitchen door to.'

Kim got to her feet and stood hands on hips looking down at the plinth surrounding the base of the kitchen cupboard unit. 'You'll have done a search course?' She looked over at him, a glint of sarcasm in her eyes. 'Unless Staffordshire Police haven't entered the twentieth century yet.'

Taylor nodded he had done such a course.

'One of the prime hidey-holes for druggies and thieves to stash their stuff is in the kitchen under the base of a cupboard. The wooden panel is never screwed on. You prise it backwards and you have a ready-made secret place that no one knows about.'

'Except for the local Drug Squad or CID officer,' Taylor said. He knew the ruse well enough, but his face portrayed his mystification with Kim's line of thought.

She pointed a finger down at the plinth she had nudged back with her toe earlier that morning. 'When I came in this morning I'm sure that was out of line. Someone's removed it overnight. The more I think about it the more I know I'm right. I cleaned the kitchen yesterday and it wasn't like that.'

Taylor got down to his knees and took hold of each side edge of the wooden plinth. Within seconds he eased the contiboard panel free and pushed it to one side. His view underneath the cupboard was aided by the torch that Kim retrieved from one of the boxes in the hall. He peered into the space which formed a six inch high by two feet square void. The green kitchen floor tiles continued beyond the edge of the plinth and into the space. A quarter inch thick carpet of dust coated these hidden tiles from the edge of where the plinth had been located. The dust had developed during the twelve years since the kitchen had been installed. The unmistakable outline of four fingers and a dragged thumb formed by a large, gloved hand were well-defined. The marks furrowed their way through the dust to the back of the void leaving traces of green glossy tiles on show. Taylor looked up from ground level at Kim, now down on her haunches.

His eyebrows lifted, the expression spelling out his disbelief.

'No doubting this at all, someone was in here last night and they've gone through this place with a fine tooth comb.'

It took some soul searching and intense conversation before they decided on their next move. Taylor wanted to play things by the book and for him that was a revelation.

'I think this should be treated with the same seriousness as Lenny Gill's murder scene,' he said. 'As if it was connected to the murder. The SOCO did her job after the burglary and very thorough she was. At that stage we thought this was nothing other than a ten-a-penny break in. A full forensic examination should be carried out as part of the murder enquiry. Now that we know that someone else has broken in here there must be an even stronger chance that it's all connected. We should be telling Ken Grainger about this.

Kim sat down at the table again with both hands resting flat on its top. She waited for several seconds until after Taylor had finished speaking before responding. 'You're right, and I know that if this didn't involve me personally I'd be straight on the phone to Exeter CID. But it does involve me.'

She looked up fixing her gaze on Taylor. 'It seems that it may also involve my father. These people… Lenny Gill and now someone else have come here looking for something. The second visitor has been careful, skilled in fact.' Her eyes widened with anger. 'We don't even know how the bastard got in.' She slammed the side of her now clenched fist down onto the table. 'For Christ's sake Doug, what was Dad doing to get such attention? What was the secret and have they already found it?'

Taylor reached over and covered the still trembling fist with his hand. 'Look, the estate agent will be here soon. I told Ken Grainger I'd see him for half one to get that statement done and it's already nearly two. We'll keep this to ourselves until we find out some more. If we *are* going to get to the bottom of this we'll have to have a serious talk about your father.'

ELEVEN

REPORTER Benedict Cappelli arrived on the pavement outside Heavitree Road Police Station in good time for the five o'clock police press release. He took up his place along with the other overcoat and anorak clad reporters. Pleasantries and nods were exchanged with a few familiar faces. Portable TV cameras bearing the logos of BBC and Sky News stood set back on the kerb edge.

DI Grainger, standing on the station's first step nervously shuffled his feet as a young lady attempted to clip a lapel microphone to his jacket. Grainger blinked a few times as the voice of a female interviewer cued him in with a question.

Cappelli scribbled onto his notepad as the DI's statement got underway marred only slightly by predictable police stiltedness. He made no mention of the burglary at Kim's father's address. No hint was given of Gill's shocking criminal record or life as a scrounging parasite. 'Mr Gill was well known in the community,' Grainger explained through slightly gritted teeth. 'He was found dead at his home at Gallway Road on the Burntwood Lane estate of Exeter on Monday lunchtime by police officers. A post-mortem examination has proved that the death was due to neck injuries. A search had been made of the property.'

Grainger gave the customary police request. 'I would like to appeal to members of the public who may be able to throw light on Mr Gill's movements over the past week. I am also interested to hear of visitors Mr Gill may have had recently and sightings of him within the past few days.'

Nothing much was given away by Grainger in the manner of detail. Cappelli kept an impassive face as the DI churned out some more of the same. The reporter's notebook page contained little – nothing more than the time, date, place and the identity of the speaker. His own knowledge of the crime scene had already been furnished with the entire gory details in much more detail. That account came courtesy of one of his police contacts garnered during his time as a freelance reporter working mostly in the South of England.

'Why were the police visiting Mr Gill?' Cappelli's voice chimed in as Grainger finished a sentence.

Grainger ignored the direct question, sticking to his own formulated plan. 'We are unsure at this stage what has been taken from the property. We visited the premises to interview Mr Gill in connection with police enquiries. I am unable at this time to disclose further details.'

The inspector then turned on his heel and tramped back up the police station steps with the TV interviewer in pursuit hoping for the return of her lapel mic. A few shouted reporters' questions went unanswered as he disappeared through the doors.

Taylor made it back to the bungalow in the late afternoon. The couple managed a little more tidying and sorting but their hearts weren't in the task. They packed in early and arrived back at Kim's apartment at seven o'clock.

Taylor made a phone call and booked a table at an Italian restaurant in Tedham for eight o'clock. They hoped to relax a little after such a manic few days and a lot of unexpected events. The worries of leaving the bungalow overnight after the two break-ins almost side-lined the idea of going out at all. Taylor's first thought had been to wait inside the property overnight for a repeat performance and then "sort the matter out," as he phrased it.

'No I'm not letting you do that. It's too dangerous,' Kim said. 'We don't know how many people there were. There may have been two or three of them.'

It made sense and anyway it was unlikely after such an intricate search that the intruders would return. 'They either found what they were after or gave up on the idea.' Kim said. She bit lightly down onto her lip as she made her unusually level-headed remarks.

After a shower and change of clothes they made it to the restaurant five minutes early. Taylor stuck with the steak: *Filetto Al Pepe*, as the menu called it. He loved that green peppercorn and cognac sauce. Kim chose pasta: *Penne Sicilia.* The choice of a deep ruby red Venetian wine, Schiopettino, worked well with both meals.

Inevitably the conversation was taken up with the latest happenings. The certainty of an in depth talk about Kim's late father was on the agenda. Taylor hoped to keep off this subject until after the food. He didn't want to spoil the evening completely. He'd met Mr Fry many times, with frequent visits to the bungalow during the four years that he had been seeing Kim. There had been meals out together. A few pints at the local pub had seen off an evening or Sunday lunchtime over the years. Fry was an intelligent, generous and humorous man, a good friend, or so Taylor thought. It was only during the past couple of days that an element of doubt had crept into his mind. *What could it be that Mr Fry had been tangled up with which had spawned so much interest from such desperate villains?*

Kim had never said much about her father's career. It was only since the recent peculiar events that Taylor realised that his own conversations with Mr Fry had never elaborated on what he actually did. The exchanges were always humorously side-stepped or the issue cleverly traded for a slightly different subject by Mr Fry.

Other than his work being connected to the NHS and based mostly in a London office, Taylor knew little. Mr Fry had only managed to enjoy twelve months of his early retirement which had been prompted by his heart condition. He was just fifty-six when he'd died.

Kim shook her head. 'Yes, looking back it's odd. Dad was open on any subject except when his job cropped up. I suppose over the years I became used to not discussing it with him. It was connected to the National Health Service.' She faltered for a second. 'Or so I thought. He gained his degree at Oxford in microbiology and later his PhD. He had a string of letters after his name but never used them. He liked to be known as Geoff or plain Mr Fry.'

Taylor listened intently. He'd given a few nods as he'd sliced himself off a piece of steak. 'I feel a bit guilty. All this probing into your father's affairs, but we both agreed that we needed to know more.'

He dabbed at his mouth with a napkin and sat back. It was time to tell her what he had found out.

'I remember when I picked up that post and found the bank card missing. We were unsure if your dad had opened the letters or if it was all down to the burglar. One was a letter from a work colleague of your dad's.'

'Yes,' Kim said. 'I remember it… a guy named Tremaine.'

Taylor kept his head down as he swilled the wine in his glass. He didn't want to look Kim in the eye at this moment. He might be accused of being a bit too nosey. 'Alexander Tremaine, Kim, Alexander Tremaine from a laboratory service… an address in North West London.'

He looked up, his expression now showing some worry. He'd been digging a bit more than he'd let on and was unsure how Kim would take it.

She stowed her knife and fork centrally onto her cleared plate and leaned back into the chair, a puzzled expression developing. 'Colindale Avenue… yes, I read it. He worked from there some of the time, but he also spent a lot of time in Salisbury as well. Years ago he would be away for weeks on end… Scotland and abroad sometimes. I believed a lot of his work was to do with the development of vaccine, for influenza and other nationwide health problems. It took me all of my thirty-one years to get that out of him.'

She gave Taylor a sideways glance, it was clear that he was keeping something back. 'You'd better tell me what you've found out.'

Taylor could sense Kim's agitation. He gave a little shrug of the shoulders before starting. 'The title is, "The Centre for Applied Microbiology and Research"… Alexander Tremaine has an office there. He's one of the main bosses.'

Kim gave a sigh. 'It sounds like something that's part of the National Health Service which is what dad said. But why do I get the feeling that you're going to upset my entire day.'

'Your father was telling the truth, the organisation is associated with the NHS and that's because it does a lot of work in the field of microbiology. So yes, what you said is also right, work on vaccines for Asian flu and other viruses which threaten the population are developed there. But Alexander Tremaine is a British Army Major and it seems that he has more than one office.'

'Where else?'

'Somewhere with a history… the Ministry of Defence facility at Porton Down, near Salisbury.'

Kim's mouth dropped open a fraction. Her eyes shifted downwards focussing on the table as she assimilated the name with some stored away memories. A jumble of different newspaper reports and TV or radio commentaries flooded into her mind as she targeted the two words: *Porton Down*. Fragments of text her eyes may have disinterestedly flitted across perhaps years ago. Some boring overheard conversation where her subconscious had selected the odd word or the odd name: *Porton Down*.

She looked up from the table and whispered the words. 'Porton Down'. Her next words were pronounced as a question… 'GERM WARFARE?'

Taylor's face remained serious and his response came as nothing more than three slow head nods.

TWELVE

THE MURDER room still buzzed with activity at half past ten. A dozen extra telephone lines had been installed as a priority job by BT. The television broadcast had generated some input from the public albeit nothing likely to earmark a particular person as the murderer. It did seem though, that Leonard Gill had plenty of enemies, plenty of people glad to see the back of him.

Five computer terminals were now installed and the major enquiry computer system, HOLMES, was up and running in record time.

Grainger rubbed at his tired eyes as he tried to get to grips with some important nuggets of information. Timson's usual maverick style had caused consternation for one or two of the by-the-book bosses. No one could deny though, that he had uncovered some useful material.

'Dykes rang Lenny on the Thursday evening to see if he wanted to meet up for a pint,' Timson said. 'From what I can work out he must have made the call not long after Lenny arrived home after his last withdrawal. That was just after eight in the evening when he used the hole in the wall at Barclays in Exeter. Dykes says that Lenny had already told him some of what he'd been up to when they'd met up on the Wednesday. He'd been paid to screw somewhere. Three hundred quid to do the job with another seven hundred ready and waiting when the goods were delivered.'

'And what were the goods?' Grainger asked.

Documents boss,' Timson replied. 'That's all Dykes knows. Obviously Lenny must have been given more detail, but he never got around to telling Dykes. Dykes says that Lenny told him that the customer specifically warned him not to take anything that might leave a trail back. The pair of them should have met up in the Hollybush and Lenny was going to tell him some more, but he never showed up. The pathologist is confident on putting a time of death between eight o'clock. and eleven. on the Thursday evening. There was no beer in his stomach and no alcohol in his blood… Lenny never made it to the pub.'

Grainger frowned. 'Hmm, so Lenny was told not to take anything which could lead back. That explains why he only took the spare cash and a few things to keep for himself?'

'Exactly and Dykes says that Lenny told him that the customer said it must look like a standard break-in. It must have been hard for Lenny to stick to the customer's rules knowing *his* track record. He pinched the sixty quid from the wallet and even managed to keep his fingers off the cheque book. He couldn't resist taking the brand new card and PIN from the doormat. He must have thought his dreams had been answered when he found them, especially when he gave the card a try and found it to be active.'

Timson furtively checked his watch to calculate if he would still make it to the pub before closing. 'It seems that the customer was well informed, as he told Lenny the time and date of Mr Fry's funeral. He described the location… opposite Tedham church. The customer told him to do the job during the funeral. He even tipped him off that the mourners would be going on to the pub afterwards.'

Grainger shook his head. 'All stuff given in the newspaper death notice. The burglary must be connected to Lenny's murder. We need to speak to Kim tomorrow and have Mr Fry's bungalow treated as an extended crime scene in relation to the murder. A full forensic examination. We must find out what Lenny was searching for.'

Timson beat a hasty retreat leaving Grainger torn between doing another half hour of paperwork or making his own dash to beat closing time. The single sheet of A4 on top of his in-tray grabbed his attention. The uniformed police woman stationed at Lenny's house on telephone duty throughout Friday evening had left her report.

The idea was that the identity of any caller and their business with Lenny may be of interest. To this end Grainger involved British

Telecom. Their latest piece of technology had been introduced to deal with long term nuisance or abusive calls. The scheme required nothing more than the authorisation of a police chief inspector and so could be instantly, legally implemented. It was a slight twisting of the rules but the fool proof system had already proved its worth many times.

The hook-up had been installed within a few hours at the local exchange and integrated with Lenny's telephone line. All that the policewoman needed to do following a received call was to press the number one digit on the phone when the call closed down. The identity of the incoming call would be automatically traced and logged at the exchange irrespective of the length of time. Even one second would be enough.

The details of only one call had been added to the bottom of the policewoman's report:

Incoming call: 7.32 pm. Friday 15th March.

Caller did not speak and closed the call down immediately after I gave my standard opening line. I did not get the opportunity to divulge my identity.

BT have given the below known details:

Call duration 4 seconds.

Caller number traced by BT as: 0710778241

Number traced to The Daily Herald Newspaper, main news office Wapping, East London (Not possible to pin point an individual phone extension).

A total of 6 unanswered calls were made to the property, between the discovery of the body and the installation of the BT trace (6.57 p.m.). The calls stopped after this (the seventh) call. BT state that it is impossible to trace the preceding unanswered calls.

Grainger muttered to himself as he read through the information. 'So we've no way of knowing who made the earlier calls. It may be that all we have is some nosey bloody reporter who has been quick out of the starting blocks and hoping for a personal police interview.'

Taylor and Harding arrived back at her apartment just before eleven o'clock. She'd had more vino than enough and a black mood had descended. She'd attempted to wipe away her thoughts with alcohol.

Taylor's revelation of who supplied his information on Major Tremaine and the association with Porton Down was Kim's given reason for her aggressive behaviour.

"Jenny Lowell." Taylor had admitted. "I rang her. No one else would have access to such info. At least no one who was likely to tell me."

"THAT BITCH." Kim had blurted out across the restaurant table. She'd said it with enough volume to make other diners turn their heads.

Jennifer Adele Lowell was a Staffordshire Detective Chief Inspector on the force's Special Branch. Lowell, a former British Army captain joined the police as a second career some nine years earlier. She'd fast tracked through the ranks. She also fast tracked through departments to land the job as an SB boss.

Taylor's own time as a Detective Sergeant on SB resulted in a short affair with Lowell. It was not one of his best thought out moves and came about when he had the black dog of his own divorce to contend with. It was an affair which Lowell was ever keen to rekindle.

THIRTEEN

TAYLOR slept on the sofa and had packed his bag by the time Kim surfaced, bleary eyed from the bedroom the next morning.

'I'll be getting back today then,' he said. He'd hoped she'd tell him not to be daft and remind him he'd still had a week of leave left. Perhaps she'd admit she was being stupid, so he could put his prepared speech into play:

I'm not interested in Jenny Lowell… she's history and that happened before I even knew you. I told you about that affair because she'd pestered me during that last case. I asked her because she was the only person likely to be able to find anything out.

Kim said nothing on the subject and so Taylor didn't get the chance to try to patch things up. Instead she picked up a bulky folder of law notes from the table and pushed it at him.

'Here, read through this. It might keep you busy until you're due back at work.'

Taylor sighed with frustration as he took the folder. It contained a lot of facts, figures, rules and regulations which he'd spent hours looking out especially for Kim. It was revision paperwork to give her a good shot at passing her inspector's exam. A note which Taylor had written to Kim and which had lain on top of the file fluttered down to the carpet. Kim snatched it up, screwing it into a ball and slamming it down on top of the file.

It was all hurtful and like nothing he'd ever seen in Kim before. It fast occurred to him that this was nothing to do with Jenny Lowell. It more likely concerned her father and what she was discovering about his past.

Taylor saw the tears welling up in Kim's eyes as he took one last look back before closing the front door on himself and walking away down the path.

Hardly ten minutes slipped by before the doorbell shook Kim

from her thoughts. She tried to ignore it until the persistent pressing stressed the fact to her that Taylor was not going to go away. She flung the door open, still in her dressing gown, her hair a mess, eyes bloodshot and cheeks tearstained.

'WHAT,' was her single half-shouted word.

It wasn't Taylor.

Two men and a woman stood back one yard from Kim's front door. The men, dark hair, dark suits and overcoats and the woman, mid-grey trouser suit and blonde bob. Kim's immediate thought was that they belonged to some kind of religious outfit. She quickly dispelled the idea. There was a professional hardness in the eyes of each of the trio. The men, square jawed and both slightly above six feet kept hands down by sides. The woman, laser cut features and untrusting expression adopted folded arms. They all watched as Kim blinked her reddened eyes and waited for them to make the first move. The woman, even in her stylish ox-blood, Crockett and Jones flat leather shoes was almost equal to the men in height. Kim scanned the three faces and a small feeling of recognition came to her about one of the men. Something told her from the back of her mind that she had seen this face before.

This man made a thin smile and accompanied it with an almost imperceptible nod of acknowledgement. 'Detective Constable Harding? he said, before pausing for effect. 'Perhaps Acting Detective Sergeant Harding would be more correct. That's the rank given to you in the recently adjusted Force Standing Orders.'

He held out a Devon and Cornwall Constabulary police officer's warrant card. 'DCI Ian Forrester, Special Branch. I don't think we've met, I spend most of my time up at HQ or in London.'

Kim remained silent, partly embarrassed by her appearance and partly stunned by the unexpected visit. She was nevertheless sharp enough not to accept the face value of the situation and held out her hand, fingers open, towards Forrester's warrant card. A more genuine smile flickered across the DCI's face as he started to accept that the résumé given to him earlier may be correct. *Harding was nobody's fool.*

Forrester accepted back his scrutinised ID before glancing left and right at the two people either side of him. 'I have with me two of Her Majesty's Security Service agents.'

Kim blinked her eyes closed and gave a little shake of the head as an *I don't believe this is happening moment* engulfed her.

'MI5,' she said, more as a statement than a question.

'We prefer to call the department Box 500 these days,' the woman said.

Ten minutes passed before Kim had dressed and tidied herself. The four were sitting around the coffee table in her lounge. The Security Service agents introduced themselves as Michael Nelson and Sheila Jennings. It went through Kim's mind that the names sounded authentic enough to be false and probably were.

The woman, Jennings, came straight to the point. 'Did you know what kind of work your father was involved in?'

Kim sat forward, the fingers of her right hand supporting her banging forehead and her eyes staring blankly at the carpet between her feet. She shook her head side to side as she answered. 'Clearly not.'

Nelson remained upright in his chair, a hand on each knee. 'We offer our condolences regarding your father's death. We do appreciate that you've been through a particularly difficult time recently, both with your father's death and other things that have happened. I'm sure that as a detective you understand the nature of our work and that sometimes sentiment has to take a back seat.'

The man watched Kim as he spoke, as did his colleague, but Kim was getting her act together now. She had tuned into the psychology being used and it wasn't that much different than the way she often played the game. They were looking for body language, fidgeting, unnecessary smiles, rapid eye blinking – rather too much detail in an answer. They were testing the water to see if she had secrets and watching to see if she was going to tell lies.

'Your father worked in a specialised field he had a DV security rating… that's the highest.' Nelson said.

Kim's poker face gave nothing away. 'He was a microbiologist… involved in some way with the NHS. I thought it was to do with inoculations for major health problems. He rarely spoke on the subject.'

Jennings got to her feet. She took the three paces over to the window and stood, arms folded again gazing out as she spoke. 'We do know that you have recently been made aware of a little more information about your father's work. Possibly via Detective Inspector Taylor?' She turned as she finished the sentence and had raised an eyebrow.

Jenny Bloody Lowell was the name that came into Kim's mind. *She's sent these here. She's started this off.*

'Incidentally where is Mr Taylor.' Jennings said with eyes on the bedroom door.

'You *just missed* him,' Kim's response was sardonic – a lengthening of the words 'Just' and 'Missed'.

'We need to search your father's bungalow,' the agent snapped back. She had turned fully away from the window to face Kim and her own sardonic face had been assumed. 'Routine you understand. Something we have to do on most occasions when an employee dies or leaves the job. We must be sure no important documents have been left lying around.'

Kim was on her feet now, arms hanging loosely at her sides, straight back and wide eyes. 'My father died two weeks ago, so it's taken you a while to decide on that.'

Neither agent reacted to her words. They would search the bungalow whether she permitted it or not. She might as well appear gleefully cooperative.

'Fine,' she eventually said. 'Do you want me to come along or would you rather have the keys and go on your own.'

'We'd appreciate you coming along and we apologise for the

trouble we're putting you to.' Nelson said this, attempting to ease the tension.

The conversation seemed to have concluded. Kim grabbed her leather jacket and checked her handbag for the keys. The sound of the doorbell stopped her in her tracks. Had Taylor come back? God how she hoped that he had.

Reg Timson stood alongside DI Grainger as Kim opened up. Grainger was keen to explain his need to search the bungalow as a part of the Lenny Gill murder. Kim made a sign with her backwards pointing thumb. Her wide eyes and mouthed words delivered the information: 'SB and MI5.'

The cosy sized lounge now seemed crowded as Grainger and Timson also squeezed in. They both recognised Forrester. Grainger's nod accompanied his words. 'Good morning Chief Inspector.'

Forrester reddened. 'Morning Ken, sorry… should have let you know we were on your patch. It was a bit rushed and I didn't get the call myself until eight this morning.'

Forrester gave a cagey résumé of their interest in the matters. It followed the lines of the excuse given by the MI5 – a routine search for overlooked government documents. It was never going to hold water with Grainger but clearly pressure had been brought to bear from higher up. The Security Service's examination of the bungalow would take precedence over that of the murder investigation.

The two Exeter detectives retreated back to their car, resigned to the fact that their search of the bungalow would not happen until MI5 were finished with it. Grainger was, to use his own description, "a bit miffed" but making waves at HQ would be pointless. He shuffled his papers on his lap as Timson drove the car into the yard at the rear of Tedham's red brick Victorian Police Station. They had decided to kick their heels there and make use of the telephones for a few other associated enquiries rather than journey back to Exeter. Grainger ordered the coffees from the tiny upstairs canteen and they settled down at a table.

'We know that Kim has had a big tidy-up right through the bungalow,' he said. 'But we do have the benefit of the SOCO examination following the burglary. The only problem is whether or not the Spooks will be willing to share anything they do find.'

'Bloody doubtful,' Timson said. 'They are looking for a particular item, or items. We're only going to find out if Kim gets to see what they take away.'

Grainger gave Timson a sideways look. 'Not even that if they hold a copy of the Official Secrets Act in front of her nose.'

FOURTEEN

SPECIAL BRANCH man, DCI Forrester followed Kim's Ford Fiesta XR2i in his own Peugeot whilst the Vauxhall Senator used by the two Security Service agents took up the rear. Within ten minutes the convoy arrived at the bungalow and Kim pulled onto the drive behind Geoff Fry's car. The other two cars were left on the roadside and the trio reunited with Kim Harding in the porch as she unlocked the door. Nelson held a large and heavy looking aluminium flight case in his right hand whilst his female colleague had a tattered looking, bulging orange folder.

Kim curled her bottom lip between her teeth and struggled against growing annoyance as the three followed her inside. Liberties were taken and a generally dismissive attitude adopted by the two agents. They both wandered uninvited into the lounge where Nelson set down his flight case on the carpet. Jennings stood spreading musty, yellowed documents from the folder across the dining table.

'You are obviously looking for something in particular.' Kim said. 'Is this the same thing that Lenny Gill was after and….'

She stopped herself in mid-sentence realising she'd been perilously close to giving the game away over the second break-in. This fact was still only known to her and Taylor.

Jennings looked up from the papers waiting for Kim to finish the sentence. 'Well…?' She said the word as a question. 'AND… and WHAT?'

Kim stepped in front of Jennings, leaning forward until their noses nearly touched. 'AND… a few manners would be appreciated, this is my property. If I can help I will, but this bloody cloak and dagger and bullying will not further your cause.'

It was quite a speech to have been thought up so quickly and under such pressure. It turned the tables, diverting attention from the near slip.

Nelson intervened, stepping towards the two women and spreading the fingers of both his hands wide in a mannerism to separate them. 'Ladies, ladies come on now. Let's try to get this done amicably.'

It defused the situation and gave the man an opportunity to divert attention to the documents on the table. 'These Kim,' he said drawing an open hand across the paperwork. 'Are the architects design drawings which were first submitted for this building to be constructed in 1957.'

He captured Kim's gaze as she glanced at the files and then back up to him. 'Okay to call you Kim?' He asked.

Kim stayed silent but gave an indifferent shrug.

'Also we have several applications which were made to the local planning department for various works and alterations carried out over the years.'

Kim centred her attention onto Nelson, side-lining Jennings. 'Impressive and very definitely suggestive of something more serious than a hunt for everyday documents. It's a Sunday today remember? You've pulled some strings to get someone from the Planning Department to turn out and dig all this stuff out for you.'

Nelson kept a poker face; he'd grasped the fact that trying to browbeat Kim was a non-starter. His tactics of information sharing and respect might be more productive. 'No point in trying to disagree, so yes, exactly that. I gather from the Scene of Crime officer's report and DC Timson's burglary file that as far as you knew your father did not have a safe?'

Kim gave a nod.

'Have you come across any keys during your clearance of the property? Keys for which there seem to be no use?' Nelson asked. 'Anything that may be a high security key? Like a safe key?'

Kim knew that all the keys could be quickly and easily inspected. The Sentry key in her bag would stand out like a sore thumb. 'Yes,' she replied. 'There is such a key on the ring with dad's car and house keys.' She rummaged in her handbag and produced the set, handing it to Nelson. 'I'd been puzzled about its use.'

Nelson separated the key and held it to the light. His facial expression until this point had been unreadable, but for a moment a flash of excitement showed. The emotion vanished in the seconds it took to hold the key up for to Jennings to see.

The woman pursed her lips as she focussed on the serrated stainless steel teeth. Her gaze glided over to meet Kim's. 'Not much doubting that… definitely a safe key.'

The agents started a visual inspection of the rooms. They occasionally took measurements with a steel tape and checked the details against the house blueprints on the dining table.

Kim formed the opinion that the two were good at their job and were leaving no stone unturned. Jennings knelt down and ran her fingers along the surface of the kitchen base unit plinth. The evidence of the unreported second break-in flashed into Kim's mind. Taylor's idea had been to replace the plinth without cleaning away the evidence, as it might prove vital to the wider enquiry. It seemed sound thinking at the time, but now she wished she'd dragged a duster over it.

Jennings pressed her fingernails into the edges of the plinth and prised it outward letting it drop flat against the tiled floor. With her cheek almost touching the tiles she peered into the space.

'Someone has searched under here recently,' she said looking up from ground level. Her eyes mistrustfully bored into Kim's psyche. 'Have you or Taylor removed this panel?'

Kim shook her head slowly. The furrows taking over her forehead could be mistaken for genuine puzzlement. The earnest quality of the expression though, had been aided by virtue of fear – *what was she getting into!* She was now down alongside Jennings looking into the space and adding realism to her act. 'It certainly looks recent. I can only imagine that the burglar has searched there.'

The two women stood back to their feet. Jennings gave Kim a

long stare. 'Doubtful, I'd say… having seen the crime file. Not a thorough search. Lenny Gill, according to his criminal record was a lump of lard with a brain to match.'

Kim swallowed hard. 'Beats me, unless dad has had the panel off at some time.'

A sideways glance at Kim followed Jennings' stare before she continued her check the kitchen. The idea was a possibility which she could not deny but the women were off to a bad start and Jennings had not been smitten with the detective's sincerity.

A search of the garage and garden generated a few more notes scribbled onto Nelson's pad. He returned to the lounge and lifted the lid of the flight case. The grey, foam-rubber mat inside had various carved recesses. An assortment of electrical devices were slotted into these. Meters, sockets and tuning dials were on display. Nelson lifted the entire top mat out to reveal another beneath it which contained an array of interlocking poles, flat discs, cabling and battery packs.

Within a few moments he had assembled a hand held scanning device and started to drift the head across a section of brickwork between the lounge and kitchen. He turned to face Kim as he adjusted the tuning. 'It's a form of penetrating radar; it can detect voids, cavities, hidden objects. Change the head and settings and it can sweep for electronic bugs or find metal.'

Kim made an impressed face as she widened her eyes. 'Drug Squad would love that toy.'

Nelson nodded. 'Yes, price is a bit prohibitive for police budgets though.' He continued to play the scanner over various parts of the building after consulting with his colleague over the notes made earlier. After less than ten minutes of this he said, 'Okay we'll check that part outside now.'

The two agents stepped out through the back door and headed across the soggy lawn to the arbour with Kim following. Nelson stood a few yards back from the construction, his head moving as he took in the build and dimensions. 'This doesn't show on the plans. It was not part of the original house build. No planning application was submitted for it and I'm gathering it wouldn't need one.' He turned to face Kim. 'Was it here when your father bought the property?'

'I think he had it built not long after he moved in. He loved it, spent hours out here when the weather allowed.'

The agent floated the scanner across some of the stonework making a glum face as no readings registered on the meter. His expression changed as he ran the device along the bottom edge of the stone seat.

'Hello, what have we here?'

Kim shuffled forward, her face showing bewilderment as Nelson's knuckle tapped against the stone front. The resulting sound gave an unexpected hollow resonance and the other agent enthusiastically knelt down alongside.

In no time the false stone front was lifted out and an eighteen inch square safe door was on display. Its matt green hammered paint finish with stainless steel handle and keyhole looked out of place against the rustic surroundings. The logo *SentrySafe* stood proud of the flat surface on a chromium silver badge fitted in the left hand corner.

Nelson pushed Kim's key into the lock and turned it the allowed one and a half times. He took hold of the handle twisting it anti-clockwise one quarter of a turn. A dull metallic *clunk* sounded as the hardened molybdenum steel bolts withdrew. The door silently swung open.

It was empty.

FIFTEEN

GRAINGER and Timson arrived back at the bungalow a few minutes in advance of the SOCO team and forensics boffins. The Security Service agents were gone, but their line of questioning to Kim over the mystery safe had been fierce.

Grainger held a copy of that morning's edition of the Sunday Herald. He'd strolled to the newsagents and purchased a few copies of the more prominent nationals. He singled out The Herald from the others and flattened it out at the relevant story onto the kitchen worktop. Kim gave the opened newspaper report nothing more than a disinterested gaze as she filled the kettle.

'You seen this?' Grainger said looking over at her. His finger pressed down onto the page where the headline read: *Former Burglar Murdered in his own home.*

'No not yet, Boss. I've had a busy day so far.'

Grainger settled his backside onto one of the tall stools against the worktop and thought for a few seconds. 'We haven't released anything over Lenny Gill's background yet. There's more in here too. This reporter… what's his name…' his finger scrolled down below the headline. 'Benedict Cappelli… seems to have some good contacts.'

Kim spooned coffee into two mugs. 'Well don't look in this direction,' she said defensively. 'Anyway, there must be dozens on the estate who know what a toe-rag Lenny was.'

'Hmm,' Grainger murmured as his finger travelled down the text of the article. 'That doesn't explain this though…' He read the passage out aloud: 'Mr Gill was found with throat wounds in a pool of blood. His hands were tied.' Grainger folded the newspaper and tucked it back into his briefcase. 'We didn't let half of that info out to the press. So where's he had that all from? Curious that Cappelli works for the Herald… the same paper that made a phone call to

Lenny's only hours after we'd found the body.'

The flashes of the forensic examiner's camera flickered through the kitchen doorway and the sound of conversation drifted in from the different rooms. Grainger's team were soon meticulously going through the minutiae of what remained of Geoffrey Fry's life at the bungalow. Kim was keen to point out the hidden safe and the kitchen plinth with its dusty handprint. Her own tidy-up hadn't left much behind in the manner of evidence though.

Grainger resigned himself to his efforts being a waste of time, but a murder enquiry demanded that no stone should be left unturned. Of course Gill had carried out the burglary, but what was he looking for and who put him up to it? The answers would almost certainly lead to the killer's identity. The revelation about the safe was interesting but nothing more, as there was nothing inside it. Grainger took Kim to one side as the search drew to a close.

'I feel a bit like Lenny Gill here Kim… hands are tied behind my back. The Spooks wouldn't have been here without good reason. I'm guessing they knew what Gill had been sent to get. It's obvious that they are not going to tell us. If they've made their minds up that Lenny Gill's murder has to play second fiddle to whatever they are looking at, then it must be damned serious.'

Grainger resumed his supervision of the search and left Kim pondering his words. She felt worse now about being so hard on Taylor. He was right to try to find out more. But DCI Jenny Lowell's involvement and her decision to tip off MI5 had opened an enormous can of worms.

Taylor made a big detour on his way back to Staffordshire. With plenty of time on his hands he could not stop his detective mind churning. Facts, suspicions and possibilities relentlessly revolved inside his head. His unplanned excursion took him on a 100 mile journey from Exeter along the A303 in the direction of Salisbury. His fleeting glimpse of Stonehenge fortified his intention to someday pay it a visit but other things were more important just now.

Nearly two hours had gone when he arrived in Porton, a quaint picturesque village nestling in Wiltshire's Bourne Valley. To the passing traveller who knew nothing of the area's history there was nothing unusual about the place. The River Bourne had made its mark, sculpting the landscape over tens of thousands of years. Those rolling grasslands with juniper scrub and broadleaved trees had been named centuries ago as "Porton Down". To all intents and purposes it was a quintessentially English part of England. It seemed criminal that in more recent times the place had been so dramatically and irreversibly associated with the horrors of germ warfare.

After pulling into the kerbside alongside a newsagent's shop he hopped out and collected a can of Coke and a Toffee Crisp. A check of his road map preceded a further ten minute drive out of the village winding him through country lanes and onto Manor Farm Road. The rural sounding road-name fitted the pastoral countryside which was on offer over the first half mile. But the sleepy Englishness dissolved abruptly as a 1,600 feet stretch of five metre high, razor-wire topped, metal fencing came into view. It made a stark contrast as it cut its way so decisively through the surrounding green fields. The line of poplar trees which had been planted as camouflage still had many years of growth ahead of them before they would achieve their mission. Tall angular, grey concrete buildings rose from different corners of the seven-thousand acre plot within the fenced enclosure. The slate grey overcast sky loomed intimidatingly and seemed the one feature capable of living in harmony with this chilling place.

Taylor slowed his car to a crawl as he passed by the huge galvanised steel entrance gates. He managed a meagre glimpse into what lay beyond: A roadway system, sentry boxes, internal barrier posts, car parks. Distant figures walking between buildings could be made out. Uniforms and the occasional white lab coat seemed in vogue.

Two British Army soldiers stood on guard inside the gates and watched Taylor's car drive slowly by. Their automatic assault rifles were supported by shoulder straps – muzzles pointing downward. Taylor quickly soaked up more information from the plethora of freestanding and fence fixed signs near to the gate. A prominent one simply bore large black lettering on a white background:

PORTON DOWN SCIENCE CAMPUS

Centre for Applied Microbiology and Research [CAMR]

Taylor's mind went back to Tremaine's letter to Geoff Fry which gave details of the same department. Another sign showed the red, white and blue of the national flag but set out as broad bands and with bold black lettering:

MINISTRY OF DEFENCE

CHEMICAL DEFENCE ESTABLISHMENT

MANAGEMENT EXECUTIVE

A third sign looked antique. It was a four feet square of rusted enamelled sheet metal supported by two equally ancient metal legs set into concrete. The once white background was now yellowed with years of age. Black, wartime styled stencilled lettering:

OFFICIAL SECRETS ACTS

PROHIBITED PLACE

PHOTOGRAPHY NOT AUTHORISED

Taylor picked up speed as he headed away with many thoughts and questions revolving in his mind:

Could it be that this entire mystery had been spawned from within that compound? A place where Geoffrey Fry almost certainly spent many of his working hours – Geoffrey Fry, the seemingly pleasant inoffensive man and father of the woman he loved.

The detour had lengthened his journey back home to Staffordshire considerably. He made good progress until he hit the unforgiving M6. It was half-past three by the time he completed the one hundred and fifty miles from Porton Down to the hamlet of Yarnstall. He pulled into his drive, switched off and reached over to the back seat for his bag before climbing out. He knew that brooding would not help but he found it difficult to drag himself from a gloomy mood. He let himself in through the back door, walked through to the lounge and dumped his bag and Kim's law notes down. A sheet of white A4 copy paper hung out from the file, it was Kim's page marker. He shook his head at the futility of it as he checked the marker. She'd already done a lot and yet now it looked as though she was going to throw it all away. He shook his head some more as he recalled how Kim had thrust the file at him along with that hurtful jibe: *"Here read through this it might keep you busy until you're due back at work."*

Taylor had a week of leave still to run before starting his new role of Acting Detective Chief Inspector at Stafford. Several possibilities entered his mind as he considered how to fill the rest of his unexpectedly blank timetable. Should he start on the paperwork sent to him by his predecessor and swot up on his new job? Maybe he could ring up, cancel his leave and perhaps get stuck into all that paperwork in his office? Perhaps he'd give the Chief Constable a call and tell him to stuff his job!

His eyes locked onto a bottle of Ardbeg whisky. The black and gold label with white lettering visible through the glass front of the drinks cabinet – a present from Kim. It was either that or coffee. The doorbell rang.

The woman, tall, slim and with a gym-toned physique stood one pace back from the door. Gleaming, well looked after teeth gave an almost sultry look to the mouth as the red glossed lips formed into knowing grin. The face though, had a certain hardness – a sallowness created by the passage of time. Solicitous use of make-up and eyebrow pencil had been employed in an effort to fight off the years. A flick of the dyed auburn hair was made before the opening line. 'Doug… are you going to invite me in?'

Jenny Lowell's perfume had an expensive classy tang that lingered in a man's nostrils.

SIXTEEN

BENEDICT CAPPELLI'S attempts to track down Lenny Gill's extended criminal family did not prove difficult. Whether or not he would get the information he needed would be a different matter.
He soon arrived in Gallway Road on the Burntwood Lane estate. The house looked different from his last visit. It had been three weeks ago when he'd made that night-time hasty call. He'd not lingered. It had only taken seconds to push the envelope containing the first £300 instalment through the letterbox. The address was not in doubt though. The crime scene was still adorned with streamers of fluttering blue and white tape along with half a dozen parked police vehicles.

Cappelli drove on past. His interest lay in the nearby pubs – Lenny Gill's watering holes.

The Hollybush, number three on his list, was a fug of smoke with a carpet so impregnated from years of beer spillage that it threatened to remove the soles of his shoes. The clatter of dominoes provided a background noise beneath several different conversations. If Cappelli had not known better he would have thought he'd walked in on a swearing competition. The contestants, red faced, mostly tattooed drinkers sat facing each other at iron legged tables. Cards, dominoes, chatter about social security benefits, dog and horse racing appeared to be the most popular interests. The Guinness clock behind the bar showed the time as quarter past two. Cappelli's enquiry regarding friends of Lenny Gill was rewarded with nothing more than a nod from the barman in the direction of a particular customer.

Several pairs of eyes studied him as he took a sip of his pint of Old Speckled Hen and then cautiously homed in on the man pointed out. The distrustful stares were dispelled as he dropped his change into the charity box on the bar – definitely not a copper!

Donald Dykes was in his usual space, a high stool with the Racing

Times spread across a sizable portion of the bar's woodwork. With his shaven bullet head, swarthy blue-jowled face and roll of neck fat bulging over his collar he appeared the epitome of a gangland crook. Cappelli suspected he was nowhere near that league. The reporter's peculiar mind-set clicked into overdrive before he made his first move. This was the exciting bit! The not knowing if he might get his teeth knocked out.

Abel Magwich was the name that came to Cappelli's mind – *the man would make a great Abel Magwich, the convict from Charles Dickens Great Expectations,* a superb casting.

Dykes slowly started to turn as his peripheral vision captured Cappelli closing in. He instantly scowled at the journalist.

'Mr Magwich?' Cappelli said.

'No,' Dykes growled completely ignorant of the mickey-taking.

'I'm looking to speak to someone regarding Lenny Gill. I've been given the name Magwich.'

'You a fucking copper?' Dykes said clenching a fist and preparing to lift himself from the stool. 'No you ain't fucking tall enough.'

Cappelli remained concerned for his teeth and kept sufficient distance between himself and Dykes in case a haymaker should be launched.

'I'm a journalist Mr Magwich. From the newspapers. I need information and I'm willing to pay.'

Dykes' eyes widened, but not now with aggression – money had been mentioned. 'I ain't fucking Mag Twitch, I keep telling you. I'm Don Dykes, but I can tell you all you need to know about Lenny… if you're paying.'

The horror of seeing the photograph of his old partner in crime was now gone. It had been replaced by nothing more than the passage of a few hours and the mention of money.

Grainger and his team had finished their search and all but packed up. Kim's options seemed to be between finishing off the remaining jobs at the bungalow or going back to her apartment and feeling sorry for herself. The doorbell rang as she signed Grainger's paperwork in the kitchen.

Benedict Cappelli gave his smile and held out his press card. 'Good afternoon, from the Daily Herald newspaper.' He extended a hand forward for Kim to shake.

She took a half-step backwards, hands remaining by sides and wordless, but with eyes fixed onto the name on the card. Cappelli hadn't known what to expect when he'd pressed the doorbell. The three police vehicles parked on the road gave him the idea that this might be a good time to call. He was ignorant though, of what family, if any, Geoffrey Fry had, and no idea of who was now in charge of the building. The police activity certainly indicated that something *had* happened at the bungalow, but who was this woman? Was she part of the visiting police team or a family member?

Grainger appeared in the hallway behind Kim. He had heard the reporter's opening line and took over the conversation. 'Can I help you,' he said, over Kim's shoulder.

Cappelli's face broke into a smug grin of recognition. 'Detective Inspector Grainger… Benedict Cappelli from the Herald, I saw you at the Leonard Gill murder press release.'

Grainger stepped into the doorway, his brow furrowing. Kim retreated down the hallway, relieved to let him take over. 'What are you doing here Mr Cappelli?'

'My question, Inspector is what are *you* doing here? I've covered a few similar stories in the past. As the investigating officer in a nasty murder, shouldn't you be spending your time with that, rather than a house burglary.'

'How would you know there had been a burglary Mr Cappelli?' Grainger fired back.

'An informant Inspector.'

Cappelli was taking a chance, but his bluff might uncover some inside police information. It could get him a step closer to understanding what the mystery file contained. Additionally it might allay his fears that the police had made a connection between him and Lenny Gill. 'I don't usually reveal my sources Inspector but I might be running a story soon and a certain Donald Dykes was happy to help. You see he's a very troubled life-long friend of Mr Gill. He's told me that Mr Gill was on a mission connected to a property opposite Tedham Church. Neighbours also told me about some police action here last Thursday. Is that when the break in happened?'

Grainger looked around at Kim. 'Okay to use the kitchen?'

Kim nodded and Cappelli followed Grainger along the hallway.

'Who's the young lady? Cappelli said. 'I'm guessing she's the owner… maybe a relative.' His raised eyebrows and tilt of the head created a knowing expression. 'Dykes said that someone died here… is that death connected to Lenny Gill.'

Grainger was in a corner. 'Look I'd rather you played ball on this, hold off your story for a while until we find out exactly what's going on.'

Cappelli was gaining confidence now. 'I can't give guarantees on that Inspector. You know as well as I do that any number of other reporters will be champing at the bit to get this into print. We must build a relationship here… a little exchange of information.'

Grainger scratched his head. 'Well the young lady is the daughter of the gentleman who passed away here a couple of weeks back. He died from natural causes… a heart attack and there is no reason to connect that with the death of Leonard Gill.' The detective paused as he decided how much more he should give without endangering the enquiry or stepping on the toes of the Security Services. 'A debit card and pin number were taken during the burglary and used to withdraw cash from the account.'

'Fairly standard burglary then,' Cappelli casually said as he drank in the new information and the reason why Lenny had been pin pointed so quickly. His mind assimilated this news and tested it against how much it affected him: *The greedy idiot didn't stick to the plan. He took that bloody bank card and pin number and it cost him his life. But who killed him and why? Did he manage to get what he had been sent for and if so where was it now? If he didn't get his hands on it, did he tell his torturers what he had been looking for? Did Lenny give them enough to uncover HIS identity before he died?*

It was an awful lot of questions and possibilities, but Cappelli felt a little easier. It seemed that the police had *not* connected him to Lenny Gill – yet! The story – the cracker – was still there to be unravelled and told, just as long as he could get hold of this mystery file. The remaining worry though, was who killed Gill, and why?

Cappelli gave Grainger a stare as he decided to try another bluff. 'So your burglar was the late Mr Leonard Gill. This must then, be the house, which according to Dykes, Lenny broke into.'

Cappelli had to be careful, he could only use what Dykes actually told him. If additional detail was mentioned, then Grainger would get even more suspicious than he already was. Cappelli scribbled the hotel address and room number he was staying at onto a page of his notepad, tore it off and handed it to Grainger. 'In case we need to talk.'

Grainger arrived back at the Murder Room, anger and frustration embedded into his expression. He could have done without this interfering journalist. It was going to generate all kinds of problems, as if there were not enough already. He plonked himself down in Angela Hewitt's vacant chair. The Scenes of Crime Officer's desk was surrounded by brown paper exhibit sacks containing items awaiting delivery to the forensic laboratory. Other recovered items forming the evidence chain, but not requiring examination, filled much of Hewitt's desk space and had yet to be catalogued. Geoff Fry's stolen clock was one of these and after fingerprinting had been plugged into a socket. It was now acknowledged as the official office timepiece.

Grainger shook his head as he glanced at the clock. 'Half past bloody five. Nearly a whole day wasted.' He turned back to Timson. 'Timmo, get some work done on this bloody nosey reporter… Benedict Cappelli. He seems to know a hell of lot more than he should do about all of this. He's even interviewed Donald Dykes. He just strolled into the Hollybush and struck up a conversation with him.'

Timson gave a nod. 'Where's he staying?'

Grainger pulled Cappelli's note from his pocket. 'He's in room 105 at the Kingsland Hotel.'

SEVENTEEN

DOUG TAYLOR sat back in his armchair and looked across at Jenny Lowell. She was cross legged on the sofa with both hands clasping a coffee mug beneath her chin.

'It was an awkward situation Doug. I didn't mind helping you out… a bit of info for an old friend.' She caught his eye as she paused. 'But the areas you seem to be getting close to are hellishly sensitive. I wasn't fully up to speed myself when I told you the bits I found out on Major Tremaine. I soon got a call from someone up on high. My interest had been noticed and I was put on the spot. I had no option but to explain who wanted to know and why. It would be more than my job is worth for me to give out more information on this.'

She flushed with embarrassment and a tinge of worry. 'I've been warned off in no uncertain terms. I've been told to keep away from you.'

Taylor made a puzzled face. 'So why the hell are you here now Jenny?'

Lowell did not answer Taylor's question. She was looking for a reason to change the subject. Her eyes fastened onto the pile of law notes on the table. Her worried look disappeared. 'What's all that stuff for Doug, I thought you knew it all, you've passed all your exams.'

It was Taylor's turn for embarrassment. 'Old stuff. I was having a clear out.'

Lowell stood and flicked open the folder. Taylor's note to Kim lay inside the cover. It showed the signs of being crumpled into a ball and then flattened back out again. The blue biro script was easily legible:

Kim,

Law notes for Crime and General Police Duties. I don't think you'll need the

Traffic stuff… ha ha.

Doug xx.

'Oooh, has someone had an argument Doug? That's why you're back home well before your leave is up. Have you and your friend had a little fall out?'

Taylor pressed his hand down on top of Lowell's, pushing the file closed. 'How did you know I'd be here?' He said, lightly keeping her hand in place.

'I didn't. I was going to push a note through.'

She turned to face him closing the few inches of space between their bodies and lifted her free hand upward. She drew a single finger slowly down over his furrowed brow to the tip of his nose. 'Don't look so nervous, I won't bite... unless you want me to.'

Taylor gave a long sigh. 'Time to go Jenny,' he took a backward step. 'Thanks for coming around specially to tell me that you're not allowed to contact me again.' He added sarcastically.

Lowell made a spiteful face and then headed for the hallway. She slammed his front door hard enough to make the stained glass panel shake and stormed off down the path. Taylor kept his long sigh and shake of the head intact until her blurred image reached the gate.

It was eight o'clock when Taylor pulled open the side door of The Crown. The two figures standing at the bar turned and watched his entrance. Detective Constable Jayne (Mo) Morrison stubbed her Number Six filter tip into an ashtray. Her other hand aligned a cherry on its cocktail stick with her mouth. She nodded a smile at Taylor before taking the cherry on board and lifting the Martini glass to her lips. The other figure, DC Dan (Cheddar) Cheeseman directed his gaze down to the bar top at the two pints of Theakston. The white foam head of one of the drinks was two inches down from the top of the glass.

'Got you one in Boss,' Cheddar said. 'Theakston okay?'

'Spot on Ched. What's with the Martini Mo?' Taylor asked turning to Morrison.

'Love the cherries, hate the bloody drink.' She said and downed the glassful. 'Do me a G and T please Alf.' Her voice was directed at the landlord who stood reading a newspaper in the doorway between the bar and lounge. 'Gin and tonic for the lady,' Alf responded putting down his newspaper.

'Strange do altogether.' Mo said as Taylor completed his summary on Kim's burglary and the subsequent murder of Lenny Gill. They had transferred for privacy into the tiny snug – only big enough for two small round tables and a handful of chairs – it was all theirs. Taylor knew the pair could be trusted and so then went on to divulge his suspicions of a second burglary after Gill's death.

The mention of his concern about Kim's father's links with Porton Down alerted Mo to a rift between him and Kim. 'Want me to give her a bell?' she asked.

Taylor shook his head before muttering into his beer. 'No, she'll do what she wants to when she wants to do it.'

Taylor's half past ten return home was watched from the comfort of a car parked some fifty yards from his house. The two spectators did not comment as they viewed the enhanced black and green images through light intensifying binoculars.

Taylor's first job, a casual check of his answerphone, revealed one call – Jenny Lowell, with another attempt to seduce him with a bottle of wine. She sounded as though she'd already had some herself. He looked at the phone for several seconds musing upon another thought: *should he ring Kim or not?* "Not" was the decision. He automatically put on the kettle and spooned coffee into a mug. He didn't really want it but carried on anyway and slumped into a lounge armchair.

Kim was two hundred miles away in her Tedham apartment – pyjamas, dressing gown and wide eyed on top of her bed. Her gaze drifted over to the bedside telephone as the thought went through her own mind: *should she ring Taylor or not?* "Not" was the decision.

The stereo soothed Taylor's tattered mind as Billy Joel's *This Is the Time to Remember* flowed from the speaker. The nostalgic thought provoking lyrics evoked contemplation: *Did you know that before you came into life, it was some kind of miracle that I survived. Someday we will both look back and have to laugh. We lived through a lifetime and the aftermath.*

He dozed off. Twenty minutes elapsed before he jolted back into consciousness and his coffee, now cold almost slopped onto the newspaper. He blinked and widened his eyes to shake off the tiredness as he looked around the room. He'd often wondered as he grew older if perhaps he had some slightly obsessive traits. He'd read about autism and Asperger syndrome with interest. He'd been fascinated by the fixation for order and organisation. Whilst he was not the tidiest of people he accepted that he could be intense about where certain everyday things in his own home should be.

The telephone in the lounge was NOT in its correct spot. It was close, but not right. Another half inch to the left of the occasional table would certainly have done the trick. It was enough for him to know. He scanned the room, eyes wide and now fully awake, looking for other pointers. There seemed nothing else and so maybe he was wrong.

He stood to his feet, still scanning until he locked onto the video recorder. It occupied a space on a glass shelf beneath the TV set. Taylor stared at the device for a moment. He adjusted the angle of his head slightly so that the room's central light fell at a more acute slant onto the glass. Two small circles could now be seen – evidence of Taylor's poor efforts with a duster. The marks had been created by the long term pressure of the recorder's rubber feet onto these two exact points. They were now on display because the appliance had recently been moved from its usual position and not returned exactly.

Taylor was still awake at half past three when the light tapping on his front door jolted him from his deep thoughts. Whoever the caller was must have worked out that the occupier was not in bed from the fact that most of the lights were on.

Fists clenched he warily opened up and stood his ground for a second staring at the figure. His deadpan expression stayed firm as he stared a little longer. Kim removed her crash helmet and her own attempt at coldness quickly dissolved as her face crumpled and the tears rolled down her cheeks. 'I'm so sorry,' she said. 'It's all been too much and now it's worse, I jumped on the bike and headed for the motorway, but why are you still up at this hour?'

Taylor made a STOP signal with the flat of his left hand. His face looked serious, angry even!

Kim's mouth dropped open. What did this mean? Why was he doing this? Was this the end of their relationship after all?

Taylor put the index finger of his right hand against his lips and raised his eyebrows. Kim nodded her understanding and said no more. She melted into his arms as he embraced her. His lips covered hers in a long kiss before sliding to her ear and softly whispering. 'Say nothing.'

He led her though to the lounge and pointed down to the skirting board mounted telephone master socket. Its lid, now unscrewed lay nearby on the carpet where he'd left it. Kim followed Taylor's finger as it directed her eyes toward a one inch circular metal disc. It hung out from the box suspended by the four coloured wires which connected it into the circuitry. You didn't need to be a boffin to work out that it was not part of BT's standard equipment.

He straightened up and gave Kim a reminder with another exhibition of finger against lips before pointing at some more of his own work. He had removed the casing of his video recorder. A couple of screwdrivers and a pair of pliers lay on the carpet nearby. Taylor knelt down and silently gestured a hand at a five inch by two inch black plastic component taped against the inside of the case. Wires trailed away from the item and disappeared into the wiring loom of the recorder.

It was obvious to Kim that it was a listening device. She shook her head with bewilderment as Taylor walked back through to the hallway and pointed to a small suitcase that he'd packed. Quietly whispered plans were agreed upon and Kim wheeled her motorcycle backwards inside Taylor's garage. She heaved it onto its stand and locked the garage doors. Taylor busied himself for half an hour restoring the phone socket and video recorder without disturbing the two devices.

Kim changed out of her leathers for some more comfortable clothes from her backpack. She dumped the other gear she had brought onto the rear seat of Taylor's Ford Orion. Taylor locked up the house and repeated his finger-to-lips warning as he started the car. The silence was broken as he ramped the stereo up onto full volume. The dashboard clock showed quarter past four as he mouthed the word, 'Travelodge?' His raised eyebrows made the location into a suggestion as Status Quo's *Never Too Late* beat from the car speakers. His next signal: two fingers pointed at his eyes, was also understood by Kim. She turned and fixed her gaze through the headrest to see if they were being followed.

The image of Taylor's car grew fuzzier in the eye pieces of the light intensifying binoculars as it drove away.

EIGHTEEN

IT TOOK a little over fifteen minutes to cover the eight miles to the Travelodge, north of Newcastle under Lyme. Kim's ears were ringing when Taylor finally switched off the ignition and silence arrived. They made their way, baggage in hand, to the entrance. The startled receptionist blinked tiredness from her eyes as Taylor reeled off his details for the room and paid up front.

Taylor gave a long sigh as he pushed open the door to their room. The sigh was followed with a shake of the head as he pulled off his jacket, kicked off his shoes and sat on the edge of the bed. 'What the hell are we into this time?'

Kim remained standing. 'God knows, but I've got a lot to tell you.' She went through the story.

Taylor looked visibly stunned at the revelation of an MI5 search and a hidden safe. The fact that it was empty added to the puzzle. His mind raced with questions. 'What is it that everyone is so keen to get their hands on at your father's? And why the hell have they bugged my house?'

He stayed put on the edge of the bed, fingers interlinked and resting on his knees. He stared down at the carpet, listening in silence as Kim gave more detail.

He looked up at her when it seemed like she'd finished. 'Is it possible that Lenny Gill found the safe and used your dad's key to open it?' He then partly answered his own question. 'I find that hard to swallow. From what I learned he was no more than a thieving fool. Do you think that safe was empty all along?'

She stared back at him. 'No… I know that it wasn't empty.' She heaved her back pack up onto the edge of the bed alongside him, slid the toggle along its elasticated band and reached inside. 'I have no idea what this means yet but I'm gathering dad had some kind of hugely important classified secret that he decided to entrust to me.

He was always planning for the worst and covering every eventuality. His health was at risk and he seems to have gone to some lengths a while ago in case he died suddenly. Lenny Gill has nearly messed up Dad's plans to pass the information on to me. I certainly did get to the safe before the Spooks did.' She pulled two hard backed books from the back pack and handed one to Taylor.

The *Anne Hill* romance novel bore a typical 1960s dust cover – a stylised illustration of a couple in some emotional turmoil. The pink banner across the top gave the title *Safe Harbour.* A paper tag hung out from between the pages and on it Geoff Fry had sketched a comical, cartoon smiley face. Taylor opened the book where the end of the paper created a page marker.

'What the hell…' he said as he looked at the opened page. He'd seen similar sights before, but only ever in drugs cases. A section of the inside of the book had been cut away. A depth of one eighth of an inch had been bored down into the pages forming a hollow. A key lay embedded into the meticulously formed cavity.

'That key,' Kim said. 'Is identical to the one on Dad's keyring, his spare… or more correctly the key he intended for me.' She lifted the book from his lap, closed it and tapped her finger against the title. 'The clue to where the safe was… SAFE HARBOUR. Or more correctly SAFE ARBOUR. He was telling me that the safe was in the garden arbour.'

'I got on to the idea quickly,' she explained. 'I went straight outside and started looking around the arbour. It took me a while to find the safe as it's extremely well camouflaged. It was only because I knew it must be there that I kept looking. The front stone panel beneath the seat is false. It's fibreglass, so when I knocked the hollow sound gave it away. The Spooks would never have discovered it without their equipment.'

Taylor silently shook his head over the revelations and prepared himself for more as Kim handed him the second book.

Again a folded piece of paper hung from within the pages. Kim flattened this onto the top of a chest of drawers in front of them. It was a brief handwritten note in Geoff Fry's writing.

Chapter 1.

Darling Kim,

Your favourite book!

Taylor was anticipating an explanation, but Kim left him to form his own opinion. He held the book in the flat of his palm feeling at its weightiness. It was a novel of standard dimensions and roughly one inch in thickness. The colourful dust cover was intact and in good condition although the faded condition indicated that it had some age. Rubbing at his chin, he took in the illustration: Two children – a boy and girl with tousled hair were clambering across rocks. Seagulls flew overhead and an enchanting seascape acted as a backdrop.

Why on Earth had Kim's father left her this CHILD'S book?

He turned the book, taking in how the spine and back continued with more of the same captivating scene – more children – more seagulls – a boat on the beach.

He shrugged his shoulders with confusion. A smile took over the mood as some boyhood thoughts came back with the author's name and title: *Enid Blyton, The Island of Adventure.*

'So where were these books?' he asked, his face a picture of bewilderment.

'Both in Dad's study with his other books… sticking out on a shelf.'

She pushed her hand back into the bag. 'This is what was in the safe.'

Taylor's puzzlement level reached an even higher plane as Kim pulled out a number of items and put them in front of him.

A great wad of bank notes was the most eye-catching of theses, but a large steel key held its own intrigue. It was a hefty piece of kit and to Taylor's eye was not far behind those needed to open the cell doors back at the police station. A standard sized stainless steel locker type key hung attached via a split ring. A slender brown envelope was the last item and seemed insignificant by comparison to the other things.

Taylor shook his head as he lifted the money and thumbed through it: twenties and tens, pinched tightly together in the centre with a thick rubber band.

'Five grand,' Kim said. 'I counted it and can only conclude that dad has put it in as expenses.'

'Expenses? Expenses for what?

Kim shrugged her shoulders. 'That's still a puzzle at the moment but dad plainly had some important task he needed me to carry out.'

Taylor cleared his throat. The sight of the money worried him. Such a wad usually meant crime but this was undoubtedly Geoff Fry's money which would have been left to his daughter anyway. He picked up the keys. 'Any ideas what they're for?'

'None at all.'

Kim lifted the remaining envelope, opened the flap and pulled out a single piece of folded white copy paper. She handed it to him.

Taylor pushed his head backwards slightly, a frown creasing his brow as he tried to make sense of the scant lettering on the page. The typed details had almost certainly been produced on Geoff Fry's Royal Model P machine:

Chapter 1
back, and° photographs. N
of a° "Oooh!" W
238
213

He looked up at Kim. 'What the hell is this all about? I'm missing something here and what does the Enid Blyton book have to do with this?'

Kim said, 'Dad collected rare books. I loved Enid Blyton as a kid, so nearly all my Enid Blytons were first editions. Dad insisted on it. He said they were more exciting… had extra character along with all the artwork that the paperbacks didn't have. I had to look after them.

I still have all my others back at my apartment, but wondered where this missing one disappeared to. I asked dad if he'd seen it anywhere a few times, but all he ever said was, "oh it'll turn up".'

Taylor opened the book and pressed his thumb against the edges of its 327 yellowed pages rippling them through from front to back. 'This book's a lot older than you.'

She nodded. 'Yes, a first edition. If my memory serves me right, printed in 1944.'

A slightly musty smell of age had been given off by the disturbed pages. Taylor rubbed at his nose before looking back at Kim. 'So what connects the book to your father's strange letter?'

She picked up the handwritten note from inside the book and held it out:

Chapter 1.

Darling Kim,

Your favourite book!

'Dad must have intended me to find both the books at some stage. I rarely used to go into his study. He could have put them sticking out on the shelf like that a long time ago. He had a heart condition and I guess he'd accepted that he could die at any time. When I found the typed page in the safe the first line struck me. It says *Chapter 1*. Now that's exactly the same as the first line in the note he'd left inside the Enid Blyton book. It's an odd thing to type or write on its own… *Chapter 1* and so I get the feeling that it connects the two.'

Taylor's eyes went from the book to the handwritten note and then to the typed page. 'So these things hold a code… and with your knowledge of how your father's mind worked he intended you… us… to find out what this is about and deal with it.'

Kim took a few seconds to analyse Taylor's sentence. 'My knowledge of how Dad's mind worked has become an uncertain skill over the past few days,' she said. 'He was a highly intelligent man – crosswords, Scrabble, puzzles, chess. He'd got the sort of mind you could imagine at Bletchley Park in the war unravelling German codes… bit before his time though. He was a real lateral thinker and perhaps he passed a little of that on to me.' She gave Taylor a serious look. 'This is *my* problem Doug. Dad has left it for *me* to sort out and I don't expect you to get involved. You're already jeopardising your career now that you know I've withheld secrets from the security agents.'

Taylor stared at the wall as he concentrated. He'd met Geoff Fry many times on a pleasant and casual basis over the past couple of years, but had never known any of this. 'So he's used some kind of protective barrier in case this falls into the wrong hands. He's hoping that only you will be able to unravel it and deal with it in a safe way.'

Kim said, 'that's the way I see it.'

Taylor's head was shaking. 'If you're going through with this then we're doing it together.'

She gave a shrug and made a heavy sigh. She felt guilty for involving Taylor in this but secretly hoped he'd help out. 'I was worried when the Security Agents searched the bungalow. I thought that they were going to search my stuff next.' She paused for a second. 'They were sharp but even if they'd found what had been in the safe, I'm not sure it would have meant anything to them.'

Taylor carried on staring at the wall as he went through the parts that he already knew. 'Those listening bugs had not been planted when I first arrived home. I'm certain of that. They can only have been installed during the few hours when I was at the pub with Cheddar and Mo. It's doubtful that they've managed to put something in my car yet, but I wanted to be sure… hence the Status Quo. I'll check it thoroughly in the morning.'

Taylor told Kim of Jenny Lowell's visit. It resulted in a long face and some silence for a few moments before she accepted that Taylor was blameless.

'Funny how she turned up as soon as you arrived home,' she said. 'Is she in league with the Security Service agents? Could they be behind the bugging?'

Taylor made a "who knows face?". 'If they're that interested in me why didn't they bug my place while I was out of town down at Tedham? The bugging seems to have been a last minute affair. That doesn't say it wasn't the Security Service people. But if whoever has done it thinks I'm worth bugging then surely your own pad would also have been on the list.'

'That's been going through my mind,' Kim said. 'And maybe I'm being paranoid, but how can we be certain that the bungalow wasn't bugged into the bargain. God, I don't know who I can trust.'

Taylor went silent. He was back to his feet. He put the book and letter down beside the room's TV set and massaged fingers deeply into tired neck muscles. 'You know when you threw me out yesterday… '

Kim closed her eyes. She didn't need reminding.

Taylor continued. 'You gave me back the law notes… virtually flung them at me.'

Kim's forehead wrinkled. 'Okay, I'm sorry I thought we were through all that.'

Taylor shook his head. 'No not that, it's what you said. The words stuck in my mind. What you said was: "Here… read through this it might keep you busy until you're due back at work."

Kim looked bewildered, but in an instant she grasped the implications. 'Someone *was* listening to our conversation. My apartment *was* bugged. So they took that sentence to mean that I was giving you a document connected to this.'

Taylor nodded. 'That fits with everything else that's gone on and with the fact that they didn't get to bug my house until they realised it might be worthwhile. I've worked SB and had some contact with the security services. Love them or hate them they do play to the rules. If they needed to plant listening devices they would have gone through the right channels.'

Kim frowned as she listened. 'Meaning?'

'They would have to get authorisation from the Home Secretary.

Look at how quickly this has all come together….' He paused. 'And the fact that they obviously hadn't searched your dad's bungalow until they did so with you. No, I don't think they're responsible for the bugging.'

It was five o'clock and a surreal sight as Taylor, a grown man lay back on the bed and started to read Enid Blyton's, *The Island of Adventure.*

NINETEEN

BENEDICT CAPPELLI couldn't sleep. He was sitting at the desk in his Exeter hotel room. A dressing gown covered his usual night attire: Superman Tee shirt and boxers. The tired carpet slippers with their crushed down backs added to the fetching ensemble. The room's radio alarm clock showed ten past five. The cup of coffee he occasionally sipped had come courtesy of the in-room facilities. It was an improvement on the machine back at Wapping. Possibilities and consequences churned endlessly through his mind and made attempts at sleep futile. He continued to slowly leaf through Andrew Prestwich's stolen address book.

Cappelli preferred to use the term "borrowed" rather than stolen in relation to the book and so far it had proved to be of no additional value at all. He looked up as a flicker of movement through the window blind slats caught his eye. A vehicle on the darkened car park, one storey below, was reversing into one of the several free spaces. The driver's methods seemed peculiar; he was carrying out the procedure without lights. The unusually thoughtful, quiet driving involved hardly any engine revving. The puzzled journalist reached over and switched off the desk lamp pitching the room into blackness. He pushed the address book into his dressing gown pocket and pressed a finger and thumb between the window blind slats for a better view.

Two figures climbed from the car and carefully pressed the doors closed before silently making their way to the rear of the hotel. It was an odd time to be arriving and odd behaviour into the bargain.

The strange display brought the inquisitive reporter to his full senses. He might be witnessing the prelude to some criminal act. A good story now became a prospect in spite of his own recent criminal deeds. He remained at the window for several minutes, but nothing else happened. The hotel was quiet and no sounds could be heard apart from a distant snoring guest in some far-away room. He considered climbing back into bed, but stopped himself upon hearing the soft bump of a self-closing corridor door.

His neck hairs bristled and his suspicious nature set alarm bells ringing. He felt his way along the wall until he reached the door. The miniscule wide angle lens of the security spy hole presented a distorted image out onto the brightly lit corridor beyond. Cappelli's heart started to pound as two figures came into view. The fact that these were the same people from the car park was never in doubt.

His heart upped its rate to a higher level as their slow tip toe manner brought them precisely to his own door. The black clothing, tight jeans and bomber jackets when coupled with the odd behaviour now very definitely spelled out the word CRIME. The unmistakable chunky shape of the semi-automatic pistols they both held compounded this notion and caused that thumping heart to go off the scale.

The distortion created by the convex lens of the spy hole blurred the features to unrecognisable until one figure closed up against the woodwork. A lean, chiselled face came fleetingly, but crisply into perspective. A perfect cut-off line of dark designer stubble ran across the cheek bones as though drawn with a ruler. The eyes seemed to bore in through the door just twelve inches from where Cappelli, unseen and unbreathing stared back.

The heart rate reached gallop level as Cappelli witnessed the man hold a finger to his lips transmitting the international signal for silence to his out of sight companion. A nod followed as some unknown agreement was reached. The sound of plastic clicking against metal preceded the muted electronic buzz of the bedroom door lock as it obeyed the command to open. The handle slowly moved downwards. Cappelli turned away from the door – his decision made. The drastic life or death choice had been running through his mind from the moment that he had seen the guns.

It was seven o'clock when DC Reg Timson arrived, tired-eyed at the car park of the Kingsland Hotel. Those early morning phone calls were the bane of a detective's life. He'd been surprised to get a call-out at all when he was already working full time on a murder enquiry. The scant information he'd been given over the phone went some way toward an answer.

He lowered the driver's window and held out his warrant card for inspection by the uniformed constable. The details were noted and scribbled onto a clipboard. The officer one-handedly lifted the fluttering blue and white police tape allowing him to drive under and park up. He pulled up the handbrake, stretched, rubbed his eyes, climbed out and headed over to where DI Ken Grainger stood with two other detectives.

The group were near to the wall of the hotel building and looking upward at a first floor window. Strips of the room's Venetian blind flapped crazily through the plastic frame of the smashed window. Small cubes of shattered safety glass littered the car park below. A huge dent could be seen to the roof of the Vauxhall Astra around which the detectives clustered. More of the chunks of glass were evident in the well of the dented roof. Smears of blood streaked against the car's white paintwork.

'Timmo,' Grainger said, acknowledging the detective's arrival. 'You'll have had a brief update over the phone and no doubt be wondering how this is connected to our current murder.'

'I got enough to work it out boss. The room was rented out to the reporter you wanted me to have a look at. The one who's been sharp enough to join the dots up between Lenny's murder and Kim's father's burglary – Benedict Cappelli?'

Grainger nodded. 'We don't know what's happened. The receptionist took a call from one of the guests just after five. He'd been woken up by shouting from another room, he said it was terrifying. There was an almighty crash and a thump outside. I guess that's when the window went through and someone… Cappelli most likely, jumped or was thrown through it.'

Timson took another glance at the car's roof. 'And landed on here.'

'Seems that way,' Grainger said. 'Whoever it was has been badly injured or worse. A car was heard driving off at high speed, but no one's seen anything worthwhile.'

'Cappelli's car?' Timson asked

'No,' said Grainger. 'That's the worrying part.' He pointed at a Ford Escort. 'That's his car… we've worked that out from hotel records. His keys and all of his clothing still seem to be in his room.'

Cappelli's room was a mess: overturned furniture, a broken lamp, wardrobe doors left open, drawers pulled out. All signs of a hurried search.

SOCO, Detective Constable Angela Hewitt was at work as Grainger and Timson looked in through the door from the hallway.

'Door doesn't look to have been forced,' Timson said examining the lock. 'And I guess that's his suitcase by the wardrobe.'

The SOCO had been photographing something on the floor on the other side of the bed. 'What have you found Angela?' Grainger asked.

The SOCO bent down to retrieve the item. 'This should interest you, Boss.' She held her biro out straight by its tip. Perched on the end was a roll of silver grey duct tape.

Grainger turned back to the detectives. 'Okay, get all the guests up… names, addresses, car numbers, statements. I want to know what's been seen and heard. See if there's any CCTV… the works.'

Timson and Grainger arrived back at the murder room just after nine. Immediate and determined efforts to contact Kim Harding continued to meet with failure. 'Still no reply Boss,' Timson shouted above the rattle of a printer. Grainger gave a nod and resumed an in depth phone call.

There were no CCTV cameras covering either the car park or

reception lobby of the hotel. A ground floor fire exit door had been forced open.

Grainger finished his call and pulled up a chair alongside Timson's desk to see if any more progress had been made.

'Receptionist from last night is giving a statement at the moment.' Timson started. 'He can't throw any light on how Cappelli's attackers knew which room he was in. He's positive that such details are never given out to anyone other than the police… He says people have been sacked for less. Thing is, I tend to believe him, but the intruders seem to have broken in and gone up the stairs directly to Cappelli's room They haven't knocked on any other doors. They knew exactly where to go and then he's either opened the door or they've had some way around the lock.'

Grainger absorbed the information with increasing concern showing on his face. 'Our Special Branch boss says DI Taylor went back up north first thing yesterday. You've had no luck trying to get Kim at home, so I'm gathering that she's now joined him. I've tried DI Taylor's home too and there's no reply. He's only got a personal pager, but Kim has a mobile phone. Keep trying both of them, it's important that they know about this business with Cappelli. Their own lives could be in danger.'

TWENTY

THE OFFICE of the Home Secretary, at 50 Queen Anne's Gate London SW1 lay almost exactly two hundred miles from Exeter. The building itself was a fairly modern concrete pile although a certain sedate ambiance existed about the actual room. It seemed, at this moment in time, to be in another dimension from the manic activity of the Lenny Gill murder enquiry. The slow ticking of the grandfather clock in one corner had, for a full two minutes, been the only perceptible sound.

Home Secretary, Walter Baker did not like gimmicky ideas such as cycling to work. Anyway, such a move would have put his police bodyguards under far too much pressure. The consequent lack of exercise and regular multi course luncheons had added many unwanted pounds since he'd taken on this current role twelve months previously. He shifted some of that weight from one foot to the other as he stared down at the street below. His hands were clasped behind his back in military fashion: right hand in the palm of the left. It was the usual way of things, but some psychoanalyst would suggest it was a give-away to his army background.

Another full minute went by, taking the time to quarter past nine and yet still Baker said nothing. The two men seated at his desk continued to look silently at his balding head and the back of his Savile Row suit.

'Serious then?' Baker finally said without averting his gaze from the hurried activities of St James's Park tube entrance three stories beneath.

'That, Home Secretary would be an understatement.' The words came from the Director General of MI5, Sir Peter Walker.

Baker swivelled to face the men. The anger which had not been apparent in his voice now showed on his face for the first time since the discussion started. 'Why in God's name wasn't I briefed on this when I came into post as Home Secretary.'

Walker sat upright in his chair, elbows on arm rests and hands clasped together over the bottom brass button of his dark blue blazer. His hair, although recently trimmed had a mind of its own with several uncontrollable tufts – grey now taking over from mousy brown at temples and nape.

'*ROSA*, Home Secretary,' Walker said. 'Was the code name given to Eleanor Thornberry. The operation to establish her activities, who she worked for and with, was given the name *CANINA*. The operation died on Tuesday 9th May 1978 along with Rosa. At least the Director General of the day, Sir Howard Smith believed that to be the case.' Walker kept a relaxed tone. 'The entire operation remained so sensitive that knowledge of it still remains strictly on a need to know basis.'

'Fuck me Peter…' The intensity of Baker's redness increased as he sat heavily back into his chair to face the men. 'And since when has the Home Secretary NOT been on the need to know list?'

Walker tilted his head to one side. 'The papers… what there were, are covered by the Thirty Year Rule. Due to necessary secrecy they are not due to be released until 2008. An application was submitted in advance requesting the usual thirty years be extended for a further ten years in the interests of national security. It must have been assumed that by that date… 2018, the situation would no longer present a problem.'

Baker folded his arms. 'And why is that? Surely this would always remain a threat until it no longer physically exists.'

'When this came to light, thirteen years ago,' Walker began. 'The Security Service officers believed that there was nothing left. Director General Howard Smith accepted his investigator's reports that Rosa's entire stockpile amounted to the contents of her car boot. The idea was that she had worked alone toward some unknown goal and in the event of no evidence to support other theories this was accepted.'

Walker's expression gave away a tinge of embarrassment as he explained more. 'There was a form of failsafe which would guarantee safety if any of the substance did remain stored anywhere in the country.' He twisted around in his chair to the man at his side prompting a contribution.

Alexander Tremaine, MI5's Principal Scientific Officer looked younger than his fifty-one years in spite of the pressure that went with his post. His hair, thick and neatly groomed, showed little sign of receding and still bore more than a hint of its original near black shade. The eyebrows fully retained both their colouring and their eagerness to grow.

Tremaine leaned his powerful shoulders inwards to speak. The left sleeve of his charcoal pinstripe suit jacket crept up a few inches revealing a broad, sturdy wrist. A flat faced silver wristwatch on an expanding bracelet nestled within a dense growth of hair.

'VX has a shelf life, Home Secretary,' Tremaine started. The resonance of his baritone voice commanded attention. 'Under normal circumstances it would turn to harmless goo after a fairly short while. If there had been other stashes they would all have become unusable within two or three years at most. Some of Rosa's activities had generated interest a few weeks prior to her death in 1978. But resulting investigations failed to prove that she had manufactured any more than the forty flasks in her car boot.'

The Home Secretary held up the flat of his left hand as he made a note.

'Being as I'm now on the NEED TO KNOW list Alex, I also NEED TO KNOW exactly what we're talking about here. Forty flasks you say… how much in each flask?'

Tremaine didn't need to consult his notes on this question. 'Two hundred millilitres Home Secretary.'

Baker looked back at Tremaine. 'A standard sized bottle of Tonic Water then,' his mind calculated. 'Forty bottles of tonic… 8000 millilitres… EIGHT LITRES.' He lengthened the words "Eight" and "Litres" to emphasise his incredulity. 'Correct me if I'm wrong. Each one of those flasks contained twice as much VX as we are allowed as a nation to produce in one entire year. Even then that would only be for research and testing.'

Tremaine nodded.

Baker set the point of an elbow down onto the desk and pressed his palm against his forehead. 'So Britain…. One of the leading lights in the preparation of The Biological and Toxin Weapons Convention….' He removed the palm and stared across the table. 'Which we signed in 1969, breaks that agreement ten years later by producing no less than seventy-nine times more VX in one year than we are allowed.'

Walker coughed before commenting. 'Thank goodness for the need to know rule.'

The Home Secretary gave Walker a stare before returning his attention back to Tremaine and said. 'Under NORMAL circumstances…?' His eyebrows elevated to their highest yet as he accentuated the word "normal". It made the sentence into a question. He repeated the words to help coax a reply. 'You said: "under NORMAL circumstances the VX would turn to harmless goo after a fairly short while." So what makes these circumstances NOT normal?'

Walker glanced at Tremaine and relaxed back in his chair. 'Our chief microbiologist of the time, Dr Geoffrey Fry was responsible for the destruction of the batch and the making safe of the area. A full inventory of everything inside the car was kept and all of the removable items were taken out. These were closely examined in the lab under the tightest of health and safety conditions. They were then incinerated in the presence of independent witnesses to ensure safety. The flasks of VX were removed and neutralised in the laboratory over a two month period. The car was considered so dangerously contaminated that it was torched on site… completely burned out. Dr Fry specifically kept one flask of the VX back for research as he'd noticed at an early stage that it bore different chemical markers from the formula Porton Down could create. Fry discovered Rosa had successfully increased the shelf life of her VX exponentially by introducing a chemical stabiliser.'

The Home Secretary gave a nod of understanding. 'So she not only concocted far in excess of our allowed output, she also illegally increased its potency as a weapon.' Baker slumped backwards into his chair before resuming. 'I breathe a sigh of relief as you tell me on one hand the batch was successfully destroyed and then hold my breath waiting for the next bombshell.'

Walker took his chance to speak again. 'Quite, Home Secretary, quite. The pathologist on the case, Mr Andrew Prestwich, a Home Office approved pathologist was specifically employed by the Government at Porton Down. He investigated Rosa's death along with Dr Fry. A perfunctory post mortem was performed and decisions reached. An in-camera inquest heard the evidence and the Coroner recorded a verdict of accidental death.'

'All good so far,' Baker remarked sarcastically.

Walker continued. 'Had it not been for the inquisitive nature of a certain Salisbury MP of the time that might have been the end of the matter, for a while at any rate. Somehow he learned a much reduced account of the story and raised it in the House of Commons. As a result, an edited version of the inquest made a few newspaper stories for a week or so. The ruse allowed the MP to garner a few extra votes from some Ecology Party supporters. He publicly expressed his disgust that Britain still produced these weapons of mass destruction.' Walker gave an annoyed shake of the head. 'That suggestion was far from the truth. We've always kept strictly to the guidelines. Rosa was acting completely independently and we have now established, as suspected, that she was acting on behalf of a foreign power. Whatever Mr Royston Heems, Member of Parliament for Salisbury would have said if he'd seen the full inventory for Rosa's car boot heaven only knows. We can only thank Messrs Prestwich and Fry for their economy with the truth.'

Baker closed his hands together as if in prayer pressing his fingertips against his lips as he thought. 'So even though the inquest was held in private it never came out about the VX in the car boot?'

'No sir,' Walker said. 'Dr Fry retired on ill health grounds in 1989. He recently died. He had a heart condition and so nothing to suggest anything other than natural causes. However…'

Baker raised an eyebrow. 'Why is there ALWAYS an *however*?'

'Exactly,' Walker said. 'The cabinet papers were filed under the thirty year rule, but one person continued to worry about the situation.' Walker turned to Tremaine, cueing him in.

'Yes Home Secretary,' Tremaine began. 'My appointment as Principal Scientific Officer for the service began in 1985. I had worked closely with Dr Fry before that appointment in my different postings. Not long after I became PSO Geoffrey Fry expressed concerns to me. He believed that both the Porton Down and Colindale laboratories had been, and possibly still were compromised by Soviet agents. He suspected Thornberry… Rosa had been a Soviet illegal… a sleeper agent with a convincing legend. I divulged this information to the then Director General. A full investigation ensued into Dr Fry's theories, but no evidence was found at that time. Rosa's illegal manufacture of the VX in her car boot was put down to her own criminal agenda. The theory being that she was plotting a blackmail attempt against the Government, or more likely a deal with a foreign power. It appears Dr Fry independently continued to pursue a line of investigation after Rosa's death. He conducted his enquires secretly… he had become paranoid that Soviet agents still held a strong presence both within the security service and the laboratory services. I suspect that the only other person with full knowledge of Fry's secret enquiry was the pathologist, Prestwich.'

'You say Fry recently died. So what happened to Prestwich?' Baker asked.

Tremaine shrugged. 'Last heard of living in care… Dementia I'm afraid. Our Pensions Department tracked him down but it sounds as though he won't be able to help.'

Walker then selected a folder from his briefcase and opened it on the desk. A seventies style of typewriter font filled the top page. He ran a finger down as he spoke, summarising and picking out required detail. 'Rosa's background went under the microscope… again! She came out clean… again! She was a Canadian; born as Eleanor Hamilton. She obtained her Master's degree at Mount Allison University in New Brunswick. Her parents died in the 1970 air crash near to Toronto Pearson International Airport.'

A few pages were turned before Walker continued. 'Rosa married in 1975 to a fellow student also a Canadian, name of Robert Thornberry. His own degree, also obtained at Mount Allison, was in Computer Sciences. He moved over here along with her to take up a job at the British Telecom's research HQ at Adastral Park near Ipswich.'

'Christ,' Baker said frowning. 'Both in prime occupations for illegals. She's working in Salisbury and he's right over at Ipswich… they can't have seen much of each other!'

'Yes Sir… another reason for the penny to eventually drop,' Walker said. 'Robert Thornberry disappeared in August of 1977; he was never seen again. The couple had only been married for two years. Recent interviews with Rosa's surviving co-workers remember the incident and say she seemed genuinely heartbroken. She later told them Robert and her had split up and he'd gone back to Canada.'

The Home Secretary's puzzlement started to turn to understanding. He picked up a ballpoint from his blotter and tapped its top repeatedly against his knee. 'Hmm Canada you say.'

'Correct, Home Secretary.' Walker said. 'I gather you're familiar with the fact that Canada has recently been identified as THE Place for the Russians to send their potential illegals. Canada is where water tight legends are created. There's little doubt that Dr Fry was right all along and when you hear what else he found out, you'll understand the frustrations he'd been going through. Fry's investigations turned up that Rosa had been acquiring large quantities of two particular chemicals… Alex, if you'd explain.'

Tremaine was looking down at his paperwork, a finger poised. 'Phosphorus Trichloride and Tributylamine. The first compound is the main ingredient of VX and the second, Tributylamine, is the stabiliser which, it seems Thornberry had developed to prolong the shelf life.'

The Home Secretary's eyebrows arched steeply. 'How did she acquire this stuff, surely it's on the restricted list?'

'Both chemicals are, but they also have a variety of other laboratory and industrial uses. She opened a business account at Barclay's in Salisbury calling itself, would you believe, *HM Government Laboratory Porton Down*. The postal address was to her private mailbox at the Porton facility. She used Government authorisation documents and collected the chemicals from the suppliers in London in person.'

Baker gave a sigh of disbelief at the simplicity of it as Walker added more. 'She paid by cheque and no one twigged on. Obviously if suspicions had been aroused she would have been detected immediately, but it never did come to that. She seems to have been moving between the two laboratories at Porton and Colindale to use the equipment and facilities. She must have manufactured the stuff when no other staff members were present who might recognise her game.'

'Easy to criticise with hindsight, but such bloody simplicity,' Baker said.

Walker took his cue again. 'Fry hinted that the quantities of the chemicals Rosa obtained over the three year period from 1975 up until her death could be huge. He believed she manufactured greatly more VX than that found in her car. He suggested that later stock checks made between Porton and Colindale did not always tie up with what she supposedly delivered. Aluminium flasks were well down on Porton's inventory and the business regarding the NBC suit in her car pointed Fry in another direction. She was probably stealing suits which had gone past their sell-by dates, rather than burning them.'

Walker pushed a sheaf of paperwork across to Baker giving details of stock movements and disposal. 'It turns out Rosa frequently took charge of such duties herself. There is no physical way of checking, as she'd written in the records that the items had been incinerated. We can never know how many used suits she's obtained in this way. From the incineration records she's made out, it could be as many as seventeen in several different sizes.'

Baker shook his head in disgust rather than examine the evidence. He was back to his feet again and looking down on the street below. 'How did Rosa die? I mean the real cause, not the one given to the papers. I'm sure there's a Post Mortem report somewhere at MI5 Peter, that didn't get hidden away for thirty years.'

Walker delved back into his briefcase and withdrew a dog-eared orange folder placing it onto the desk. The title printed on the cover read: *"Eleanor Thornberry Post Mortem. Pre-Lim Dr A Prestwich"*. He handed the file to Tremaine. 'Summarise please Alex.'

Tremaine opened the file and selected a few of the top sheets of paper. 'The pathologist only went as far as body fluid samples together with other evidence from the car. 'Rosa certainly died from the effects of VX.'

Tremaine then flattened his hand down onto the paperwork. The action indicated that he was about to add information not given in the file. 'The blood samples also tested positively for the presence of Tributylamine. Her own VX killed her. Dr Fry proved that Rosa's new formula drastically altered the composition of normal VX. It reduced the viscosity and the volatility and so made it much more soluble in water. It made it more effective in the poisoning of large bodies of drinking water, such as reservoirs. It could also be used in aerosol form successfully. The altered volatility meant that it had a lower boiling point and would fume at much lower temperatures than the original version.' He gave a nervous cough. 'Of course this information was withheld from the inquest.'

Baker held station at the window. His shake of the head coincided with a long sigh which momentarily misted the pane of glass closest to his mouth. 'So she converted a genocidal nightmare into an everlasting doomsday weapon.'

'In a nutshell yes, but it's not everlasting.' Tremaine said. 'It does degrade and the changes she made were ultimately her own undoing. One of the failings of her formula is its reaction with plastics. The chemical, Tributylamine is used industrially as a stabilizer in the production of plastic and synthetic rubber. Rosa was obviously involved in a spillage whilst wearing that particular suit during the creation of some of the last batch. She probably stepped into the liquid with one of the over-boots of the suit. It shows how careless she'd become.

'The Tributylamine component of the altered VX reacted with, and soaked into the crepe rubber over-boots of the stolen NBC suit. Dr Fry was satisfied that she went through the in-suit showering process meticulously. This is carried out in cold water and it undoubtedly washed away the VX residue. However, the rapid cooling effect of the cold water closed up the pores of the softened boot and trapped some of the VX. It would stay there undetectable until the suit had lain in her car for several hours on that warm summer day.

'The temperature change softened the crepe rubber soles and also released the altered VX as fumes. As soon as Rosa sat into the driving seat she would have started to inhale those fumes. VX has no smell or taste and the effects would commence within thirty seconds or so. Not as quickly as a droplet onto the skin. It would therefore allow enough time for her to climb in, put on her seat belt, start up and drive the few yards that she did.

'The inquest was given some of the truth as to how she died, although it never came out about the altered, new formula VX. The business over the suspected spillage, the reaction of the rubber boot sole and effect of the hot temperature inside the car were all disclosed as evidence. The idea that the suit had reached the end of its life and that it was stolen did not get a mention. It gave the Coroner the opportunity to justify his existence. He suggested that suits should be disposed of on a more frequent basis and that the material used for the boots be re-evaluated.'

Baker was still watching the traffic down below when Tremaine completed his lengthy explanation. 'All nicely swept under the carpet, but the happy ending you have described is not the happy ending we would all like… right?' Baker's shoulders stiffened and his hands clasped more tightly as though he had been ordered from the *Stand Easy* position by some unseen Sergeant Major. It indicated his anger.

'No Home Secretary I'm afraid not,' Tremaine replied. 'From the quantities of the chemicals he believed Rosa had obtained, Dr Fry was confident that she had manufactured a large quantity of the long life VX. He remained convinced that the bulk of this was secretly stored somewhere for later use. He felt it likely that Soviet agents had infiltrated the Government laboratory facilities and possibly even MI5. When he retired he suggested that if further information came in he be consulted. He felt sure that his inside knowledge of the case may be helpful.'

Walker edged forward on his chair, keen to make his point. 'Everything was fully investigated and nothing ever came to light… until February this year.'

The Home Secretary turned away from the window to take on board the worst of the news so far. The buzzing intercom halted the conversation and caused him to lean across the desk to flick a switch upwards. 'I said no interruptions Janet.'

A female voice came on the loudspeaker. 'Apologies Mr Baker, an urgent call for Director General Walker. He could take it out here. It's Devon and Cornwall's Chief Constable.'

TWENTY ONE

MI5 BOSS, Peter Walker left the office to take the Chief Constable's call and Alex Tremaine began to explain how another incident had recently been connected to the affair. 'On Wednesday 12th December last year, a worker was attending to a problem inside a ventilation shaft at Vickers Armstrong shipyard at Barrow-in-Furness in Cumbria. The ducting had been blocked for years and the only way to get at the problem was by crawling into it. The man found a human body inside the duct close up by the fan which draws air from outside and blows it into one of the submarine construction workshops. I think you visited a few weeks back, one of our new Trident subs is under construction there.'

Baker gave a nod.

Tremaine took a wad of photographs from his briefcase. He tapped them down onto the woodwork of the desk and squared the edges as if he was about to deal cards. He then got on with his tale. 'The police had one hell of a job extracting the body. They broke in through the roof. It looked at the beginning like a nutty burglary attempt gone wrong. Over the years similar cases have made the news with bodies found inside chimneys, some dating back over twenty years. This one, a male, must have climbed a derelict metal access stairway outside the building and pulled back the fan assembly which is fitted on a hinge system.'

Tremaine selected and placed a couple of the photographs down in front of the Home Secretary.

Baker looked down at the two pictures. They showed views of the crumbling outside brickwork and the rotting metal staircase.

Tremaine continued. 'The police thought the fool had been trying to get into the building to see what he could steal. The motor unit was found to be locked firmly back into its housing. It probably slammed shut on him and could not be opened from inside the shaft.'

Two more photos followed. These were of the massive fan motor in open and closed positions.

'The pathologist could not pin down the man's age any tighter than between twenty-four and thirty-five. The body had completely dried out… mummified due to the air duct conditions. The PM result is rather open-ended and does not help the case.'

Tremaine set another photograph onto the desk:

A brown skeleton with cling-film skin stretched over its bones lay upon a stark white mortuary slab. Apart from the mop of dusty dark hair still attached to its scalp it could have passed as the twin brother of Egyptian Pharaoh, Tutankhamun.

Tremaine ploughed on. 'After some painstaking laboratory work fingerprints were recovered but no match could be found on criminal records.' Tremaine sighed. 'Now that in itself is unusual; you'd expect such a bumbling burglar to be on file. The corpse's full head of thick hair remained as the only distinguishing feature. Scrape marks found at various points along the ducting indicated the man had been trying over a period of time to escape. Some of the metal plating showed signs of attempts to pull it back here and there. The pathologist noticed corresponding damage to the hands and finger nails resulting from desperate attempts to escape. His cries for help would never be heard. It's far too high and the racket from the shop floor is twenty-four seven.'

Tremaine flattened some more images down in front of the Home secretary:

A close up of the severed right hand with its jutting brown bones and tattered fingernails was shown lying on the slab close to its rightful place with the body. Other shots showed items of crumpled bleached clothing, a rail ticket, some loose change and four ten pound notes. The remarkably preserved paper money bore a stiff crease across the middle resulting from all those years in the man's pocket.

Baker sat back into his chair with his interlinked fingers resting upon his stomach. 'So the poor bastard died up there.' His face showed his distaste at the idea.'

'Seems that way Tremaine said. 'But let's reserve the "poor bastard" phrase until after I've told you some more. A rail ticket found in a pocket covered a return journey from Euston to Barrow-in-Furness. It had been purchased on Friday 19th August 1977 at Euston Station and this would suggest the man died no earlier than that date. The outgoing journey… Euston to Barrow had been taken on that same day, but the return part was unused. It became invalid after four days. The Pathologist's report states that the latest date of death is an awkward one. The closest he'd go is no less than eight years ago.'

Tremaine used a finger to guide the photograph showing the paper money in front of Baker. 'We can track the ten pound notes down a bit more tightly. First issued in 1975 and known as the Series D… still current today, but these are signed by J. B. Page who was Chief Cashier between 1970 and 1980. The serial numbers close the net a little tighter.'

Several more photos remained face down on the desk top. Tremaine turned them over one at a time to reveal sharp glossy eight inch square colour prints:

The first showed a pair of orange, arm-length hazmat gauntlets and the second an orange hazmat face visor.

Baker seemed unfazed at these images but when the next ones were turned a flicker of horror appeared on his face.

Three aluminium flasks had been lined up on a desk top. A twelve inch ruler lay next to them to give scale. Black and yellow skull and crossbones hazard logos adorned the front of the flasks. Red screw tops were fitted.

Tremaine explained. 'One of the flasks, the gloves and visor were discovered in the shaft around the corner. They would not have been seen by anyone later opening the motor casing for normal maintenance. The other two flasks were found underneath the body. Fortunately the police officers were wary of the hazard logo and did not try opening them. Everything eventually went off to Cumbria's forensic science laboratory. There was no rush as there was no suggestion of murder. It was nothing more than an unusual case. The exhibits joined a long queue for forensic examination behind more obviously serious cases. Thankfully when the Cumbrian forensic scientists started on it they took heed of the warning on the flasks. They opened the first one inside the confines of a vacuum cabinet on Wednesday 2nd January. Their mass spectrometer set to work and in no time the entire building was evacuated and out of action until a team from Porton Down arrived.'

Baker shook his head as he digested the information.

'Anyway,' Tremaine continued. 'Our scientists immediately recognised them as old Porton Down stock. All of Porton's flasks are serial numbered. These three disappeared back in 1977. Rosa signed them off along with another seventeen as having been incinerated.

'I was informed and gave the warning about what they might be dealing with although none of the past history was divulged. When the results came back they showed a full 600 millilitres of VX in a usable and only slightly degraded state. The chief scientist pointed out the odd readings from the initial mass spectrometry tests. He described it as: "being unlike any other VX sample he had ever tested". I checked the read-out myself against the test done on Rosa's surviving sample. It was a perfect match. It was hers.'

Baker picked up the photo of the gauntlets. 'And this stuff?'

Tremaine nodded. 'Yes, this is all Porton Down gear. Old serial numbers prove that conclusively. It's been customised; made from original NBC suits. It was no doubt all part of the gear spirited away by Rosa.' He paused for a few seconds. 'With Director General Walker's agreement I sent a coded letter to Dr Fry…the intention being to arrange a meeting. Fry's input would have been invaluable, but sadly he died. The Cumbria incident has identified what Rosa was up to. This was a *Dead Drop* in the truest sense of the phrase. Dead drops between foreign agents would normally be nothing more than a secret exchange of information… a safe location to secrete messages which could later be collected by another agent. In this case it was the covert storing of a weapon close to a strategic target. In the event of imminent war, illegals throughout the country would be directed to the various dead drops to initiate these weapons.'

The Home Secretary had silently digested Tremaine's theory. Several seconds passed before he responded. 'The various dead drops…?'

'Yes sir,' Tremaine said. 'The dead man was almost certainly depositing the VX, the gloves and the visor for some later use, possibly years into the future. If the liquid were to be poured into the duct its altered composition would soon generate fuming. The powerful fan would blast the fumes into the shop floor. Without doubt it would carry along other subsidiary air ducts feeding into the offices of draughtsmen, scientists and anyone else connected to the projects currently under way. An entire arm of our nuclear defence would be lost in an instant… hundreds of our most important workforce killed within minutes.'

Baker repeated his initially selected words. 'The VARIOUS dead drops…?'

Walker had re-entered the room and took on the Home Secretary's question as he returned to his seat. 'If Dr Fry was right, then a huge quantity of VX could be hidden away throughout the country. It's unlikely that the dead drop we've stumbled across is the only one. What we can learn from this episode is that the targets were politically and strategically important. They would be military bases, defence projects, weapons and ammunition factories, vehicle, marine and aero factories, reservoirs…'

Baker held up a hand for Walker to stop. 'Yes Peter, I get the message, but is there no suggestion of a record being kept by Rosa of the places set as dead drops. She was a scientist for God's sake.

There must have been a record kept or no one would know where to go to set these bloody things off.'

Walker glanced at Tremaine before explaining another worrying aspect. 'Quite, Home Secretary,' he said with sigh. 'As I mentioned earlier everything from inside the car was listed and destroyed under lab conditions inside Porton Down's high temperature incinerator. The car was set fire to on the car park.'

Walker took a glance down at his notes. 'The initial list of contents included a secure metal file container. 'It was described as a Vaultzsafe document holder and bore the name Dr E Thornberry. The list of laboratory destroyed items does not include that container. Dr Fry has written up his notes to the effect that the document holder was left in the boot of the car and destroyed along with it.'

Baker saw through the anomaly and added his own input. 'The reason for removing the car's contents before destruction inside the lab was so that they could be examined. Clearly any paperwork would be of immense interest. You're surmising that the file was kept to one side by Fry and that it could contain a list of more dead drop locations?'

'Exactly that.'

'God above is there any good news?'

'Maybe Sir, maybe. You see it does begin to look as though this was a fairly small operation only involving a handful of people. If that is the case it's unlikely that many dead drops were actually set.'

'Hmm,' Baker mused. 'That's a rather fingers-crossed presumption Peter… something that experience tells me you are not prone to. Are we back in the realms of the need to know rules again?'

Walker raised his eyebrows and a rare smile fleetingly crinkled the corners of his eyes.

Baker tapped his index finger down hard onto his desk. 'I need to know Peter.'

Walker gave a *please yourself then* shrug before beginning. 'Vladimir

Pasechnik, Home Secretary. You are familiar with the name?'

Baker nodded as he recalled the details. Pasechnik was a senior Soviet biologist and bioweaponeer who had defected from the Soviet Union via France to the UK the year before. The fifty-three year old had taken his chance during a never-before-allowed visit to Paris and fled to Britain. His revelations served as a wake-up call to the West. He brought with him, not only a plethora of unknown technical information, but also a worrying tale. The Soviets had completely side-lined all of the anti-biological and chemical conventions. The research, improvement and production in all of their biological weapons programs continued apace.

Walker said. 'Without going into the complex details, Pasechnik has proved to be the goose that laid the golden egg, or in his case, eggs! I'm sure you will remember that he was a leading scientist involved in the production of Soviet biological weapons. He specialised in the plague.'

A silence enveloped the room at the mention of the chilling word before Walker continued. 'It is down to him that we realised how much we'd got to pull up our socks to get on top of the Soviet biological threat. Pasechnik now works at Porton Down. He was fully debriefed when he first arrived, but still continues to surprise us with some ad-hoc snippets. His favourite English phrase seems to be 'Oh zat old chestnut.'

Walker's poor mimicking of the defector's accent sounded more German than Russian. 'Pasechnik had known that an illegal was in place at Porton Down throughout the seventies. He didn't know the person's identity. He confirmed our suspicions that many illegals are paired with a suitable second illegal as a spouse. This, of course, goes a long way towards strengthening the legend of both agents. He suggested that Rosa's extended reach to take in the Colindale lab spoke volumes for her initiative. She would have been looking at a comfortable lifestyle along with medals of honour and all the trimmings if she'd eventually made it back to the Soviet Union.

Pasechnik suggested that the missing husband must have been the man in the air duct. We'd already looked into this idea as soon as this all started to come together.'

Walker slid a close up facial photograph of the mummified body to the centre of Baker's desk. The features were horribly distorted into something akin to that of an Amazonian shrunken head. He continued with the explanation. 'The only remaining feature is the hair. The legend provided by the Soviets for the man we knew as Robert Thornberry stood up well until we picked closely at it. The real Robert Thornberry died in Canada aged seven after contracting meningitis. A birth certificate was applied for in his name in 1971… eighteen years after his death! No photographs now exist of our Robert Thornberry… it is after all fourteen years since he disappeared. Even his security pass photographs at his workplace have long since gone. A couple of his former workmates have been traced and remember his sudden disappearance.'

Walker tapped a finger down onto the image of the corpse's face. 'Both mentioned in their recollections of his appearance that he had a mop of dark hair

The MI5 boss withdrew another file from his briefcase and consulted it occasionally as he spoke. 'A Strontium isotopic analysis was carried out on the corpse's teeth. It proved that he was brought up as a child in the region of the Angarsky Mountain ridge in Russia. We haven't got the luxury of having Rosa's body to carry out such tests, but once we started into the enquiry we quickly smashed her legend. The parents of Eleanor Hamilton *did* both die in the 1970 air crash near to Toronto Pearson International Airport. That little snippet fitted nicely into Rosa's legend and prevented anyone from asking for a reference respecting young Eleanor. The fact is however, that the real Eleanor Hamilton was also on that plane. She died in that same air crash with her parents and another one hundred and six people. A birth certificate was requested in the name of the dead girl in 1971.'

Walker closed the file and filled in the Home Secretary with more information. 'Pasechnik is confident from these details that both Rosa and Robert were well placed top grade illegals. His suggestion is that they were officially sleepers waiting to be woken. The biological dead drop scheme had been discussed at length in Moscow, but no plans had been formulated to get it off the ground. It would be normal for illegals to lie low without contact from Moscow for three to four years. Pasechnik is convinced that what Rosa did in the manner of production and the setting up of VX dead drops she did entirely without instruction from Moscow. He added that enterprising agents who take a few risks and get ahead of the game could expect encouragement from Moscow rather than retribution. He is satisfied that the pair worked on their own scheme for some time and may well have set up several bio dead drops.'

The MI5 boss took a pause before throwing in one more worrying aspect. 'Rosa continued producing the VX after her husband disappeared. That is borne out by the stash found in her car boot. She must have concluded by then that he'd died in action and that she was on her own. She can't have considered that she was physically capable of setting up more dead drops on her own. So was she on her own or were there other illegals… even within MI5 who were working with her? This seems to have been Dr Fry's theory. It must also have been the reason why he conducted his own enquiry.'

Baker's face showed his worry but he'd also guessed that there was even more bad news from the way that Walker shuffled forward in his chair. The note in his left hand had been taken during his telephone conversation with Devon and Cornwall's Chief Constable. It would add an additional dimension to the narrative.

'There has been an incident in Exeter,' Walker said, with eyes fixed on the slip of paper. 'Dr Fry's home was burgled on the 13th of March. Initially there seemed no connection, but it now seems certain that the burglar was sent there looking for something in particular. That burglar was later found murdered. A journalist, name of

Benedict Cappelli, has acquired a remarkable amount of information about the case. I have been informed that a violent incident happened in the early hours of this morning at Cappelli's hotel room in Exeter. It seems that he has gone missing. He's been abducted or even murdered.'

Baker now leant in across the desk. 'You knew about this burglary and the burglar's murder before you came here Peter. The need to know rule has been a prominent feature today, but from now on it finishes. I want to know everything and I want to know it as soon as you do. I think we can be confident that Dr Fry did, as you suspect, retain Rosa's file and hid it somewhere. This reporter probably hasn't got a clue what he's got himself into. We need to track him down… if he's still alive and find out what he does know.'

TWENTY TWO

BY HALF past ten Taylor and Harding had checked out of their Travelodge room and taken the one minute stroll to the Little Chef restaurant next door. The two businesses shared the car park and this allowed Taylor to keep an eye on his car. Their breakfast order of a bacon sandwich and mug of tea was now a memory. Taylor's twenty minute examination of his car had been fruitless and he'd declared it clean of listening and tracking devices.

The Enid Blyton book and the typed page lay on the table between them as a second mug of tea arrived. They both stared down at the text hoping for inspiration, but nothing came quickly:

Chapter 1

back, and° photographs. N

of a° "Oooh!" W

238

213

Kim ran her index finger along the top line of text reading out loud. 'Chapter one.' She then pointed to the book which was opened at its contents page and said: 'Chapter one is titled, "The Beginning of Things".' She looked around at Taylor. 'So this is perhaps a starting point; maybe we even have to stay within chapter one of the book to find everything we need.'

Taylor nodded in agreement. That bit seemed feasible. He'd already familiarised himself with all of the wording on the sheet, but had failed to come up with ideas.

Kim wrote the first two words of the code onto a sheet of note paper before starting to talk. 'Not capitalised and all lower case with a comma after the first word. The odd use of degree sign… does that stand for an angle or a temperature?'

She continued to reproduce the line of text and think aloud at the same time: 'Then a space before the second word… a full stop and then a letter N.'

Taylor watched her biro form the letters. 'So the information is in the detail,' he said. 'How the word is formed… upper, lower case, commas other punctuation?'

'Must be,' Kim said. 'Dad was a real stickler for detail. Even his typewriter was a special high-tech one in its day. He ordered it from America because it had additional maths symbols.'

Taylor tapped his fingers down onto the book. 'I only reached chapter nine of this before I fell asleep.'

'Hmm, A Strange Boat,' Kim responded.

Taylor looked puzzled. 'Pardon.'

'A Strange Boat… the title of chapter nine. Think so anyway.'

They slowly drove back to Taylor's house discussing their next moves with some confidence that the conversation was private.

Taylor pulled the car into his driveway. 'I'm not happy telling the authorities about the bugging or about what your father left you.'

Kim unfastened her seat belt. 'I'm glad you said that. We still can't be sure who to trust with this. I need to keep in touch with what's going on in Exeter and they'll think it odd if it looks like I've just vanished.'

'Agreed,' said Taylor. 'But at the same time I wish we could make some inroads into what your father wanted you to do. Whoever we are up against seems keen to get hold of this same secret and without doubt for different reasons. Lenny Gill got himself murdered because of this and we might be similar targets.'

Taylor's home phone was ringing as they opened the back door. He shook his head at Kim; he'd left the listening devices in place and had no intention of answering. A silent check through the house was made as his suspicious mind-set considered the possibility of another break-in, but he was left undecided on the issue. They wordlessly started preparations for what they'd planned. It was going to be a trip to who-knows-where with a small overnight bag each. The panniers of the motorcycle dictated what they could take. It would be little more than a few clothes and toiletries along with a road map, note pads, credit cards and cash. They would be putting distance between themselves and Staffordshire before discussing their next move.

Kim collected a few things together in readiness to load up and they both changed into their motorcycling gear. A check on the bike before setting off seemed sensible and Kim made her way through into the adjoining garage from the kitchen. A quick start-up of the engine was a preliminary step. The machine fired up quickly despite the unusually sluggish note of the starter motor. She pursed her lips as she switched off, puzzled by the uncommon issue and wondered if the battery might need testing.

She met Taylor back in the lounge, his pager had beeped for the umpteenth time and he was checking the message: *Ring DC Timson Exeter CID.*

Taylor rummaged in his pocket for change. 'I'm going down to the phone box. It's too dodgy using your mobile; they've probably already arranged to intercept the calls.' He mouthed the words into Kim's ear. 'I'll take the car… I'm not walking down in these motor cycle leathers. I'll pick up some sandwiches and cokes from the corner shop. I'll be ten minutes… fifteen tops. You okay with that?'

Kim responded in an equally clandestine whisper. 'Okay, I'll load up the bike and we'll get out of here as soon as you're back.' She gathered up the bags and her crash helmet and quietly stepped back from the kitchen into the garage. The possibility that someone might be listening to every sound and trying to work out their next move was on her mind. She gently pulled the kitchen door closed as she heard Taylor's car reverse out and then drive away down the road.

The Yamaha TDM 850 with its metallic scarlet paintwork rested on its side stand facing the doors. Taylor's silver and red Schuberth crash helmet was on the pillion fastened to the seat bracket.

Kim had never been a fan of side panniers; she thought they spoiled the look of the bike and affected the aerodynamics at speed. Most of her journeys were at speed. Her advanced riding skills had been acquired from her time as a traffic cop and as a consequence she now also had some enviable success on the race track.

She loaded the hated but necessary panniers before leaning quietly against the workbench for a moment. Her mind drifted back to some of the details her father had so meticulously typed onto that sheet of paper. She'd stowed both the book and the paper into the bike's back box, but knew the words off by heart. She leant back against the workbench; arms folded trying to get a grip on what it meant. This was the first chance she'd had at uninterrupted private thought for some time. It did not last long...

The noise she heard was slight but enough for her brow to furrow with puzzlement. She slowly turned her head and decoded that the sound had been that of the house back-door handle being pressed down. It was almost imperceptible; nothing more than a delicate rumble from the complicated mechanism of the UPVC door as it disengaged. The door had not been locked.

The manoeuvre appeared so intentionally furtive that it sent a shiver down Kim's spine. It was too soon to be Taylor; he could hardly have started his phone call yet. The stealthy quietness of the action brought with it a feeling of dread. A second, almost identical and equally clandestine sound followed as the door closed and the handle was pressed upwards. The third much lesser sound was actually the one which struck real fear into her heart. If Kim's senses had not been so acutely tuned by the sudden rush of adrenaline, that extra noise might have gone unnoticed. The almost inaudible dragging sound originated from the peaks and troughs of door key's high tensile steel cuts travelling over the tumbler pins of the lock. The door had been locked and the key removed!

Kim slowly unfolded her arms, conscious of possible noise made by her stiff leather biking jacket. Her eyes scanned the garage for something to use as a weapon. She looked directly at the door leading into the kitchen and although she could hear nothing knew that someone was on the other side. Her neck prickled as the thought came to her that this was almost certainly one of the people who had murdered Lenny Gill. It also occurred that without doubt the person had seen her and Taylor enter and had watched Taylor leave alone. The visitor had come for her.

Her choice of weapon seemed to fall between a long screwdriver and a ball peen hammer, both of which lay on top of the workbench. She'd dealt with a couple of stabbings where a similar screwdriver had been used almost as effectively as a knife. But the dull screwdriver tip would not have the penetrating power of a sharp knife and the disabling properties were likely to be slow acting. She knew of serious assaults and even murders where a hammer had been the weapon of choice, but many blows were often required before the target succumbed.

She turned her head to the right as her peripheral vision caught some movement. The blurred outline of a man had now come into view through the opaque window glass of Taylor's rickety wooden garage doors. This second person had taken station on the driveway to watch the front of the house. He would be concealed from prying eyes by the shrubbery and tall hedges.

Kim's mind raced as she considered her options. Neither the intruder nor his look-out knew where in the house she was or that they had lost the element of surprise. The door between the kitchen and garage was unlocked and its mortice key was slotted in on the other side; she could not lock it.

She lifted the hammer slowly from the bench and crept silently to the side of the door. The next noise was tiny. She perceived it as nothing more than a well-engineered metallic *click*. She had undergone extensive firearms training with the police over the past few years. Her deep and silent intake of breath came unevenly as her heart thumped. The click seemed identical to that of a pistol safety catch! The anxiety level rose further as she heard one more identical click. She looked straight ahead at the opposite wall as a feeling of dread enveloped her. The last noise was not the safety catch going back on – why would it be? It was the catch being clicked over into *Position 2*. The gun was a machine pistol and now set to automatic.

There were only a few such guns available, but the one that she did know of was the particularly inhuman Russian 9mm Stetchkin APS. It was a fully automatic pistol which held twenty rounds. With its fire rate of 750 rounds a minute it could blast the door to matchwood in seconds.

With eyes wide and at their most acute of angles Kim waited. Her left palm now flattened against the wall to the side of the door whilst her right hand gripped the shaft of the hammer. The will to survive formed desperate plans as she quickly thought through what she would do if the door started to open. She considered swinging the hammer upwards from knee level and smashing it into the intruder's face. But the door would have to be allowed to open sufficiently for her to hit the target. The man would be on his guard and expecting trouble. How could she even be sure of his intentions or if he did actually have a gun? What if she was wrong? There might not even be a gun. She'd then be the one in court and perhaps even on a murder charge.

Her vision concentrated onto nothing in particular as she cocked her head to one side and listened. Another slight sound came. It was nothing more than the dull rustle of clothing and the stealthiest of footfalls as the person crept through into the hall. He had overlooked the door leading into the garage. He'd either considered it to be a cupboard or had made a conscious decision that she was in another room in the house.

Kim allowed herself one small sigh of relief but knew that the reprieve was only temporary. She was still trapped. She bent her knees and carefully crept over to the double garage doors keeping her outline below the level of the row of opaque window panes which formed the top half. A thin band of brighter sunlight shone through between the right hand door and the thick frame onto which it hinged. She pressed an eye up against the crack, taking in the front garden and then the figure.

Standing with his back towards her and no more than ten feet away the man was well-built and over six feet tall. The corner of his unzipped black windcheater hung loosely as he arched his back and retained a tip-toe stance, neck craning, looking above the hedge - watching for nosey neighbours or even Doug Taylor's premature return. He swivelled his shoulders slightly to look at the house, perhaps readying himself for the action which would surely come.

As his body turned a little more his right hand was fully seen from Kim's awkward viewpoint. The square thick outline of a Browning 9mm semi-automatic pistol pointed down at the ground. The man's index finger ran in a straight line along the barrel waiting to snatch down onto the trigger in a fraction of a second.

The man twisted a few more degrees and set his eyes upon the front door of the house. Kim stared at the face and a shockwave of disbelief rolled over her.

She crept back to the kitchen door and listened some more. A creaking stair tread gave the clue that the intruder was on his way upstairs. The backdoor was now locked and the front of the house was a definite NO-GO. An escape through a window would take too long. She'd get a bullet in the back of the head before she'd struggled halfway through the narrow slot allowed by the double glazing. She opted for a possible delaying tactic and crept back to the door leading to the kitchen. A slow downwards press of the handle allowed for the merest opening of the door. A fraction of an inch at first, and then a little more until, with breath held, she peered through into the kitchen and on into the hallway.

She captured movement on the staircase through the gaps between the wooden balustrades in that last available triangle between ceiling and stairway woodwork. The intruder's final furtive upward step gave away little detail before the leg disappeared. It was brief, slight even, but there was no doubting that the stylish black trouser and flat court shoe belonged to a woman.

TWENTY THREE

KIM'S trembling hand reached around and delicately took the key from the other side. With the handle kept upright she noiselessly pressed the door back closed and carefully lowered the handle back to rest. Her staccato open-mouthed breaths produced the only sound as she then inserted the key in from the garage side and slowly turned it until the mechanism engaged. The door was now locked, but if the intruder did have a Stetchkin APS then there would be no need for a key.

The dull low buzzing sound which then began came in sync with the vibration Kim felt in the left breast pocket of her leather jacket. Her eyes widened as she slapped a hand against the pocket – fingers fumbling to get at the off button of her mobile phone. It was a small sound but had it been enough to alert the intruder upstairs?

The answer came with the sound of feet tramping down the stairs. Stealth had been cast aside. The intruder knew she was hiding downstairs and there was nowhere for her to go. It wouldn't take long to find her. The crashing of cupboards being wrenched open, furniture being tipped to one side and doors being kicked open lasted for a short while before an eerie silence. There was only one place left – the garage.

Kim had her own agenda and she wasn't going down without a fight.

The door-handle slowly edged downwards and was followed by a pause before the slight pressure of a hand on the other side tested the slack between door and frame. A noisy rattle was the next action as the handle jolted sharply north to south showing the intruder's agitation.

The scuff of a backward taken footstep away from the door was the prelude to a chilling few seconds of silence – and then the trigger was pulled. A deafening explosion of sound reverberated through the building. The door splintered into chunks of flying timber as the Stetchkin sprayed a burst of 9mm Makarov rounds. Sparks and ricochets filled the garage as the bullets struck the wall opposite.

The deafening sound did not stop with the release of the trigger pressure – it increased to a thunderous roar as Kim yanked the throttle of the Yamaha open. She'd waited astride the machine, helmet on, first gear selected, clutch held in and thumb on the start button until the door exploded. She was head down and knees in close as the bike's front wheel slammed into the double garage doors on full power and burst through onto the drive. Both doors cartwheeled outwards, ripped free from their hinges in an eruption of glass and timber. The unprepared outside gunman staggered off balance to dodge one of the flying doors but was caught in a spray of debris.

The Yamaha's front wheel lifted from the surface momentarily as it reached the pavement and then slammed back down as Kim thumped her foot onto the rear brake. Her right hand squeezed at the front brake, locking it and lifting the bike's rear end. She shifted her weight up off the seat and outwards to the right, swinging the bike around into an impossibly tight left hander. With the back wheel down again she opened the throttle and tore down the centre line of the asphalt road under brutal acceleration.

The sound of gunshots travels, and although he was in a phone box two hundred yards away Taylor heard the commotion. Alarm spread across his face as he pushed open the kiosk door with the phone still pressed to his ear and peered up the road. The blazing headlight of the Yamaha appeared at the top of the road as Kim rounded the left hander. She set her sights on the red phone box and the figure standing in its open door.

Taylor let the phone drop from his grip as he took in the situation. Only snippets of information had yet been exchanged. The tinny sound of Timson's voice from the telephone earpiece could not be heard as it swung on its cable – 'Hello… Doug…. Mr Taylor…

what the hell's going on?'

Taylor was already out onto the pavement, standing between the phone box and passenger door of his car. Kim mounted the kerb and skidded to a halt alongside him with the engine still roaring. 'Get on NOW,' she shouted above the din. He leapt onto the pillion seat pulling up the spare crash helmet on its retaining cable, trapping it with his stomach against Kim's back. He interlinked his fingers in around her waist and bawled into her ear… 'GO... GO.'

The acceleration compared with a punch in the chest as the G-forces pushed him backwards. The bike lunged forwards out onto the main road, topping one hundred miles an hour in less than eight seconds.

Kim quickly put distance between Taylor's house with a three mile north bound, main road sprint and a further two hair-raising miles along country roads. She succumbed to Taylor's repeated rib digging and pulled into a secluded field gateway. She switched off and heaved the bike up onto its stand as they dismounted.

As the noise of the gunshots had reached Taylor in the phone box he'd instantly known that it was connected. He'd also grasped that whatever actions Kim had taken had saved her life. 'You okay?' was his first question.

Her crash helmet nodded twice before she pulled upwards to remove it. She shook her hair back into place. 'You'll be needing some new garage doors,' she said before explaining what had happened.

'Christ,' Taylor said after the tale was told. 'This all just got a lot worse. These people have almost certainly murdered Lenny Gill and now they've come within an inch of murdering you. I'd only just started to speak to Reg when I had to cut the call. It seems that something equally serious has happened down there concerning the reporter Cappelli. He's disappeared from his hotel. He's been attacked, kidnapped… murdered even.'

Taylor went silent as he stood looking down and thinking for a moment. 'Cappelli has uncovered information on this. I'm sure that he doesn't understand the seriousness of it but his digging has attracted some nasty attention. These people are capable of anything. Your father was protecting a secret that they're desperate to get their hands on. They'll take on anyone who might lead them to it and eliminate anybody who stands in their way.' Taylor grabbed Kim by the shoulders and turned her to face him eye to eye. 'Look, you already know that MI5 have their noses in this, so we're talking national security. After what's just happened at my house we can't go vigilante on this any longer. We MUST hand it over.'

Kim looked up at Taylor; she lifted her hands upward and pushed outward breaking his grip. 'I saw one of them Doug… I recognised him.'

'What?'

'We can't trust anyone over this. The man I saw was Nelson, the MI5 agent. His partner, the one who tried to kill me was a woman… it must have been Jennings.'

TWENTY FOUR

A LOCAL police response car quickly arrived at Doug Taylor's house. The uniformed officer's steps up the driveway to the open garage were cautious; the report had suggested automatic gunfire. The splintered garage doors lay in pieces on the front garden. Shards of window glass littered the lawn and drive and a thick black tyre mark led out from the garage toward the road. More shattered woodwork could be seen inside the garage from the internal door. Deep pockmarking and displaced bricks where the powerful machine pistol had hammered in bullets were on show. The officer backed out to the refuge of his car and within minutes local CID officers DC Dan Cheeseman and WDC Jayne Morrison arrived. Their attempts to start an investigation were quickly thwarted by the rare and speedy arrival of Special Branch.

DCI Jenny Lowell's Vauxhall Carlton with its magnetic blue flashing roof light followed three police armed response cars, klaxons blaring and roof lights flickering to a tyre scrunching halt. In no time blue police tape had been stretched and knotted to lampposts. Burly officers with flak jackets and Heckler and Koch sub-machine guns stood with stock-in-trade menacing stares.

The events were unquestionably serious and that condition was aggravated even more as they involved the private home of a serving police officer. But Special Branch would only show an interest where the matter touched upon national security. Lowell's immediate taking command of the situation seemed bizarre. Her forceful ushering of Cheeseman and Morrison off the property, in no way fitted with usual divisional procedure.

'A boss is a boss Ched,' Morrison advised. 'She's a DCI and we are mere DCs.' Mo rested her back against the door of the CID car and lit up a Player's Number 6.

'Our DI is on his way,' Cheeseman bellowed down the driveway to Lowell. 'I'm told shots have been fired and he's going to expect us as the first CID officers to have secured the scene.'

'Don't worry yourself constable,' Lowell sarcastically replied. 'You won't be in trouble and I can assure you that your DI won't be going any further either.'

Cheeseman's anger level reached an even higher plane when additional Staffordshire Police Special Branch officers arrived and appeared to be coordinating an investigation of the incident. The local CID had effectively been relieved of duty.

'What's going on Mo?' Cheeseman grumbled. 'They're doing our job. This is Doug Taylor's house and this needs looking into properly.' He craned his neck, watching as the Special Branch officers could be seen inside the wide open garage inspecting the scene.

'Why are you keeping CID out of this serious crime scene?' Cheddar shouted to Lowell.

'Your interference is verging on a disciplinary offence now Cheeseman,' Lowell shouted back. 'I am ordering you back beyond the police tape. You can take it up with your boss when he arrives.'

Cheddar wandered back to where Mo still stood against the car. 'Annoying cow,' Mo said.

Cheddar gritted his teeth and made a low growl. It was something he only did when he was angry. 'I can think of a better description Mo.'

Within minutes Little Stoneleigh's CID boss, DI Pete Noonan arrived and received an update from Cheddar. His attempt to get to the bottom of the issue collected a similar rebuff from Lowell. She was talking into a mobile phone as Noonan purposefully approached her. His expression portrayed his intent to find out what the hell was going on. This was after all his patch. Lowell stabbed an angry finger at Noonan and quickly changed it into a flat palmed stop signal as she continued to talk into her mobile. Noonan, not normally one to back down was stalled by the venom in Lowell's expression. He stopped five yards short to await an explanation. Lowell swung around in an attempt at privacy. Noonan caught a glimpse of the shoulder holstered semi-automatic pistol beneath her jacket. Special Branch officers would occasionally be armed. Their infrequent cloak and dagger appearances typically came and went without explanation. Noonan understood that there was usually a good reason but only Special Branch, MI5 and the top execs at Police HQ would be in on these secrets.

A muttered conversation continued for a moment before Lowell turned full circle and held out her phone at arms-length towards Noonan. He accepted the offer and immediately recognised the educated voice of Chief Constable Sir Henry Charles.

'Sorry Peter, I'm going to have to ask you to leave this scene entirely in the hands of Special Branch.'

Sir Henry was not in reality asking. He was ordering.

A black Vauxhall Senator pulled up kerbside outside Taylor's house as Noonan made his retreat. Cheddar commented on the driver. 'There's a spook if ever I've seen one.' His words were delivered from the corner of mouth to Morrison. 'Looks as though he's upset someone recently.' The additional observation referred to the piece of sticking plaster beneath the man's right eye.

Morrison nodded in agreement with the suggestion. 'Yes, and here's another,' she said, as a VW Golf pulled in behind. The woman at the wheel set a stony stare onto the group of detectives.

With their participation completely axed the Little Stoneleigh detectives made their way back to the police station. Taylor's car was still parked by the phone box but was now being guarded by one of the armed officers.

Benedict Cappelli was sitting on a filthy tiled floor with his back against a wall. Remnants of wallpaper were still attached here and there. Bare brickwork showed in other places where the plaster had parted company and dropped down. A similar story was evident above his head, gaping holes showing the underside of upstairs floorboards. The overcast sky successfully dulled the weak March daylight down lower than the usual norm. As quarter past two approached it seemed that the sun had already given up for the day. The gloomy interior of the derelict house had been left to the spiders, the damp and the ghosts.

Cappelli was cold, uncomfortable and in pain. His right ankle hurt like hell. One or two of his ribs might be cracked and his left wrist had seen better days. The pain in his jaw indicated another injury, but at least he was alive. Had it not been for his desperate quick thinking that would not be the case. The word desperate certainly fitted. The fact that his hotel room was only on floor one had also played a part. His running drop kick straight through the window did not cause his injuries other than countless small cuts to his legs and face. The landing onto the car's roof broke his fall, but also contributed to his ailments. Adrenalin had been quick to combine with logic inside Cappelli's mind and had made it clear that the two hotel room visitors were not there for a friendly chat. What a stroke of luck that he'd been awake.

The attackers were never going to throw themselves out of the window to get him and so they had to take the stairs and corridors. By the time they made it on to the car park lights were being switched on, alarmed voices could be heard and phone calls were being made. Cappelli fled, twisted ankle or not! He knew he was a dead man if these people caught him. Their tyre squealing exit from the car park was dramatic but necessary. They knew that the police would soon be arriving.

Cappelli shook his head with disbelief as some of the incident came back to him. He had bounced off the roof of the car and fuelled by adrenaline managed to stagger away towards a row of derelict houses.

The semi-comatose vagrant, "Ossie", as he liked to be known had the fright of his life when Cappelli lurched noisily in through the broken down door and tripped over him. Ossie was an unlikely

Good Samaritan. He'd even extended an arm and proffered a swig from his bottle of cheap whisky. The concussed and dazed Cappelli declined the offer, but did take the man's advice. It was after all, very cold. The tattered, flea infested sleeping bag which had been abandoned in a corner by some earlier visitor was now his to use as he wished. Dressed in his Superman T-shirt, boxers and dressing gown he hoped that the sleeping bag would keep out the chill until he felt well enough for his next move.

'You in some kind of trouble?' Ossie had casually enquired. It was a stupid question to ask an injured, blood spattered man in a derelict house at quarter past five on a March morning.

'With the police I mean.'

'Something like that,' Cappelli had mumbled through his painful jaw before lapsing into unconsciousness.

Several hours passed before the battered reporter focussed his blurred vision onto the face of his saviour. The towels which Ossie used to tidy up the wounds seemed to be genuinely clean and freshly washed. 'Borrowed 'em from the hotel,' was the explanation. 'They won't miss 'em.'

Cappelli's strange mind-set fired up again as his lucidity fleetingly returned. Even though his predicament was serious his thoughts went back to Donald Dykes in the pub. Now he himself was the fugitive Abel Magwich from Charles Dickens' *Great Expectations* and Ossie was young Pip – looking after him.'

'You're going to need some clothes and some food eventually,' Ossie said.

'Thanks, but I've no money with me, I can't pay you.' Cappelli croaked.

'I didn't ask for any did I? Make yourself comfy and get some rest. You can use my bedroll for a bit more warmth. I'll be a while.'

Cappelli had floated in and out of consciousness over the next few hours as different degrees of pain circulated between his ankle, jaw and ribs.

The sound of broken glass crunching under foot broke the silence announcing Ossie's return. He was a peculiar individual: gaunt and slightly stooped with a full head of silver white hair scraped meticulously into place. The unwashed scalp provided all the necessary oils to keep his locks permanently in situ. The overcoat he wore could well have seen its first days in the trenches of the Great War.

Ossie stood over Cappelli holding a bundle of clothing under his right arm and a wad of newspaper in his left hand. The reporter's senses were quickly restored as the smell of vinegar percolated through the dilapidated surroundings – chips!

A bottle of milk was pulled from the greatcoat pocket. 'Nicked that off someone's step earlier,' Ossie explained as he handed over. 'It ain't proper chips… bits of fry that the chippie gives me. He chucks in one or two fish bits and the odd chip.'

Cappelli tucked in. 'Thanks Ossie… what about you?'

'I'm okay. I nicked some bread and cakes from around the back of the baker's earlier. That's where I got you these.' He handed over the clothing. 'Can't have you wandering around in your underwear…. Oh and this.' Ossie proffered a black fold-over wallet at Cappelli. 'It's the baker's… no money mind you. He's a working man, probably has a wife and kids, I wouldn't pinch his cash, so I left that behind.'

Cappelli made a frown of puzzlement as he accepted the wallet. He opened it and plucked out two cards for inspection. There was a library card and a credit card in the owner's name: *Raymond Meigh*. 'Hmm,' Cappelli said. 'I don't want to commit any more crimes.' He delved a little deeper into the wallet and pulled out Mr Meigh's driving licence. He stared at it and then said. 'I see your thinking Ossie and I appreciate it, but I think I'll pass.' He put the wallet down onto a rotting window sill and began to examine the clothing.

TWENTY FIVE

HALF PAST TWO arrived as Kim rode the Yamaha up the off-ramp of the M6 onto Forton Services seven miles short of Lancaster. Their ninety mile journey had taken them far enough from the action to allow them the confidence to relax a little. A toilet break and some food were also on the list.

The quietest corner of the eating area proved to be a lot noisier than they would have liked, but they made do. The pizza and chips was just fuel to keep them going. Coffee washed it down.

Taylor voiced his concerns over leaving the Yamaha on show. 'We're the victims in this, but I've an awful feeling that the focus of some people is on finding us. If this security agent, Nelson, is working for the other side he'll be pulling some official strings to get that done sooner than later.'

Taylor pulled out his pager and scrolled through the half dozen messages which had come through since they'd set off. Most seemed to be followed with the instructions "Ring me now". He pressed the off button and flicked out the batteries.

Kim needed no prompting and followed suit with her mobile phone before spreading the cryptically typed page of instructions onto the table between them. They stared down at it hoping for inspiration. Taylor's first question had been running through his mind for some time. 'Why here… why this direction?'

Kim nodded her forehead at the paper and then pressed a finger down upon the first line of puzzling letters. 'I think these are coordinates, for a map, perhaps for a particular place even. This letter N at the end tells us it's to the North.'

Taylor frowned. 'That's hit and miss. If your dad wanted you to go to the North, then he'd need to know where you were starting from. If he'd planned on you starting from home then we may already have overshot the mark.'

Kim rolled her eyes. 'I had thought of that and I know it was a gamble, but we had to get away while we could. We need some time to work this out.'

Taylor glanced over his shoulder at the surroundings. It was what you'd expect from a busy motorway service station, drivers, businessmen, reps, families with kids, queues of people and the general hustle and bustle. 'We're not going to get much thinking done here,' he said.

Kim stood to her feet. 'Agreed and I don't fancy another Travelodge. Seeing as how it's my problem we're trying to sort out it'll be my treat and Dad's provided the funds.'

A scan through some local information brochures at the onsite newsagents gave them ideas for a few fairly handy possibilities. After a couple of payphone calls and a twenty minute drive they found themselves in the small coastal town of Heysham. It lay sufficiently distant from the holiday resort of Morecambe to retain a little of its old world charm.

Kim pulled in at the kerbside and they sat on the bike for a moment with the engine ticking over. They gazed up at the Heysham Port Hotel.

Taylor said, 'It looks great, but it won't come cheap.'

'Already told you, it's my treat.'

With the Yamaha discreetly parked on the rear car park Kim's deliberate mistake with the registration number for the hotel register went unnoticed by the manager. The room on the first floor was generously sized with a wide bay window looking out towards Morecambe Bay. The pseudonym of "Mr and Mrs Tresilian" had been Kim's idea of a joke.

'Stuart Tresilian was Enid Blyton's artist,' Kim explained. 'He did the artwork in The Island of Adventure.'

It was Taylor's turn to roll his eyes as they made their way up to their room. 'Hmm, not the easiest of names to sign onto a hotel register especially if you don't know for sure how it's spelt.'

Kim laughed and fell back onto the bed. 'You did a great job.' She was at ease for the first time in days. She held out her arms to him. 'Come here.'

Home Secretary Walter Baker arrived home at Dorneywood in South Buckinghamshire from his London offices at six-thirty that evening. MI5 boss Sir Peter Walker landed on his doorstep an hour later. The Cabinet Minister was due to attend a social event that evening and the one hour of home time had been spent in the usual rush to get ready.

Walker was impressed by the strict security checks before he was allowed into the grounds. The armed police officers on the gates to the estate passed the test and so too did the Special Branch detective who answered the door.

Baker stood inside a reception room off the main hallway as Walker made his entrance escorted by the detective. The huge room was brightly lit by two crystal chandeliers. The massive gilt framed over mantle mirror reflected back the light, creating a dazzling effect.

Baker wore a dinner suit minus the jacket which was draped over a nearby armchair. His paunch had been tightly stowed inside an evening dress shirt but still seemed comparable to four months of pregnancy. Mrs Baker, in full-length, dark blue, sequined evening gown glittered under the lighting as she tottered on tip-toe to adjust her husband's bow tie.

'I'm short on time Peter,' Baker said, making a grab for the jacket. His face was flushed from a recent shower. His eyes directed Mrs Baker to the doorway indicating a private conversation. 'Two ticks darling,' he added in an attempt to soften the rudeness. A beckoning of the thumb was enough for the Special Branch man.

It was the second meeting of the day for the two men. Walker would not invoke the need-to-know rule again. This latest news must be shared.

'Yes a little birdie tipped me off… automatic gunfire in a

Staffordshire village,' Baker said as he slipped on the jacket. Walker's continuing summary of the events generated increasing puzzlement on the Home Secretary's face. 'So the policewoman who was there is Dr Fry's daughter?'

'Correct Home Secretary. Kimberly Harding, she's a detective with Devon and Cornwall. Her partner, Doug Taylor who owns the house, is a detective inspector himself with Staffordshire Police. The woman crashed straight through the garage doors and Taylor's car was found abandoned nearby. They have a pager and a mobile phone between them but nothing has been heard of either of them, despite numerous attempts at contact.'

Baker made an alarmed face as the more violent and desperate threads of the incident were related.

'Fortunately the neighbours kept their heads down,' Walker said. 'There was a hell of a commotion. A man and a woman were spotted jumping into a car and chasing after the motor cycle.'

'Baker flicked fingers across the shoulders of his jacket as he examined his appearance in the mirror. 'And do we think that these people may have caught them?'

'Doubtful Home Secretary, Harding had a head start and from all accounts she's a highly experienced pursuit trained rider. We've only allowed Special Branch onto the scene along with a forensic team and scenes of crime officers for the moment. A meticulous search has revealed the tiniest trace of blood on glass from the garage doors and so someone has sustained an injury.'

Baker turned back from the mirror to face Walker. 'So the two police officers have been missing for several hours now. Is there some possibility that... what's-her-name... Harding has inherited some of her father's vigilante genes? Is she intent on getting to the bottom of this herself?'

Walker made a frustrated sigh. 'From what I've learned, both of these officers have track records suggesting that is entirely possible.'

'Thing is Peter, both you and I know that the people behind this are not your run-of-the-mill crooks.'

Walker had more to add but delayed for a moment as Mrs Baker's face peered around the door in an effort to remind her husband of the time. As the lady disappeared back into the hallway he began. 'It seems that someone believes that Dr Fry's daughter possesses valuable information. Now, that could mean she already has that information or that she has the key to finding it. If what was discussed in our earlier meeting is correct it may be the location of Rosa's file. It could contain a plan of other VX dead drops or the location of a large stash of unused VX.'

Baker's urgency to be on his way had now been side-lined by the significance of Walker's words. The security of the nation was of greater importance than his timely arrival at the Central London Arts Club. The other guests and hosts attending the annual dinner of the Community Security Trust would be forced to accept his late arrival apology.

Baker waved a palm in the direction of his wife's peering-around-the-door face and nodded a "soon-as-I-can-darling" expression back to her. He turned back to Walker. 'What steps are in place to trace Harding and Taylor? I doubt if they realise what they are up against.'

'We've been attempting to track them through Harding's mobile phone. It's all relatively new technology. If they're out of range of a base station mast or switched off then we haven't a hope in hell. It's a lot more difficult with Taylor's pager but we're working with the network providers. They were last tracked through Harding's mobile to Forton services on the M6, close to Lancaster at two forty-five this afternoon,' Walker said with a grimace. 'Unfortunately we lost them after that so they've either switched off or headed into a dead area. I've committed two particular agents to find them. They will see to it that an interest flag is initiated on the police national computer for the motor cycle. If a police officer spots and checks it an instruction will inform him to report it immediately and keep it under observation. There is still no more on the missing journalist. The agents have also taken on finding him as a priority.'

Baker nodded his understanding as he hurried toward the door. 'If we get no luck soon we'll have to use the media to broadcast Harding's motor cycle registration number. We need to find them before the other side do. Chances are this reporter is already dead.'

It was seven o'clock and dark when Taylor awoke. He blinked a couple of times as his eyes adjusted. The dull orange glow of a street lamp shone through a chink in the curtains allowing outlines of a table and wardrobe to be made out. He turned on his side catching the silhouette of Kim sitting up, two pillows behind her and wide eyes fixed onto the opposite wall.

He gave a little cough to give his voice resonance as he reached over to switch on the bedside lamp. 'What you doing?' he said.

'Thinking… thinking about Dad's note. I've an idea what it might mean.'

They were soon seated side by side at the room's oval dining style table. The Enid Blyton book took up the centre and Kim set the page of typed details down beneath it. She drew a bold biro cross on a page of her notepad, nothing more than two intersecting lines covering the entire length and breadth of the page. She then printed a letter "N" at the top of the vertical line and a letter "W" on the left side of the horizontal line.

'A compass?' Taylor questioned.

'Better than that I think,' Kim said. 'Latitude and longitude, unless I'm mistaken.'

Taylor watched her, stunned at the way her mind was working and surprised at her knowledge.

'Dad did a lot of sailing whenever he was allowed away from work,' she said. 'We had a small boat at one time. I did the basics of latitude and longitude at school, but learned more from dad than I did at school.'

Taylor nodded as his own brief school time understanding of the subject was trawled. 'So if I remember correctly latitude measures how many degrees north or south of the equator you are.'

He moved his finger across to rest it down onto the second line of Geoff Fry's typed words:

back, and° photographs. N

'So this is code for a latitude coordinate?'

'If the letter 'N' at the end stands for North then that's how I see it,' Kim agreed. 'And the other line of letters ending with W for west is going to be for the longitude.'

Taylor positioned the point of his elbow down onto the table and rested his chin on his palm before starting to speak. 'The first line of text says, "chapter one", so is the answer in chapter one of the book? I've read through that already and I'm none the wiser.'

'Well perhaps all the details are contained in chapter one.'

They both fell silent for a while.

'Hmm,' Taylor eventually mused. 'So we must be looking for numbers, as in latitude and longitude?'

'That must be it,' Kim interrupted and opened the book randomly with her left hand. 'It must be page numbers.' Her left index finger was pointing at the centrally positioned number at the bottom of the yellowed page. 'If we find that the words that dad has typed are also within the story, then that page number should form part of the map coordinates.'

'Possibly,' Taylor agreed. 'But we're pretty limited if we can only use chapter one. That's only ten pages long. I'm gathering that your father has been very precise. He's typed an exact copy of a piece of text and even included punctuation marks. It must mean that we have to find the words he's typed reproduced exactly.'

Kim starting turning the pages of the book and looking through the text. She restricted the check to the first 10 pages of the story which made up chapter one. It wasn't long before they realised that some of the groups of two words together appeared several times whilst others did not appear at all.

TWENTY SIX

WITH A tattered hooded anorak, carpet slippers and a pair of black and white chequered chefs trousers Benedict Cappelli looked ridiculous. It was eight o'clock when he took his first steps back into the outside world. He'd left his departure until this time for a couple of reasons. His injuries restricted his movement and his hobbling might attract attention. The twisted ankle and intense pain from his ribs were the worst and the cuts to his face made him look like a car crash victim. The clothing seemed even more likely to draw attention than the injuries, but he was not complaining at Ossie's efforts.

Cappelli's thank-you to the elderly vagrant included a hug which generated a searing pain in those ribs before he ventured out. His uncomfortable shuffling lasted fifteen minutes before he emerged from a side alleyway out onto Heavitree Road. He resolutely started off in the direction of his goal: the three storey concrete block on the other side of the road which was Exeter's police station. He felt certain that his entry into that building would afford sanctuary away from the people who wanted to kill or capture him. It could also provide a portal back into his normal world.

Two figures approached the police station's entrance from opposite directions as Cappelli mustered the courage to make his move. *Members of the public,* was his first thought, but that idea was quickly dispelled in favour of *detectives.* The height and build was a good pointer. The overcoats with hands thrust deep into pockets and heads bowed into upturned collars against the weather added substance to the guess.

The men stepped from the pavement and climbed the few steps up to the doors in unison. A courteous exchange took place before the door was opened – a handshake and some unintelligible conversation.

Cappelli slunk back into a nearby bus shelter for a moment. He never forgot a face and the one that he could now see was unquestionably that of Detective Inspector Ken Grainger. Holding back in the shadows he watched a little longer as the handshake finished. Grainger politely pushed the door inwards for the other man as more inaudible, but apparently civil dialogue drifted across the road.

Cappelli's spirits lifted a little. A direct approach to Grainger would by-pass a delay at the enquiry desk. An immediate face to face with the detective in charge of Lenny's murder enquiry would hopefully put a quick end to his suffering. He lifted his painful ankle and made to set off across the road intent on catching the pair before they had cleared the internal security door.

The reporter's first step stalled as the profile of the second man came into perspective. Cappelli never did forget a face and as the man rotated his shoulders slightly a brief and distant full facial came on view. Here was one face which would live with him forever. An instant flashback came to him and his heart thudded with the power of a steam hammer. The last time he had seen that mug had been through the spyhole in his hotel bedroom door. Yes, the image had been a little distorted then, rather like looking into the reflection given from the side of a chrome plated kettle. The smiling and somewhat arrogant expression that the man now wore was at odds with Cappelli's aforementioned brief glimpse. On that occasion it had been both vicious and determined. A small alteration had been also made to his appearance. A piece of sticking plaster now showed beneath his right eye. Had it happened during Cappelli's daring escape? The reporter wasn't that interested as there was no question about the identity.

The man pulled momentarily away from the held-open door and settled his eyes upon the oddly dressed and bedraggled hobo on the other side of the road. The wretched individual was rummaging in the waste bin attached to the bus stop pole – no doubt after fag ends.

Cappelli breathed a sigh of relief as the two men disappeared inside. He wiped his sticky hands down the sides of the anorak and retraced his steps unsure of his next move.

By nine o'clock Taylor and Harding were hungry and suffering from eyestrain.

'I think we're on the wrong track with this idea,' Taylor said. 'Let's get some food. I can't think straight on an empty stomach.'

A severe chill in the air belied the fact that it would soon be the first day of Spring. Kim gripped her arm tight in against Taylor and they set off along a narrow street lit by lantern style streetlamps. The shops were mostly in darkness, windows crammed floor to ceiling with cheap dusty trinkets and all forlornly awaiting the return of the holiday season. Their ten minute stroll from the hotel landed them outside Mr Wang's Chinese restaurant, one of the few places open.

Taylor pushed on the restaurant door. A waiter, almost certainly also the owner, checked his watch from where he sat on a tall bar stool behind the central counter. The otherwise empty eatery suggested that for tonight he was also head cook and bottle washer. He delivered a smile before outstretching a hand over at the vacant tables. 'Evening Sir… Madam… anywhere you like.'

The lack of other customers caused Taylor some concern that the food would not be up to the mark, but he was proved wrong. They decided on a set meal for two: chicken and sweetcorn soup, salt and pepper ribs and exotic main courses that arrived on sizzling platters. A glass of Shiraz for Kim and a pint of Tsingotao beer for Taylor complimented the meal.

The conversation immediately turned to their progress in unravelling Kim's father's instructions. It had appeared promising at first, but now they accepted that they were no further forward. The book and page of code lay on the spare seat next to Taylor.

Kim started from memory. 'So… two lines of code. One presumably for latitude ending in N for north, and the other for longitude ending in W for west.'

'The trouble is,' Taylor said. 'If we stick to chapter one, we simply can't find some of those words to match those given by your father. There are also a couple of the other ones that are duplicated no less than three times.'

Kim was nodding. 'I still think we're on the right track, but we've missed something important.' She sat back in her chair, took a sip at her wine and then stared at the ceiling for several seconds. 'What if… where dad puts "Chapter 1" has a hidden meaning? What if the title of the chapter is the clue or instruction to what we have to do?'

'The Beginning of Things,' Taylor said recalling the title of chapter one. 'We were thinking it was a starting point and that everything was in chapter one.'

Kim kept her gaze on the ceiling. 'So maybe, just maybe, *The Beginning of Things* is an important instruction to follow for each piece of the code.'

'The first words on a page…' Taylor murmured the sentence, hardly sure if his idea was worth a mention.'

Kim's hand had gone to her mouth. 'The first words on a page… the first words on the relevant page?' Her efforts to snatch up the book from the spare chair almost knocked over her wine. She was thumbing through the book, checking only the first words of each page. It did not take her long.

'Here,' she said holding the open book toward Taylor. 'Page five the first letters are *"of a"* and that fits the first letters of the second line of code. That must be part of the longitude.'

Taylor peered at the page. 'Well yes, it does, but that piece of code also has a degree sign after it and there's certainly nothing similar to that in the book.'

'Elementary my dear Taylor,' Kim said, her face now beaming. 'It would be nonsense to put a degree sign after the word "a". The degree sign goes after the number five to indicate that the longitude starts with five degrees. We're onto it Doug, I think we know how to do it.'

They paid up and hurried back to the hotel eagerly setting out their stall on the table. Kim started to thumb through each page of the book and both of them focussed their vision firmly onto the first words as every page was turned.

The formula for both coordinates kept running through their minds:

back, and° *photographs. N*

of a° *"Oooh!" W*

238

213

Page 5 quickly confirmed the idea with *"of a"* as its first two words and Kim jotted down the number 5 which she followed with a degree sign. Page twenty-eight was the next page to give up its secret when they discovered that it began with the matching code words *"Oooh!"* complete with identical spelling and punctuation.

Page fifty-three then delivered the second part of the code for the latitude with the identically produced word *"photographs"*. This allowed Kim to add the letter "N" for north.

It was twenty minutes past one by the time they had unravelled and triple checked their work which began with the starting figure given by page fifty-seven of the book. The page's beginning words of *"back, and"* were a perfect match and so the degree symbol was added.

They both stared at the two decoded coordinates:

57° 53 N

5° 28 W

The additional numbers *238* and *213* which appeared beneath the two lines of code was an anomaly which they had yet to spend time on. These seemed completely dissimilar to the puzzle that they had already unravelled.

Taylor looked down at the decoded answer. 'Now we need to work out where the hell it is.' He added another thought as they climbed into bed. 'The two numbers must be significant, but at least we've made headway.'

TWENTY SEVEN

THE NEXT morning came all too soon for Benedict Cappelli. After his failed attempt to get back to civilisation he'd returned to the only sanctuary he knew. The cold dampness throughout the night made comfort impossible. It was now seven o'clock and still dark as he stood to his feet and stepped over the still snoring Ossie. He checked out the weather through a broken pane. It seemed as chilly inside as out and there was rain in the air. He gnawed at a piece of stale bread filched from the hotel bins by Ossie and then checked out his various injuries. Perhaps the cold had numbed his senses but his aches and pains didn't seem so bad now.

He'd kept as quiet as possible; he didn't want to disturb Ossie. He pulled back the sleeve of the tattered anorak to check his wristwatch. It was the only reminder he had left of his former civilised life. The time showed as ten past eight and he had to make a move. Going to the police was no longer on the list, not after seeing one of his attackers talking with the detective investigating the case.

He needed money. His stupidity suddenly dawned as he did a double take at his wristwatch. The Van Der Bauwede Magnum Commander, a present from his former wife was not a Rolex but almost in the same league. Even on the second hand market it could still be worth in the region of £600. He looked around to see that Ossie had woken and was sitting up in his sleeping bag yawning and stretching arms upwards. The tramp finished his yawn and stared at Cappelli through squinting slits.

'Yes, you've cottoned on then Benedict. The watch is your ticket out of here.' Ossie lay back down putting his hands behind his head. 'I spotted it straight off. You'll get a few quid for it, but nowhere near what it's worth. The jewellers on the corner of Mace Street buy second hand. They'll buy from anyone… even me, but you'll not get top dollar.'

Cappelli was stunned by Ossie's knowledge and quick train of thought. 'You spotted it straight off?' he questioned, copying the tramp's phrasing. 'How so?'

'Survival son, survival. If I'm to be honest with you…' Ossie stared at Cappelli again. 'Yes if I'm to be honest, which I'm sometimes NOT. I'd thought about slipping it off your wrist while you were out for the count and rambling.'

'Rambling… what do you mean?'

'Such a tale… journalists and murders, scientists, gunmen. The leap through the window. I thought it was all bollocks at first and then again… the state you were in. You certainly looked as though you had jumped through a window, but it was when you mentioned Porton Down that I sat up and took notice.'

Ossie paused for a swig from his milk bottle. 'I was a young soldier when I first heard about Porton Down. They used to send out requests for volunteers to go there and have tests done on them. I suppose they were guinea pigs really. They would send out invitations in our pay packets and anyone who put in for it would get ten bob and three days leave. I considered it myself a couple of times. I was always skint, but I never did put my name down. A story hit the newspapers later. The real truth never came out but a young airman died; they'd tested some kind of nerve gas out on him. There were stories floating around that dozens of people had been affected long-term and probably lots of deaths over the years.'

The gaunt features of Edward Olivant had come sharply into perspective in Cappelli's mind by the time Ossie finished the tale.

'I went off the rails without the help of mad scientists,' Ossie said. 'When I saw your watch it added some credence to your story.'

Cappelli shook his head at Ossie's sharp mind and intellect. The use of the word "credence" coming from the down and out added even more weight to his opinion on the man. There was an educated human being hiding inside that filthy exterior.

'I told you then? I didn't know I had.' Cappelli shook his head in disbelief.

'You were well out of it for a while… concussion at a guess, but Dr Ossie looked after you. Incidentally, I sold your dressing gown at the second hand shop. It was a Polo, Ralph Lauren. I got £4.50 for it… put it down to expenses. I didn't know people still wore dressing gowns.' Ossie was sitting up again. A big grin had overtaken his face.'

Cappelli winced at the thought. The gown had cost nearly fifty pounds, but he was in no position to complain.

'I found an address book in the pocket. It's not yours and so I gather that it's connected to all this. I assumed that you'd… acquired it.' The pause and raised eyebrows reinforced Ossie's suggestion.

'Where is it?' Cappelli said; he'd forgotten about the book.

Ossie rummaged in the depths of his sleeping bag and produced the item. 'I've been looking through,' he said as he handed it over.

'And?'

Cappelli's question accompanied his frown. The book felt warm and this caused him to wonder exactly where it had been stored.

'Well, it is what it is… an address book. The names mean nothing to me, but I was in the military and some of these people have initials after their names, indicating high rank.'

Cappelli wandered back over to the window and looked out at the grey day. He gritted his teeth as he stared down at the address book in his hand and his mind tumbled back to the devious methods used to obtain it. A feeling of guilt was inevitable, but other emotions triumphed over the guilt. The fear that someone was out to kill him for what he knew, or what they thought he knew was one such emotion. But he still held a craving to get to the bottom of the mystery. He turned back to Ossie. 'I'd love to go through the book with you, but I need to see if I can cash in this watch. Where is this jewellery shop?'

Ossie scrambled out of his sleeping bag and stood to his feet. 'That watch is worth a lot, but don't expect much more than two hundred. They won't be open until nine o'clock. I'll come with you.

You'll get ripped off otherwise.'

Taylor and Harding had finished their light breakfast at the hotel by eight-thirty. Last night's late Chinese left them without much need for food. They were also eager to try to unravel more of the mystery. Taylor switched his pager back on as they took the steps down from the hotel's front door to the pavement. He was well versed with the difficulties in tracing pagers and also keen to see who'd been after him.

'Best leave your mobile off,' he said. 'Too easy to get our coordinates if you turn back on, pagers are a lot harder. The device buzzed for several seconds as it updated with all the new messages. The latest list contained several repeat attempts by the same callers from yesterday. Some new names also appeared. Taylor's main boss, Detective Chief Superintendent Burrington was one. Burrington was due to retire next month but Taylor felt sure that his message would not be an invite to his leaving party. *Ring DCS Burrington NOW*.

'No can do just yet Boss,' Taylor said in a low voice as his thumb continued to press down on the back button. He stopped scrolling as he came across another line of text. The sender had used the name Gordon and the message read: *Usual time, usual place!* Taylor raised his eyebrows and even managed a little smile as he realised the identity of the caller. He switched the pager off.

The walk to Heysham's Victorian library took them ten minutes. They'd left the motorcycle back on the hotel car park and the rest of their gear in the lobby. Their covert wait across the road from the library's front doors had been thought out. The librarian's timing was exemplary. She unlocked the doors at nine o'clock on the dot. Taylor and Harding left their entrance into the building for two minutes. To have been openly waiting for the keys to be pushed into the lock could have been something which may have lingered in the lady's mind. They headed toward the stairs following the signs marked *Reference Library*. They were unsure how to deal with their next task but one thing was agreed on: The fewer questions they asked the fewer clues they would leave behind.

After browsing the rows of double sided bookcases and mentally working out how the place worked they homed in on the Geography section. There was little that would easily help them. Several books gave lectures on how latitude and longitude worked, but they already understood that. What they needed was a map of the world with full latitude and longitude. It seemed too much to hope for at the small branch library. The available maps were road atlases and fold out tourist guides which were calibrated with nothing more than a simple letter and number grid system.

Taylor nodded over at a large antique looking, wall-hanging, poster map of the world. The pair examined it, trying to summon up that long since learned and now rusty knowledge of latitude and longitude.

The multi-coloured chart was faded, but boldly pronounced its maker's name in the bottom left section which covered the Pacific Ocean. It read: *Stanford's General Map of The World.*

Their earlier conversations optimistically concluded that their objective lay in the British Isles. It was a tongue-in-cheek idea and mostly down to Kim's recall of the basics of navigation. Taylor had kept quiet on that part of her theory, but Kim was eager to test the notion. This map did show the lines of latitude and longitude, albeit in large twenty degree sized boxes. It was never going to accurately pin point the location of their decoded coordinates but it should give a vague, fingers-crossed idea.

Kim targeted her finger at the bottom of the chart on the zero degree vertical line of longitude and moved it half an inch to the left to make a best guess at five degrees west. This was as close as she could get to the first part of Geoff Fry's decoded longitude numbers. She then carefully drew it straight up the chart whilst Taylor kept a finger just down from the sixty degree horizontal line of latitude on the left edge of the chart. It was his own estimate of the required fifty-seven degrees.

As Kim's finger climbed steadily up through Western Africa and Spain Taylor's traversed in across Canada and The Atlantic Ocean. Their two digits met high up in the Scottish Highlands of the British Isles toward the West coast. It was nothing other than a very rough guide, but it was a starting point.

A check of other maps from the library's shelves on the imprecise location did not help other than to make it clear that the destination was an isolated part of the country. Only a few minor towns and villages showed up as small red dots in the midst of sparsely inhabited terrain. Their best target before pin pointing where they needed to go was the name of the Ross-Shire village of Garve.

W.H. Smith's was another short walk from the library. The shop assistant quickly selected a decent road map from which a route could be plotted to the general area decided on. The young man was helpful, but explained that large regional maps were only held in stock at stores local to that area. He had several comprehensive maps covering Lancaster, Morecambe and Fleetwood, but as for the Scottish Highlands, it would be a special order. 'Perhaps get you one for Monday sir.' The young man said.

With the hotel bill paid in cash Mr and Mrs Tresilian donned crash helmets, zipped up leathers and made off for the M6 motorway. Their planned journey to Garve in the centre of the Scottish Highlands and then on towards the West coast lay 350 miles ahead of them. After Kim's terrifying incident at Taylor's house there remained an unspoken urgency to get as far away as possible. The puzzle of the two numbers at the end of the coded message could wait.

TWENTY EIGHT

OSSIE AND CAPPELLI sat opposite to each other in Bridley's Breakfast Café on King Street. Both men were in the process of cleaning the last traces of brown sauce from their respective plates with a piece of toast. Every mouthful of the mountainous full-English had been savoured and devoured. Cappelli pressed his fingers into the side of his painful jaw and made a wide-mouthed yawning expression in an attempt to exercise away the pain. It felt a lot better and he reckoned there were no lasting injuries. He turned towards the girl at the counter as he continued to scrape at the now shining plate. 'Another pot of tea for two please love and some toast and marmalade when you're ready.'

The girl took a puzzled glance over at the men as she dropped a couple of teabags into a stainless steel teapot and filled it from the boiler. The amount of food the two rough looking chaps had eaten must have been close to the café's record.

The owner was wary and managed nothing more than a suspicious stare. He'd seen Ossie around the town many times and knew him as a local character. Rumour suggested he'd been a warrant officer during his army service with considerable responsibility before going off the rails. He could be troublesome in drink and was renowned for a little petty thieving, usually for food.

Local people now tended to turn a blind eye to Ossie's shortcomings since his appearance one Remembrance Day sporting a dazzling array of medals on his tattered great coat. The anecdote garnered a little compassion and understanding amongst those previously fed up with his antics.

The tramp's battered friend was a new face on the block though. The café owner's request for payment up front from the two men seemed prudent in view of the state of them. He'd been surprised when the one with the cuts and bruises peeled off a fiver from a good sized wad of notes to pay for both meals.

Cappelli had Ossie to thank for the £225 squeezed from the jeweller. If he'd been on his own, he would have been at least a hundred down on the deal. The conversation had been taken up with the contents of the notebook. Ossie's sharp mind and general knowledge continued to baffle the reporter.

When the third pot of tea arrived Cappelli changed seats to sit alongside his companion. Prestwich's address book now commanded the centre of the table and Ossie turned pages and made comments. 'See that… ' his blackened fingernail pointed to a name in the book. 'See the abbreviation next to the name.' The finger tapped against where the word "Capt" had been written. 'There are several captains mentioned and some high rankers.' He flicked a few more pages over, tapping down here and there. 'A Lieutenant Colonel, a Brigadier and even a blinkin' Lieutenant General.'

Ossie picked up on Cappelli's blank stare and explained. 'The Lieutenant General would have been God. He'd be the Commander in Chief of an entire military district. But what makes all this so interesting Benedict my boy is this….' Ossie's gravelly laugh followed before he added more. 'All these place names, from what I can remember, are in Wiltshire in the Tidworth Garrison. Now the closest I ever got to that part of the military world was at Denison Barracks in Berkshire. Only forty or fifty miles from most of these places. Ossie turned more pages. 'Look here… and here.' His finger darted from one piece of text to another. 'See this… Prestwich has put the initials P.D. against some of these senior officers. Now that must stand for Porton Down.'

Cappelli gave his head a little shake as he took in the information but also considered the sadness of what had driven such an intelligent man away from society.

They continued to go through the book until the page fell open at the entry for Geoff Fry. It showed Mr Fry's full address, postcode, phone number and date of birth. It was all straightforward and the shortening of the Christian name to "Geoff" showed the friendly bond between the two men.

Cappelli's eyes landed on the opposite page. It looked as though Prestwich used this space for notes. It contained some writing and beneath this three bold letters had been written. It appeared to be an acronym and was followed by a series of exclamation marks: "*Q.E.D.!!!!*". The feature had been spotted by Cappelli during his first examination of the book but he'd no idea what it signified.

He looked up at Ossie. 'So what's that mean then?'

Ossie sat back in his chair and gazed up to the ceiling. 'Q.E.D. Now that takes me back. That really takes me back.' He turned to Cappelli with a confident expression before delivering an answer. 'Quod erat demonstrandum.'

Cappelli stared back wondering for a moment whether Ossie had gone mad.

'A Latin phrase… roughly translated it means: "which is what had to be proven".'

The lines of confusion consuming Cappelli's brow spoke volumes for his lack of understanding of the situation. Ossie's wide grin exposed his two rows of discoloured teeth and empty sockets to their fullest. The expression indicated the tramp's enjoyment of the moment. His now familiar laugh preceded his explanation.

'The phrase in its abbreviated form…' He said, with his finger tapping down onto the page. 'Is traditionally used by boffins after working something out. It might be a maths problem or a philosophical argument.' He repeated the words: '*Which is what had to be proven…*' He gave more. 'Prestwich had come to a conclusion. He'd worked something out… found the answer to a puzzle. The way he's written the exclamation marks after it show that he was pretty pleased with himself.'

Cappelli's face showed a mixture of enlightenment and astonishment. 'How the hell do you know such things?'

'I studied at university before the army… maths. I was going to go into teaching but that never happened. I ended up working out calculations for aiming gunsights instead.'

'The words which Prestwich has written above where he's put Q.E.D. must be the solution to the problem he'd been working on,' Ossie said.

It was a vague explanation and Cappelli's puzzled face conveyed his own bemusement. He reached over and traced his finger along the wording above the Q.E.D. It read:

Geoff Fry, a partial anagram, but a complete guardian.

Several lines of thought started to coincide within Cappelli's mind as he read through the wording a few times. His mind drifted back to the file on Geoff Fry, the one he'd shredded. Something rang a distant bell. The phrase that Prestwich used just before they parted company also now came back to him: *Geoff Fry… a Guardian of Lies.*

Ossie was already shrugging before Cappelli asked the question. 'What's it mean?'

'Who knows… it might be a crossword they were working on. But he seems to be talking about Geoff Fry… as though he's the subject of the puzzle.'

TWENTY NINE

KIM kept the throttle open. They now had a target, albeit a vague and distant one. Garve in the Scottish Highlands was still three hundred and fifty miles away and they both knew that even then it would not be journey's end. They needed to put some of those miles behind them so that they could unravel this mystery before anyone else.

The last thing they needed was to attract the attention of the police. Kim's eyes forever searched both the road ahead and the rear view mirror. The Yamaha's speedo registered a near constant 110 mph. The occasional reduction down to a sedate 70 became essential with the infrequent appearance of a police patrol. An hour and twenty minutes passed taking the time to ten past eleven before Kim chose the exit lane off the A74(M) for Abington Services. It would be a tea stop and a chance to check out the newspapers.

Kim ordered drinks at the Coffee Primo counter while Taylor grabbed a copy of the Daily Herald from the news stand. He'd read the newspaper headline before he'd picked it up and had studied the story by the time Kim returned. She manoeuvred the tray of coffees and chocolate muffins into a space and settled herself in a chair at his side.

Taylor turned to her. 'Big story in about Cappelli going missing from the hotel, but not a mention of the action back at my house. I think someone at the top has managed to stifle the papers on that one for the time being.' He left the paper open at the Cappelli story for her to read as he gave an opinion. 'Automatic gunfire in the suburbs of Little Stoneleigh would be a big story and should have made the nationals easily.'

Kim pushed Taylor's coffee and cake towards him. 'The fact that it's not made the papers yet might help us. If they start publishing our details and descriptions we'll soon get spotted.'

Taylor stood from the table. 'I need to make a call.'

Kim frowned. 'Is that wise, there seems to be a lot of earwigging going on at the moment. I wouldn't want anyone to get an idea where we are.'

'Agreed,' said Taylor fumbling in his pocket for coins. 'But we need to know what's going on and pass on some information to the right people ourselves. It's a calculated risk, but if I phone from here rather than where we are heading, we might still protect our backs for a while longer.'

Reg Timson only allowed the telephone on his desk a half-hearted attempt at ringing before he snatched it up. He was stunned to hear Doug Taylor's voice, but also sharp enough not to give the game away to anyone sitting nearby.

'Let me stop you there,' Timson whispered into the mouth piece. 'You got a pen? Okay then, call me back in three minutes.' He reeled off a phone number that he had committed to memory years before for occasions like this – occasions when conversations must be held in private.

His casual stroll from the murder room could have been taken for nothing more suspicious than a visit to the gent's, but as he turned the corridor corner he lengthened his stride. The single flight of stairs up to the ground floor were taken at a jog, a rare thing for Reg Timson. He made it to the call box on the corner of Gladstone Street next to the Nick in just under the allotted three minutes. He was still gasping when the phone started to ring.

Taylor needed the inside story on Cappelli's hotel room episode along with any news on his whereabouts since the newspaper report. There was nothing new.

'Jesus.' Timson sighed as Taylor related the terrifying episode involving Kim.

Taylor felt awkward discussing Geoff Fry's work. Up to this point he'd kept quiet on the subject but the one-way-traffic was unfair on

Timson. He gave a brief summary of what he knew of Geoff Fry's background.

A stunned silence came from Timson's end of the phone when Porton Down and biological weapons came into the conversation. The fact that Taylor's own house in Staffordshire had been bugged drew another astonished intake.

Taylor joined Kim back in the restaurant area after the phone call. He'd only been away for fifteen minutes but was keen to get back on the road. He went through the conversation as they made their way out to the car park. 'There's been no sign of Cappelli at all,' he said. 'The hospitals have been checked and no one fitting his description has visited. His clothing and belongings were left in the hotel and his car was still on the car park. He's not contacted his work.'

They pulled on their helmets, zipped up jackets and climbed back onto the bike. Kim took the pillion for a change. Taylor was a good rider, he couldn't match Kim's skills but it was sensible to share. Midday arrived as he took the exit lane from the Services onto the M74 and settled the bike into a steady eighty miles per hour. A journey of 220 miles still lay ahead before they would reach Garve. All but fifty of those miles were along poor quality, non-motorway routes. At Taylor's current speed, even without stops the ride would take around three hours.

Ossie and Cappelli turned their late breakfast appointment into more of a midday conference. The café owner's concerns about the rough looking pair had been needless. No one had paid much attention to them and with his legs beneath the table Cappelli's most noticeable feature, his trousers, remained hidden from view. They'd even settled up in advance for their additional pots of tea.

The usual lull in customers between breakfast and lunch allowed the owner to take a well-earned break. He stood behind the counter reading through a copy of The Daily Herald spread out in front of him. His mug of tea had fashioned a brown circle onto the corner of the newspaper; he took a sip as he leafed through.

The face staring back at him looked familiar. The front page lead story gave a summary along with a small photo. He'd been alarmed as he read about a violent incident at a local hotel, but that small front page picture didn't grab his attention. This bigger one did the trick though. It showed Princess Diana taken in 1989 during a visit to HIV patients at an East London hospital. It had been edited to focus in specifically on the reporter standing behind her. The headline read: *Fears For Missing Herald Reporter.*

The proprietor kept his head firmly in the reading pose but moved his eyes slowly upward until they locked, like magnets onto Ossie's new found friend. Regardless of the cuts and bruises there was no doubting that this was indeed Benedict Cappelli. Those recent injuries tied in with the story of the hotel episode.

The man considered approaching Cappelli direct, but the article gave specific instructions:

Information on Mr Cappelli should be reported immediately to Exeter Police Incident Room.

A direct line number was given in the report. He looked back at the newspaper for a moment as he decided what to do. The clunk of the café's heavy glass entrance door caused him to look back up. Ossie and Cappelli were out onto the pavement and casually heading off down King Street. He lifted the telephone and began to dial as the self-closing door slowly settled back.

Cappelli glanced at his friend, 'I'm going to get tidied up now Ossie, so point me towards Boots for some toiletries. I'll get kitted out with some decent clothes as well. My editor will be wondering what's going on but I'll keep my head down for a bit.' He dipped his hand into his trouser pocket as Ossie made clear the directions. The thought came to mind of how he would relish binning the ridiculous chequered slacks. He pulled out the wad of bank notes and peeled off thirty pounds. 'Thanks mate,' he said as he held out the cash you've been such a friend… saved my life and restored my faith in humanity. It might not seem like much but I've a feeling that I'll need the remainder if I'm going to get through this on my own. As soon as this lot is sorted I'll be back to see you. I think my paper would jump at the chance of doing a story on you. It could set you up for life.'

Ossie nodded a thank-you face at Cappelli. He'd never turn down the money but as for the other idea, he would take a lot of convincing.

The pair stopped alongside an alleyway off the main road and Cappelli knew that this was the route that Ossie would take back to the derelict house which he called home.

'You had second thoughts over the wallet, then?' Ossie said, adding a knowing wink. 'I saw that you'd taken it from the window sill.'

Cappelli's blush was noticeable even through the grime. 'Yes,' he said, conscious of the stolen wallet pressing against his thigh. 'In case I need to prove who I'm not.'

The vagrant set off down the alleyway at his normal ambling pace. He raised an arm aloft showing the back of his hand with a spread of open fingers in a gestured goodbye. 'Thanks Benedict, see you around.' The statement was followed with one of those gravelly laughs. It was as though Ossie had added, "but I doubt it."

In the Murder Room, as lunchtime approached, Reg Timson and Angela Hewitt had been left holding the fort. The other investigators were either out on enquiries or in the canteen for their own butties. Timson offered to take the stroll to the nearby sandwich bar and collect his and Angela's rations for the day. The healthy tuna mayo on brown for Angela contrasted with his own choice of a cholesterol raising cheese toastie and a vanilla slice.

Hewitt's phone started up once again as the door closed behind Timson. 'Hello, Murder Incident Room, WDC Hewitt speaking. How can I help?'

Café owner, Mr Bridley was puzzled at the response. 'Sorry, I've been put through to the wrong extension,' he said. 'I needed the team who are investigating the missing reporter.'

'Oh,' Hewitt said. 'That's okay, I'm a Scenes of Crime Officer. All the investigators are out of the office at the moment. I can take the details of your information on Mr Cappelli though.'

Bridley related his tale about the extended breakfast meeting between the tramp and the reporter as Hewitt jotted details onto a pad and verbally confirmed facts as she went along.

'Yes I know Ossie… who doesn't?' she said with some humour to her voice. 'The last time I heard he was living in one of the derelict houses in Watson Street? You're sure it was Mr Cappelli then? And you say he looked injured.' Hewitt continued to jot as the story was told. 'Limping …? Chequered trousers…? You're sure it was the missing reporter? Okaaay… and they turned right when they left your café. So chances are they were heading back to Watson Street. Right I'll ring Control Room and get a patrol around straight away… '

The café owner had told all that he knew, but was surprised at how abruptly the call ended without so much as a thank you. He shook his head at the policewoman's brusque finish to the conversation and replaced the handset. 'Thanks a lot… I don't think.'

Timson grumbled under his breath as he descended the steps to the Murder Room. The sound of those ever ringing telephones created a discord of three or four different bell tones and gave warning of another disturbed working lunch break. 'No peace for the wicked,' he said as he pushed a hand against the door. He had a plan in mind. He usually did have.

He visualised Angela Hewitt with one phone pressed to her ear whilst the others continued to demand attention. His intention was: *place Angela's food parcel in front of her, hang his jacket on his chair and then fill and switch on the kettle.* This would all happen before picking up a ringing telephone. It was how Timson's mind worked. The other callers would all have to put up with listening to a ringing tone for a few more moments. If the information was important they would hold on or ring back. Timson surmised some more: *his conversation would probably last no longer than the time it took for the kettle to do its job. Hopefully, as he replaced the receiver, his urgently needed brew would be as good as ready. Both Angela and he could juggle more telephone calls whilst consuming the necessary sustenance to continue with life.*

As the door to the room opened up his conception of the scene and what would take place could not have been more wildly wrong.

Angela Hewitt lay sprawled on the office floor. Her eyes wide and bulging and her mouth gaping. Almost her entire face and throat were coated in a thick bubbly froth of saliva which seemed to have erupted from her mouth and nose. The only areas of skin on show, patches of her forehead, hands and calves were a deep purplish blue. A smear of blood tinged some of the froth around Hewitt's nostrils. Pools of vomit and urine had been spread haphazardly across the floor as the woman had thrashed about in her death throes.

Timson checked his own natural response to rush to help his colleague. The scene was more horrific than anything he had ever laid eyes on in all his twenty-seven years as a copper. It resembled something from hell. Doug Taylor's final words in that brief phone call smashed into the centre of his mind like a road drill into a rotten melon: GERM WARFARE.

Angela was dead and whilst germ warfare in its strictest sense could hardly be the cause, some form of highly toxic chemical or biological contact almost certainly was. Timson took several backward paces. He dropped the sandwiches, turned and made for the stairs. Giant steps, three at a time, a loudly shouted 'HELP'.

The sound of voices on the floor above stopped, indicating that someone had heard. Another shout from Timson now, but with more thought attached to it – an attempted warning. 'Stay away. Don't go down there.' His voice not so loud now. What was happening to his speech, it suddenly had no power in it. He was only halfway up and for some reason his three-stairs-at-a-time were reduced to just one as his trembling legs tried to lift themselves upward. It seemed to be going dark, it made no sense it was midday.

Two blurred silhouettes appeared at the top of the stairs, alien shapes, featureless faces, like something from a science fiction film. He could barely pick out their shocked expressions. He managed to hold up a hand. 'Angela's dead… dangerous don't go in there.'

Timson dropped down to his knees, retched a few times and then slumped forward onto his face.

THIRTY

BENEDICT CAPPELLI pushed open the door to Debenham's on the corner of Sidwell Street and stepped inside. He was now showered and shampooed courtesy of the facilities at the local swimming baths. He still cut an odd figure in the strange clothing and his battered face made shaving impossible. If he was to continue with his investigation independently he would have to be careful with his cash.

The eyebrows of a few staff members rose as he made his way towards the gent's clothing department. This may well have worked to his advantage for a while as the shop floor girls were more taken-up with making giggling comments about his peculiar attire than concentrating on his face. Fortunately none of them were avid newspaper readers.

The store manager watched Cappelli's arrival from a distance. He kept an eye on the man's clothes-rack browsing with growing interest. The vagrant's disappearance into the changing rooms with arms full of gear added more concern. The word *shoplifter* came quickly to mind. There seemed little doubt that the awful ensemble the man had been wearing would be dumped in the changing room in exchange for the new clothing selected.

The transformed down-and-out eventually reappeared smartly kitted-out in Tee shirt, jeans, crew necked sweater and grey hooded duffle coat along with matching scarf and gloves. A pair of tan suede Hush Puppy boots completed the outfit and several other garments hung over an arm.

Surprise took over the manager's face as he watched the suspect make his way to the checkout clutching a handful of price labels. These had been removed from the garments he now wore. Relief engulfed him as the former tramp, now valued customer gave an explanation to the cashier.

The manager, Mr Selwood, moved forward as if on wheels, smiling-faced and hands behind back. He watched from close range as Cappelli tendered the bundle of price tags and added arm gestures to the clothing which he now wore. With everything accounted for and the bill paid in cash the neatly bagged additional items were handed back to him.

Cappelli looked over at the watching, blue-suited Mr Selwood, quickly deducing his status and accepted his interest as understandable. The reporter's smile and nod received the routine: 'Thank you for your custom sir,' from the manager.

Selwood though, unlike his staff, *was* an avid newspaper reader. As he turned away from his closer encounter a memory from his recent fifteen minute toilet break and additional read of the Daily Herald came back. Within a minute he had the newspaper opened on his office desk at the page showing the picture of Benedict Cappelli. He reached for the telephone.

Oddly, the number rang out without answer. Over the years Selwood had made dozens of calls to the boys in blue from Heavitree Road. The number was there on a notice board with the reminder to only use the 999 system for genuine emergencies. Shoplifters, the most usual reason to call the police, did not fall into this category unless the thief became violent. Selwood did not judge this as a 999 situation. Cappelli, although acting oddly did not appear to be at risk and so using the police station's ordinary phone number was the correct action. This was the first time that he'd ever known the police not to answer their telephone though. After six more unanswered tries he replaced the receiver. It passed through his mind that a complaint to the Inspector regarding the poor service would also be something to mention.

The arrival five minutes later of one of the store's cleaning ladies provided a part answer to the tardy service given by the local police. As she pushed open the shop's entrance door the impatient blare of car horns flooded momentarily inside. The klaxons of several different emergency service vehicles could also be heard approaching the area from different directions.

'Town's grid locked,' the lady said, pointing a thumb over her shoulder towards the street. 'They've closed Heavitree Road off completely. All the bobbies and the other staff from the police station are out on the pavement. There's a line of ambulances and three fire engines.'

Mr Selwood made an alarmed face. Something serious had happened. Perhaps even a fire at the police station itself. His information over the missing reporter would have to wait; the police clearly had their hands full with other things. He stepped out onto the pavement and looked in both directions. The closing off of the main Heavitree Road had indeed caused chaos; traffic was at a total standstill throughout the main town centre. Being a local man he knew the rough whereabouts – as the crow flies – to the police station itself. The noise of the klaxons homing in towards that spot fitted with the cleaner's summary.

Selwood now also saw a great pall of smoke rising from an entirely different part of town. Evidently this was a significant building fire. He shook his head and used his local knowledge to calculate the location. It seemed to be the slum clearance area on the edge of the old town, near to where his late grandparents used to live. He hoped he was right as most of those two-up, two-down terraces in Watson Street were empty and awaiting demolition.

Cappelli now resembled a respectable human being again and felt a great deal the better for it. He'd been puzzled by the traffic chaos which had ground Exeter centre to a complete standstill. He had thought of popping back to see Ossie before making a move. But after what had happened at the hotel, and then the sighting of the same man at the police station he needed to put some miles between himself and Exeter. With all public transport out of action he decided to walk the one mile to Exeter's main rail station: St David's on

Bonhay Road. The exercise seemed therapeutic to his injuries and by the time he arrived he was managing with some degree of normality. Fortunately the biting wind along with the prospect of rain allowed him to blend in with other travellers with his duffle coat hood up and scarf drawn across his face.

It began to dawn on him that by now his colleagues at the Herald would be concerned about his wellbeing. The hotel incident must have generated worries. It remained a fact that some extremely violent people were also searching for him. His walk gave him the opportunity to think straight and accept that he had become a wanted man by some people and reported as missing by others.

A railway station is not the best of places for a fugitive to be. With his pulse rate a little higher than the suggested norm he stepped through the doors into the bustle of people. The placard outside the news stand fixed his attention. His slightly raised heartbeat was quickly traded for a crashing steam hammer as he read the words: *HUNT FOR MISSING REPORTER*

He pulled the scarf up a little further to cover his nose as he wandered over and picked up a copy of the Herald. The front page with that small photograph taken eighteen months ago jumped out at him. The steam hammer registered an even higher rate as he opened up and took in the large photograph of himself standing with Princess Diana. He carried out a head down mumbled purchase of the paper and gritted his teeth as he took the short walk to the ticket counters. He was now more determined than ever to get the hell out of there.

THIRTY ONE

AS twenty past one approached Taylor and Harding's journey continued to take them further north. With Taylor still at the handlebars his average speed of between seventy and eighty had been no mean feat when the frequent roadworks and traffic snags were taken into account. Kim's dig in the ribs meant that the time had arrived for another stop. It would be a chance for some coffee and a check of the map. Their agreed destination of Garve would, they both knew, be nothing more than a generalised area. It was certainly still many miles from the pin-point accuracy of Geoffrey Fry's latitude and longitude coordinates.

Taylor steered the bike off the A9 as the name sign for a never-before heard-of small Scottish town came into view. Another sign gave the news that a further mile would have to be covered before they would actually arrive in Dunkeld. The square steeple of the town's church could be made out in the distance on the other side of the River Tay.

A petrol filling station provided their first stop. They made a bee-line for the extensive array of Scottish Highland maps which were displayed along with the usual newspapers, sweets and chocolates.

Kim's questions about the maps included a hopeful query that at least one might show latitude and longitude references. The enquiry went completely over the head of the bemused owner. His Scottish accent was broad in any sense of the term. The rising and falling lilt and the extended rolling of the letter R was almost song-like.

It seemed that the flat English accent used by the two tourists came over with equal difficulty for the owner. He stared, puzzle-faced across the counter for a few seconds before a flash of recognition came. 'Nay… never hearrrd of it. There's a Loch Lochy up near to Loch Ness, but I canna say I've err heard 'O a Loch Itude…'

As well as the full tank of petrol, a map *was* purchased in spite of the breakdown in communications. They had to hope that this one, an individual fold out affair, might get them a little closer to their ultimate goal as it did show lines of latitude and longitude. Whether it would give the necessary small detail to pin point the exact location still seemed doubtful.

The conversation with the garage owner became the subject of laughter between the two as they made their way back to the motor cycle and then headed into the town.

Taylor pulled the bike into a parking space at the back of the post office and after locking their crash helmets in place they set off to find somewhere for lunch. It had stayed dry throughout their journey although the sky over Dunkeld had yet to make up its mind. Huge boulders of grey nimbus clouds tumbled and rolled over to the east of the area. Thin streamers of cirrus pushed in from the west. Without their helmets they soon became aware of the March temperature nibbling at their cheeks.

The Tayside Arms was a traditional pub with a welcoming log fire crackling inside a smoke stained stone fireplace. A plump rosy-cheeked barmaid smiled at Taylor as he enquired if they were still in time for food. 'Not a problem,' she said handing him a couple of menus and nodding over at the daily specials chalked onto a blackboard. Taylor opted for liver and onions whilst Kim decided on steak and ale pie with chips.

The newly purchased map showed only Scotland rather than the entire British Isles and so presented the supposed target area in more detail. The most exciting features though, were those lines of latitude and longitude. They appeared as a sweeping broad pattern of vertical and horizontal lines across the entire single page. Printed down the left hand side were the degrees of latitude from 55° to 60° North, whilst the bottom edge gave longitude from 1° to 11° West. The map now lay unfolded on the pub table between their cleared plates.

The decoded location devised by Kim's father had been the

subject of a good deal of conversation. Their original knowledge of latitude and longitude had been pooled and between them they now had some reasonable understanding. The new map would help them home in more accurately, but it still covered a truly vast area. It was inevitable that this was still nothing more than a rough estimate – almost certainly tens of miles out in any direction. The spot where Taylor's biro tip now rested supported their first idea of making for Garve in the centre of the Highlands. But the disconcerting feature was that it had settled in the Atlantic Ocean off the West coast. The nearest piece of mainland appeared to be the very Scottish sounding Mungasdale, a journey of another one hundred and sixty miles.

It was three o'clock when the pair stood from their chairs and took in the view from the pub window. The heavy clouds were prematurely adding a darkening tone to the northerly Scottish sky. It wouldn't be long before the street lamps of Dunkeld came to life. They needed to press on with the journey but also had to find a bed for the night at some stage. It was uncharted territory in several senses. With no tourist information centre or travel brochures covering the route ahead everything was a gamble. They agreed to get as far as they could and would have to keep their fingers crossed for a hotel.

Taylor paid the bill, zipped up his leather jacket and started to make for the door. Kim's hand, gripping his forearm, stopped him. The wall mounted TV was showing a windswept, overcoated presenter with a microphone held to his mouth. In the background a wide town centre street had been closed off. Strips of blue and white incident tape thrashed wildly. Two uniformed police constables were in camera shot, hands clasped behind backs reinforcing the no go area. The TV volume was muted but the outline of the buildings grabbed Kim's attention. The shot slowly panned away from the reporter's face to focus on the front of a building halfway along the deserted street. Kim frowned, eyes still glued to the screen, and gripped Taylor's arm even harder, but he'd already recognised the scene.

The barmaid, alerted by Kim's interest in the news report, paused from her beer-pump-polishing.

'Can you turn this TV up please?' Kim asked, eyes still fixed.

The woman picked up the remote from the shelf to oblige before joining the two customers in watching what was clearly a serious incident unfold.

The building now centre screen was Exeter's Heavitree Road Police Station.

The reporter's words came through mid-sentence as the volume button was pressed:

"… evacuated the entire police station and have taken the additional steps of removing everyone from sixteen other nearby properties. Exeter's Chief Superintendent, Mr Trevor Bartlem has stated that a serious incident has taken place at the police station which necessitated evacuation. The police refuse to make further comment. But twenty minutes ago a large vehicle was allowed through the police cordon and is now parked outside the police station in the centre of the road."

The camera shot then moved to the right and fixed onto the vehicle as the commentary continued:

"The figures you can now see with that vehicle are the only people who have been allowed to approach the area."

The shot was distant, but the TV camera zoomed in with reasonable clarity. Two figures emerged from the side door of a large white box van. They both wore one piece, olive green coloured protective suits. The pointed topped helmets had full face visors. Darker green boots and bulky looking black gauntlets completed the outfit. Hesitant paces were taken toward the front of the police station. The lead figure started up the steps with his arm outstretched. He was holding some sort of device.

The camera briefly panned back to the presenter who had been joined by a second man. An introduction was given and the microphone was swung over:

"I now have with me Mr Roger Lloyd a retired army captain who may be able to explain some of what is going on."

Lloyd began:

"Thank you, yes… the suits which the two men are wearing are what we jokingly called in the army, Noddy Suits. The correct title is an NBC suit. It is designed to protect against nuclear biological and chemical substances."

A repeated clip of the two men walking from the van up the steps to the police station now showed as Lloyd's voice continued:

"You will see that the leading figure appears to be using some kind of sensor. From the images available I'm confident that it is a biological and chemical particle detector. These instruments are in use by both the American and British armed services and at research facilities. I note that the second person is holding a clip board. This is probably a map or description of the inside of the police station to help him get around and inspect what he needs to."

The camera centred back onto the reporter who then expanded on an earlier part of his report:

"The Police will not comment further on the identity or condition of a man who was seen to be taken away in an ambulance at an early stage. Neither will they comment whether this man is the only person affected by what has happened here today."

Short on real detail the broadcast quickly developed into conjecture. Taylor turned back to face Kim. 'Come on let's go.'

Their mood was serious as they walked back to the Yamaha. 'What the hell has happened?' Kim said.

'Serious stuff... serious stuff involving exactly what we're looking into, but how the hell it's suddenly affected someone in the nick I cannot imagine.'

THIRTY TWO

AT LITTLE STONELEIGH Police Station in Staffordshire DC Dan Cheeseman was unaware of the tragic circumstances unfolding in Exeter. He hated the slow seepage of information and urgently wanted a chat with Doug Taylor after the dramatic incident at his home. Taylor and Harding seemed to have vanished without trace and nothing new on the episode had escaped any further than the Chief Constable's office.

Cheeseman decided on a call to Exeter Police station. He'd met and worked with Reg Timson years before and knew that he would be tuned into the events. The unending ring tone presented a puzzle in itself. He came to the conclusion that a major line fault must be the reason. His idea to keep trying occasionally seemed sensible as BT would be treating the problem as an emergency.

He eventually did get an answer, but quickly realised that the call had been automatically diverted to Tedham Police Station, a smaller facility, a few miles outside Exeter. The constable whose voice came on the line sounded on top of the job despite his workload having increased many times over. His adamant refusal to give Cheeseman any idea why calls were being diverted added to the mystery though. An exchange of information was usually par for the course for a colleague from another force, but PC 1527 Scotton had undoubtedly been told to give nothing away at all.

Name rank and number was Cheddar's first thought, but the officer's whispered comment potentially threw some light on the situation. 'BBC news,' he said.

The doorway to Little Stoneleigh's police canteen gave a good line of sight to the television.

'What the hell,' Cheddar said in a low-voice as he watched the same news broadcast that Taylor and Harding had seen.

The commentary sharpened Cheddar's appetite for more

information and his next call, to Devon and Cornwall's Middlemore Police HQ, was answered quickly. He'd already decided on the name to ask for.

Pete Lacey was a former detective sergeant at Exeter. Together with Reg Timson he'd been a major player on an enquiry involving both the Exeter and Little Stoneleigh CID units several years earlier. "Mr" Lacey, as he was now known, had held a civilian post since his retirement twelve months before. He worked on old unsolved major crimes. If anyone could and would help it was Lacey, but the serious and troubled tone in his voice caused Cheddar to worry. Had Lacey been warned not to speak to anyone? If so, this wasn't the Pete Lacey that Cheddar knew!

'No, that's not it Ched,' Lacey reassured. 'It's Reg… bad news I'm afraid.'

Taylor was demoted to the pillion seat for the remaining 120 miles journey through to Garve. This stretch took in the fast A9 and it had been agreed that if a hotel or guest house could be found in that area it would be a sensible end to the day's travel. For a skilled rider like Kim the A9 on a decent day made for enjoyable riding but the blustery cross wind and bouts of drizzle squeezed the fun out of it. The last twenty miles of the day took in the two-lane winding A835 and slowed their progress.

It was five o'clock when the name sign for the village of Garve came into sight. Kim steadied down to the 40 mph limit as they entered the boundaries of the area. With little daylight left, the bike's headlight reflected back from the Black Water River which ran parallel to the right of the road. The remoteness of the region was reinforced by the complete lack of other vehicles.

Within another half mile the flat waters of Loch Garve could be seen over to the right of the road. On the left, trees and steep hills disappeared up towards the clouds. Garve's tiny railway station came into view, an unexpected sight in an area without business or entertainment. The large white painted Garve Hotel was an equal surprise. It sat on the offside of the road and was doubtless the only accommodation for miles.

Kim steered the bike onto the car park without a second thought and turned off the engine. 'We seem to be approaching the end of the world. It'll be properly dark soon and we've still got forty miles before we reach Mungasdale, so that'll be a job for tomorrow. The roads get more like tracks from here on.'

Taylor dismounted and pulled off his crash helmet. He pushed his fist into the small of his back and straightened up. 'Agreed, we're not going to find anywhere else to stay tonight and even when we get to Mungasdale we could still be miles out.' He looked up at the hotel building. 'Fingers crossed they're not full,' he joked.

As expected the hotel was quiet. The only other guests were a group of fresh air fiends who had booked in the day before to use the place as a base for their hiking expeditions.

Taylor gathered from the friendly and casual way that the manager noted his details that passing motor cyclists would often be overnight guests.

'Yes Mr Brown, we get a lot of bikers staying over, although usually a little later in the season,' the man said.

Taylor had opted for an easy false name to book in with. He'd not been comfortable with Kim's Tresilian joke the first time around.

With a table booked in the hotel's restaurant for an evening meal they struggled out of their leathers and flopped, worn out, onto the king size bed as six o'clock arrived. The bedroom's en suite shower wasn't designed for two people but they managed well enough. After the love making which followed a deep sleep robbed them of consciousness.

The more mileage Cappelli put between himself and Exeter the better he felt. His hasty departure North did have some thought attached to it though. Any journey south would soon peter out at the coast! His choice of Bristol came easily. He knew the area from his time working there as a journalist. There were facilities close at hand which might be useful, but he had to keep his head down; someone might recognise him.

It is surprising what plans can be formulated during a simple one hour train journey. To be accurate the journey from Exeter St David's Station to Bristol's Temple Meads Station appeared on the timetable as a mere 59 minutes. But those uninterrupted moments were enough for Cappelli to temporarily clear his mind and think properly for the first time in days.

Raymond Thomas Meigh, was the name on the green paper, fold-open driving licence. Mr Meigh was the true owner of the trousers Cappelli had so despised; he was the Exeter baker. The given driver number showed as: MEIGH 504193 RT9ZA. It was amazing what inconsequential snippets one could pick up as a journalist. Whilst Cappelli did understand how to work out the date of birth from the number, he never understood why the licencing authorities had gone to such trouble. It took him a few minutes to reach the conclusion that Mr Meigh's birthdate was the 19th April 1953, making him thirty-eight years of age.

At the age of thirty-three, Cappelli figured that it could have been worse. With his battered face temporarily piling on the years he decided that he would pass. Mr Meigh had been a careful driver and not yet accrued penalty points. Such stains on the character might result in a refusal for car hire.

He would have to use Mr Meigh's credit card to pay for a hire car. This meant reproducing a signature which in some way matched the scrawl applied to the card's plastic strip.

Numerous attempts at the signature were made during the train journey. His forgery efforts at *R. Meigh* soon filled up the margins of the newspaper which also showed his photograph on its front page.

After mastering the signature he mulled some more over Prestwich's address book and the ideas Ossie had come up with. In doing so his mind went back to the file which had been compiled for him back at his office on Geoffrey Fry. He cursed himself now for shredding it in a moment of blind panic.

Now calm, his fertile mind started to make a connection with a particular entry in the address book and the loose fragments he remembered from the destroyed file. He looked out at the passing countryside as the train's repetitive *clackety-clack, clackety-clack* morphed with phrases going through his mind: *an anagram… a guardian – an anagram… a guardian – an anagram… a guardian.*

THIRTY THREE

TAYLOR woke with a start, his hand scrabbling on the bedside table for his watch. The yellow glow of the table lamp showed the time as twenty-five minutes past seven. The hour and a half they had managed was more a doze than a sleep and something at the back of his mind had roused him long before his body would have liked.

He grabbed clothes in seconds. 'Supposed to be making a phone call at half seven,' he said.

Kim sat up, weary eyed. 'What… who… I thought we were supposed to be careful.'

Taylor had thrown on enough clothes to make him decent and grabbed a handful of coins from the pocket of his biking jacket. He exited the bedroom shoeless as he shouted back. 'Tell you when I get back.' He made it downstairs and into the reception's phone booth with seconds to spare.

Cheddar and Mo, the only customers in The Crown, were perched on high stools against the bar. Landlord Alf, in his favoured spot, stood with his back against the wall between the lounge and the snug. The newspaper held down at waist level suggested that those tip-of-the-nose spectacles were no longer of the correct prescription. He squinted over at the two detectives between pages. They usually had a joke to tell or some interesting gossip to exchange. Tonight the pair looked troubled. Mo had decided against a Martini and lemonade as Alf had run out of cherries. 'G and T it will have to be then,' she'd proclaimed with half-hearted humour. Cheddar stuck with his pint of Theakston. The wall mounted telephone behind the bar interrupted the silence.

Alf muttered a few words as he picked up and then turned to Cheddar.' Take it upstairs Ched,' he winked. 'It's Mr Taylor.'

Cheddar settled himself onto the sofa in the lounge of Alf's upstairs flat. He heard the click as Alf replaced the receiver in the bar. 'Boss… you there?'

'Yes, Ched, thanks for this, I understood the cryptic message and I'm confident that no one can be listening in.'

'Okay, but have you seen the news. Have you heard what's happened at Exeter Police Station?

Taylor described the scant detail he had seen on TV. 'It's obviously serious Ched. Has someone been hurt?'

'Worse than that. A scene of crime officer named Angela Hewitt has been killed. Reg Timson's had a lucky escape. He's in hospital, but the word is that he's okay. Some kind of toxic substance seems to be the cause. The theory is that the SOCO has collected something as evidence and that has been the source. Pete Lacey filled me in, but all off the record of course. Everyone down in Exeter has been sworn to secrecy and even threatened with the Official Secrets Act. The entire nick is still off limits until whatever has caused it is identified. The murder enquiry has ground to a halt and the Spooks are all over everything.'

Taylor listened quietly to Cheddar's dreadful update knowing the impact it would have on Kim. He had to make the best of the phone call and pumped in more coins before detailing what had happened at his home the day before.

'Jesus,' Cheddar said. 'This is even heavier than I'd thought. We've not been allowed on site. Some forensics and SOCO people now have, but all with the strongest of warnings to say nothing to anyone. The enquiry into it is being dealt with by Special Branch… absolutely no input from Division at all.'

Cheddar had nothing new on the missing reporter but it made sense that Cappelli's violent disappearance from the hotel was connected. 'They have their hands full down there,' he said. 'If Kim's right about this MI5 agent being part of the attempt on her life then I don't know who we can trust. There was another serious incident in Exeter around the same time that Angela died and so that's gummed the wheels up a bit more for them.'

Taylor shook his head at this news. 'I don't like all these coincidences Ched they don't add up. Tell me about this other thing.'

'A derelict house went up in flames and when the fire service searched through they found a body. It's believed to be a local tramp'.

'Hmm,' Taylor mumbled. 'That would take up more man power, but it's hardly going to require a lot of undivided attention.'

'That's just it though. Pete Lacey has told me that the post mortem has shown the poor blighter's throat had been cut, so that's turned into another murder enquiry.'

Taylor arrived back in the room within half an hour. He explained the cryptic pager message from Cheddar which had prompted his call. 'Gordon had to be Ched… another of his nicknames… Gordon Zola! Usual time usual place had to be The Crown at half seven.'

Taylor now dealt with the most awkward part: Angela Hewitt's death.

Kim slumped down onto the edge of the bed and stared blankly at the wall. 'Angela… not Angela, she was getting married in a couple of weeks.'

She looked up at Taylor, tears welling up in her eyes and rolling down both cheeks. 'Is my father responsible for all this? All this… and then this fucking wild goose chase we're on.' Her recently applied mascara had smudged into black, wet streaks running down to the corners of her mouth.

Taylor sat on the bed beside her, put his arm around her shoulder and pulled her in tight. 'We're not on a wild goose chase. The only way we can find out about your father is by uncovering the whole truth. We've been in tight corners before and come out with the right result. I'm more determined than ever to get to the bottom of this.'

Kim said nothing. She stood, took a deep breath and hurried through into the bathroom pushing the door firmly shut. Taylor, now by the window, gave a long sigh and gazed out. A single security light illuminated the hotel's car park and a distant yellow street lamp twinkled in the frosty air near the front of the hotel. There were no passing cars and no people. He was now unsure of the evening's plans. Should he tidy himself up for dinner or was that part of the evening cancelled? He picked up the Enid Blyton book and settled back into a chair.

Fifteen minutes went by before Kim stepped out from the bathroom. She managed a smile although her eyes showed redness. Jeans, sweater and trainers were the best she could do from the few clothes they had been able to bring, but she looked good.

'Well aren't you ready yet? I'm starving!' she said.

Taylor explained the entire conversation he'd had with Cheddar as he finished a quick shave and dressed. They made it downstairs and into the bar for ten to nine.

It was a big hotel and in the high season would be busy with ramblers, hikers, sightseers and tourists. Twelve people was the sum total on this evening, six couples including Taylor and Harding.

Two couples, who were on a joint hiking break for five days stood against the bar taking an after-dinner drink. Conversation was unavoidable. Taylor and Harding knew that they had to employ what would be considered customary behaviour. They'd both been in enough undercover situations to appreciate how quickly suspicions might be raised by being too tight lipped or offhand. The sociable approach from the four people instantly inferred that an amiable exchange of information on the "who, why, where and when" was the norm in these circles.

'Hi, Terry Bowers,' said one of the men extending his open right hand to Taylor.

'Doug… Doug Brown,' Taylor said gripping and shaking the hand. He'd booked in under the name and was paying in cash so there'd be no requirement for ID. He wasn't expecting that he'd have to come up with a Christian name for Kim, other than: *Mrs Brown.* His mind went into overdrive. He quickly concluded that it would not be good on any covert operation – official or otherwise – to use names which might register with someone. He could get away with Doug, but not Doug and Kim.

He smiled at the man and by way of introduction raised his left hand toward Kim. 'My wife… Enid.'

Kim was unfazed and responded with a broad grin. 'Hi Terry, nice to meet you.'

The other three members of the group shuffled forward eager to chat with the newcomers. Terry introduced his companions. 'My wife Anne and our friends… Matthew and Susan Jervis.'

Matthew joined the conversation. 'Ah, you're the motorbiking pair. Saw you arrive... used to do that ourselves a few years back, until we fell off a couple of times.'

The comment raised a ripple of laughter amongst the group. 'We all stick to the hiking boots nowadays,' Matthew continued. 'You tend to see more, we've covered many miles in this area. Where are you two heading? Do you have a plan?'

Taylor increased his sip from the pint of beer that he'd purchased and altered it into a large gulp as he attempted to extend his thinking time. Kim was ready to step in but decided to leave Taylor to it as a punishment for her new name.

'West coast,' Taylor eventually answered. He'd decided to stick with the truth as he could come up with an actual place name to back up his answer. He'd also considered that these people may be able to unwittingly help. They certainly seemed to know their way around.

'West coast is beautiful but those sudden weather changes can catch you out,' Terry advised. 'Especially this time of year. We did a lot of it a couple of years back. You selected a base camp yet?'

Taylor understood the hiker's jargon. 'Well we were going to make for Mungasdale tomorrow.'

'Hmm if you want to get away from humanity Mungasdale's as good a place as any to start.' Terry replied. 'What do you do… stick to the bike or get off and go for a ramble as well?'

'Yes a bit of both usually, but only if the weather stays fine'. Taylor lied.

'Important to be prepared for bad weather, particularly out that way,' Matthew said. 'Not too many folk around, but I guess you know all that.'

The woman named Susan joined the conversation. 'We always plot our intended routes out before starting off,' she said and gave the sheaf of paperwork in her hand a little wave in the air. 'We've sorted out tomorrow's trek over dinner. We stick to accredited walks planned by the Rambler's Association.'

'It's supposed to stop us getting lost,' the other woman, Anne, chimed in. The comment created some more laughter amongst the friends. There was undoubtedly a story or two at the heart of it.

'If you two are sticking to the motorcycling you'll not be needing this.' Terry interjected.

'No it's interesting,' Kim said, revitalising the conversation. 'We might be able to consider it for our next outing. What sort of maps do the Rambler's Association provide?'

'Oh very extensive,' Anne said. 'You can pick on the amount of difficulty as well. They go from Easy up to Strenuous and from three miles to ten plus. We used to do the Strenuous Tens when we were your age, but now with Matt's dodgy knee we're on Leisurely Fives.' More laughter followed.

'Here take a look,' Anne said and spread out tomorrow's planned route onto a side table.

Taylor and Harding held their breath as they continued the charade of interest in the subject and stared down. Garve and even the hotel showed in the map's right hand corner. Contours and footpaths were marked out. Dots, crosses and arrows pinpointed danger spots. Derelict buildings and other features were listed and reference numbers corresponded to information which could be consulted in a small separate booklet.

The two detectives exchanged a glance as they simultaneously twigged the purpose of those sweeping vertical and horizontal lines. They were the deadly accurate lines of latitude and longitude. The larger scale of this map also showed much greater detail. Instead of only giving the vastly spaced lines of single degrees it included a series of fainter lines – fifteen minute segments of degrees.

Taylor caught Kim's eye again. They were both thinking the same: *If only the map had taken in that part of the western coast around Mungasdale. It would be infinitely better for accurately calculating their destination.*

Kim was in like a shot! 'This looks great; we ought to get into this Doug.' She turned back towards the group. 'Would we be able to get one of these covering where we are thinking of going tomorrow?'

Terry shook his head. 'No they take a couple of weeks to come through usually, but each one covers a sizable area and you can plan several different walks from them. I'll tell you what I'll do.... We're off first thing after breakfast, but I'll leave you some paperwork at the reception desk and you'll be able to join.'

Taylor thanked Terry for his kind, but under the circumstances useless idea and the pair bid their goodbyes before heading through for their evening meal. The sharp dig in the ribs Taylor received accompanied Kim's muttered sentence. 'Bloody Enid.'

A decent meal with a bottle of Shiraz drew the long day to a close. The pair made their way out onto the car park for a breath of fresh air, chunky pullovers fighting against a bitter chill. A cloudless, charcoal black sky teemed with bright points of white – dots of fainter yellow and red stretched out from the infinity of the Milky Way. A swathe of flickering green and pink swirled up from the horizon, as the Northern Lights made a brief appearance. The fluorescent colours swept left and right with the spontaneity of a gigantic flock of starlings. Kim pushed her arm in around Taylor's waist and pulled him in close as they watched in silence. The setting was romantic, but their minds were filled with the uncertainty of what the next day would bring. How many more people would suffer before they uncovered the full facts?

THIRTY FOUR

THE NEXT MORNING Benedict Cappelli gave a covert grimace. He was checking out after his overnight stay at the Holiday Inn on Pump Street, Bristol. With the hotel just two hundred yards from Temple Meads Rail Station the decision to book a room there had been an easy one. The Raj Indian Restaurant in nearby King Street proved equally handy and that Chicken Jalfrezi deserved top marks. He would have happily paid the bill from his traded in wristwatch funds, but the importance of retaining ready cash for future use stopped the idea. Mr Meigh's credit card had footed the bill.

The grimace Cappelli so successfully hid from the receptionist had been prompted by his additional use of Mr Meigh's account to pay his hotel bill. He seriously wanted to stay within the law after his devious treatment of Dr Prestwich and involvement with Lenny Gill. *Needs must,* he reminded himself as he watched the girl drag the machine's flat-bed roller across the card and proffer the credit slip to him for the addition of a near perfect *R. Meigh* signature.

His conscience cleared ever so slightly some fifteen minutes later with the handing over of real cash for the taxi journey which landed him at his current destination at ten minutes past nine.

Cappelli stared up at the ceiling of the reading room of Bristol's College Green Reference Library and silently cursed himself again for shredding that file on Geoff Fry. How he wished that it now lay open on the desk in front of him.

His scan through it had been less than brief, and he only held the vaguest of recollections. Strangely his thoughts kept pushing him back to yesterday's train journey. Those repetitious words which fitted the train's *clackety-clack* came into his mind again:

An anagram… a guardian.

Cappelli altered his thinking pose from ceiling gazing to elbow points on table and head in hands, as he wrung out his memory like a pair of sodden swim shorts. He remembered fleetingly reading through the first few pages of the dossier. It was filled with Geoff Fry's glowing Oxford University achievements. The work on virus strains and vaccines looked very impressive even though the reporter had no idea what it all meant.

An anagram… a guardian.

Cappelli changed back to ceiling gazing as he picked further into his subconscious.

An anagram… a guardian.

An image emerged from the depths of his memory: *Half a page of photocopied newsprint – something he'd briefly seen in that dossier. Old seventies typeface, a years-old edition of some regional Scottish newspaper.*

An anagram… a guardian.

He couldn't recall the detail. The article was in the file solely because Dr Fry's name had been mentioned.

A handful of words from the passed-over story came to him as his mind strained to find dots and join them up: *An island – World War Two.*

Why did he keep going back to Prestwich's address book?

An anagram… a guardian.

Ossie's clever interpretation that a puzzle had been solved by Prestwich now entered the fray along with the retired pathologist's words in the address book: *Geoff Fry, a partial anagram, but a complete guardian.*

Cappelli stared at the wall, deep in thought before going back to the microfiche machine. He spun back and forth through copies of the Inverness and Highlands Daily News one more time – nothing.

His prediction that he would NOT be able to locate the actual article in the library archives seemed correct. He didn't know what he was looking for and was only guessing at dates from his recall of the old typeface used. He could be fifteen years out!

He sat back into his chair and twirled his pen between his fingers concentrating onto what he COULD remember from the article.

Thirty-five minutes plodded slowly by before his grey matter provided a possibility.

A pair of white cotton gloves accompanied the weighty eighteen inch high book which was delivered down to the desk in front of him. The leather bound copy of *Macculloch's Highlands/Western Isles/Hebrides-Scottish Antiquities* had been published in 1824. The bespectacled aging librarian appeared sufficiently elderly to have been the book's author. He carefully opened the tome at a helpful page and pushed the gloves forward as a reminder.

A grateful thank-you was delivered as the old boy made a painfully slow return to his distant desk. Cappelli then stared down at what was a comprehensive list of the names of Scottish islands. The record included nearly three hundred mounds of rock and earth which were dotted around the Northern coastline and large enough to actually be called islands. As his white cotton gloved finger ran down the list the retired pathologist's written words kept going through his mind:

Geoff Fry – a partial anagram, but a complete guardian.

That strange disjointed conversation with Prestwich came back to Cappelli. The old man's explanation that he was never actually supposed to know of the location of the secret. The puzzling sentence he'd used: *"His secret was safe with me though… he was the Guardian."*

That word again: Guardian.

Twenty minutes passed before his finger overshot the mark and then went back to rest alongside the name of an island of the Inner Hebrides off the North West coast of Scotland.

An anagram… a guardian.

Cappelli's eyes had widened to their maximum as he slowly whispered each letter of the Latin acronym. 'Q.E.D.'

He had found what had to be proven. He had solved the puzzle. The island's name was after all, a near perfect anagram of GUARDIAN: *GRUINARD ISLAND.*

THIRTY FIVE

FIVE HUNDRED and fifty miles to the north, in the village of Garve, the Wednesday morning was cloudless. Kim looked from the bedroom window at the bright stillness which evoked thoughts that Spring had arrived. The hotel's central heating was working hard to fortify the idea against the reality of a three degree outside chill.

They made their way into the dining room as the waiter cleared a table recently vacated by the four hiking enthusiasts they had met last night. The breakfast's description of a *Full Scottish*, proved accurate and after packing up their meagre luggage they arrived back in reception at nine forty-five to settle the bill. Kim gave Taylor the necessary cash and left him at the desk as she went out to load the panniers and check the bike over.

The Yamaha had been left in a sheltered corner tucked under a lean-to designed for the hotel's rubbish bins. She turned the key and pressed the start button. The resulting unhealthy, solitary *click* from the starter relay suggested a flat battery. Kim shook her head and made a puzzled face. 'Can't believe that,' she grumbled, heaving the bike off its stand and pulling it out from under the shelter. In no time she was freewheeling down the slight gradient of the car park. She toed the gear shift pedal upwards and released the clutch. The bike lurched forwards a shade and the engine immediately roared into life. After returning it to the shelter and finishing the packing she left it quietly ticking over as she made her way back inside to the lobby.

It had all taken a just few minutes and Taylor was still completing the payment. 'Thank you sir,' the receptionist said. 'I'll get you some change. Oh, Mr Bowers left something for you.' He turned and pulled a bulky envelope from one of the pigeon holes behind.

Taylor recalled Terry Bowers' plan to leave some information on the Rambler's Association. He expected a one sheet flyer but the envelope was certainly more than that. He decided on a quick look before they started on the journey. He indicated his intention to Kim with a wave of the envelope as he headed for a table in the lounge.

Kim mentioned the bike as they pulled up chairs. 'It was a bit slow when I checked it out in your garage before we set off. It's a pretty new bike, it shouldn't be doing that. It's a bit nippy outside but not cold enough to affect the battery.'

Taylor frowned as he pulled out the paperwork. 'We don't want it letting us down out in the middle of nowhere. It's okay now though?'

Kim made a hopeful face. 'Hmm seems okay. It fired up straight away on a push start. Thank God it didn't do it when I had to demolish your garage doors.'

Taylor gave a nod but wasn't listening. He'd already spread the three feet square map across the table. 'Think we'd better shout up for some more coffee before we set off. Our friend may have solved a problem for us.'

An accompanying note from Bowers clarified the situation:

Dear Mr & Mrs Brown,

Hope this comes in handy and gets you on board for a Rambler's Association membership. It is one of the guides we used on the West Coast a couple of years back and it covers where you're heading. The booklet explains about places of interest. We won't need it again.

Good luck and best wishes

Terry & Anne Bowers.

By the time the coffee arrived they had already worked out how the map could help. It was much more detailed than anything else they had seen and was confined almost entirely to the latitude lines between 57 and 58 degrees. A series of other fainter lines crossed the entire chart between those degree markers. These ran both left to right and top to bottom. They were an indication of the much more accurate *minute* divisions – sixty in every degree.

Each faint line on the map was a fifteen minute line. It segmented the degrees like minutes on a clock, from zero to fifteen, then thirty then forty-five and finally to the next full degree. The latitude coordinate they needed was 57° 53 minutes. The closest marker line on the map was therefore the complete 58° line.

Taylor borrowed a ruler and pencil from the reception desk. They then calculated that the precisely accurate 57° 53 minute line would lie just under halfway back between the given full 58° line and the lower 45 minute line. Taylor drew a long pencil mark from left to right across the map along this agreed position.

The closest line of longitude shown on the map to the line they needed of 5° 28 minutes was 5° 30 minutes. Setting the ruler a fraction back from the 30 minute line to take account of the small difference Taylor drew the pencil line from top to bottom.

They settled back a little in their chairs and stared at the point where the two lines crossed. They now knew their destination. Their idea to home in on the desolate area of Mungasdale had been a good choice. It was the closest named place on the map to their final destination. But even though they had now worked out a target, getting there was not going to be any easier than it had been so far. In fact it looked to be almost insurmountably more difficult.

The lines crossed almost exactly in the centre of a small island sitting off the western coast of the Scottish Highlands. The oval shaped landmass showed as nothing more than a featureless red outline, but it did have a name.

Written inside the outline was that name:

GRUINARD ISLAND.

They'd found it!

The pair remained silent for a moment as they took in the terrain and difficulties that chart suggested. The body of water surrounding the island was a sea channel of the Atlantic Ocean which also had an individual name in neatly scrolled print: *The Minch.*

Taylor broke the silence, tapping the pencil down onto Gruinard Island: 'The Island of Adventure?'

THIRTY SIX

IVY TIMSON sat in against her husband's hospital bed. The blood/oxygen sensor pegged to the index finger of his left hand made it difficult for her to hold the hand and so she made do with Reg's wrist. The initially strict regulations regarding his admission to Exeter Isolation hospital had already been lifted and he could now have visitors. He'd only received a minute dose of the toxin which had killed Angela Hewitt. His hasty retreat from the room saved him. An oxygen mask covered his mouth, nose and a good deal of his face hiding his expression from the view of his visitors. In addition to his wife two other figures were present. DI Ken Grainger had originally occupied a chair on the opposite side to Mrs Timson. He had now positioned himself at the end of the bed alongside the latest arrival, Devon and Cornwall's Chief Constable, Steven Dudman.

Dudman, a good looking 44 year old stood six feet tall. His neatly trimmed dark hair was lined with a series of steel grey streaks – too symmetrical to be natural. A discreet application of gel held the well-groomed look firmly in place. His athletic frame was packaged neatly in a well-tailored grey suit. A snow white, crisply ironed shirt presented the backdrop for a burgundy tie. A hint of expensive aftershave had followed the Chief into the room.

Timson had accomplished a full four hours without the oxygen mask during the night and had succeeded in retaining a high blood/oxygen level throughout. He had snatched hold of and refitted the mask after a tip-off that the Chief was on his way down the corridor. There wouldn't be any awkward questions at this stage of the proceedings, but better safe than sorry was the adage that Reg always adhered to.

A copy of the Daily Herald lay folded on the edge of the bed. Reg had pushed it to one side when he saw the headline:

DETECTIVE'S SINISTER DEATH

Police station evacuated. Was it nerve gas?
Timson's warning had saved lives and probably prevented others from being affected as he had been. The Chief was keen to mention this and took the detective constable's slow head nods as comprehension of his praise.

'Thanks for what you did Reg,' Dudman repeated, confident that his use of the shortened Christian name was appropriate. He delivered a squeeze to the officer's right hand. 'Must be getting back to HQ.' He cleared his throat before a word of warning. 'These matters have taken over the newspapers and TV. There's a lot of speculation, none of which help our enquiries.'

A short and uncomfortable silence followed before Dudman added his final words. 'We must be aware that the Official Secrets Act applies to us all.'

Grainger had managed a private session with the patient before the Chief's arrival and recognised Timson's humour as an attempt to cover his emotions. He was broken hearted over the dreadful event which had taken the life of fellow officer Angela Hewitt. He'd shed some tears when his return to consciousness allowed him to distinguish reality from hallucination. The sight of the woman, not only a colleague, but also a good friend, would live with him forever. The death brought the true nature of the situation to him. He decided to keep the information about double agent Nelson to himself for the time being as Taylor and Harding needed more free rein to unravel this story. Another worrying factor had been pointed out by Taylor which reinforced this decision: WHO could be trusted?

Timson kept the face mask on a while longer as the door closed behind the Chief Constable. *He was confident that Grainger could be trusted, but ANYTHING and EVERYTHING he told him would unquestionably have to be divulged by him to the Chief. Ultimately that would also get back to the MI5 agents.*

Timson pulled off the facemask and shook his head. 'Any idea what the poison was yet Boss or how it came to be in the office?' His use of the word poison seemed a good term under the circumstances.

Grainger sat back down. He didn't want to discuss theories on the subject especially after the Chief's additional warning. He side-lined the question. 'We've now got access to the building back Reg, but they're still not letting us into the Murder Room. The military are in control of the whole operation and the boffins from Porton Down are the only people allowed in. They've been in consultation with the doctors looking after you. They've taken all sorts of stuff away… all of Angela's exhibits and even her desk!'

Grainger started on a different police incident. He hoped that the chat might steer Timson's troubled mind away from Angela's death. 'Something else has turned nasty,' he said. 'It came in around the same time that we were evacuating the nick.'

Mrs Timson was on her feet making a tactful departure from the room. 'I'll see if I can get us a cup of tea,' she said.

Timson listened as Grainger related the story of the murder of an old vagrant in a derelict house close to the town. 'You'll know him,' Grainger said. 'Ossie Dennis. He used to get locked up occasionally for pinching food.'

'My God, that's dreadful. I knew old Ossie same as most of us did. A real character and never much trouble. A clever bloke actually. I can't understand why *anyone* would want to kill him. The only thing of value he had were his war medals, but I guess that a good enough reason in today's awful world.'

'Well whoever did it set the place on fire but his medals survived, they were in his pocket.'

Timson looked thoughtful as Grainger gave the full details. 'Throat cut you say? That's hard line and I can't say that I've been involved in too many similar cases in all of my career. Lenny Gill's cause of death springs to mind.'

'Thought you'd say that Reg… a pretty nasty coincidence.'

Mrs Timson soon returned with the tea. Reg shuffled himself upright whilst she fussed with pillows, plumping and rearranging. Reg sipped his drink and then reached over to the bedside table for his spectacles as Grainger stood to his feet preparing to leave. 'No tea for me thanks Ivy. I'd best be getting back.'

The Inspector only made it as far as the end of the corridor before Ivy Timson called him back. Reg was now properly upright, spectacles perched nose-end and newspaper spread across the bed. His finger rested upon the large inside photograph of missing reporter Benedict Cappelli pictured with Princess Diana in the foreground. The image and an update on the story had been repeated from the day before. A sub heading asked intriguing questions: *Was this reporter on to something? Has he been kidnapped because he knew too much?*

Grainger made a despairing face when he saw the newspaper in front of Timson. 'Yes, I've seen it Reg, hence the Chief's warning. The papers have blown it wide open and as I said earlier, Exeter is crawling with reporters.'

'No, that's not what I'm on about Boss.' He tapped a finger repeatedly down onto Cappelli's face. 'Remember that house burglary initiative me and Pete Lacey ran back in the mid-eighties… Operation Pane?'

Grainger nodded. 'Well I wasn't the DI then, but yes I remember. A successful job and we've got all the files out again at the moment. It forms a big part of the background in Lenny Gill's murder. He was the offender.'

Timson continued to tap as he spoke. 'Correct. He burgled fifty-three houses in and around Exeter, Tiverton, Newton Abbott and Oakhampton over a ten month period and what did he get? A measly twenty-six months. Nine charges and the rest taken into consideration, but that's not the point. You'll remember that one newspaper made a big thing of it.' Timson rolled his eyes with annoyance. 'It made Lenny out to be local hero… a desperado. The wording used in the paper was: *Daring crimes and audacious acts.*'

Grainger did some more nodding as the story came back.

Timson ploughed on. 'That was how Lenny got his nickname, *The*

Ghost. One of the people whose house had been screwed brought it up in court.' Timson took a moment to think. 'The man said that he'd been asleep on the sofa and the burglar must have been in and pinched stuff from the same room. "It was as if a ghost had been in", was what he said. The reporter even used the headline: *Lenny the Ghost puts the willies up the police.*'

Grainger managed a smile at the accuracy of Timson's account but remained puzzled over the point being made. 'Okay Timmo,' he said. 'What bombshell are you going to drop now?'

'This reporter...' Timson's finger took another stab at Cappelli's face. 'Is the same one who did that story, but he wasn't calling himself Cappelli then. I can't, for the life of me remember what name he used but that article gave Lenny his nickname. Cappelli, or whatever is real, visited the police station a couple of times while Lenny waited in our cells for court remands. He interviewed him there a few times while he was concocting the story.'

Timson's eyes fastened onto the ceiling as he thought out aloud. 'Now what the hell was his name?' He shook his head with annoyance and looked back at the newspaper to slide his finger to the sub headline:

Was this reporter on to something? Has he been kidnapped because he knew too much?

After a moment's concentration his eyes returned upward and he spelled out his idea. 'Cappelli has to be the person who put Lenny up to screwing Kim's Dad's place. He's got wind of there being something at the house involving a big story and he's employed Lenny to break in and find it. He's used Lenny because he knew his credentials… thought he was the best man for the job.'

Grainger nodded throughout the theory. 'And that explains the phone calls made to Lenny's house while we were at the murder scene. One was traced to the newsroom of the Daily Herald. It must have been Cappelli after an update. I'll bet he crapped himself when he found Lenny had been topped.'

THIRTY SEVEN

AT quarter past ten that morning Charles Selwood, the manager of Exeter's Debenhams, decided on another try at ringing the town's Heavitree Road police station. The place had opened for business again and so a reply was likely.

Things did seem to be back to normal and within seconds he found himself talking to Detective Constable Bob Dixon. Selwood could not have known though, that the officer was actually sitting at a desk in Exeter's Town Hall. The original Murder Room was still out of bounds and being treated as a crime scene due to Angela Hewitt's death. In addition, Porton Down boffins continued to monitor the air quality to be absolutely sure of safety.

'Hmm,' Dixon murmured as Selwood gave his account. 'Why didn't you ring up immediately?'

The phrase *assault on police* ran through the annoyed store manager's mind as he found himself justifying the delay.

'I see,' the detective replied as he listened to the full circumstances. 'I'll pop over to see you shortly for a statement.'

At around the same time a scientist at Porton Down's microbiological research laboratory sat at a desk within the depths of the facility's complex. Detective Inspector Arthur Hancock and DC Barry Cliffe occupied seats opposite to him. The men were Scenes of Crime Officers from Devon and Cornwall's Criminal Investigation Department. A mock-up of Angela Hewitt's last moments had been reproduced within a safe area of the facility. This was being used to establish exactly how the woman had died and to determine if the event had been anything other than a terrible accident.

The actual physical cause of death had now been positively established, but not how it had come about. Top level talks had taken place before an agreement was reached that even the Police could be made privy to this detail. The ever-present Official Secrets Act swung out again with an additional warning to the two SOCO detectives: IF THE PRESS GET HOLD OF THIS HEADS WILL ROLL.

The toxin which killed Angela Hewitt was an organophosphorus compound officially classified as a weapon of mass destruction – Sarin.

The blood, tissue, and hair samples from the woman's body were obtained under the strictest and most cautious of regimes. The same guarded and vigilant approach was used for the swabbing of the items that she'd been in contact with. This included everything on her desk and near to her.

The body samples conclusively proved Sarin as the cause of death due to the changes created within her blood. The Porton Down specialists were dumbfounded by the complete lack of Sarin residue from the room or the items in it. If Hewitt came into contact with it from something inside the room it must have quickly evaporated. It seemed that the quick evaporation feature was designed especially for this particular batch and had been conjured up in an attempt to conceal the cause of death.

The scientist explained, 'Sarin even in its crudest form evaporates very quickly. This batch included a cleverly engineered feature which speeds up that characteristic, making it difficult to establish a cause of death.' He then held up a heat sealed polythene bag. 'This might interest you,' he said handing the item to Hancock.

Inside could be seen a page of note paper. The ragged top edge suggested it had been torn from a spiral wire bound booklet.

'Found crumpled in the lady's left hand,' he said. It seems as though she wrote it moments before she died. The writing has already been identified by our expert as being hers. Her telephone was found hanging at the side of her desk as though she'd been a making a call.'

Hancock and Cliffe both knew Angela Hewitt; they'd worked closely with her over the years. The paper had been carefully smoothed before being inserted into the bag against a stiff card backing to allow inspection without contact. Hewitt's distinctive neat lettering was legible even in this hastily jotted note and filled the single page:

Info from: Mark Bridley, Bridley's Breakfast Café, King Street

Bridley phoned in – pretty sure that the missing reporter Cappelli was in for breakfast with Ossie Dennis, the vagrant last heard of living in derelict house in Watson St.

Cappelli looked knocked about and was wearing peculiar clothing – chequered trousers!!! They seem to be making their way back to Watson St.

THIRTY EIGHT

TAYLOR and Harding's route from Garve to Mungasdale was an uncomplicated but twisting journey of over forty miles. To say that they saw half a dozen other vehicles would have overstated the issue. The ribbon of pothole repaired tarmac took them through a few small hamlets and gave occasional distant glimpses of single cottages out in the hills. The A835 and the subsequent A832 could have been the blueprint for a theme park roller coaster ride. Twists, turns and steep ups and downs took them through valleys and ravines all of which belied the road's "A" classification. Swathes of open country with mountains climbing away on either side stretched to a distant line of white capped peaks. The still and black waters of several lochs seemed close enough to lap the edges of the road in places. Loch Glascarnoch, Loch Droma and the tiny Loch A Bhraoin lay before them under the cloudless sky.

The motorcycle's exhaust note pitched from a high revving whine down to a burbling throb as gear changes assisted braking and Kim negotiated sharp bends and differing gradients. Little Loch Broom, an eight mile sea loch appeared on their right. The Atlantic Ocean and The Minch sea channel rapidly took over the entire vista in front with awe inspiring rugged beauty.

Kim dropped the bike into an improbably low gear for the near flat stretch of terrain that ran alongside Little Loch Broom and slowly cruised. They drank in the sights for a few hundred yards before she opened the throttle again. A tattered metal road sign gave notice that they had arrived in Mungasdale. Its weather beaten, rusted surface evidenced the harsh climate endured over the years.

They came to a halt and dismounted in a lonely pebble strewn natural pull-in where the road ran close to the shoreline. Kim rested the bike onto its side stand as Taylor straightened up and stretched. Helmets and gauntlets were removed and left with the bike. They had not seen another human being for over twenty miles.

A narrow strip of coarse turf separated the parking spot from where the beach began with gorse bushes, heathers and ferns amongst moss encrusted rocks. The growth petered out as the ground sloped towards the ocean. Pebbles and then swathes of golden yellow sand were interspersed with jagged rocks and boulders.

They picked their way, hand in hand and arrived on a patch of seaweed strewn, tide-rippled sand a few yards from the water's edge. Standing, protected from the chill by their leathers, they looked out across the slowly rolling blue grey waters of The Minch. The unhurried and solid heaviness of the swell had a formidable aura. Strangely it produced nothing more than a regular procession of small lapping wavelets. These perpetually furled over at their feet before draining backwards with a thought provoking whisper.

The wind caught Kim's hair, tousling it and causing her to shield her eyes with a flat hand against her forehead. She looked out across the bay taking in her first focussed view of the hump of one mile long undulating grass covered rock. It sat forebodingly over half a mile out into the Minch. She now knew that this was their intended destination, this was Gruinard Island.

Craggy, jagged outcrops and low cliffs could be made out along its coastline where the deep swell of The Minch rose and fell. White horses of foam rode back over the retreating water with each cumbersome steady heave.

Taylor also had eyes fixed on the sight as he took in the distant geography and summed up the difficulties of getting there. Could it become a reality? What would they do if it did? They had decisions to make and ideas to discuss. The weather was being kind to them considering the time of year, but the biting chill and the occasional gust served as a warning that it may not continue. With only the motorcycle, they had no immediate shelter and nowhere to sit and plan their next move in comfort. Hardly any buildings, let alone cafés had been seen along the final part of their journey. The last sign of civilisation had been a full eight miles back as they had passed the Dundoon Hotel.

Taylor bent and picked up a couple of flat oval stones. 'Good skimmers,' he said as he looked around. 'Never seen so many good ones. I used to love doing this with my dad… Rhyl or Llandudno on holidays… Abersoch sometimes. We'd spend ages skimming… seeing who could get the most bounces.' Taylor laughed. 'He taught me the optimum angle "Twenty degrees Douglas," he'd say.'

Taylor crooked his arm, bent his knees and hurled one of the stones hard and low. Kim watched as it sped out and dipped to meet the surface of the water then skipped up and repeated several times before disappearing beneath the waves. 'Not lost my touch,' he said and then looked skywards. 'Thanks Dad. Not sure it'll ever be much use to me though.'

There was nothing more to be learned by standing on the beach and they were soon back on the bike and heading further along the coast road.

Within a couple of miles they saw the name sign for the hamlet of Second Coast. A handful of distantly spaced cottages and a couple of semi derelict stone buildings hinted that there were at least some other people in the vicinity. A wooden sign had been hammered into the roadside turf alongside one property. It simply read: *Bed and Breakfast.* Another sign, next to it read: *Closed until April.* They journeyed on for a couple more miles before coming across the road sign for the similarly named, First Coast. Again a handful of cottages and farm buildings being the only signs of life.

They had travelled a little over six miles from Mungasdale before the marker for the village of Laide showed itself amongst heathers. The sturdy looking cast iron sign had been recently repainted. In spite of its windblown tilt from the horizontal it gave the impression that the few people who lived here cared.

Laide possessed a scatter of old farm buildings, boat houses and some recently refurbished cottages. A small post office, a general store and a tiny school stood side-by-side in the village's single street. Several of the cottages gave the feeling that they might be holiday rents or holiday homes. A couple more bed and breakfast notices showed along the roadside, but each one had an additional fold-over board showing: *Closed for Winter*.

A narrow junction came up on the left along with a brown and white chevron board: *Laide Caravan Park*. It included the symbols for a tent, a caravan and a petrol pump along with the words: *200 yds*. Deciding there was nothing to lose Kim took the tight left hander off the coastal road and kept the bike in a low gear for the steep climb that followed.

More cottages appeared as she drove slowly up the single track road away from the sea. The road sign was predictably inaccurate. They covered 400 yards before they encountered the petrol station with its two rusted pumps. The outlines of caravans could be seen within a neatly laid out area but the gated and locked entrance gave the clue that this was also closed for winter.

A small provisions store also served as the cash desk for petrol sales. A wire fenced enclosure at one side was stacked with blue metal gas bottles. There was no one about.

Kim pulled the bike onto the little gravel forecourt. Taylor hopped off and made a bee-line for the entrance to the store. A sign etched onto a piece of cardboard with green marking pen took up part of the door glass. It showed that the place was closed, but additional wording advised: *Knock at Bungalow*. An arrow pointed in the general direction of an adjoining property.

Kim switched off and pulled the bike up onto its stand. Taylor commented on the situation. 'Good job we don't need anything yet, everywhere is closed. Pity there's no café.' he added.

'Aye, closed we are… until April,' a voice said.

Taylor spun around to see that a bulky figure of a similar height to himself had appeared from around the side of the building. The man was grey haired and perhaps 65 or 70 years of age. In spite of the weather he wore a shabby looking grey and red check patterned open necked shirt. The sleeves were rolled to the elbow and showed broad hairy forearms. One arm supported three decent sized logs clutched in against his torso. The other hand held a full sized, heavy looking axe with such casual effortlessness as to suggest that it was a plastic theatre prop. A grey unkempt beard matched the hair.

The man unceremoniously downed his cargo onto the gravel and stood to his full height brushing his hands together. 'If it's petrol you're wanting I can switch on the pumps.'

Taylor recalculated the man's height at around six feet, six inches – a full two inches taller than himself.

Kim pulled off her crash helmet. 'No, we're still fine for petrol. We're doing a bit of touring. It's a beautiful part of the world. If we could find somewhere to stay we might hang about for a few days and take a closer look.'

The man nodded a few times, looking from Taylor to Kim and back as he summed up the new arrivals. 'Yes, it's a fine place to live, but it can get wild when the bad weather comes in. Most bikers usually plan in advance and the season doesn't start for a couple of weeks. Having said that I've seen one or two walkers already.'

Taylor had now also taken off his helmet. 'It was a last minute thing, we had a few days to kill and found ourselves up here in the Highlands.'

'I heard you mention a café,' the man said to Taylor. 'If you ride down onto the site…' his finger pointed toward the gates of the caravan park. 'You can use our café. The wife's in there at the moment smartening things up for holiday makers. She'll make you a drink or whatever as long as you don't mind the smell of paint.'

The pair nodded in unison and the man produced a set of keys from his pocket to unlock the gates. 'I'll bring you down some details of a couple of places which may be able to put you up.' He leant in to Taylor with an outstretched shovel sized hand. 'Brice Guaire. Nice to meet you.'

Taylor shook the hand. 'Doug Brown,' he lied and then: 'Nice to meet you too.' He turned to Kim holding back a smile. 'My wife… Enid.'

Kim narrowed her eyes giving Taylor a covert *just you wait* look and then turned back to Guaire. 'Do you sell newspapers?' she said.

Guaire shook his head. 'No, most people who come here want to get away from all the trouble and strife in the world. I never buy one, but you'll get one in the village.

Mrs Guaire seated the couple at a table and took their order of coffees and biscuits. The cleverly named *Tables Laide Café* was a converted farm building providing limited amenities for campers and caravanners. With no other potential customers within miles Taylor and Harding took the prime window seat. It gave a spectacular view 150 feet below out over The Minch and the distant Gruinard Island.

'Are we your first of the season?' Taylor said as the woman delivered their tray.

'You are indeed,' the lady said brushing back a ringlet of grey hair which had fallen across her forehead. The ringlet together with the forehead showed a small smudge of white paint which appeared to be well dried and possibly from yesterday's decorating efforts. She was a stout woman, perhaps ten years junior to her husband with a round face and a complexion which seemed more red than rosy. The tattered jeans and green pullover she wore bore evidence of a multitude of other painting undertakings and a complete rainbow of colour samples. 'No doubt come April you'll not be the last visitors we get.' She made her way back to her paint pot and brush and squatted to the floor.

Her husband pushed open the door and a cold breeze followed him in. He strode over to their table. 'Try these,' he said handing out two business cards. 'It'll say closed or no vacancies, but I know the owners. They're not likely to turn business down now that we're close to season's start anyway.'

Taylor nodded a thank you and then decided on some discreet digging. He pointed a finger at Gruinard Island. Its plump oval shape solidly defying the swell of the Atlantic. 'That place looks interesting, does anyone live there?'

Guaire's expression had changed from that of pleasant affability to one of incomprehension. He looked down at Taylor, his head now thrust backwards into his collar and his eyebrows steeply arched. 'Live THERE!' It was an exclamation rather than a repeat of Taylor's question and considerable emphasis had been driven into the word THERE. He shook his head as he added more. 'No one would want to live THERE, my friend.'

Taylor was taken aback by Guaire's reaction to what he considered a good pretence at pleasant conversation. He quickly assumed that the conditions on the island were too hostile even for the likes of the hardy looking Scotsman. 'Oh that bad, eh?' Taylor said. 'It looks idyllic from up here. Just used for sheep farming then I suppose?'

Guaire blew out forming his cheeks into two cricket ball sized spheres as he did. He shook his head. 'No sheep would last long on Gruinard and you certainly wouldn't want to be wearing a coat made of their wool anyway.' His face resumed its smile. If it's a leg of lamb you're thinking of taking home, then I'd advise you to steer clear of Gruinard Lamb… if there is such a beast.' He uttered a wheezy laugh and turned to walk back to the doorway. He shook his head again and mumbled as the door closed behind him. 'Gruinard Lamb. Never hearrrd of such a thing.'

Taylor looked across the table at Kim. He didn't need to speak; her bewildered face portrayed her own mystification over Guaire's comments. She turned in her chair towards where Mrs Guaire was down on her haunches applying white gloss to a skirting board near to the café's counter. A low volume portable radio was playing sixties music and the lady had been occasionally overheard to participate with a droned off-tune attempt at the chorus line. Clearly she had overheard the conversation and so Kim was confident that her one-line question would be enough. 'Is there a problem with Gruinard Island Mrs Guaire?'

'Aye there is that,' she said standing and admiring her work. 'There certainly is a problem.' She looked up from the paintwork and across the room at the pair. 'It's a painful story and not one that you're likely to tease from local people. We'd all rather it had never happened and so it never gets discussed. It's a beautiful sight to see from up here, but up here is as close as you're best getting. There's things written about the island and occasionally folk come because of what they've read. We even had people asking for a boat trip over there a few years back. They had no takers.' She shook her head as she resumed back into the haunches stance. 'I ask you… a trip to Gruinard Island… mad.'

Taylor's face said it all as he took on board the information which said so much but also said nothing. He stirred his coffee and spread out the map they had used earlier to home in on Gruinard Island. He looked over at Mrs Guaire, now thinking that she'd best not overhear their conversations about Gruinard Island. His concern was unnecessary, the lady was now absorbed again in her painting. Her youthful memories keeping her from the present day as she mumbled and hummed along to *Bus Stop* by The Hollies.

Taylor aligned the map on the table putting it in sync with the real world down below. The two took in the detail of the coastlines of both the mainland and the outline of Gruinard Island itself. The contour rings on Gruinard showed in differing shades of green becoming darker at the centre where a named summit, "An Eilid", rose up to 348 feet. Taylor's earlier pencil lines crossed over close to this point.

Their study of the map before they set off had been hurried. Their one objective had then been: to accurately plot the location of the decoded latitude and longitude. They had achieved that, but now they needed to glean as much information as they could especially after their worrying conversations with the Guaires.

'What do you reckon to this?' Taylor said. His finger was tracing around the outline of the island. A series of red coloured, inwards pointing, block style arrow heads formed a chain completely encircling the entire landmass. The finger progressed over the map and down to the lower right section where the Ordnance Survey legend appeared. He scrolled through the scale and the various icons and signs. The list was extensive but confined to three main headings: Public Rights of Way, Other Public Access and finally Access Land.

Taylor's finger stopped on *Access Land.* He moved it down until it came alongside where the identical series of red, inward facing block arrowheads were printed. The legend simply translated the representation as: *DANGER AREA.*

'What the hell…' he said in a whispered voice as he started to read through some smaller print alongside: *Usually denotes firing and test ranges in the area. Danger! Observe warning notices.*

Kim took the foolscap envelope which had contained the map and pushed her hand down inside. 'We've yet to look at this.'
She pulled out a well-thumbed six inch by four inch pamphlet titled on its cover as:

Ordnance Survey Map 47, Hikers and Rambler's Guide.

Produced by The Rambler's Association.

Suggested Walks, Points of Interest, Associated Features, Dangers.

The booklet contained a dozen pages giving several designated walks of varying difficulty. Historical and other curious topographies and structures got a mention as well as some particularly noteworthy views. The last page was dedicated specifically to Gruinard Island:

Gruinard Island, a small, oval shaped island approx. 1.2ml long by 0.62ml wide located in Gruinard Bay halfway between Gairloch and Ullapool. Its closest point to the mainland is 0.68 ml. The island was made dangerous for all mammals by experiments with the anthrax bacterium during WW2. Gruinard is owned by The Ministry of Defence and is listed as a place of danger. Entry onto the site is strictly forbidden, illegal and highly dangerous.

The two looked up from the paperwork to meet each other's eyes as disbelief swept over them. Kim's slow head shake joined forces with her blank expression. 'Where in Hell's name has dad brought us to? Even if we can get over there it's a bloody suicide mission.'

Taylor went quiet for a moment as the situation sunk in and another idea started to come to mind. 'Hang on a minute,' he quietly said and rose to his feet. He disappeared out through the door.

He arrived back at the table in less than a minute, holding the Enid Blyton book which he set down on top of the map. 'I took another look at this while you were in the shower last night. I came up with an idea over the number 238 but it didn't make sense then. But now that we've seen where we're expected to go… it must be connected.'

He thumbed through the pages. 'Your father would have known all about Gruinard Island and what went on there. It was his job, he surely knew of the dangers that still existed there.'

Kim looked thoughtful as she processed Taylor's ideas and then gave a firm nod of the head. 'I'm sure that you're right. The thing is, as I've said before, he spent a lot of time in Scotland. Often weeks on end and thinking back he had to take a lot of outdoor clothing with him. It can't have been for a conference.

Taylor opened up the book at page 238 and then drew his finger up to the top. 'The original instructions are the same… *the beginning of things*. We already have the answer with the page number. What we have to do is go to the beginning of things… the beginning of page 238 and then read the first words.' He tapped his finger against the first words as he read them. 'BE SAFE HERE'.

THIRTY NINE

DI KEN GRAINGER'S return to the temporary murder room at Exeter Town Hall was ambushed as soon as he pushed open the double front doors. Chief Constable Dudman was waiting for him in the foyer. The Chief's opening line failed to allay the concern given away by Grainger's expression. 'Nothing to worry about Inspector, I need a word.'

Grainger's qualms were not lessened as the Chief turned on his heel and directed him toward a reception room off the foyer. Some string pulling had been done beforehand to commandeer this council owned space.

The room was a good size with a central table and a dozen chairs but only one figure occupied a seat. The man stood to his feet and thrust an open hand at Grainger. The DI nodded as he shook Michael Nelson's hand. They'd met before; this was the security service agent who had turned up unannounced on the police station steps one evening. The name dropping he'd used on that first meeting remained in Grainger's mind: *"Steve Dudman, your Chief Constable", "Ian Forrester your Special Branch boss".*

The Chief Constable made an arms-outstretched gesture for the trio to take a seat before starting. 'As you know KEN...' some emphasis was put on the use of Grainger's Christian name. 'Mr Nelson is a member of Her Majesty's Security Service. He has proposed that as the officer investigating the murder of Leonard Gill it's only right that you are made aware of the Service's interest. I understand that Mr Nelson spoke to you in connection with the disappearance of the reporter Benedict Cappelli. There's now a firm connection between the burglary at the home of WDC Harding's father and the murder of Leonard Gill. The idea that Gill was the burglar seems credible and of course property recovered from his home fits with that. The abduction, or attempted abduction of the reporter Cappelli, once again seems likely to be connected.'

Dudman applied the side of a loosely clenched fist to his mouth and coughed before continuing. His voice held some out-of-character nervousness. 'Mr Nelson believes that several years ago Mr Fry uncovered a serious threat to national security. Instead of dealing with it in the correct manner he kept it to himself. The theory is that Fry had been attempting to sell the secret to a foreign power. These matters only came to light after Fry's death.'

Grainger retained an impassive face. He'd met Geoff Fry a few times and was shocked to the core by such revelations. He decided on nothing more than a nod.

The Chief looked directly at Grainger as he spoke. 'The death of WDC Hewitt is almost certainly down to contamination from a biological agent. Without question something that she unwittingly picked up as evidence either from Mr Fry's home or from Leonard Gill's place.'

Nelson leaned in, giving notice that he was about to speak. 'WDC Harding and DI Taylor disappeared from Taylor's house in Staffordshire on Monday 18th March… it's now Wednesday. An automatic firearm was discharged. Forensic tests show no less than seventeen bullets were fired. Taylor and Harding made off at high speed on her motor cycle. The weapon has not been recovered and neither of them have responded to pager or mobile phone calls.'

Nelson sat back in his chair and set a cold stare onto Grainger. 'I believe that Harding now has possession of some information from her late father. It's something which is vital to the security of this country. If she doesn't yet have it then she knows where to find it. The incident at Taylor's house probably resulted from a meeting with foreign agents or foreign criminals intent on buying the secret from them. Clearly things didn't go according to plan. Taylor and Harding's actions throughout this entire matter spell out their own criminal involvement. Miss Hewitt's death from a nerve agent which was almost certainly hidden in Mr Fry's house show that Mr Fry was in this up to his neck. Harding and Taylor must be found before they make a deal with a third party or before that third party takes the secret by force.'

Grainger was shocked. The revelations that Harding and Taylor and even Kim's father could be criminally implicated in such ways seemed absurd.

Nelson added more. 'The reporter… Cappelli, he's either been abducted or has gone renegade from his newspaper on this. The circumstances suggest that he knows a lot more about this than I would expect through normal channels. We need to work together on this. You may think this is all one-way traffic, but there lies at the heart of this matter a feature which seriously affects national security. The murder of a no-hope crook like Lenny Gill is the least of our problems.'

Nelson made an open-handed gesture towards the Chief Constable. 'Mr Dudman has assured me of complete cooperation.' He fixed his stare upon Grainger. 'As the officer in charge of the Leonard Gill murder you have the contacts and all the background information which could help us with our immediate goals. We need to find Taylor, Harding AND Cappelli, if he's still alive… NOW.'

DI Grainger squeezed behind his desk in a side office at the temporary murder room as the fingers of the wall clock showed midday. Of course he knew that the pre-planned hospital visit to see Timson would make a dent in his already lined-up schedule but wasn't expecting the meeting with Dudman and Nelson. The revelations, insinuations and bossy attitude of the MI5 agent not only spoiled his plans even more but also ruined his appetite. He pushed the sandwich box his wife had put up for him into a drawer and started to thumb through the documents piled on his blotter.

Only a few minutes of pen-pushing were allowed before Grainger's concentration was broken by DC Bob Dixon's return from his visit to Debenham's. The detective dumped a large, bulky polythene bag down to the floor. His statement pad with Mr Selwood's account of yesterday's events remained clutched in his hand as he slumped onto his chair.

'Any use Bob, was it Cappelli?' Grainger said through his open door.

Dixon swivelled to face Grainger and gave a shrug of the shoulders. 'Well the store manager seems positive on it. The bloke had certainly been knocked about, which is to be expected if he'd been chucked through a window.' He made a doubtful face as he continued. 'Thing is Boss… the guy turned up at the store dressed in a bunch of rags which he left behind after buying a load of new gear. He paid for it in cash,' Dixon added as he leaned over and lifted the bag. 'None of this is stuff a journalist would wear and I'm sure you won't want to open it in here, there could be fleas or anything in it.'

Grainger arrived alongside Dixon. He took hold of the transparent bag at arms-length and eye level, turning it to inspect the contents. A pair of carpet slippers came into view. 'Well, we're suspecting that when Cappelli went through the window he'd got nothing on. He may well have been in his nightclothes and possibly even carpet slippers, so I guess it remains a possibility.' His eyes then fixed upon the black and white chequered material of the stolen baker's trousers. 'What the hell is that?' he said pointing.

'It's a pair of trousers Boss… thin cheap things, like a chef wears. The big wholesale outlets sell them. I've seen similar in Makro.'

Grainger looked at the wall opposite as he concentrated his mind. 'You're ringing a bell somewhere with this Bob.'

A discreet female cough interrupted Grainger's thoughts. 'Phone call for you Inspector,' the uniformed police woman said and held out a telephone handset. 'It's DI Hancock; he's still down in Salisbury and he has something important to tell you.'

Grainger took a convenient seat and listened to what Hancock had to say. His jotted notes were accompanied by a few *"Hmm's"* and *"yes I see's"* along with a couple of *"go on's"* before the call ended. He then turned back to face DC Dixon. 'Bob, get around to Bridley's Breakfast café on King Street. We need a full statement from Mr Bridley. Apparently Cappelli was in there yesterday with the tramp Ossie and was wearing, would you believe, black and white chequered trousers. It seems that Bridley was on the phone to Angela about this a few moments before she died.'

Grainger turned back through 180 degrees to face the police woman. 'Wendy, go through the crime reports since the incident at the hotel when Cappelli disappeared. I'm damned sure we had a sneak-in theft somewhere around the town centre at a food outlet of some kind. You'll have to check thefts and burglaries. I'm not sure what it'll be classified under.'

Grainger did another 180 back towards Dixon as the detective gathered his statement forms together. 'Get onto Cappelli's newspaper when you get back. Reg reckons that the reporter who did the story on Lenny Gill a few years back was none other than Cappelli himself writing under a nom de plume. Cappelli was actually responsible for Lenny getting nicknamed *The Ghost.* Now if that's true it'll definitely tie Cappelli in with Lenny. It MUST have been him who paid Lenny to screw Kim's father's. If we're going to find Cappelli we need this information.'

FORTY

KIM SLOWED the Yamaha to crawl as the sign board for *Cliff View Guest House and Lodge* came up on the left. They'd followed Brice Guaire's directions out from Laide back to First Coast. The solitary location of the place made it difficult to miss. A roadside notice board was accompanied by an additional: *No Vacancies* sign, but Guaire had advised them to ignore this.

The large dormer bungalow sat solidly at the top of a steep driveway facing over the road and toward the beach one-hundred feet below. Two other, much more ancient stone block outbuildings also stood within the extensive drystone wall boundaries of the property. Taylor's eyes took in the proportions and likely use of these structures.

Kim parked the bike on the stone chip driveway next to a smart black Range Rover. The owner opened the front door before crash helmets were fully removed. He was both red haired and red faced. The strident colour scheme matched the man's impatient manner. He quickly identified himself as 'Mr James Boyle'. A tip-off from Guaire had forewarned him of a possible visit from the two early season customers.

Dressed in his overcoat, complete with scarf and gloves, Boyle had good reason to be rushing. Mrs Boyle, similarly attired, peered puzzle-faced from behind him in the hallway. The large grey suitcase she towed had a label attached to its handle. Their imminent flight abroad seemed to lessen the chances of room rental for Taylor and Harding considerably.

First impressions are not always accurate though. Boyle took a small step backward into his hallway and gave the pair a quick once-over before rapidly delivering his firm and uncompromising offer. 'You can take The Lodge, it's self-catering. The gateway is fifty yards down the road. There's everything you'll need and you'll be able to get your provisions from Mr Guaire or up in the village. It'll be a minimum of one-weeks rent… so £200 cash. There's a full gas bottle and the price includes all of that. We're away to Tenerife now for two weeks. Take it or leave it.'

Taylor looked at Kim – she was the one with the funds.

'We'll take it.' She pulled a wad from the zip pocket of the jacket and peeled off the required twenties.

Boyle pocketed his supplementary holiday spending money and then took a further step back inside to rummage in the drawer of a hall table. 'Now if you've got one of those new-fangled mobile phone gadgets, be warned that they don't work anywhere around these parts. There's a telephone box along the coast road by the turn-off to Laide.' He pulled out a set of keys from the drawer and handed them to Kim before delivering a final proviso. 'Push them in through the letter box when you leave. I've memorised your registration number so look after the place and leave it as you find it.'

Mr Boyle then kindly held the door wide so that his wife could haul the heavy suitcase out over the step and off toward their Range Rover. After pulling his front door closed Mr Boyle gave a nod of the head to his new tenants. His assistance to Mrs Boyle with the heavy case amounted to no more than ensuring that the boot lid was properly closed. Taylor and Harding wished the Boyles a happy holiday and waved them off from their own front garden as the vehicle made a quick departure back along the A832.

Taylor complied with Mr Boyle's parting order and closed the bungalow's double drive gates. He then gave his head an overemphasised scratch. 'Did I dream that, or have we really shelled out two hundred quid to someone we've never met before for a week's stay in a place we've not even viewed?'

Kim nodded. 'Err, yes… and didn't it all happen in the space of two minutes? Aren't I right in thinking that we're both supposed to be back at work by Monday as well?'

The gateway to The Lodge was found, as Boyle had said, fifty yards from the bungalow down a steep section of the road. Screw-on brass letters fixed to a white painted wooden board spelled out: *The Lodge*. This nameplate had been fixed to one side of a pair of five feet high, green painted metal gates which were recessed from the coastal side of the road. A chunky padlock and chain held the gates together and Taylor took a moment to select the correct key. Not until he pushed the gates open could he see the building properly. It lay another seventy yards down a steeply sloping rough driveway. A natural depression in the landscape along with a thick growth of gorse bushes hid the structure from the road.

They free-wheeled down the drive and Kim squeezed the bike under a lean-to erected for the storage of gas cylinders. The ancient building with its varying shades of clay roof tiles and patched stonework had clearly undergone changes since it was first built. The brickwork showed signs of other now redundant doorways and windows from many years before. The outline of an earlier large double doored entrance faced out to the sea. This and the building's rectangular shape hinted at its origins as a boathouse.

A number of similar structures had been seen during the journey, both in changed and original form. Nets, ropes, riggings and other seafaring paraphernalia were a standard spectacle around the coastline along with boats of varying size and condition near to the sporadically sited homes. The picture as a whole suggested that fishing and boating still played a part in the lives of the thinly distributed population.

The driveway from the road down to the side of the building was made from beach shingle and pebbles. 'Look at all these skimmers,' Taylor joked as his footsteps delivered a crunching sound.

The back door yielded to another of the keys and swung open onto a neat, recently decorated two bedroomed modern style accommodation. The Boyles had left the central heating on a low temperature timer to combat the possibilities of a freeze-up. A little tweaking of the controls soon made everywhere comfortable.

A large picture window fitted into the end of the structure had replaced the boathouse double doors many years ago. The outlook across Gruinard Bay was spectacular. If they had wanted somewhere to sit and contemplate the raw beauty of Gruinard Island, then they had found it. The island was now much more distant than their first, water's edge view from near to Mungasdale and looked to be almost two miles across the grey rolling water. The problem was that they didn't just want to contemplate the view.

FORTY ONE

KEN GRAINGER'S hunch had been right and he now had the crime report open on his desk. It was a pretty impressive feat to have dedicated a portion of his grey matter to this piece of trivia. Dozens of similar minor offence incidents went through his CID admin office each day. The fact that most of his time was currently taken up with a murder enquiry made his recall of this insignificant case all the more remarkable.

The incident which stuck in his mind had been reported by telephone during the afternoon of Monday 18th March, over two days before. Mr Raymond Meigh was described in the report as the proprietor of a bakery in a back street close to Exeter centre. From this building some Eccles cakes and a French stick had been stolen. It was certainly not a crime to warrant the skills of a detective and if those had been the complete facts, it's doubtful that Mr Meigh would have noticed the crime.

Meigh's parents held no connection with baking. The fact that their son entered the trade upon leaving school was unexpected. Their christening of him with the name Raymond seemed a reasonable choice to go with the surname of Meigh. It did however, lead to some mickey taking at school. This began when fellow students started to get a grasp upon musical scales. The melodic chant: *Do Ra Me Fa So La Te Do* became particularly annoying when the emphasis was put on the RA, ME. In a twist of fate it also provided the inspiration for his eventual profession and the name of his new business: Dough Ray Meigh (Bakery Ltd Court Street Exeter).

Meigh's knowledge of the crime first came about at around lunchtime. Someone had sneaked in whilst he was busy with the ovens and taken his spare work togs. The loose fitting white shirt and the black and white check pattern chef's trousers were taken from a cupboard near to the unlocked back door. The items held little value and did not warrant a police report, but the old quilted anorak, which was also missing, put a different light on the issue. The baker's black leather wallet containing £35, a Barclaycard, driving licence and library card had been in the pocket.

Grainger rested his forehead onto the palm of his hand as he picked through the detail given in the report. The account had been compiled by a probationary constable, a rookie with six months service. Hopefully the young man would continue with such detail for the next thirty years, as he'd missed nothing out.

The discovery of the missing cakes and bread along with descriptions of the clothing were all religiously written onto the crime report by the officer. The surprising feature being that the £35 was not actually taken. Although removed from the wallet it had been left on a shelf in the cupboard.

As a safeguard against the breeze when the door was opened, the thief had thoughtfully left an Eccles cake down on top of the notes. A large crescent shaped bite was missing from the counterweight.

'Ossie… you bugger.' Grainger muttered under his breath. There was no doubting the identity of the thief. The tramp's aversion to taking the cash of the working man had previously served as the linchpin to solving other crimes committed by him.

Mr Bridley's café sighting of Ossie accompanied by Cappelli wearing the stolen clothing clinched the matter. There would be no need for Sherlock Holmes on this case. Ossie must have stolen the clothes for Cappelli. The additional theft of Mr Meigh's driving licence and other ID documents was unheard of for Ossie but the deliberate leaving behind of the £35 definitely pinned the crime onto him. Grainger concluded that the now deceased vagrant had taken those out-of-character ID items for Cappelli.

Commendably, the constable dealing with the theft had correctly circulated the details to the bank and to DVLA. Under normal circumstances, even with the card being stopped, it would still take days or even weeks to stop illegal use or find where it had been used.

It was now certain though, that Cappelli had not been kidnapped. He was at large and operating independently. A good description of him, right down to his current clothing was also available.

Grainger's last conversation with the Chief Constable and the security agent ran through his mind. He fingered Nelson's business card which included a mobile phone number. He stayed put at his desk for a while as he thought things through a little more. Cappelli had been seen with a wad of cash. This could have been his own, but Grainger doubted it as Cappelli's own wallet, cards and cash were found in his hotel room. Enquires with Benedict Cappelli's estranged wife had been made soon after his dramatic disappearance. Grainger already possessed a good description of a watch she'd bought as a present for his thirtieth birthday during happier times. No such watch turned up in the reporter's hotel room.

Two and two were quickly put together and DC Dixon was dispatched hot-foot onto the town centre to speak with likely dealers in second hand property. Fortunately Dixon knew the ropes – he was a Reg Timson protégé! The Mace Street jeweller's was his first port of call.

His exclamation in a loud voice of 'BINGO!' caused a couple of people to turn heads. *Whatever could be so exciting to the man peering into the shop window?*

Cappelli's gleaming Van Der Bauwede Magnum Commander took up the centre with a spot light focussed upon it. The price tag of £625 was one hell of mark-up from the paltry £225 which had been paid.

'That's life,' the jeweller said when challenged by Dixon on the morality of it all.

Dixon returned to the Murder Room within the hour. The door to Grainger's temporary office was partially ajar. Figures could be seen inside. Dixon applied a knuckled rap to the doorframe and waited until Grainger's edgy sounding voice called him in.

Security Service agents Nelson and Jennings along with Special Branch boss DCI Forrester stood around the seated detective inspector. Dixon sensed unease in the room – intimidation even. He delivered the watch, now in a polythene evidence bag, down in front of Grainger. The jeweller's witness statement and some connected paperwork accompanied the consignment.

Nelson waited until Dixon received the praise due for a job well done from his senior officer. He pushed the door closed as Dixon left. 'So we now know that Cappelli IS alive AND also up to his neck. He's not contacted his newspaper and he's changed his appearance. He has a false identity along with a pocket full of cash. It seems likely he'll hire a car on Meigh's licence and credit card.'

Nelson moved around Grainger's desk to stand in front of him. 'The machinery to reach some of these small hire firms is slow moving. Broadcast an urgent telex message to all police forces, route it through your Chief Constable. It will be authorised by MI5's Director General. I gather that Barclaycard have put a stop on the card. It usually takes days to get info back on whether it's been used. I'll speed things up on that score.'

The Special Branch DCI adopted an arms-folded posture and did nothing other than give a straight-mouthed single nod at Grainger. It augmented the suggestion that heads would roll if the orders were not complied with.

Nelson continued with more detail. 'The telex should suggest that Cappelli is wanted in connection with the murders of Leonard Gill and Oswald Dennis.'

'WHAT…' Grainger couldn't help his outburst. 'That's ridiculous.'

'I haven't finished Inspector,' Nelson snapped back. 'It's an absolute necessity that all car hire firms throughout the country are visited by a police officer. Every possible effort is to be made, as a priority over all other work, to get details of a vehicle rented in the name of Raymond Meigh.'

'On whose authority?' Grainger demanded.

Nelson placed both hands down onto the edge of Grainger's desk and leaned in closer. 'How about the Home fucking Secretary?' 'It doesn't stop there inspector,' Nelson added moving even closer. 'I want a police interest marker putting on PNC for DC Harding's motor cycle. I don't want it stopping and checking but I want to know where they are. I want it doubling up with an additional telex to all police forces.' Nelson made a "speech marks" gesture with his two index fingers in the air: 'Urgently and covertly locate the rider and passenger. Do not approach. They are not to be made aware of police interest. Sightings immediately to ME.' He turned toward his partner. 'Miss Jennings here will be in charge of the Cappelli side of things.'

Grainger looked up at Forrester. The DCI raised his eyebrows and added a shrug of the shoulders.

FORTY TWO

DOUG TAYLOR had been on the bike up to Laide Village. He'd decided to use the village store for their provisions rather than Mr Guaire's campsite shop. There seemed a better chance of getting everything on Kim's list. He'd also hoped for a newspaper, but the few which formed the small shop's daily quota had already been sold.

They ate tuna sandwiches with a pot of tea and gazed out through the end window as a gloomy evening approached. Dark rolling clouds swept in from the sea to obliterate what a couple of hours before had been a clear sky. The first fat drops of rain struck the window with a sharp *tap – tap – tap* intensifying by the second into a background roar. A wall of rain thrashed at the glass and bounced stair-rods up from the stonework of the patio. Gruinard Island disappeared into a grey gloom that almost reached the beach. The speed of the weather change served as a warning.

Their conversation inevitably turned to the last parts of Geoff Fry's code and those numbers, 238 and 213. Taylor's interpretation that the answer followed the original decoding principles in reverse seemed plausible. The first words of page 238 had given that message – Be safe here.

It seemed crazy after reading the history of Gruinard Island that Mr Fry would be so blasé about the situation. He, more than anyone in the world, would have known of the shocking dangers of the island.

They pondered on the idea for some time, but Kim conceded. 'Yes, on such a critical issue he'd not want to leave anything to chance. He was telling me that it is safe whatever I might think.'

If they *had* arrived at the correct result with the number 238, it seemed common sense to apply the same rules to the remaining number 213. The result fazed them a little though. A single word enclosed in speech marks was printed at the top of page 213: "Look".

All that they could deduce was that Geoff Fry was perhaps saying "It's up to you now… LOOK."

'So… we're going then,' Taylor said. 'Only one minor detail remains. How are we going to get there?'

The question had only one answer. This was something which neither Taylor nor Harding wanted to suggest as it went so firmly against their principles.

Their conversation with Mr Guaire and the worrying details in the map guide suggested that no locals would be willing to provide a boat trip to the island. They also concluded that no boatman would hire out his craft to unskilled people.

Taylor's reluctant suggestion was made tongue-in-cheek. 'So we borrow someone's boat?'

'As in, *pinch someone's boat* you mean?' Kim said.

'Well… ' Taylor stretched out the word. 'I didn't want to put it like that.'

'Hmm, I can't disagree and I can't come up with another scheme, but there are a lot of snags that go with the idea.'

'You mean like going to prison and losing our jobs.' Taylor's eyebrows were raised.

'That crossed my mind. On the other hand though, if we take into account that a Security Service agent is working for the other side and has already tried to kill me…. Then according to your law notes...' She stifled a laugh. 'We could claim that as police officers, we were commandeering the boat to carry out our lawful duties.'

Taylor rose to his feet and rocked back and forth pinching the material of his shirt collar between fingers and thumbs. It was his impression of a barrister. 'Oh, I understand now officer… so you *have* been studying for your exams after all.' He was speaking with a plum-in-the-mouth accent. 'Well let me see now…' He sustained the performance for another sentence: 'There may be some difficulties Sergeant Harding, due to the differences with Scottish law.' He caught hold of her and pulled her toward him tightly. Their noses touched and they burst into laughter. 'And so we'll do it *our way*… like we always do.'

It was half eight when Kim padded across the carpeted floor from the bedroom and through to the kitchen to make coffee. A low wattage table lamp was the only illumination as she filled and switched on the kettle. The storm had disappeared inland across the hills leaving an odd stillness behind. She peered through the window. A half-moon hung almost at the top of the sky, looking tiny but still managing to cast a shimmering silver reflection down onto the Minch. The squat outline of Gruinard Island fleetingly showed itself as Kim's eyes adjusted. Nothing more than a black bulge against a blacker backdrop. An indistinct glimpse of white horses of foam was made out as the swell rose up at cliff edges. Clouds quickly blotted the moon's weak light and the entire scene was lost again.

Taylor wandered out from the bedroom, T-shirt and boxers, bare footed and rubbing sleepy eyes.

'Coffee?' Kim said the word as a question but had already held the mug out to him.

'Thanks,' he said walking through to the lounge and settling down onto the sofa. He pressed the pile of the hearth rug between his toes, stifled a yawn and made extra wide eyes to waken himself properly. His mind had been working though.

'So, chances are that we've now been declared the bad guys by your friendly MI5 chums. The bike's almost certainly on PNC with a report-sightings flag attached. We still don't know what's behind your father's secret, but someone seems to have a good idea and wants it at any cost.'

He went quiet as he thought some more. 'We can't be sure how long we have before local gossip gets around. Mr Guaire at the caravan park has seen us and the bike. I know he said he doesn't read the papers, but he's bound to hear something. It won't take much for him to put two and two together. Our landlord, Mr Boyle is not a problem. He'll be sitting in a bar in Tenerife with a cool beer right now.'

Kim was standing by the window; she listened to Taylor's ideas. 'Sooner we get over there, the better,' she said.

'Hmm,' Taylor mumbled. 'Even if we get a boat, it's bloody chancy. That's the Atlantic Ocean not Trentham Gardens Lake.'

Kim looked puzzled… 'Where?'

'Doesn't matter… How much sailing have you done, I mean, can you handle a boat?'

Kim shook her head. 'Very little, and nothing in years, I was a schoolgirl when dad had the boat. So only basic stuff anyway.'

'Same here and even if we do get a boat and manage to get to sea, we've got to find somewhere safe to land. Most of what we've seen is all rocks. It looks terrifying.'

Kim turned to look back through the window. 'If the weather's good, I think we can make it. There's a long bar of sandy beach which comes right out from the island, you must have seen it. If we could get across I'm sure we'll be able to land safely there.'

Taylor closed his eyes and nodded. 'Sure I saw it. It's plain enough for anyone to see. The thing is even if we get close enough to land there, someone will definitely see us. The island is completely off-limits to everyone remember? They'll be on the phone to the Coast Guard or police straight away. From what the Guaires said all the locals know about the island. There'll be helicopters, boats and the entire balloon will go up.

Kim turned back to face him. 'So we go at night.'

Taylor flopped back into his seat. 'At night… are you crazy?'

'Yes.'

FORTY THREE

IT WAS half past eleven and The Lodge was in darkness when Taylor and Harding hiked up the drive to the road. Street lamps didn't exist this far from civilisation and the moon's faint blur of silver aided their steps only slightly.

Jeans and chunky pullovers had been decided upon. The motorcycle leathers would be too restrictive for their plan. Cautious left and right glances were taken when they reached the gates. The closest human being though, was fast asleep and two miles away in the village of Laide. The rhythmic distant sounds of the sea carried on a chill breeze as they made their way up the narrow, steeply inclined road towards the outline of Boyle's bungalow. Kim gave a shudder as apprehension joined forces with the cold temperature.

Taylor pushed open Boyle's gate and they started up the driveway. Two powerful security lights abruptly clicked on jolting the couple to a wide-eyed halt. They should have been prepared for this. Taylor shook his head and blew out a gasp of icy breath, convincing himself that no one could possibly have witnessed the event.

The fact that they now trespassed on Boyle's property was down to an idea conjured in Taylor's mind during their earlier meeting with the owner. One of the two outbuildings in the grounds had caught his eye. In his normal world these actions were completely taboo and would have led to dismissal from the Police. But there seemed something so serious and so threatening about this whole affair that Taylor had not struggled for long with his conscience.

Kim overcame the doubts even more easily than Taylor and when he suggested that one of Boyle's outbuildings was probably a boathouse her response was instant: "What are we waiting for then?"

Taylor quickly identified the location of the security lights and their sensors. He worked out a route to approach the elongated building which might avoid the lights even though they did not really present a problem. There was certainly no one to see them, but it felt better doing what they were doing in the dark.

The boathouse – if that was what it was – had been built with its large double doors in line with the property's exit gates out onto the road. A smooth freshly laid strip of tarmac connected the two.

As soon as the lights timed out the pair worked their way around the back of the garage intending to head for the side of the boathouse. A torch was something they had not brought with them. Fortunately Mr Boyle had covered the eventuality. Complete with fresh batteries it had been left in a kitchen cupboard. Boyle's complexion would undoubtedly have deepened in redness had he known it would be used to break into his own property.

A peek in through the window of the first building produced the expected result – a neat, tidy and empty garage. Its usual occupant, Boyle's Range Rover, would now be sitting in an airport car park for the next two weeks.

Still unsure if their target building was indeed a boathouse and even less sure of what was inside, they silently made their way over. Yet another security light caught them unawares and lit the front doors up like a lightning strike. 'Damn' Taylor muttered stepping close in against the building. He quickly made use of the light to examine the doors: Wooden, seven feet high, twelve feet wide and with a recently applied coat of black gloss paint. A two inch circle of shiny brass fitted halfway up one of the doors glinted back from the security light. The lock's predictable name, *Yale*, could be seen stamped into the brass-work. It was a standard, front-door style, night latch, which looked to be fairly new and in sound condition. Taylor reached up squeezing his fingers into the small gap between the top of the frame and the door. His attempt to shake the door back and forth resulted in hardly any movement at all.

'Hmm, really secure, and it feels like its bolted top and bottom, so there must be another door.'

The security light went out as they crept along the side of the building. There were no windows and so the contents remained a mystery but sure enough a second, single sized door was discovered facing the bungalow. This entrance was lower in height than the double doors but again had a recent coat of black gloss and a similar night latch. Using the same test as before, Taylor tugged the top edge of the door. The woodwork was older and more worn. A loose clacking sound was produced as the latch moved back and forth within the metal keep. With no security light to help or hinder them Kim shone the torch down between frame and door. She saw a glint of brass where the latch protruded into the box keep.

Taylor rested his head against the frame for a few seconds and continued to move the free play. He watched the fingernail sized portion of the latch which could be seen and tried to work out a way to press it backward. In the movies this was where the deft use of a credit card produced instant results, but not this time. Taylor shook his head and took a step backwards as he worked it out. 'What tools do we have?'

Kim reached into her pocket for the handful of items that she'd brought along. Some had been borrowed from The Lodge, others from the motor cycle tool kit and the remainder from her handbag. It was not the best of burglar's kits – three differently sized screwdrivers, a small box spanner, a flat bladed butter knife, eyebrow tweezers and a metal nail file.

Taylor selected a slender, long-shafted screwdriver and following his instructions Kim shone the torch down into the gap where the lock met the door frame. He probed the screwdriver downwards jiggling it until it met up against the rounded keep box edge of the brass latch. He then slowly pressed the screwdriver handle over to his right so that its tip eased the latch back into the body of the lock. The door swung silently open.

'You're in the wrong job,' Kim whispered.

The torch beam shone into the darkness and picked out the rounded coarse inflatable collar of a RIB boat. The vessel, with its rigid fibreglass hull sat on a light tubular metal "A" frame trailer. Its general overall appearance was dirty, well-worn and stained. The red top tube was scuffed and tatty and bore the boat's name in faded twelve inch, white lettering near to the bows – *Angry Boyle.*

Kim directed the beam slowly around to reveal more of the sorry situation.

The boat was open-topped with two seats up front and a bench seat behind. A big black Mercury outboard at the rear sat at an angle lolled over to one side. The steering wheel and dashboard with dangling central ignition keys, a start button and a choke knob seemed reminiscent of an old car. A throttle lever took up space to the left of the steering wheel along with a couple of circular instrument dials and some switches. Lifejackets, buckets, a mound of thick rope and an old-fashioned red painted, heavy fibreglass life ring had been piled inside.

'Been out of action for ages,' Taylor said.

'Pull the door to,' Kim said. 'There are no windows in here, let's get the lights on and have a better look.'

The torchlight located the switch inside the door and then four powerful fluorescent tubes flickered before brightly lighting the entire scene. Things looked even worse with the full detail on show. The engine cowling had been removed and lay on a bench. Tool boxes and socket sets stood opened on the floor along with an assortment of oil coated nuts and bolts. A service manual for the boat's Mercury 115 horsepower motor lay open on the bench. Oily finger-marks plastered its dog eared pages. A cardboard box stuffed with new parts including filters, spark plugs, coils and a five litre can of Lucas outboard oil rested on the bench. It seemed that Mr Boyle's last attempt to get the boat seaworthy again had been abandoned some time ago.

Kim silently gazed at the engine for a few moments. After some thought she gripped the propeller and gave it a little back and forth tug. 'Well it's not seized. I've never worked on marine stuff, but it can't be too much different than a motorcycle engine. I wonder if we could get it running. It's our best bet.' She pressed the palm of her hand down onto the boat's top tube. 'Hmm under pressure so we'll need to sort that out as well. Boyle's not back for two weeks and so that must be a bonus… no one's going to miss this boat.'

Taylor shook his head a few times before giving his opinion on the situation: 'Sometimes I despair of you!'

Kim paced around the vessel eyeing it from different angles. 'Trailer's in better nick than the boat,' she said. 'It looks pretty new.' She patted her hand down onto a third wheel fitted near to the trailer's towing knuckle. 'It even has a rescue wheel, so that would make it easier to push and pull on the beach… and a handbrake in case it starts getting away from us.' She pointed at a long handled lever also mounted in the same area. She got down on her haunches inspecting where the rigid hull of the boat sat on the trailer. 'Wow, Mr Boyle's splashed out for us… rollers and a strap winch. This will help with the launching. All we need now is a decent boat.'

Taylor's head shook some more.

Kim took fifteen minutes to investigate the mechanics and try to get an understanding of what did what. Taylor in the meantime checked out the electrics of the boathouse itself. The wiring leading to the fluorescent tubes and the wall mounted power points all looked new. He tracked it back to an electricity consumer unit fitted near the door. Several different switches and contact breakers led out to grey coloured cables branching off to the various circuits. Each one was carefully named in felt-tip onto a paper stick-on label. After reading the labels for a few seconds he made a satisfied smile and pressed a finger against a switch marked: *Outside Security Lights.*

Kim had discovered that the boat's battery, a standard 12v car-type was stowed inside the hull near to the motor. She tentatively brushed a spare piece of cable across the two terminals producing a weak and half-hearted spark along with a small audible *crack*.

'The battery's not completely flat; there's still a bit of power in it.

It's a good sign. It means it should charge up. Looking at Mr Boyle's tools there's bound to be a battery charger here somewhere.'

She was right; Taylor reached up to a high shelf and within a few minutes the device was connected and producing a low hum.

The marine engine turned out to be quite different from the road versions that Kim was so familiar with. The grubby service manual proved invaluable as she worked her way through different procedures, fitting new parts, adjusting, checking, cleaning and testing.

By half past three with the help of Taylor's much lesser mechanical knowledge and his more powerful physical strength a complete overhaul had been carried out. All the new spare parts including filters, coils, timing belt, leads and spark plugs had been fitted. Kim suggested at an early stage that the major problem with the boat seemed to be water contaminating the fuel. It may well have been a theory that Boyle himself had been working on. The service manual remained open at the relevant page and two full containers of fresh fuel had been left inside the door of the garage. Taylor found a small, mains operated compressor under the bench and got to work reflating the boat's five air chambers to what felt like a sensible pressure.

After checking the recharged state of the battery Kim gave the nod to Taylor for one last check on the outside world. Nothing had changed. The blustery wind and the regular sound of waves were still there but no lights and no signs of life.

Kim settled herself into the driving seat, pulled out the choke, gripped the throttle lever with her left hand and twisted the ignition key. She looked over her shoulder to where Taylor stood on look-out peering through the partly open door.

'Okay give it a try,' he said.

Working on the recharged battery the motor spun rapidly for several seconds creating a mechanical whirring, but not a single sign of combustion. Kim turned the key off and sat thinking for a moment. 'Nothing, and I can smell petrol so it must be the electrics… no spark.'

She slapped her forehead as the answer came to her. 'Of course,' she said resting her finger onto the red plastic dome shaped knob next to the start button. 'A kill cord… all boats have them. It clips onto your clothing and pulls out to stop the engine if you get flung into the water.'

The bright red cord was found on the floor of the boat and in no time Kim slotted its metal key end into the dashboard knob.

A deep *pop-pop-pop* started as soon as the second try began. A couple of near starts came with rush of explosive noise. Kim turned off the key and sniffed as a strong smell of petrol filled the air. She adjusted the choke, pushed the throttle lever forward and tried again. Two almighty backfires followed a splutter of engine noise. The steady roar of the outboard firing perfectly took over and filled the entire space along with the thick blue exhaust.

Kim only ran the engine for a few seconds. Just long enough to be sure that it could produce healthy looking exhaust before switching off.

'Christ that was loud,' Taylor said. He then killed the inside lights and opened the side door wide to let out the smoke. They both looked out towards Laide, wondering if anyone could have heard the racket from such a distance. It seemed unlikely.

Quarter past four arrived and Taylor, unhindered by the now redundant security lights, walked down to where the property's gates met the road. He opened them and stood watching and listening for a while. The moon had long since disappeared and his eyes had taken some time to adjust. Kim carefully slid back the top and bottom bolts on the boathouse front doors and pushed them open as Taylor arrived back alongside her. She took a long stare over towards Laide, but there seemed to be no sign of life. A gust of wind caught one of the doors, almost pulling it from her grasp and encouraged her to quickly bolt them both down into their stays in the tarmac.

Taylor lifted the tow bar of the trailer upwards so that the third wheel came up from the concrete floor. He gave a tug and felt at the weight. He knew he had to keep the rig under control as he attempted the downward slope to the gates. It looked easier to turn the trailer around and slow it with the handbrake until he reached the slightly lesser gradient of the road. He pulled it out from the boathouse with ease before swivelling on the remaining patch of level ground outside the doors and then gave the first tentative push onto the gradient. The weight jarred at his shoulders and stretched his arms out to their fullest. He dug his heels down onto the tarmac and grabbed for the handbrake jolting the entire outfit to a lurching stop. He soon mastered the technique of letting the gradient do the work whilst gently applying the brake. Within a couple of minutes they were out onto the road.

Kim jogged silently on in front to open the gates of The Lodge as Taylor carefully let the trailer creep down the steep incline whilst holding it against the brake. He pushed the trailer's tow-bar left and right to slowly, but inch perfectly steer into The Lodge's opening. The gradient down from here was equal to that from Boyle's boathouse, the only advantage being that the rough pebble surface offered some added braking. They arrived panting, alongside the building and then pushed the trailer further around onto the seaward side of the building. Hopefully, here, it would be hidden from all but the most prying of eyes.

It was another fifteen minutes before the exercise was over: Boathouse doors closed and bolted, side door left unlocked but wedged shut with a handy house brick, drive gates closed.

They stood over the kitchen sink, cleaning the worst of the oily grime from their hands aided by washing up liquid and a nail brush. Skinned knuckles and a few cuts were war wounds they'd both sustained. 'Only did my nails last night as well,' Kim joked as she examined the damage. After a shower and a hot drink they both crashed into bed exhausted.

FORTY FOUR

A LOUD cheer went up as Timson made a nine o'clock appearance the next day in the Town Hall's temporary murder room. His quick discharge from hospital had been more down to insistence on his part than decisions by doctors. His regular suit and tie had been substituted for jeans, sweat shirt and cardigan. The visit had been made on the journey home from hospital and the clothing he'd worn on the fateful Tuesday was with the Porton Down scientists – never to be returned.

Wife Ivy, had rolled her eyes at Reg's persistent pleas to call in for a ten minute catch-up and she now waited in the car, sighs of frustration combining with more eye-rolling at her husband's doggedness.

A couple of pats on the back were delivered as Timson eased down into a chair. 'I'm fine,' he said. 'I don't think the wife will put up with me for a fortnight though. If I can get the Doc to sign me off I'll be back within the week.'

'Don't rush back Timmo,' Grainger advised. 'You've had a lucky escape. You were right with your idea about Cappelli. We've found a copy of the newspaper article in Gill's CRO file.'

Grainger pushed the cutting across the desk in front of Timson. It was sealed in a transparent plastic folder. Timson read the headline. It was exactly as he'd remembered:

Lenny the Ghost puts the willies up the police.

By Kevin Lawton.

'That's it LAWTON, I've been racking my brains all night.'

Grainger explained the situation. 'The newspaper has confirmed that he used to write under that name as a freelance.'

The other team members tried hard to stay cheerful throughout their colleague's short visit, but Angela's death dented their best efforts. The gloomy mood returned as soon as the door closed behind him.

Ivy Timson was the only person privy to her husband's hunch and what he intended doing about it. He would certainly not be putting his feet up and taking it easy. He expanded on his ideas and intentions as soon as they arrived home. He knew the CID bosses would not approve but Ivy also had an opinion. 'You'll get yourself into trouble and you've still not properly recovered.'

'I'll be okay,' he said as he picked up the car keys and delivered a kiss to her cheek. 'If anyone rings or calls around tell them I'm convalescing at my brother's in Dorset.'

The first leg of Timson's journey took in a six mile drive out to the village of Broadclyst. Retired Detective Sergeant Peter Lacey was waiting on the doorstep for his old work buddy. He took a furtive glance up and down the road as Timson opened the garden gate. It was an *old-habits-die-hard* impulse formed from years of doing things *not* by the book. He had been expecting Timson but the fewer people who knew of the visit the better.

'Glad to see you're okay son,' Lacey said ushering the forty-eight year old veteran detective indoors. 'You've had a lucky escape. I've done a bit of unofficial digging and found out lots... fancy a brew?'

Up in Scotland, after their late night Taylor and Harding sat looking out from the end window. A pair of binoculars discovered in a kitchen drawer now stood next to the coffee pot. Gruinard Bay remained deserted throughout their half-hour breakfast. Not so much as a solitary beachcomber had been seen, nor a single craft out at sea. The swell of The Minch rose and fell against the rocky coastline of Gruinard Island. It inspired interest but heightening unease.

With biking jackets over pullovers they stepped outside. An icy breeze coming in across the water cancelled out the bright sun's best efforts. Hands in pockets they wordlessly contemplated the product of last night's work. Boyle's boat on its trailer was completely shielded from the roadway by the building. On the other hand that fat red top tube with its broad white lettering *Angry Boyle* might be seen by passing boats. It would only become a worry if there should be a local on board who might recognise this as out of the ordinary. Taylor decided on a little extra camouflage and made use of some brushwood, piling it against the boat.

Their trek down through what now served as the back garden of The Lodge and onto the sand took a few minutes. The slight gradient must originally have been used as a causeway during the building's time as a boathouse. A few obstructions including a garden seat and a couple of large earthenware flower pots were quickly dealt with by Taylor. Several medium sized rocks on the beach itself he also hauled to one side. The resulting cleared pathway went some way to restoring its original function.

It had been a late and tiring night but the crystal clarity of that chilly Scottish air created a heady invigorating tonic. It was what they needed for the decisions in front of them. The past few days had been a near constant adrenaline rush and some of the choices they had made *could* and maybe *would* be viewed in different lights. The words foolhardy and even criminal became fixed in Taylor's mind. The stimulating walk they took helped toss what doubts they might have held out of the window. They were in deep now and determined to go through with it.

The clear sky suggested a spell of decent weather, but the gusting wind required a firm, legs-apart stance as they stood at the water's edge taking turns with Boyle's binoculars.

The spit of smooth yellow sand which pointed out from the island toward the mainland looked to be about three hundred yards in length. Judgement of its average width proved difficult. A couple of mounds of grass could be made out running down the centre. It seemed likely that the spit was safe from the tide and their best calculation made it no less than fifty yards wide. It was undoubtedly a permanent feature and the best, if not the only place to land with a degree of safety.

The binoculars strained to their limits to produce the outlines of numerous notice boards dotted here and there. No writing was legible from such distance, but it was a good bet that the words DANGER and KEEP OFF formed part of the text. Three fairly intact looking, but crazily off-centre notices could be made out along the sand spit. Others could be seen on the land high above the rocks facing the mainland to warn off foolhardy individuals. A refocussed view showed rusted stumps which had been defeated by the weather.

They strolled back to The Lodge and followed up their beach recce with more coffee and an in-depth conversation on their next moves. They would need provisions and some equipment. It was unlikely that they would be able to buy the gear locally. The map and tour guide pamphlet donated by Mr Bowers gave the largest nearby settlement as Ullapool.

'We're not going to get all this stuff on the bike,' Taylor said as he checked through the list which had been written onto the back of Bowers' envelope.

Kim gave a nod. 'My thoughts too; we need a car.'

Taylor rested an elbow onto the table and plonked his chin down into his palm. He came straight to the point. 'Three options… hire, buy or borrow.' He didn't give Kim the chance to make a choice. 'Borrow, as in STEAL, is a non-starter,' he firmly added. 'We can only go so far in justifying what we're doing. A stolen car up here in the middle of nowhere would also raise a huge amount of police interest and it would be quickly spotted. No, we'll have to hire or buy.'

Kim gave another nod. 'Hiring will present more problems than buying.' She added some weight to her point with examples: 'They'll want proof of identity and a driving licence. They'll probably require payment on a credit card. It's all stuff that could put the authorities on to where we are.'

Taylor agreed. 'Yes and you can include the other people who are after us as well as the authorities. Can we buy a decent banger for a few hundred quid?' He successfully turned the suggestion into a question. It was after all Kim's cash they'd be using.

She shrugged. 'Best plan… but Ullapool's only small. It might not even have a car dealer.' The decision was made though!

Within half an hour they were ready to go. Kim straddled the Yamaha and teased it backwards from the lean-to onto the steep drive with her toes as Taylor locked up The Lodge. She gave a puzzled shake of the head at the bike's reluctance to easily fire up at the first press of the start button again. The parallel twin engine turned sluggishly for a couple of seconds before its throaty roar took over. 'Shouldn't be doing that,' she said. 'I only serviced it a couple of weeks ago.'

Their journey to Ullapool didn't take much working out on the map. It was the scenic route or nothing. The narrow potholed A832 would be followed by the slightly better A835. It was a mere ten miles as the crow flies but the meandering roads around two lochs and through mountainous regions lengthened the outing to a full thirty-five miles.

As ten past eleven arrived the *Welcome to Ullapool* sign came up on the nearside verge. Taylor's idea that the motorcycle's registration number had been flagged on the Police National Computer seemed probable. However, it would still require the presence of an inquisitive cop to spot the bike and run a PNC check to get that particular ball rolling. They'd only seen a handful of cars on the journey and certainly no police vehicles. With the pager and mobile disabled and lying on the table back at The Lodge keeping a low profile should do the trick. Consequently the electronic signal which *was* generated as they entered into the fringes of Ullapool was an event which would not even have rated as possible in their thoughts.

Six hundred miles away in the headquarters of the Vodafone Telecommunications Company in Newbury Berkshire a chain of automatic computer commands were initiated by that signal. The cascade of pre-programmed instructions which then followed spawned the robotic transmission of a message via the latest method of communication: *Electronic mail.* This sequence of events had been set into motion by a criminal action now popular with the secret service agencies of countries throughout the world: *Hacking.*

Behind permanently drawn blinds in a semi-detached house at New Eltham, London, a Macintosh Classic computer monitor blinked into life. The string of green text which robotically scrolled from the top left hand corner of the black screen had been eagerly awaited:

Mobile 0532167258 connected to Vodafone base station 200361 Ullapool South 11.10 hrs. Thursday 21st March 1991.

The firestorm of activity following that message led to a series of telephone calls which put wheels into motion in the broadest sense of the phrase.

Within thirty minutes of the message coming through two men clad in black leathers and helmets sat astride a high powered motor cycle. They headed along the A96 out of Aberdeen with the speedo held steady at 110mph. Their intention of quickly covering the 158 miles to Ullapool and tracking down Taylor and Harding would not be for a friendly chat.

The pillion passenger carried a 9mm Glock 17, semi-automatic pistol. The threaded barrel conversion allowed for the screwing on of a silencer. More correctly termed a "suppressor", the precision engineered component was a product of the *Advanced Armament Corporation.* It not only increased the overall length of the weapon to an unwieldy sixteen inches, but also obscured the gunsight at the end of the real barrel.

The assassin could simply have screwed the suppressor into place after arriving in Ullapool. He had been content though, to ride with the bulky weapon zipped inside his leather jerkin, ready for immediate use. The unusable gunsight was not a problem – a head shot from six inches would not require much of an aim.

FORTY FIVE

AFTER A half hour chat with his old partner in crime Reg Timson set off on the second leg of his journey. His mind churned with the events of the past few days throughout that one hundred mile drive. The further fascinating facts illicitly uncovered by Pete Lacey added even more intrigue.

With his hospital breakfast forsaken in favour of an early escape Timson's rumbling stomach gave notice of its emptiness well before his half past twelve. arrival. He climbed the two steps to Salisbury Leigh Nursing home firming up on his decision to play this role with a straight bat. After all he was indeed a police officer making enquiries into a crime which may have involved a resident at the home. Neither the local police, nor his own bosses knew of his agenda. The fact that he was on official sick leave might also raise eyebrows. He gave a shake of the head as he looked down at his jeans and T-shirt, as an old-school detective he felt very underdressed. He pushed these thoughts to the back of his mind, confident that his warrant card and statement pad would be enough to confirm his authenticity.

Duty nurse and receptionist Janice Hopkins listened with interest from across the other side of the counter as Timson explained. 'I'm from the CID in Exeter. I'm making enquiries into crimes committed in that area which may be connected to Salisbury Leigh Residential Home.'

Timson's nose blowing allowed for a little more thinking time as he bluffed his way onwards. 'In particular a resident by the name of Mr Andrew Prestwich.'

Janice looked instantly puzzled. 'Good heavens, Andrew is elderly, he suffers with dementia. I can't understand how he could be connected to anything in Exeter.'

'Yes it's a little complicated. One of my colleagues at Exeter is the daughter of a friend of Mr Prestwich…'

Janice interrupted. 'You're talking about Kim, Geoff Fry's daughter. I met Mr Fry several times when he visited Andrew. I even took Andrew over for Mr Fry's funeral and met Kim. We spent a good half hour chatting.'

The conversation looked likely to develop and so the pair settled down at a table in the foyer. The pot of tea and plate of biscuits supplied by Janice would help to stave off Timson's hunger pangs for the time being.

Timson started. 'Mr Fry lived in a bungalow almost opposite the church and it seems that during the funeral someone broke in and stole a few items. They made an extensive search...' He paused. 'I understand that a burglary also happened here in Mr Prestwich's room. Now that in itself is not particularly odd, but some other features may link the cases.' Timson shook his head. 'Excuse me for being so vague, but this is confidential stuff.'

Janice made an anxious face. 'Yes I can tell you about Andrew's break-in and I'll help however I can. I do know that Andrew and Mr Fry worked together and that Andrew had been a pathologist. He never discussed where he worked from. I always presumed that Mr Fry held a similar top flight job… NHS or something.'

Timson nodded as he listened to Janice's thoughts on the issues. 'How did the burglary here come to light?' he said.

'It was my day off, but I know the facts well enough. Andrew went back to his room after his evening meal… around half six or quarter to seven is his usual time. All the rooms are ground floor here and Andrew's backs onto the garden. Someone had smashed the window by the handle and then opened it to climb in. They'd made a right mess… drawers pulled out cupboards rifled. A lot of stuff emptied onto the bed.'

Timson jotted a few notes onto his pad. 'What date was this?'

Janice stood to her feet and collected a diary from under the counter. 'End of February, I think.' She flicked over pages and scrolled a finger down. 'Yes, here it is. Wednesday 27th February. He'd only been out of his room for an hour or so. Police arrived quickly and did all the usual stuff but nothing came of it.'

'Taking into account Mr Prestwich's memory problems, how can you be sure what was taken?'

'Well we can't exactly, but we do keep an inventory of the ready cash that dementia patients have. We're particularly careful when they have no regular visits from relatives who would normally take charge. The evening duty nurse is certain that he'd had around £40 taken.'

Janice sighed and sat back into her chair. 'Strange though, you see Andrew kept his wallet in a trinket dish on a table by the window.' She gave a shrug. 'It must have been the first thing they found when they climbed in. They still searched through everything though, so perhaps they thought there'd be more cash hidden somewhere else.'

'You're saying *they* when you talk about the burglar. I know we always seem to use that phrase as though presuming there was more than one thief. But I'm picking up that you seem certain on that.'

'Oh yes. The police came back the next day and did a thorough outside search. I was back on duty then. They found two sets of shoe prints in the border outside the window. The window pane had been taped over with that silver coloured sticky tape. The policeman said they'd done it to deaden the sound. He said it was a professional method for an otherwise junkie style break-in.'

'Sound thinking,' Timson muttered as the thoughts of the use of the same tape on Lenny Gill came to him. The abandoned roll found in Cappelli's hotel room also flagged up in his mind. 'Mr Prestwich had a lucky escape.' Timson added in the same low tones.

Janice heard the remark but said nothing.

'Anything else missing?'

'Well as I told Kim at the funeral, Andrew lost his address book and in his muddled state he's convinced himself the burglars took it. In point of fact it disappeared a few days before that. He had us all searching for it.'

'Okay. You mentioned that Mr Prestwich has no regular contact with relatives.'

Janice gave another nod. 'That's right. There's only a small family group and no one has been to see him in all the time he's been here apart from his nephew Bernard. I didn't know, but Bernard told me that some of the family emigrated to Australia years ago and so I guess that's why no one visits.'

'When did Bernard visit last?'

'Oh he's only been the once. I'd never heard of him until then.' She flicked through the pages of the desk diary again and quickly landed on the relevant date.

'Here we are: Friday 22nd February so a few days before the break-in. I made them a pot of tea.'

'You say his relatives didn't keep in touch?'

'No, not at all. That one visit from Bernard is the only one.'

'From Australia you say?' Timson raised his eyebrows at the thought. 'Do you have a record of Bernard's details?'

'Yes it's all here.' She pushed the book across for him to examine. 'He's written it in himself. We don't do an ID check. It's never been thought necessary and anyway with him being a nephew...' Janice smiled. 'They soon got chatting away and Andrew even recognised Bernard, which is a rare event with how his mind has gone.'

Timson narrowed his eyes with suspicion as he examined the scant details. The record showed that Bernard had spent an hour and a half of that morning with Uncle Andrew.

The name *Bernard Prestwich* had been entered legibly into the book but the address was quite the opposite. The best interpretation Timson could make of it read as:

27 Worraloada, Fakitown, Melbourne, Aus.

Timson instinctively but discretely shook his head whilst keeping his thoughts to himself. He didn't want to embarrass the pleasant natured nurse, but the address was obviously false. Another thought came to mind. 'I see you have a CCTV system. Would Bernard

Prestwich's visit be on tape?'

Janice stuck out her bottom lip. 'Well the tapes run on slow and the policy is that we only keep them for a month before reusing. I'm sure we'll still have it.' She returned to the counter and momentarily disappeared from view as she rummaged beneath. After a few seconds she surfaced, placed a green bound book on the worktop and opened the pages. 'You're in luck,' she quickly declared. 'Tape 26.'

Timson joined Janice at the counter and threw in another question as she now explored a cupboard behind her for the tape. 'How about other cameras covering the outside which might have caught the burglars?' he said.

Janice turned, tape in hand, 'no, the police thought of that one too. The CCTV only covers the entrance.'

She slotted tape 26 into the player and fast-forwarded through to a time setting prior to Bernard Prestwich's recorded visit. She pressed the play button and the pair looked upwards at the wall mounted TV screen as a colour image showed a fairly reasonable picture of the back of her own head.

'God… I needed my roots doing,' she commented as they watched, necks craning upwards.

In addition to Janice's head, the counter, reception area, glass front entrance doors and some perception of the car park beyond were all visible. There was no sound recorded with the images and they watched in silence for a few moments until a car pulled onto the car park. The driver's door opened and with each step closer to the entrance the grainy outline of a man came increasingly into focus.

Timson made up his mind even before the door opened. As the figure sauntered, smiling to the counter he was left with no doubt. Cappelli had altered little since that newspaper photograph.

'Benedict bloody Cappelli,' he said.

Janice turned to him, her face reddening.' No, that's Bernard Prestwich.' Her faltering voice gave away her own developing suspicions on the issue.

Timson did not dwell on the matter. He was sure that the circumstances would result in a tightening up of security anyway. He threw in a question though. 'So the address book went missing between Bernard's visit and the burglary then?'

Janice reddened some more. 'Er, yes that would be right.'

'Is Mr Prestwich in? I'd like a quick look inside his room.'

'He's having his lunch now but I'm sure it'll be okay for a quick look.'

Janice, keys in hand, led the way along the ground floor corridor passing a number of identical green painted doors and stopping outside number 12. A small aluminium mount was affixed to the door alongside the numeral. Slotted inside this a white cardboard name tag spelled the occupant's name: Mr Andrew Prestwich.

The door swung inwards and the nurse stood back gesturing for the detective to lead the way. Timson hesitated at the threshold, preferring to eye the space from the corridor for a moment.

Andrew Prestwich's clock on the mantel shelf caught his eye. He'd only ever come across one like it once before. He ran through the chain of events as his eyes stayed riveted onto the clock. Geoff Fry's own stolen clock had been seized by the police when Kim pointed it out at Lenny's murder. The Scenes of Crime Officer, Angela Hewitt had taken possession of it as it formed part of the evidence chain. It linked the murdered Lenny Gill to Kim's father's burglary. Now Timson found himself staring at an identical clock which had also been in the possession of another of Porton Down's retired top men. It was an odd coincidence.

A blurred part memory started to come back as Timson's eyes stayed glued onto the clock. The awful sight of Angela Hewitt lying spread-eagled on the office floor lit up inside his head like a firework. Some of the minor details of the dreadful episode had been erased by the delirium which had followed. But as he gaped, open-mouthed at Prestwich's identical timepiece the death scene began to crystallise sharply, complete with all that missing detail – *the entire front of the clock on Hewitt's desk had glistened with a misting of clear liquid.*

Timson looked away for a moment as he plunged deeper into his subconscious: *Droplets had also been speckled onto the woodwork where the clock had rested… too far from Angela's body to have been contamination from her death throes.* THE CLOCK HAD KILLED ANGELA. The clock was the source of the nerve agent.

Timson held his left arm outwards barring Janice's way into the room. He reached forward and pulled the door closed without saying a word. His hunch now snowballed rapidly down a steep, snow covered mountain. If Geoff Fry's clock was indeed capable of killing Angela Hewitt then this one was equally lethal.

'Keep this room locked?' he ordered. 'No one is to enter. I mean NO ONE and that includes Mr Prestwich.'

Janice made a confused face. 'Okay… but the cleaner is due to do it today.'

'NO… no cleaners. NO ONE AT ALL until further notice.' He turned to look at Hopkins; the seriousness of the situation intensified his expression.

'Okaaay…?' the nurse said, stretching out the second syllable. It turned the word into a question which matched the two vertical worry lines furrowed into her forehead. Surprise joined her confusion at the detective's sudden sharpness. She locked the door and led Timson back to the reception area. 'I'd better speak to my manager. I'm not sure what's going on here.'

'Sorry,' Timson added his apology as he took a chair. He recognised that his instructions, although well-meant came over harshly. 'Could you tell me how Mr Prestwich acquired the clock on his mantel piece?' The question was fired quickly. He needed to deter the participation of anyone who may not be so helpful. He wanted answers.

'His CLOCK?' Janice's bewilderment seemed to increase tenfold with everything Timson said. 'Well…' she started. 'I do remember it.

Andrew didn't get much post at all. Royal Mail delivered it. The correspondence said that he'd won it in a competition. He did enter a lot of crossword contests and that sort of thing. He couldn't remember entering, but with how his memory had gone that wasn't unusual.'

Timson knew he could not allow the second clock to remain, even though involving the authorities would expose his vigilante enquires. Janice allowed him to use the reception telephone to make a couple of urgent calls. One was to Porton Down's Microbiological Research Establishment. The other, an update to the local detective inspector included an apology for trespassing on his patch without permission.

The gravity of the warnings he gave were, he hoped, sufficient to convey the seriousness of the situation. He did not intend hanging around until the authorities arrived. With thanks given to Nurse Hopkins he headed for his car. He tossed his clipboard over onto the passenger seat and started the engine. He needed to make another phone call and was not prepared to use the nursing home's line for this one.

FORTY SIX

DC DAN CHEESEMAN had two days off ahead of him. He intended using the time to indulge in one of his favoured pastimes – lying full stretch on the sofa watching TV. There were no feelings of guilt for leaving the sinking ship. The way that Special Branch had side-lined the CID over the affair at Doug Taylor's house strengthened his *well-up-yours-then* resolve. Taylor and Harding's situation worried him though, especially after yesterday's TV broadcast.

Cheddar did not like gardening or housework and so his divorce five years before brought with it a culture shock. The many tasks now added to his daily routine were things previously taken for granted. He'd always been good at ironing, but never managed to master the washing machine. Last night's take-away cartons would remain on the kitchen worktop until a trip out to the dustbin became completely unavoidable. His new fitness regime had faltered after one day and he blamed Doug Taylor for this. His decision to have no beer for a week wasn't working out. He was now obliged to pay a visit to the Crown pub each evening in case Taylor needed to call again. "You cannot enter a pub and not drink beer," he had told himself.

The lunchtime news on the TV showed images of the new Prime Minister, John Major, with a recording of his earlier speech, but the spiralling events had diverted Cheddar's mind from politics. The ringing telephone made him hit the TV off button. A call-out to work would always be a possibility and official days-off were no exception. He feared the worst as he heaved himself up from the sofa.

Cheeseman answered in a guarded tone. He could usually put a name to a voice even on the phone and that southern accent had a familiar ring, but he couldn't identify it.

'It's Reg Timson Ched… from Exeter… been a long time mate.'

The name made Cheeseman raise his eyebrows. 'Hell fire Reg, I've heard a little of what's happened to you… sounds awful, but I thought you'd still be in hospital!'

'I escaped this morning. I'm fine, but there are a few things going on mate. Pete Lacey found me your number… and before you say it… yes, I know we should be careful on the phone. I figured you're the only person likely to know how to get hold of Doug Taylor. I had to take a chance on your home phone being safer than the one at work.'

Cheddar scratched his head. The doubtful security of his own phone was one of the reasons he arranged for Taylor to ring him in the pub, but there seemed no option. 'I'm all ears Reg,' he reluctantly said.

Taylor and Harding parked the Yamaha in an out-of-the-way Ullapool back street with their crash helmets locked onto the seat bracket before setting off toward the shops. The place felt several degrees warmer than the coastline around Gruinard Bay and even this early in the season it looked busy. It was clearly a hub for hikers, climbers and ramblers and looked likely to provide most of the things they needed. An outdoor clothing store kitted them out with a couple of changes of warm weatherproof clothing before they split into different directions. Taylor would take on the car-job whilst Kim would track down the other gear.

Taylor's first port of call was a newsagent's where he hoped to grab a copy of the local weekly rag which may just include ads for second hand cars. Along with this copy of the Ullapool News he also splashed out on a notepad and biro.

The North West Pioneer store in West Argyle Street looked a good starting point for Kim. She quickly dropped into shopping mode and set off along the aisles of camping and outdoor pursuit equipment. By half past twelve and with the shopping mission well under way several pencil lines had been scored through items on the list.

Taylor was disappointed with the number of local car adverts in the Ullapool News – a measly ten and none suitable. He ran his eyes over the shop's cork-backed noticeboard checking out the free adverts and jotted the particulars of three potential cars onto his note pad. After checking a few more likely shops for similar ads he made his way to the telephone box on the corner of Shore Street. His list did not look that promising and showed just four cars worthy of a phone call. An additional draw-back existed in that the seller was likely to be out at work and Taylor needed a car pronto. He tried a couple of the numbers without answer before he spotted a card tucked in behind the Perspex of the phone box's information board.

'This looks more like it,' he said to himself tapping out the phone number of *Ulla Motor Pool.* A young lady answered.

The car plot was a one hundred yard walk from Taylor's phone box and held six cars in stock. Bangers might have been an overall description, but they were all taxed, MoT'd and cheap.

The manager, Debbie, greeted Taylor with a smile and waved an open hand over at her assortment of *good runners*. 'Keys are in them if you want to start any up. You'll get a three months guarantee with anything that's over £1000.'

The one car which took his fancy, a 1981 Vauxhall Cavalier looked in better nick than the one he'd owned a couple of years back. With six months MoT, two months tax and a recent service the advertised £450 seemed reasonable. A guarantee didn't interest him. A little haggling seemed par for the course when the cash appeared from his pocket. The price of £420 with half a tank of petrol quickly closed the deal. His current insurance would cover him.

He drove the car the short distance back to their agreed rendezvous and parked up. Kim was sitting at a table inside the Forge Café surrounded with bags and boxes. She was leafing through a recently purchased copy of *The Powerboat and RIB* magazine. In front of her was a now empty tea mug, a folded and as yet unread copy of the Scottish Daily Mail and two packs of sandwiches. One pack was empty. 'Couldn't wait any longer, I was starving,' she said.

Taylor nodded down at Kim's boating magazine. 'Doing a bit of swotting?'

She made a comical expression of apprehension – bared teeth and rolled eyes. 'Yes, it could come in handy if we do actually make it out onto the open sea. How've you got on with the car?'

He held up the keys. 'A Cavalier…seems okay. How about you?'

Taylor opted to eat his sandwiches on the move as he wanted to get back. Kim summarised on her success with the shopping as they carted the bags out to the car park and loaded up. She quickly ran her eyes over the car and gave an approving nod. More positive comments were made during the short drive to where the Yamaha was parked.

'Looks and sounds a bargain for that money.' She planted a kiss onto Taylor's cheek before climbing out and unfastened her helmet from its retaining cable.

'You carry on at your own pace,' Taylor said through the open window as Kim pulled on her helmet. 'I'll only slow you down in this. No doubt you'll overtake me on the way.'

Taylor started off, leaving a small cloud of blue smoke behind as Kim mounted the bike, turned the key and pushed the button. The bike started, but once again not healthily. A possible breakdown was now on her mind – disastrous in these circumstances! She remembered the sign for *Vin's Motorcycle Repairs* on the way into Ullapool and decided to get the problem checked out.

Vin, mid-thirties, overall clad and with an Elvis hairstyle stood in front of the roller shutter doors of his single storey pre-fab workshop. He eyed Kim with interest as she rode the Yamaha onto the cobbled forecourt and pulled up in front of him, engine ticking over and toes on the ground.

Vin dropped his half smoked cigarette down onto the cobbles and pressed his boot onto it.

'Can I help?'

'It's been a bit sluggish starting… battery I think. It let me down the other day, but it's a newish bike and it's not been that cold. I can't understand it. I wondered if you might run the tester across it.'

Vin raised his eyebrows as Kim climbed off and pulled the bike onto its stand. The woman seemed to know something about bikes. He returned from the workshop with his battery analyser – a hand held gadget with a meter, buttons and trailing cables.

Kim took off her helmet and watched as Vin quickly removed the bike's seat. He probed his fingers amongst the cables easing them to one side allowing access to the metal contact lugs. The analyser's meter needle flicked firmly over to the right as he pressed the red and the black copper tips down onto the positive and negative connections.

Vin's first word: 'Good,' was followed quickly by a confused: 'Hmm… a slight power drain. Not much at all, but overnight in cold weather it could flatten the battery.' He looked up and ran his eyes over the bike's controls. 'Lights haven't been left on?'

Kim shook her head. 'No, it's played up over the last two nights and that's with a couple of good runs as well.'

The mechanic fiddled some more with the cabling and bent in closer for a better look. As he straightened up his expression had become even more perplexed. 'There's some non-standard wiring fitted, I can see it above the gearbox. You've not had an alarm put in have you?'

Kim shook her head again. 'No, they offered me a factory one as an option but I didn't bother. I certainly wouldn't have a Mickey Mouse one put in.'

Vin got to his haunches and shone a torch into the recess under the battery. 'It's all very tight, but there's definitely something wired in. Shall I fetch it out?'

Kim joined in with the puzzled face competition and gave a nod of consent. 'Please do.'

It took Vin some time to gain proper access but eventually the cause of the power drain came on show. Self-tapping screws had been fixed into the thick insulation of the main power cables. A pair of small red and black wires led away to a two inch square plastic transformer/charger. This was taped to and separately wired into another rectangular bar-of-soap sized device.

Vin unscrewed the self-tappers and then forcibly ripped the rest of the hodgepodge out. 'Damned strange,' he said as he handed it all to Kim. 'Maybe a boyfriend who doesn't trust you or something? Looks suspiciously like a tracking device to me.'

'Something like that,' she replied, deciding that the least she said the better.

Kim declined Vin's suggestion of a drink later that evening with smile. 'Must press on sorry, heading back down South now.'

Vin wouldn't take any payment for the work. 'Cost me nothing… strange though,' he added as Kim climbed back on.

A new email had been generated on the computer screen at New Eltham in London:

Mobile 0532167258: Signal lost at 14.27 Thursday 21st March 1991.

FORTY SEVEN

TAYLOR had been expecting Kim to quickly pass him by and as the minutes ticked on he started to wonder where she'd got to. He pulled into a lay-by and made a grab for the sandwiches and the newspaper Kim had bought. He intermittently checked the car's rear view mirror as he munched his way through the cheese and pickle on brown and started to worry. There was only the one route back to Gruinard Bay and so she would have to pass him. The thought of the motor cycle's poor starting came to mind.

His half-hearted newspaper reading became more focussed when the article on page four reached out and grabbed his attention.

Police Hunt Bikers.

Police took an unusual step yesterday by asking the public to look out for two motorcyclists. The couple may be connected to a shooting incident in the village of Yarnstall in Staffordshire on Monday 18th March. The man and woman were seen near to the incident riding a red Yamaha 850 motor cycle registered number H32NJY. Police ask that they be notified of sightings immediately and state that the couple should not be approached.

'Christ… that's all we need he grumbled as he started up the engine.

He turned the car around and set off back towards Ullapool. It would be stupid to drive all the way back to The Lodge if she *had* broken down and this latest twist threw even more possibilities into the mix. They'd parked the Yamaha in an out of the way corner for their shopping trip to lessen the chances of a sharp-eyed cop spotting it. The publishing of the registration number in the national newspapers effectively engaged the wider public on the case. A distinct possibility now existed that Kim had been detained.

Taylor backtracked half a mile and was travelling along one of the few straight stretches of road when a mirror check caught sight of a distant speck. The image of a motorcycle heading in toward Ullapool rapidly grew in size as it bore down on the rear of the Cavalier at 95 mph. Taylor blinked in astonishment at the frightening speed and bumped his nearside wheels up onto the grass verge to give the crazy rider and pillion some more of the narrow road. The car physically jolted as the blur screamed past and the Doppler effect dragged its deafening high revving engine note down an octave. In no time it became the same sized speck as when he'd first seen it – then it was gone.

'Bloody maniac,' he shouted as he pulled back onto the road. A moment of worry entered his mind. Kim handled a motorcycle better than anyone he knew, but with idiots on the road….

Kim saw the oncoming two-up motor bike a little over a mile outside Ullapool. She'd become even more untrusting since discovering the tracker but a motorcycle being ridden by a madman was not particularly uncommon to her.

The way the rider slammed on his brakes and initiated a shuddering slow-down as the two bikes passed each other was unusual though. Her eyes glanced down several times at the mirror as she continued to draw away. She seized each decreasing image like a separate photograph and unscrambled what it all meant: *A skidding halt with the back wheel slewed around and the machine almost facing back up the road. A two word conversation and a half pointed hand. A brutal two-feet high wheelie start. A heads-down, asphalt burning piece of acceleration.*

She instantly knew that this was part of it. They were after her.

She kicked the bike down a gear and twisted the throttle around to its maximum in one flick of the wrist. Her front wheel lifted as she accelerated from 65 mph up to 90 in the blink of an eye. She held the bike steady for a moment watching the chaser in her rear view. She was testing him, watching how he was coping, trying to identify the blurred outline of the bike.

Her puzzled frown soon gave way to astonishment as she accepted that the following bike was catching her. The Yamaha's engine note started to climb as she pinched the throttle further round and the speedo needle fluttered towards 110 mph. With another flick of the eyes down onto the vibrating mirror she recognised the outline. A Kawasaki Tomcat ZX-10 – a 1000cc bike with a top speed of 165mph. If she was going to win this race and survive it would have to be on skill alone.

A straight stretch of road lay ahead. Beyond this she knew that the terrain changed significantly – twisting, winding, climbing and descending. A series of bad potholes were randomly strewn and any one of these could spell death at such speeds.

Another hazard now showed itself 400 yards into the distance as an approaching car rounded the first bend where the landscape changed so significantly. Split seconds flashed by before she was close enough to identify Taylor in the Cavalier. He'd surely recognise her bike and work out the situation.

She concentrated as she closed in on the tight right-hander, working out the best line of attack for the bike, eyeing the upcoming camber and looking out for potholes.

'Jesus Christ,' Taylor spluttered as he determined the speed of the oncoming Yamaha. His added comment came within the same breath that he recognised the bike and Kim. 'What the hell are you doing woman.' The sight of the following Kawasaki hurtling into the bend and catching up on Kim gave him some of the scenario. The long barrelled gun which the pillion passenger rested one-handed onto the shoulder of the rider provided the terrifying fuller facts.

Kim banked over at forty-five degrees to take the right hander in the self-same instant that Taylor pulled the car around the bend. Her crash helmet blurred past within inches of his driver's door.

His eyes locked onto the oncoming Kawasaki as it started to bank for the corner. Another snatched glimpse of the gun came as the pillion passenger levelled it at Kim.

Taylor gritted his teeth and then purposefully nudged the steering wheel right-hand down with the merest of tugs. The action caused only the slightest of twitches in the Cavalier's line as it left the bend, but the perfect timing spooked the oncoming Kawasaki rider. An instinctive reaction triggered a tiny yank of the handlebars and a minor easing of the throttle. The gunman's hand involuntarily jerked just as the trigger was pulled. The unmistakable crack of gunfire punched the air regardless of the silencer and engine racket. The weapon lifted even more from its supporting shoulder with the recoil as the 9mm bullet flew harmlessly into the sky. The rider regained full control, took the bend and started to open up the throttle again.

Kim's skill added yards to her lead through the series of bends which followed. The Kawasaki's extra raw power could never compete with her on this type of terrain as she leant in at impossible angles and pushed the bike to its limits. A sudden flash of sunlight upon the roof of a slow moving waggon several bends ahead was *not* what she wanted. She rammed the gear pedal down into third. The rev counter momentarily shot around to 8000 rpm and into the red section. She lay low across the tank taking up the racing position, banking left, then right, then left again. A cloud of diesel preceded the back of the waggon. A check of the mirror showed the heads of the chasers two bends behind. She inched out to the offside of the road, looking and getting a view to overtake. Apart from Taylor there had not been a single oncoming vehicle, but now was not the time to take chances. ALL CLEAR and maximum throttle up to fourth gear as the engine's power peaked. A mirror check showed that the chaser *was* taking chances and his overtaking of the waggon *didn't* include that vital last moment check for oncoming traffic. He got away with it and hunched his shoulders lower as he drew even more power from the massive engine with slight turn of his right wrist.

The landscape now took on a different shape, flattening and straightening. Kim maxed the bike out in fifth gear. The engine screamed for mercy as the speedo topped 130 mph, but the juddering mirror started to fill with the shape of the Kawasaki as it closed in. The gun now rested back on the shoulder, but any shots would be more by instinct than design. It gave all the more reason to get closer.

A bullet smacked through the bike's front fairing causing a slight tug on the handlebars. A chunk of carbon fibre wheeled away into the air.

One medium left hander lay up ahead before the miles of mostly straight roads to Inverness. Kim knew that her last chance to shake them off would be if she could take the junction which also lay beyond this bend. Here, the A835 met with the lesser A832. This was the route back towards the coast and Gruinard Bay. It was a full right-angle, a complete ninety degree turn carrying the A832 via a bridge across a ravine where the Abhainn Droma stream flowed fifty feet below. She fixed her eyes and mind on what she had to do. She calculated how long she could maintain this speed before she had to slow and alter attitude for the first left hander.

She shoved out onto the road's offside and in the same moment jarred back in, almost clipping the verge. A puff of smoke and a spray of gravel lifted from the road surface in front as a bullet ripped into the tarmac. Chippings peppered her visor and the bike's windshield. She leant into the left hander, footrest almost touching down as she pressed the bike and her skill to the utmost. A check of the blurring mirror showed the Kawasaki fighting to compete as the rider crazily forced more power from the motor and leant into the bend. Kim straightened the bike and took in all the detail of the upcoming junction. NO TRAFFIC – DECISION TIME – THE STRAIGHT ROAD AHEAD OR THE RIGHT ANGLE ONTO THE BRIDGE?

The point of no return was yards away. Kim was now bolt upright and still touching 80 mph. She needed fierce braking if she was going to fling the bike into the bend.

The handlebars dived down hard over the front wheel as her right fingers heaved back on the brake lever. She felt her body lifting from the seat with the G-force of the intense deceleration. Careful feathering in of the rear brake with the sole of her right boot pulled the speed down some more. Another mirror check showed the

Kawasaki had left the bend but was completely out of position. The pillion rider's gun pointed skywards as he fought to hang on. The rider wrestled for control as a wheel wobble set in. His only option was to keep a straight line and take the A835.

Kim touched at the rear brake again and then threw the Yamaha into the ninety degree turn to the right. It was incredible that the bike could lean so far from the vertical and still stay under control. The tyres bit down into the tarmac pulling on every ounce of adhesion. A shudder pulsated through the machine, signalling to her that she'd reached the absolute limit – a hair's breadth from disaster.

She straightened up and twisted on the throttle, leaving the bridge under full power, but gave one more glance down at the mirror. The wheel wobble had ripped control from the rider. His foolish attempt to follow Kim into the right hander had brought about a lethal ending to the situation. The bike was in the air turning over and over. The two figures – black leathers and helmets – had been flung into a writhing blur of flailing arms and legs. The entire spinning mass crashed through the wooden fencing in the centre of the bridge. The Kawasaki's engine note leapt up to a high pitched scream as it disappeared down into the ravine along with the two smashed bodies.

Kim slowed to a stop, putting down one foot to hold the bike upright as she looked back. The orange glow of flame down below preceded a mushroom of smoke which quickly drifted up to the bridge and then carried on skywards. There were no witnesses.

Blue-smoke generating gear changes followed Taylor's handbrake turn as he thrashed the living daylights out of the tired old Cavalier. He made a decent job of covering the miles which had grown between him and the motorcycles, only overtaking one vehicle during the impossible game of catch-up – a lorry some good way back along the road. The sight of the thick pall of smoke which now rose in the distance worried him.

As he rounded the left hand bend to take in the sight of the bridge junction with the A832 he worried some more. The bridge fencing was shattered. A twenty feet gap had been torn open, broken staves and wooden posts hung precariously out over the edge. A fierce fire blazed fifty feet below. He drove onto the bridge, stopping adjacent to the gap for a view through the passenger window. His heart pounded as he took in the information that the tangled remains at the heart of the flames had been a motor cycle.

The image he caught in the corner of his eye accompanied the note of the Yamaha's engine. He looked up as Kim pulled alongside his driver's window. 'I'm okay, but they must be dead; we'd better beat it.'

The reflection of the Vauxhall Cavalier remained in Kim's mirror throughout the slow cruise back to The Lodge. The fact that she felt physically sick was not because the motorcyclists had been killed – they were, after all, intent on killing her. It was more the sheer overdose of adrenaline coupled with the entire terrifying sequence of events.

Half past three arrived as Kim pulled in through the open gates to The Lodge and coasted down the drive. Taylor followed suit. By the time he joined her in the lounge she had stripped down to her underwear. Her crash helmet, leathers and T-shirt lay dumped on the floor. She was soaked in sweat and shaking as he put his arms around her and held her tightly.

FORTY EIGHT

IT WAS seven o'clock and dark when Kim emerged from the bedroom to join Taylor in the kitchen. She was bare legged, with his chunky roll neck sweater hanging halfway down her thighs. Her fingertips poked from the cuffs. He stood in against the cooker stirring soup in a saucepan. She put her arms around him from behind and pressed the side of her head against his back.

'Okay?' he asked, still stirring.

'Will be, yes.'

The pile of wiring ripped out from Kim's bike lay on the worktop.

'I've had a good look,' Taylor said nodding at the tangle. 'I've read some Special Branch paperwork on the idea recently. It's essentially a mobile phone. The battery, screen, keypad and speaker have all been removed to make it smaller. As you've already worked out it was running full time from your motorcycle battery hence the poor starting. Secret Service agencies around the world are using the idea. The usual function is as a simple listening bug. It'll be legally registered with its own phone number on the network, but it's always switched on. Whoever wants to listen in simply rings the number and it automatically connects as if someone has answered the call.'

He raised his eyebrows as he continued with the explanation. 'That wasn't the intention with this one though, as they'd never hear a thing because of the engine noise. You see it also serves as a good tracking device. The network provider would be able to pinpoint the actual phone mast it's hooked up to. Connection to a single mast would be enough to give a rough bearing. If the device entered a built up area with several masts, then the location could be worked out fairly precisely.'

Kim's expression indicated her knowledge on this part. 'Hmm, but surely the only people who could access that information would be police or security services?'

Taylor poured the soup out into a couple of bowls on the worktop. 'Yes, but money buys info. If they've got someone on the inside or they'd worked out how to hack the system then anything's possible.'

He nodded down at one of the bowls of soup and Kim took the hint. He followed her into the living room with his own bowl and continued with the explanation as they settled at the table. 'Mobile phone coverage hasn't reached much of the Scottish Highlands yet. The tracker must have been installed either while the bike was at your apartment or in the garage at my house on Sunday night. I can't see MI5 being responsible, it happened too quickly. Nelson or the people he's working with must be behind it. Whoever it is didn't locate us until we got close to Ullapool. It's probably the only place for miles around with a mobile phone mast. The motorcyclists were probably assigned the job of finding us as soon as the mobile phone connected to Ullapool's mast. They'd been sent in from somewhere outside Ullapool.'

'So the tracker stopped as soon as the mechanic disconnected it from the battery,' Kim said.

'Yes, it hadn't got its own battery but we're safe here. Mr Boyle pointed out to us that there was no mobile phone coverage for miles around. So they'd never get a fix on us here anyway.'

Taylor took the empty bowls back and left them in the sink. Kim stood from the table, her face almost touching the window pane as she peered through. A nearly full moon and cloudless sky allowed the silhouette of Gruinard Island to be picked out. Her hot breath condensed on the glass, misting it. 'Calm as I've seen it so far,' she whispered.

She flinched, startled by Taylor's hand now in around her waist unaware that he had come back into the room.

'Okay.' He whispered the word, accepting the inevitable and then checked his watch – twenty minutes past seven. 'We'll go tonight, but I must make a phone call.'

Taylor soon arrived at the pull-in alongside the solitary vintage red phone box. The remote place lay close to a branch in the road leading off to the village of Laide. The dim yellow bulb inside the box was the only light for miles. It seemed doubtful that he would see or be seen by other members of the human race, but to be careful he had used the car. The bike was now hot property since the newspaper article. He fished in his pocket for the change he'd put to one side during the day.

The phone in the bar of the Crown started to ring at seven thirty-five. Landlord Alf recognised Taylor's voice without the need for an introduction and gave a single knowing head nod to Cheeseman. 'Want to take it upstairs Ched?'

Cheddar rested his pint of Theakston down onto the bar before squeezing through the narrow doorway to the stairs.

The two men had tales to swop. This pooled information would give a better understanding of the bigger picture and even an insight into what lay ahead.

'Jesus.' Cheddar breathed the word as Taylor recounted the tale of the fatal motorcycle chase and the tracker attached to Kim's bike.

'The clock which Gill pinched from Mr Fry's bungalow was a cleverly put together bugging device,' Cheddar said. 'It sounds as though it was much the same idea as the one you've described attached to Kim's bike. Its prime function though, would be to listen into conversations involving Mr Fry or visitors to the house. Presumably the aim would be to find clues which might lead to whatever Mr Fry was protecting.'

Taylor gave a mumbled 'Okay'.

Cheddar continued. 'Seems that the clock had been delivered through the post as a free gift or competition prize and even relied on the home owner unknowingly installing it himself. It then sat there plugged into Mr Fry's electricity in his living room picking up every conversation and one half of every phone call he had. It also doubled as a tracker in the same manner that the motorcycle bug did.

When Lenny pinched it and took it home they pretty quickly knew where to go.'

Taylor interrupted with some doubt in his voice. 'Why have they gone around to Lenny's and tortured him for information though? What's suggested to them that it was anything more than a tin pot burglary? How did they know that he had been sent to look for special documents?'

Cheddar related some of the tale given to him by Timson. 'The identical clock which Reg discovered in Mr Prestwich's room must have been installed at about the same time, or even before Mr Fry's clock. Prestwich and Fry had both been targeted. There's little doubt that the story Cappelli spun Prestwich was earwigged through the clock. Cappelli made a phone call to his newspaper requesting research on Geoff Fry and probably gave away his real identity to the clock when he did that. Nelson and his team knew all along that Cappelli was tangled up with it and that he'd put Lenny up to the burglary. When Lenny took the clock home with him as well, it made their job even easier as it told them exactly where he was. Presumably they tortured him because they believed he'd found the file.'

'Must be,' Taylor said. 'But why didn't they take the clock away with them after they'd killed him. They left it sitting on Lenny's mantelpiece waiting to be recovered by the police.'

Taylor paused for a moment as more of the jigsaw slotted into place and then answered his own question. 'We fell right into their trap. They were listening in when Ken Grainger, Kim and I were investigating the murder scene. They knew the clock would be taken back to the nick as evidence. They also knew it would run on battery for some time and that they might even be able to continue to tune into detective's conversations at the police station. When someone even plugged it into the mains they might as well have been sitting in the bloody office.'

Cheddar agreed with the theory. 'That figures, Reg has explained to me that he spoke with Ken Grainger about Cappelli while they were in the office together. They even discussed his hotel and room number. That conversation must have been earwigged through the clock and that's how they nearly got their hands on Cappelli.'

'When did Cappelli visit Prestwich?' Taylor asked.

'Reg was able to pin point that from the home's CCTV and the visitor records. It was Friday 22nd February.'

Taylor took a moment as he recalled dates and made calculations. 'Okay, Geoff Fry died around the 28th February, hardly a week after Cappelli had conned Dr Prestwich and realised he was onto something big. We'll never prove it but Cappelli probably put pressure on Mr Fry. He had a heart condition remember… perhaps that was the final straw. He'd been using the phone when he died.'

Cheddar was slow to agree with Taylor on this possibility. 'Well maybe,' he said. 'But there's another feature of these clocks which I haven't yet discussed. Reg Timson has had to draw on some seriously big favours to get to this information. You see the clock killed Angela Hewitt.'

There was silence from Taylor as he tried to comprehend this.

'It wasn't just a bugging and tracking device,' Cheddar continued. 'It had another nasty sting in its tail. The mechanism from an automatic air freshener had been included inside the casing and connected via some altered circuitry into the mobile phone innards. If an earwigged conversation led the listener to the opinion that his plan was becoming compromised he could take some pretty drastic action. It simply required the pressing of a series of pre-programmed digits into the listening phone. When the phone unit in the clock receives that radio command it would operate the air freshener's motor. That releases an aerosol type spray through an aperture at the front of the clock.'

Taylor was a step ahead of Cheddar's explanation. 'But it wasn't Lavender or Forest Pine which squirted into Angela Hewitt's face.'

'No Boss, the air freshener capsule contained Sarin nerve gas.'

'God above.' Taylor said. 'Why kill Angela; how had she

jeopardised their plan?'

'Angela Hewitt took a call from a witness who spotted the journalist Benedict Cappelli in Exeter with a local vagrant. Angela was in the process of arranging for a patrol to quickly find them. By killing her before she told anyone else it gave them the time to get to the derelict house where the vagrant would be and hopefully get Cappelli. Cappelli wasn't there though. These bastards take no prisoners… They cut the vagrant's throat and then torched the place.'

Another few seconds of silence from Taylor's end of the phone followed as he took in the dreadful facts. The penny also dropped about Cheddar's reluctance to agree to the theory that Cappelli's phone call triggered Geoff Fry's heart attack. 'My God Ched… you're thinking that Geoff Fry may have died in the same way.'

'I'm not saying it's a certainty Boss, but his phone was off the hook. I gather the clock was nearby.'

'It was.' Taylor's voice had become a whisper.

'Perhaps best not to mention this to Kim.' Cheddar added. 'It's only a theory.'

Kim had her coat on and was ready for the outside weather when Taylor arrived back. They had decided earlier that the car must not be left on the driveway of The Lodge. A strange car could raise the suspicions of locals. The idea to hide it inside Mr Boyle's now empty boathouse did the trick. With all of the garden security lights off from their last visit, the operation went without a hitch.

They were back at The Lodge and drinking coffee by ten o'clock

FORTY NINE

AT ten minutes past ten a hired Ford Escort pulled onto the carpark of the Dundoon Hotel eight miles east of the coast and Gruinard Island. The hotel complex had been built from a series of farm buildings and cottages and formed a sizable development stretching along the roadside for a distance. Only a narrow pavement separated the actual building from the kerb. A line of trees on the opposite side of the road hid the large car park from view.

A couple of the hotel's windows showed lights, but the general look was that the place had already closed for the day. No doubt in a few weeks things would start to change as tourists and holiday makers began to appear. The two other cars taking up spaces on the car park probably belonged to staff.

After locking the car the single occupant trudged wearily across the road to the hotel's front door; it had been a long day. The man bent his knees and peered in through the front door glass catching a glimpse of a distant figure behind the bar polishing and repositioning glasses. A try of the handle gave the expected result – locked. A respectful knuckle gave a loud-enough to be heard, but soft-enough not to be intimidating tap to the door glass.

The startled manager strode over and peered suspiciously through at the figure on the other side. He would not often get customers so late in the evening during March. The suggestion of a room for the night in such circumstances was rare.

The top and bottom bolts were slid, but the security chain remained in place as the door opened up two inches. Apprehensive thoughts accompanied a frown when the stranger's healing cuts and bruises came into view. It looked as though he had been fighting.

Benedict Cappelli's cunning attained overdrive as he delivered his sob story through the gap left by the security chain. 'Sorry to trouble you. I can see that you'd already locked up for the night but I've gone and got myself lost. It's been a bad few days all round. As you can see I've been in a nasty road accident. White Van Man pulled out in front of me… wrote my car off. I was lucky to get away so lightly. I spent a night in hospital back at Inverness and now I've taken the wrong turning and the blasted car's running on vapours. The car hire people never put fuel in these things. Seeing your hotel sign appear is the only decent thing that's happened to me in a week.'

Cappelli complemented his tale with a mournful expression. 'I'd hoped I could book a room for the night.'

The manager, Mr Munroe, had been hooked when Cappelli added that last piece of soft soap. He unfastened the safety chain. 'My word you have had some bad luck. 'Where were you heading?'

Cappelli soaked up the inference given by the: *where WERE you heading rather than where ARE you heading.* He felt that he was almost home and dry as he gave his answer. 'My sister's place in Ullapool. It's the first time I've been. It took ages to get the car hire fixed up and I guess I should never have started out at night.'

'Well it's a fairly simple journey, but as you say it's a good job you pulled in here if you're low on juice. There's certainly nowhere for petrol at this time of night.'

Munroe was now hook, line and sinker. 'Settle yourself down over by the fire Mr…?

'Meigh… Ray Meigh.'

'Yes warm yourself by the fire whilst I make a room up for you. Would you be wanting a wee dram Mr Meigh whilst you wait?'

'Lovely… thank you.'

Cappelli was provided with sandwiches to accompany his wee dram before showering and nestling down in a comfortable bed for the night. He fell into a deep sleep before midnight arrived.

Taylor and Harding's chances of turning in for the night were never on their list of things to do. Most of the planning had been done when the madcap scheme was agreed upon the day before. Taylor kept the awful theory that Kim's father may have died as a result of nerve gas to himself. The idea could easily throw her completely off the rails.

They kitted themselves out in the weatherproof clothing bought during the Ullapool outing and packed all the additional gear into the back seats and floor of the RIB. Taylor lashed it down and waterproofed it with polythene sheeting.

Boyle's lifejackets had seen better days, but two new ones were ready for the launching. A pair of old waders, found inside the boat would come in handy for Taylor to cast off even though they were a little on the small size. The rope and life ring were also thrown in. Everything was set by half past eleven, but it seemed like sound thinking to wait until the locals were tucked up in bed.

At ten minutes past one Taylor released the trailer's handbrake and gave it a nudge. With a couple of grunts and some hefty pushing the wheels began to revolve over the firm but uneven turf of The Lodge's back garden. The slight gradient at this point didn't help much as the loaded boat was now a hefty weight. The task became more difficult as the wheels met the strip of pebbles which signalled the boundary of the beach. Kim joined in the pushing over the last forty feet of wet, hard packed sand up to the shoreline. They pushed the trailer out into the water until the boat's stern started to lift under its own buoyancy. Taylor tied the rope through the metal ring on the boat's bow and knotted it around a large boulder as a temporary mooring point. Kim unwound the strap winch holding the bow of the boat up on the trailer. A steady *click, click, click* came as the broad flat strap reeled out. The Angry Boyle inched its way backwards off the trailer with each *click* until it separated and started to loll back and forth with the incoming tide.

No words had been necessary up to this point as the plan had gone like clockwork. Taylor pulled hard on the rope and kept the bow of the boat nudging up against the partially submerged back of the trailer. It allowed Kim to use it as a stepping stone and clamber over the inflatable tube and into the driving seat. She watched his outline give the thumbs-up sign signalling her to start the motor. The next few minutes would be crucial. If anyone was in earshot the whole venture could be at risk. She slotted in the kill cord, pulled out the choke, turned the key, crossed her fingers and pressed the starter.

An instantaneous roar came from the motor as it fired into life. She pushed the throttle forward a little to test the response and heard it reply with an eager increase in revs. She thumbed the choke back in a little and let the motor tick over before selecting reverse and inching against the tide keeping the bow line taut.

Taylor grabbed hold of the towing knuckle of the trailer intent on quickly getting it off the beach. His expectation that this would be an easy job with all the weight removed was shattered when his first attempt nearly pulled his arm out of socket. The realisation quickly came that the now submerged road wheels had been deeply pressed down into the wet sand. The incoming tide started to engulf the entire trailer as Taylor gritted his teeth and heaved backwards. Kim watched on through the gloom unsure of the exact circumstances and frustrated that she could not help. The trailer had to be removed from the beach.

Taylor was now almost up to his waist and the backward flow of the waves threatened to take him off his feet. The freezing water bit into his hands as he took a firm double grip onto the framework. He dug both heels of his waders down deep into the sand, straightened out his arms and slowly pushed his quivering back into the job. The impossible was suddenly achieved with the additional help of a larger incoming wave and the wheels dislodged. Taylor staggered to regain his balance against the sudden momentum and then quickly pulled the rig free of the water. The wheels bounced over the hard packed sand as he ran back up the beach easily pulling it along one-handedly and disappeared into the darkness.

Kim nursed the boat gently back and forth with the occasional touch of throttle as she attempted to keep tension on the bow line.

Taylor made easy work of the next part of his task and hardly five minutes passed before he had dragged the trailer back up behind The Lodge. He threw some of the brushwood back over it and set off back to the beach.

The time took an age to go by for Kim as she feathered the throttle back and forth. Eventually she made out his figure bundling up the bow line and running back to the water's edge. He waded out to the side of the RIB and tossed the rope over down onto the passenger floor before clambering over. The boat wallowed to one side as his weight combined with the incoming waves to momentarily shift its centre of gravity. He took up his seat gasping for breath and slamming his icy hands together to help circulation.

Kim kept the motor in reverse and opened the throttle a little taking the boat steadily backwards into darker, deeper water. Taylor patted his hand down on top of hers. They exchanged gritty looks with each other and then both instinctively turned their heads in the direction of Laide. The Angry Boyle's engine note, even on tick-over seemed aggressive and strident – surely the sound would carry.

Kim pushed the gear lever through neutral and into forward. This was the first time since being a teenager that she'd done anything similar and even then nothing on this scale. Her heart pounded as she eased the throttle forward feeling the boat start to move and gather a little speed.

The difference to the swell of the sea in the deeper water became alarming as the small craft rode up each wave and then thumped back down. Clouds had blown in, the moon had all but disappeared and blackness threatened to take over the entire landscape. The smudged, almost invisible outline of the mainland blended imperceptibly with the sky. The view out to sea seemed no different. The slow heavy weight of the water rolled smoothly and silently past the boat like folds of glistening black tar as it effortlessly lifted and dropped them. Kim swallowed hard. *This was dangerous.* She glanced over at Taylor as his features fleetingly sharpened in a rare flicker of moonlight. His hair was windswept, his face wet with sea spray, but his jutting jaw proclaimed his determination to get the job done.

Kim squeezed the throttle open a little more and pulled the wheel right hand down. She watched as the flat colourless horizon started to give way to the murky outline of Gruinard Island. The ragged east facing coast could be made out from the series of white wave tops crashing onto rocks. They needed to go further out to sea before they could even guess at the position of the spit of sandbank on the southern tip.

The engine purred on for fifteen minutes pushing them further out to sea. The shape of Gruinard Island slowly altered from the memory they both still held. The new perspective lacked that daytime detail and showed as nothing more than a sketchy outline against a vague backdrop. A splash of white wave on rocks or sand made the difference. Taylor stared hard, eyes stinging from salt, hand shielding face. 'THERE,' he bellowed – his arm pointing. 'The signs… the notice boards. Can you see them? It must be the sandbank.'

It was the sandbank. The spit of sand on the southern edge of the island.

Kim looped around and slowly started to approach. 'We must be careful, there could be rocks.'

Taylor's shout of agreement went unheard on the wind as Kim fought against the current to manoeuvre the boat and edge nearer to the shore. He leaned in to her and yelled in her ear. 'Anywhere along the sandbank will be good, but as close to the main island as possible. We'll still have to drag the boat and hide it.'

Kim's overemphasised nod indicated her understanding and augmented her level of concentration. Now she was doing the pointing. 'How about there?' she bawled indicating to a patch which in the gloomy conditions appeared to be devoid of rocks.

'Okay, what's the plan?' Taylor shouted back.

'I'll go in close. Then if it still looks good I'll back off and give it some gun. I'll try to mount it up onto the beach.' She then lifted

Taylor's right hand and plonked it firmly down on the boat's "Trim" lever. 'Be ready with this and when I shout "NOW" jam it hard forward. It lifts the engine up and stops the propeller from smashing into the sand.'

Kim completed the first manoeuvre feeling the boat rock end to end on the waves as she inched as close as she dared. The beach at this point steeply shelved away into deeper water. It meant that she had to run the boat in hard. There may not be a second chance.

She back tracked thirty yards out to sea, looked over at Taylor and yelled. 'You ready for this?'

His fist gripped tightly onto the trim lever. He gave a casual nod and decisive 'Yep' through gritted teeth.

The engine snarled into life as Kim pushed the throttle lever up to the maximum. The boat's rear end sat back down into the water and the bows shot almost upright with the surge of acceleration. A white V shaped wave cut through the liquid blackness and the beach rushed toward them.

'NOW,' Kim screamed.

FIFTY

TAYLOR jammed the trim lever hard forward and in that same instant there was a bone jarring thud. The boat's rigid fibreglass hull slammed into the sand bank and skimmed on for several yards. The pair lurched forward against the dashboard as the craft jolted to a stop with the intensity of a minor car crash.

They both flopped back in their seats. They'd made it.

'Sorry,' Kim said. 'I think I overcooked it a bit.'

Taylor climbed out onto the sand. 'You did a great job, and to prove it we're here.'

The landing put them in close to where the spit of sand connected to the rocky foundations of the island. Their earlier daylight assessment through binoculars suggested that this area on the far side of the sand bar would keep the boat hidden from the mainland around Gruinard Bay. It was likely though, that a view from the shores near First Coast or Laide could still give a distant line of sight to the spot. Signs of activity on the outlawed island would set alarm bells ringing.

Taylor's wader boots scrunched down into the wet sand as he quickly got to work unloading the gear. They needed to lighten the Angry Boyle before attempting to shift it. Within ten minutes they had removed everything and stashed it in a temporary safe corner of the beach.

The boat, even minus its cargo took all of Taylor's muscle, it was a dead weight. After some trial and error attempts the two of them perfected a method of part dragging and lifting. The temperature hovered in the region of two degrees, but the biting wind chill and sea spray worsened the situation many times over. By half past three they'd dragged the craft a full thirty-five metres to the edge of the beach and hidden it amongst bushes.

They sat next to each other on a rock, heads down and panting with arms resting on knees, breath vapour curling upwards into the gloom. Sweat glistened on their faces but the plummeting temperature continued to eat into them.

A lot of work had to be done before daylight arrived, but they needed a break. Kim broke out a pack of sandwiches and flask of tea. Much of the cloud had pushed across to the mainland and onwards to the mountains. Their ten minute break benefitted from the occasional silvery flashes of moonlight. It gave them their first peek at the terrain of Gruinard Island and a half-chance at understanding the character of the place.

Evidence of rusting metal signs showed here and there. Some had survived the years of pounding storms better than others. The phrases and wording used were subtly chosen and even the partially legible signs seemed to radiate a chilling aura of menace:

DANGER OF DEATH

DO NOT LAND ON THIS ISLAND

MINISTRY OF DEFENCE PROPERTY KEEP OFF

An additional warning on several signs increased the hype:

ENTRY ONTO THIS ISLAND IS FORBIDDEN, ILLEGAL AND EXTREMELY DANGEROUS.

A scattering of the notices had been reduced to nothing more than skewed rusting stumps poking from solid concrete bases embedded into the turf and sand. One larger sign, close to where they sat, had survived relatively intact. It served as a good wind break and for this reason it was chosen as the spot for their tea break. Kim gulped at a mouthful of the hot drink and swivelled to read the still legible words. Thick streaks of brown rust had meandered downwards from the edges and bolt holes of the sign's yellowed enamel face. This one sign spelled out the whole terrifying story:

GRUINARD ISLAND

This Island is Government

property under experiment.

The ground is contaminated

with anthrax and dangerous.

LANDING IS PROHIBITED BY ORDER.

They looked away from the notice, both staring down at the sand between their feet and silently gulped more tea. The wording confirmed the passage given in the Ramblers' Association guide booklet. It also confirmed to Kim her father's part in this frightful slice of Britain's history. Geoffrey Fry's coded message told them that the island was safe to visit. The sign said the exact opposite.

Kim caught Taylor's eye and an unspoken agreement immediately went between them: *They were here now – so what the hell!* They scrambled back to their feet intent on sticking to the rest of the hare-brained plan. They needed comfort, warmth and proper rest before they could start the search for the answer to all of this.

The sparing use of their torches had nothing to do with conserving batteries. The possibility existed that someone might be peering through a distant cottage window far across Gruinard Bay and they were not taking any chances on that score.

The camouflage pattern of the small tent Kim had purchased in Ullapool would help if the right place could be found to pitch. It was identical to one she'd bought a few years back for a pop festival and she hoped this might make it a little less confusing to erect.

Any camping rules barring the pitching of tents under trees would be ignored. They needed trees to keep hidden. The night time view available to them though, inferred that the island was severely lacking in the tree department. The clump of stunted elders which they did discover was one hundred yards from where they'd landed. Taylor used some more of his muscle on the scattering of rocks and quickly produced a usable concealed space. A hectic windblown forty-five minutes of chaos followed before the tent was fastened down and the rest of their gear collected and stashed nearby.

Five o'clock arrived before they collapsed into their double sleeping bag and immediately dropped into a state of unconsciousness.

FIFTY ONE

BENEDICT CAPPELLI made an early start that Friday morning. With breakfast behind him and his bill paid on the baker's credit card, eight o'clock chimed as he left through the hotel's front door. He wandered across the road to the car park. Apparently the sun had risen, but thick cloud hid it from view and this seemed like the yardstick for the rest of the day.

The manager's helpful pencil drawn plan of the closest petrol station was tucked safely into his pocket, but the car had plenty of fuel and Cappelli wouldn't be heading for Ullapool and his non-existent sister. His real goal lay on the coast and hopefully his first sighting of Gruinard Island.

The opaque white frosting to the car's windows evidenced last night's low temperatures. He pressed the key into the door lock and opened up. He slung his bag over onto the passenger seat, grabbed the tin of de-icer from the door's side pocket and gave the front windscreen a liberal squirting. The other windows would fend for themselves as the car warmed up. He settled into the driving seat and fumbled in the gloom for the safety belt before readying himself to start the car.

The business end of a Browning 9mm pistol pressed against Cappelli's temple. The dark outline now sitting upright on the back seat nudged the gun in with a little more force, but said nothing. Oddly the barrel felt more rectangular than rounded in shape. It was a feature of most semi-automatics, created by the heavy metal casing enclosing the gun's return spring.

The shape of the weapon's muzzle was not something Cappelli concentrated on for long though. The fact that it *was* a gun and *was* undoubtedly loaded did more to focus his attention. The coldness of the metal struck through the close cropped hair above his right ear. It nudged in hard squeezing that thin and tender strip of flesh and veins which separates the skull from the skin. The forceful action made him incline his head inwards in the manner that a person will do when puzzling over something.

No words were said as his open hands progressed slowly upwards until the fingers touched against the car's roof lining. His head stayed put as though clamped in a vice, but his sight locked onto the rear view mirror. The outline of the balaclava covered head moved forward slightly in the gloom. A flash of eyes – wide, determined and menacing filled the two eye holes.

The thirty seconds of silence which followed lasted a full hour in Cappelli's mind before the single word instruction came.

'Drive.'

In the circumstances the command was predictable, but the fact that the order had been delivered by a female voice was almost as unexpected to Cappelli as the event itself.

'You know where to go,' came the follow-up command as the tip of the gun slowly dragged around to the back of his head. It momentarily parted company to reposition through the centre of the headrest and relocate in that natural hollow at the base of the skull.

Cappelli with shaking hands remained wordless as he started up, switched on the wipers and screen blower and steadily edged the car out onto the road and off toward the coast.

After a few minutes the pressure of the gun was removed and the reporter's nervous mirror checks showed that the woman had sat back into her seat.

'No false moves Cappelli.'

He did not need the warning; he'd already made up his mind on that score. 'Okay… okay,' came his shaky reply. 'But I'm not sure exactly where I'm going. It's an island off the coast. I hadn't worked out how to get to it.'

'Drive.'

At twenty minutes past eight the sea came into view. 'That must be it,' Cappelli said nodding at the distant mist-shrouded landmass.

It's called Gruinard Island.'

'Pull in here.'

The gun returned and pressed even harder into his temple as the featureless head nodded towards a lay-by. Cappelli followed his orders.

It was half past eight when Taylor zipped open the tent flap and stepped outside to look at the slate grey sky. The pair had managed around three and a half hours of poor quality uncomfortable sleep.

Taylor's first worry focussed on the possibility of someone on the mainland or in passing boats seeing them. With this in mind he nestled down between some small sand dunes and pointed Guaire's binoculars across the half a mile of slow rolling grey water which he now knew as The Minch. He turned the focus wheel as the distant ribbon of tarmac that was the A832 came into sight. A sprinkling of isolated cottages dotted its length. He could see no signs of human life other than the teeny outline of a parked car on the same layby they had used when they first arrived. It was unlikely to be connected to anything, but reinforced the wisdom of keeping their heads down. It wouldn't do for them to be spotted even by an innocent bird watcher or fresh air fiend.

After the ten minute recce he returned to the seclusion of the campsite and gave a hopeful shrug. 'Not bad, but we'll have to be careful especially if we have to go out into open spaces. There are one or two people about.'

Kim cooked up a decent breakfast of bacon, eggs, sausage and tomatoes within the tent on three Camping Gaz burners, temporarily transforming the flimsy sanctuary into a hothouse.

They kitted themselves out for the day ahead with the combat style gear and sturdy boots purchased in Ullapool. Their small rucksacks held a few provisions and equipment. They set off at half past nine without much idea of what they were actually looking for.

Cappelli had followed more instructions and now found himself shackled to the steering wheel with a pair of shiny ratchet style handcuffs. The woman's orders put the reporter in no doubt as to what to do. 'Put one cuff on your right wrist then pass the other through the steering wheel before you do the left hand.'

Her additional advice made Cappelli believe that she'd done this before. 'Tighten the left one up two more clicks,' she snapped. 'And don't try anything else.'

The handcuffing had followed a further half mile drive to where they now were. The out of the way branch from the road was a dead end which lay adjacent to a stone bridge over the River Gruinard. The short but steep gradient from the road made the point completely hidden from passing traffic – not that there had been any. No doubt the place occasionally served as a car park for river anglers although the likelihood of that, at this time and on this day, seemed slim.

Cappelli's eyes landed on the only view available to him through the windscreen – a ten feet high grass covered embankment up to the road above. He wondered if this might be the last sight that he was destined to see. His pathetic attempt to leave one half of the handcuffs loose had been as far as his escape plan developed.

The woman settled back into her seat, lifted her right hand to the back of her neck and yanked the balaclava forward and off her head. Cappelli's picture through the mirror was limited, but clearly the idea of staying anonymous had been dispensed with. *Could this be another reason for him to worry over his own prospects?*

He could see that she was blonde with an expensively fashioned bob cut with fringe. A weariness showed in those almond shaped brown eyes – the ones which flashed with forceful determination not long before. It didn't take much working out to conclude that she'd spent an uncomfortable and sleepless night waiting for him to arrive.

The reporter's limited analysis secured an overall impression of a lithe and strikingly fit young woman. Had the circumstances been different he felt sure that he would have been making a considerable effort to examine the bigger picture regarding his captor. Having already survived one determined, gun-toting attempt on his life it now seemed likely that this woman was part and parcel of the same group.

She tossed the balaclava to one side and spoke. 'You wanted a big story Cappelli. I wonder if you ever realised how big it would be. I don't think you have a clue what you've got yourself into, but now you are going to tell me exactly what you DO know.'

The square ended gun muzzle jabbed hard back into his temple again and he heard his own voice shouting inside his head: *"You are so fucking right lady."* The attempt on his life at the hotel and now THIS had underscored his ignorance of the facts many times over. An adage known as the "iceberg syndrome" compared well with the situation. A full ninety percent of the floating mass lies hidden beneath the ocean's surface. Only the tip is visible. Cappelli's delving had exposed nothing more than that tip. The tip may be as far as he would get! There seemed no point in holding back on the few facts that he did know. At least this might buy him a little more time to stare at that embankment.

The woman eased back into her seat as he began his tale.

FIFTY TWO

TAYLOR AND HARDING had quickly accepted the evidence given in the Rambler's guide that Gruinard Island had not been inhabited from around the time of WW2. The fact was corroborated by the beach signpost with the worrying use of the term "contaminated with anthrax". The Guaires' unwillingness to discuss the issue added an even more mysterious aspect.

The eerie, lifeless feeling of the place fitted with the story that no one had set foot there for almost fifty years. The ruins of the derelict cottage which they had now discovered added even more weight to this idea.

The pair stood in the blustery wind gazing at the crumbling mound. Little remained of what once, many years ago, must have been a farm cottage and family home. Only a shell had survived – walls a few metres high surrounding a mound of broken tiles and rubble from where the roof had collapsed inwards. An overgrowth of thick turf coated much of the shattered stonework. Two well established self-set trees grew from the middle.

They left the place behind after finding nothing of interest and started to make their way further inland and west of where the central highpoint rose to almost 350 feet. Occasional fragments of dry stone walls gave rise to the idea that sheep farming had provided a livelihood decades ago.

Thirty more minutes passed before they came across what appeared to be traces of a farm-type track. Again an overgrowth of turf had all but obliterated the feature, but strangely its state of dilapidation did not match that of the old cottage. Saplings and bushes sprouted, but had yet to take on a firm grip and were still saplings rather than established trees. The track also looked much wider than was to be expected. If Gruinard Island had not been farmed since WW2 it would then have been a place for a horse and cart rather than a tractor.

Taylor stopped and puzzled at this feature. He stood in the middle of the track looking down towards the west coast. 'This is a bit odd. It's far wider than you would expect, and at some stage was fairly smoothly surfaced under this grass.' He got down to his haunches and tugged at a lump of turf. He peeled back a one-foot square section. 'Look at this… hardly any roots. The grass has grown on top of few inches of soil that's blown in. It's concrete.'

Kim looked down. 'You're right it's been a makeshift roadway, probably made with a bulldozer.'

They decided to follow the route down to the sea and arrived at an open space looking out across a sandy beach. A rocky outcrop stretched into deeper water on one side. Signs of a small, makeshift and now derelict harbour could be made out. The concrete and brickwork was crumbling and discoloured, but there seemed no doubting the idea. The remnants of two ship's mooring bollards, some stone steps down into the water and corroded handrails supported the theory.

'So this must be where the boats moored when the anthrax experiments were being carried out.' Kim said.

'Yes,' Taylor agreed, but it's seen some work in the not too distant past as well. Those handrails are all pretty shot now but don't come close to the dilapidation you'd expect from nearly fifty years since the end of the war.'

'So more like in the years when dad worked for the Government in the seventies and eighties.'

'I think that would fit,' Taylor said and turned back toward the track. 'Shall we retrace our steps? This must lead somewhere if it was important enough to make a proper route.'

They set off and soon bypassed the spot where they'd first encountered the track. Within fifteen minutes the ruins of another stone block cottage and a cluster of outbuildings came into view. Taylor eased the rucksack from his back, dumped it to the ground and gazed up at the front of the building. All four walls were still standing and parts of the roof remained intact. A bush had taken root in a mortar crack on the side of the chimney and thick clumps of bright green moss grew in random patches on the brickwork. Several of the glass window panes had survived within rotted frames.

'This place has seen some use since the war as well.'

He skirted around the side taking in the remains of several outbuildings. A few dilapidated, wooden doors were still attached, each one bearing fragments of peeling, green paint. Taylor tugged at one of the doors and felt it slump in his hand. The hinges had given up supporting the weight years ago. He stepped back as it crashed out onto the ground.

'What the hell's all this?' he said as he peered inside.

Dozens of empty, two feet high plastic liquid containers lined the walls. They were stacked three high into separate numbered bays. Each bay was labelled with a faded, black painted numeral stencilled at the side. Several of the containers had toppled to the floor. The remnants of discoloured paper stickers still adhered to some.

'What is this stuff?' he said stooping for closer examination.

FORMALDEHYDE

(Aqueous) CH20 40%

S1 Poison

6 Gallons

Taylor backed off. 'Formaldehyde! What's been going on here?'

They took in the sight of the lines of containers. 'We used that stuff in the school lab,' Kim said. 'It's only harmful if you're not careful.'

Taylor's own school laboratory sessions came back. 'Yes, we preserved dead frogs in it. All this stuff's old, but it's not been here since the war.'

Kim pulled open another outbuilding door. 'More here,' she said stepping aside so that Taylor could see the rows of empty containers in their numbered bays. 'And even more still over there.' She pointed at a further crumbling door-less building.

Taylor shook his head. 'Each bay contains six of those plastic drums, the bay numbers go up into the hundreds. Whatever has been going on here? They must have used thousands of gallons.'

They took another look at the cottage itself. The back portion had survived the elements better than the front. Taylor shouldered the rotting remains of a jammed door to one side and looked upwards before stepping inside the gloom. Chunks of crumbled ceiling plaster lay everywhere. Rotted upstairs floorboards were on display, chinks of dull grey sky peeked through gaps. Rubble and wooden laths filled most of the floor space. An old stone sink remained firmly on brick pillars by a window suggesting the room had been a kitchen. A carpet of glistening moss covered the wreckage which had accumulated inside.

Taylor picked out the best spots to place his feet and Kim did likewise behind him. 'What a mess,' she said. 'But you're thinking there's been activity here since the war?'

Taylor's downturned mouth was out of sight to her but his slow nod indicated a solemn "yes".

Another door led from the kitchen, almost certainly to a parlour. This room seemed fairly intact; its old Bakelite handle turned easily. Taylor shifted some of the debris away with his foot and then carefully pulled the door open. It was darker inside. The floorboards of the bedroom above had survived and given protection from the worst of the elements. The window panes also fared well, but their grimy condition kept out the meagre daylight.

Kim clicked on her torch and shone around. The bare lime-washed walls were streaked with brown stains where rainwater had crept in from above and run down. Mould and clumps of green moss sprouted in patches. The metal frame of a 1960s office table took up the centre of the room, but its fibreboard centre had long since decayed and dropped to the floor. A chair of similar design and condition remained pushed in underneath by its last user.

Two rusted filing cabinets had endured the years. The drawers were unlocked but jammed. Taylor's repeated efforts won through but they were empty. A tattered light fitting still hung from the ceiling. A mirror, a wall chart and a single A4 sized framed photograph adorned the walls.

Taylor peered at the wall chart with the light from his own torch. 'A year planner… a calendar.' He rubbed some of the grime from the all-important date. '1978, I think…' He spun around as he heard Kim's sobs.

Tears streamed down her face as the light of her shaking torch illuminated the framed photograph.

'What, what is it?' Taylor said putting an arm around her shoulder and squinting for focus onto the photograph.

The glazed framed picture had somehow survived. Three figures could be made out beneath the dirt. A young man and woman in summer clothes stood together with a toddler – a little girl. The background suggested a seaside holiday – a sandy beach and a small boat lying on its side.

Taylor's forehead pinched with puzzlement as Kim turned full face to him. 'It's me with my mum and dad.'

FIFTY THREE

CAPPELLI'S ACCOUNT of what he knew and how he came to know it proved to be full and unabridged in every detail. The woman quickly saw through his attempts to prolong the agony with unnecessary detail. 'Skip the bullshit Cappelli and get to the point,' she said. But when he got to his skin-of-the-teeth escape from the hotel, she sat back up and showed interest.

'You saw this man then… through the spy-hole. Could you describe him?

'You bet I can. The thing is I saw him again on the police station steps talking with DI Grainger. Definitely the same man.'

'At the police station?' the woman quizzed. Her voice held some scepticism.

'Yes same man, I'm confident of that and this time he had a piece of sticking plaster on his face… below his right eye. I reckon he got that when he burst into my hotel room. Flying glass from me jumping through the window at a guess.'

The gun returned into the nape of Cappelli's neck. The hard push was even more aggressive than before and jolted his head forward. 'If I thought you'd made this up I'd blast your brains out through that windscreen.'

Cappelli didn't need to be that smart to realise he'd touched on a raw nerve and quickly considered that it may also be his ticket to a longer life expectancy.

'It's the truth,' he spluttered. 'It's also a fact that I haven't got a clue about the full picture.' He turned his head as far as the shackles would allow, straining to make partial eye contact. It was his effort to reinforce his honesty. 'I don't know enough about any of this to make something up that will help me anyway.'

She sat back in the seat again with the gun now resting on her lap. A head shake accompanied her derisive smile. 'No, I think you're telling the truth on that score.

Cappelli puzzled over this remark. *Was she going to kill him?* He flinched as he sensed her lean back in towards him. He felt her right hand outstretching to his head. He closed his eyes and waited for the end to come.

The hint of perfume heightened the soft warmth of the woman's cheek as she unavoidably brushed against him. His eyes opened like dinner plates to see that she was leaning forward and pressing the handcuff key into his clutching fingers.

'You're not my enemy Cappelli. I never intended harming you. I just needed the truth.'

The reporter struggled for a full two minutes unaided, to release the handcuffs. He slowly twisted in his seat to make full eye contact. It was a careful almost respectful action. She did after all still have a loaded pistol by her side.

'Remember who's the boss around here Cappelli. I think you've only now started to get a grip on the seriousness of all of this.'

He blinked and gave a sincere nod. He now knew what the woman did for a living and her next statement confirmed the idea.

'I'll spell it out Cappelli. The security of our country rests on the outcome of all of this. The file which you have been searching for is… or at least possibly was on that island.' MI5 agent Sheila Jennings shuffled for comfort back into her seat before giving more. 'I'm going to need some help with this.' She viewed Cappelli with a shake of the head. 'You certainly wouldn't have been my first choice, but beggars can't be choosers. The fact is this… you've been a prick. You've broken the law… serious offences which have had serious consequences. Lenny Gill was not much of a loss, but he'd still be alive if it wasn't for you.'

Cappelli's mouth formed a tight line and his gaze firmly fixed down onto his knees as Jennings gave away some of the background to the case. When the bombshell of Ossie's murder was dropped he gave a despairing sigh. 'God, that's awful. He was so good to me, but how did they find out I'd been with him. How would they know where to go to get me?'

The additional horror of DC Angela Hewitt's death was outlined. 'They listened to her taking a call suggesting you were with the tramp. She was killed to stop her passing on the information… to give them time to get you and when you weren't there Ossie had to be silenced.'

FIFTY FOUR

TAYLOR'S arm held Kim in close. They were back outside in the yard and Kim had regained her composure after seeing the photograph.

'This place must have been abandoned when Gruinard was declared dangerous during the war,' Taylor said. 'I can only imagine that your father came to the island in the late seventies on some Government sponsored project. It seems crazy with the very real threat from anthrax. Then again he knew better than anyone did back then. I'm guessing his team used these empty buildings as a temporary base and that room must have been his office.'

Kim sniffed and wiped at her eyes. 'I knew he came up to Scotland, but I never knew where exactly, or what it was he was doing. He must have been in charge of a Ministry of Defence operation here.

They wandered around to the back of the cottage and took in the better preservation of the buildings in this spot. One particular single storey structure warranted a closer inspection. It had been built from the same hewn stone blocks and slate tiles as the cottage but had been shielded from the worst of the weather and looked fairly intact.

The sturdy squat design measured roughly five metres long by three metres wide and had no windows. The bleached green paintwork of the relatively intact wooden door had a chalky weather-worn texture. A similar stencilled marker appeared on this door to the others. Faded but legible:

BAYS 208 - 218.

He leaned inwards turning the handle and pushed the door. It was stiff on its hinges, but not locked. It swung open revealing more individually numbered bays of the same stacked Formaldehyde containers, but these were full.

They took the cautious option and shone a torch beam inside. It looked similar to what they'd already seen. They turned away intent on a more detailed search elsewhere, but then Kim stopped and turned back into the room, her eyes opening wide with hope as she focussed on Bay 213. She walked down to the end of the room and pointed a finger at the bay number. 'Look?' she said with raised eyebrows. They stared at each other both grasping the possible significance of the number.

Their torch beams flashed upwards to the ceiling, along the wall and between the rows of containers. Had it not been for the number 213 they wouldn't have even ventured inside, but there didn't seem to be anything other than stacked containers.

Taylor remained stationary in the centre of the room stroking a gloved hand across his unshaven chin. His suddenly widened eyes indicated a eureka moment before he turned and hurried outside. He positioned himself several yards back from the brickwork taking in the overall construction of the building as Kim watched him through the open doorway. He was soon back inside.

Bay 213 was stacked three high with full Formaldehyde containers. Taylor took hold of one and heaved it down to the ground. Within five minutes he'd transferred all the containers from the end wall and piled them outside. Kim soon cottoned on to his discovery. The end bay covered a false end to the building. With the canisters removed the outline of a sturdy metal door could now be seen.

'You can work it out when you stand outside,' he said. The building's longer outside than it is in here.'

The door stood less than six feet in height and about three feet in width. It had no handle, but did have a one and a half inch long keyhole. It took no thinking to conclude that the large key for this lock now lay inside Kim's rucksack in the yard. Kim quickly collected it together with the attached small locker type key. She slotted in the big key and gave it a try. The years of damp and the cold conditions since the lock last turned had gummed up its brass innards to the point of seizing. Taylor took over and after a few back and forth twists he felt the mechanism shift. A hollow *clunk* came as the deadbolt shifted backwards. The door remained solidly in place though, held fast by nothing more than weight and corrosion.

Taylor bumped a shoulder against it and then pulled back on the key. A *crack* of separation followed before he could haul the door fully open on its stiffened hinges and shine his torch inside.

The musty smell of stale air drifted out as they gazed in at a three feet deep void stretching back to the real end wall. A series of floor to ceiling solid wooden shelves ran over the entire length of the space. It appeared to be a secure cupboard or walk-in safe, clearly designed not to be found by accident.

Taylor's torch flashed back and forth over the empty shelves landing upon the one single item. It had the outline and size of a slender briefcase and sat pushed back out of sight in a far corner of a middle shelf. He reached over to lift it, but the weight belied that of a briefcase. It was heavier and made from metal.

They moved back outside the building to gain some advantage from the gloomy half-light. Twelve years-worth of dust coated what was a secure metal document container. A beige Hammerite style paint finish showed through beneath the grime. The logo *Vaultzsafe* stood out in red lettering beneath a sturdy looking stainless steel press-lock. The small key would be the one to open this lock. A piece of red Dymo tape still adhered to the lid. The passage of time since it was first applied had caused the ends to curl slightly. The wording was obscured with dirt. Taylor rubbed a thumb across the tape to expose white raised lettering:

Dr E Thornberry.

The key opened the lid effortlessly and the pair looked inside to see the edges of several yellowing documents. Some were separated by faded coloured cards. A brown manila envelope had been pushed down in front of this paperwork. This arrangement implied that it should take priority over the other paperwork. Taylor half slid it out exposing a line of biro written text which simply said:

Director General British Security Service.

'Dad's handwriting,' Kim said.

A standard sized envelope was paper-clipped to the larger one. It's pale blue shade was recognisable as Basildon Bond. Kim shook her head. 'Dad always used that.'

The theory was supported by more of Fry's handwriting – one underlined word:

Kim.

'So this file is the one that everyone's been after,' Taylor said. He looked up, taking account of the worsening weather. The wind blew in steadily, carrying flecks of rain. 'Let's get back to the tent and some comfort before we look at all this. It's been waiting for twelve years. Another half hour won't make any difference; we don't want the weather damaging it.'

Across the bay in the Mungasdale lay-by Cappelli sat at the wheel of his hire car, with Jennings now in the front passenger seat. They had reached an agreement: He would do whatever he could to help and she would put a good word in for him in the event of a later court appearance. A sweetener was added: He may be allowed to use the story if they managed to see it through to the end alive.

The Minch looked bleak. Lashing rain barrelled in sideways across the sea, buffeting against the car. Relentless waves pounded the beach. Each thunderous crash was followed by the surging roar of retreating shingle.

Gruinard Island had vanished in a soaking grey shroud, as churning nimbus clouds sagged heavily overhead. The actual whereabouts of the sun were unknown. Only the fact that it was four o'clock in the afternoon supported any suggestion that it was still daytime. Jennings and Cappelli stared silently out through the rivulets streaming down the car's windows.

Jennings had necessarily updated Cappelli on the suspicions that

Taylor and Harding were believed to be close to discovering the secret and probably already in the area. 'If they're here they must have stayed over somewhere,' she said. 'They're only on a motor cycle. From what we've seen all the B & B's are closed. There are only two hotels in the area, the one you stayed at and one further back in Garve.'

Cappelli nodded. 'Well I passed the time of day with the manager at the Dundoon where I stayed. He said I was the first customer to stay over for the night in nearly a week.

Jennings gave Cappelli a harsh sideways stare. She still didn't trust him. 'We need somewhere to stay overnight… don't get any fucking ideas.' She thought for a moment. 'Better still don't get ANY ideas. Now get us to the Garve Hotel.'

FIFTY FIVE

THE BRITISH LIBRARY newspaper archives were to be found in Colindale, North London. The supervisor of the day had watched the young man occupying a seat in the reading room with some interest.

Almost certainly a student, he thought, *and clearly dedicated to his research.* He hadn't moved since the doors had opened at nine o'clock.

There was irony in the location of the ongoing search for clues. The newspaper archives were only a short walk from the Government Laboratory which had been Thornberry's supposed destination on the day that she died in 1978.

The supervisor pushed his antique rubber wheeled trolley silently down the central aisle between the twenty-four wooden desks. Closing time now approached and he was taking his chance to collect discarded research copies for refiling back onto the shelves. His inquisitive sideways glance focussed on the stack of yellowed newspapers in front of the customer. His knowledgeable eye identified that the young man had been working his way through small, regional Scottish editions. The adverts and general print layout of what he could see allowed him to perceive a date range of the seventies and eighties. The poor chap must have trawled through hundreds of these old copies since his arrival and with closing time minutes away he remained as the sole customer.

Undeterred, the young man selected yet another copy from the top of his batch. He lodged it down onto the base lip of the wooden easel affair which sat upon each leather topped desk. A quick glance at the wall clock confirmed his notion that this would have to be the last of the day – he was out of time.

The copy of the Inverness and Highlands Daily Times was dated Saturday 5th August 1978. It bore a banner headline concerning the arrest of politician Jeremy Thorpe on charges of conspiracy to murder. Two other pages held more of this bombshell story. The man quickly turned these as they were of no interest to him. His eyes – now tired and sore – darted over the print searching for specific words or names. He had not possessed this skilled and honed technique when he'd arrived that morning.

When he reached page five his head jolted forward as if it had been swatted with a rolled-up copy of the newspaper he was scrutinising. The name and title of the man he had found formed nothing more than three miniscule words in the two inch column, but came into focus like a front page banner headline.

The insignificant lead to the story read:

ISLAND CAN NEVER BE MADE SAFE.

This meant nothing to him. But the name of the Government Microbiologist who had attempted and failed to rid the place of anthrax spores after WW2 experiments did:

DR GEOFFREY FRY.

He quickly jotted down the account verbatim, rose to his feet and headed for the exit as the closing time bell started to sound. His dash to the nearest payphone on the corner of the street would add a little more security to his attempt to pass on what he'd discovered. Mobile to mobile calls would be easier to spot than a landline to mobile call.

The recorded voice message he heard, gave the situation in monotone clarity: "*The person you are calling is unavailable*". For the Cambridge University student whose twisted idealism had been born out of naivety and a search for adventure it came as an annoying delay. His considerable acumen had been devoted throughout the day to discovering the possible whereabouts of Harding and Taylor. It had paid off. Gruinard Island must be the answer. The automatic recorded response to his phone call meant that double agent Mike Nelson was still travelling. It seemed likely that Nelson was, by now, well north of England and inside one of the gaping cell-phone dead spots, which were the drawback of a technology still in its infancy.

On Gruinard Island as six o'clock approached the day's light had all but gone. Kim sat cross-legged inside the tent surrounded by documents and folders from the Vaultzsafe. The lantern hooked centrally above her head gave off a strong white light and swung back and forth as the tent was buffeted by the gusting wind. Taylor crawled back inside to the semi-comfort. He had taken a cautious look to be sure that the light would not be seen from the mainland. He pulled the door flap zipper closed and settled down awkwardly alongside Kim.

She had selected the one envelope that her father had addressed to her. She slit it carefully along the top with a penknife and pulled out four sheets of matching blue letter paper.

August 1978

Darling Kim

As I write this letter you are barely twenty years of age and have just started out in life as a police officer. If you do ever come to read this it will almost certainly be after my death.

My coded instructions for you to play a part in this and to recover Dr Thornberry's file are a backup plan devised to cover the possibility of my early death.

My priority (in an ideal world) is to keep the details of this (Thornberry's file) unknown until 2018 (by which date I will be 83 and by which date the threat described in the file will have become harmless).

If I have not died before 2018 I will be able to inform the authorities myself allowing them to take the remaining necessary action in the knowledge that the details contained in Dr Thornberry's file no longer present a problem. If on the other hand, the date has not been reached a serious threat could still exist to the security of this country. Many lives may be in danger.

I have placed a heavy burden upon you. The secret HAD to be protected by complex means. Only you could be trusted with this. If 2018 has not yet arrived and you find yourself on Gruinard Island reading this letter then you have my permission to read the letter addressed to "The Director General". This will enlighten you to the threats posed by Dr Thornberry's file and will reinforce my warning that no one can be trusted by virtue of their position alone. The contents and details held within Thornberry's file can only be dealt with by the authorities. It is now your responsibility to pass this entire file to the current Director General.

Dad x

Taylor had read the words at the same pace as Kim. She looked around at him, raised her eyebrows and sighed before picking up the Director General's envelope and tearing it open.

The three full typed sheets of foolscap paper had become yellowed with age. They were stapled together in the top left hand corner. A brown rust stain had crept into the paper from the corroded metal staple.

The manual typewriter font looked ancient compared to that which Taylor and Harding were now accustomed. Those twelve years since Geoff Fry had hammered out the document on his own old machine gave the script a personal and more caring feel:

To the Current Director General, Military Intelligence Section 5

I am Geoffrey Fry, Senior Microbiologist employed by Her Majesty's Government. The date as I write is Tuesday 15th August 1978.

Included in this document container are the following:

1. This letter (To Director General).

2. Letter to my daughter Miss Kimberly Jayne Fry.

3. A dossier compiled by the late Dr Eleanor Thornberry.

The military intelligence file, code named ROSA (1978) will be available to you. It will provide details of the circumstances surrounding the death of Microbiologist, Dr Eleanor Thornberry at Porton Down in May 1978.

I am confident that Dr Thornberry was working as a Soviet agent in 1978 in spite of a lack of evidence to support this theory. You will note that her actual aims were never officially ascertained by British Intelligence. My involvement in the death, however, led me to uncover what her intentions were. The serious risk to national security posed by Thornberry's actions caused me to take the unusual and clandestine steps I have taken.

Together with Dr Andrew Prestwich (incumbent Home Office Pathologist at the time) I was tasked with the investigation of and the making safe of Dr

Thornberry's death scene.

You will see from the inquest findings that Thornberry died from the effects of a nerve agent commonly known as VX. The cause of the death was correctly judged to be accidental although I confess that Dr Prestwich and I kept back some details from the Coroner. Our reasons for this were driven by a strong suspicion that Thornberry had been working in concert with others including at least one MI5/Soviet double agent. The identity and status of these people was not known. It was impossible to ascertain who could be trusted to deal with what was a matter of the gravest concern to national security.

A huge quantity of VX was recovered from Thornberry's car. This had been illegally produced by her and made to her own recipe. A non-standard ingredient had been added giving the substance a much longer shelf life than its normal three years.

Dr Thornberry's dossier contains the formula and procedure for concocting her own variety of VX, which you will see she has titled VX(T). It is a complex procedure involving specific temperatures at various points of manufacture.

Thirty-one sites throughout the UK where "dead drops" of long-life VX {VX(T)} have been made (or were to be made) are identified in the dossier. These strategic locations include seats of government, military installations, water supplies, nuclear power stations, armament factories and certain university buildings. The goal appears to have been to secrete a quantity of nerve agent in such a manner that it could be administered covertly upon the unsuspecting subjects. I believe this was planned to be phase one of a pre-emptive attack (in the event of an imminent war).

It is impossible to say how many, if any, of these dead drops were actually "set". An interesting feature remains that Thornberry's husband, Robert, went missing in 1977. My own enquiries also suggest that he too was a Soviet agent and concerned with his wife in this venture. It seems most likely that his part in the scheme was to set the dead drops for later use. His sudden disappearance indicates that he was abruptly taken out of the game for unknown reasons.

The formula and procedure for producing VX(T) is hugely important. It seems unlikely that Thornberry has had an opportunity to pass the details of this to her Russian counterparts and I believe this copy is the only one in existence.

It was vital that the file be retained so that each possible dead drop is known and can be dealt with. My concerns regarding a double MI5 agent have forced me to keep the secret of the existence of Thornberry's file between myself and Dr Prestwich and knowledge of its hiding place strictly to myself.

Whilst VX(T) has a hugely longer shelf life than ordinary VX, I am confident that a safe date for the expiry of its potency is mid-2018. I arrive at this date through scientific research on Thornberry's last batch and as she died in 1978 no more of the long-life toxin could have been made after then.

I have found it necessary to burden my daughter (Kimberly) with safeguarding the file and passing it directly to the Director General of the day. This situation should only arise if the existence of Thornberry's dossier becomes known before 2018 (but after my death)

Between May 1975 and August 1978, in my role as Government Chief Micro biologist I was tasked with overseeing the cleansing of Gruinard Island following its contamination with the Anthrax bacterium during WW2 experiments. You will note that in my final report on the procedure (delivered in July 1978) I state categorically that the island remains severely infected in spite of all the work. Consequently I further point out the ongoing threat to all mammal life forms continues. I additionally state that the island should not be visited for further tests until the year 2018. I also add in the report that by this date, scientific advances and the passage of time MAY enable Gruinard to be declared safe.

The truth of the matter is that the work WAS a success and the island became completely safe from June 1978. The charade was necessary to provide a safe haven for the storage of the file.

I believe that at the time of writing, security at both Porton Down and the Colindale (London Lab) was compromised by the infiltration of Soviet agents. I also believe that at least one person of high standing within the liaison between Porton Down and MI5 was also in the pay of the Soviet Union. Should the contents of the dossier fall into Soviet hands or indeed the hands of another individual set upon an idea of a form of blackmail against the nation the consequences would be dire.

Geoffrey Fry.

Taylor and Harding looked up from the paperwork, their expressions exhibiting the horror and gravity of the situation. The events of the past few days spelled out that someone else did know about the file and was keen to get their hands on it. The motorcycle chase also proved that these people were getting close.

FIFTY SIX

THE MARCH climate in Tenerife suited Mr James Boyle to a T. The daytime temperatures usually hovered around 18°C – ideal for the fair skinned Scot. The Boyles were now three days into their holiday but already Mr Boyle's face and forearms matched the bright red hue of his hair.

By seven o'clock that evening Boyle was relaxing after his evening meal. He sat – T-shirt and shorts – on the balcony of his Costa Adeje hotel, a cold beer close at hand. The puzzles formed by time differences on holidays abroad did not apply in Tenerife. The same time applied as that back in the United Kingdom. "It's one less job for you to do my dear… altering my watch." Boyle had made the comment to his wife upon landing.

"See how I think of you. It's your holiday as well," supposedly served as his half joking addition.

The similarities to the UK ended with the matching times. It would be dark back in the Scottish Highlands by now, but Tenerife still held the prospect of perhaps another hour of light. Boyle sat back in his chair, sighed with satisfaction and took another sip at his drink. Holding the glass up to eye level for a moment he watched the droplets of condensation meandering down the side. He reached across the table for his copy of the Daily Mail. It was nearly always old news by the time you managed to get sight of a UK paper abroad – usually a day behind. You could get one same-day if you did your homework, but the earliest for a UK daily would be around the 6 p.m. mark.

Martha Boyle's list of things to do took on board the task of locating a reliable source for her husband's Daily Mail. She discovered a shop a quarter of a mile from the hotel. The newspaper recce was carried out as soon as she unpacked on the first day whilst James enjoyed a snooze after the arduous journey. A firm agreement made with the shop owner secured her a copy each day.

Boyle unfolded the tabloid and started his normal routine – reading every word from page one. His arrival on page four at seven thirty-five coincided with Martha's kindly switching-on of the balcony lights. A good sized gulp of beer was taken prior to his vision landing upon the small heading:

Police Hunt Bikers

His eyes grew wide and his sun ripened cheeks increased to balloon-like proportions as he attempted to hold the gassy liquid inside his over full mouth. The explosion of beer which followed preceded a violent coughing fit. Both events had been prompted by the registration number of the wanted motor cycle.

Martha – alarmed face – appeared through the balcony doors in time to see her husband now standing, scarlet features drenched in beer, with finger pointing at the sodden newspaper in his hand. 'It's those bastards… the ones who rented out The Lodge.'

Taylor and Harding now understood the facts and had the all-important file. They also knew that some people were prepared to gamble everything to get their hands on those papers.

Geoffrey Fry's explanation and his fears from all those years ago still seemed relevant. What had happened over the last few weeks supported his original notion that double agents *had* existed. The revelation that Nelson was a foreign agent proved conclusively that the problem had not gone away.

Thornberry's dossier pinpointed the locations of the intended individual dead drops precisely, but did not confirm which ones, if any, had actually been seeded. Each possible site needed to be checked and made safe if necessary. They needed to get off the island and deliver the file into safe hands. Geoff Fry's explicit instructions nominated that this must be the current head of MI5 – the Director General.

They walked down to the sea's edge and stood on the sand near to where they'd landed. The importance of getting back to the mainland consumed their thoughts as they gazed across to where a couple of twinkling lights could be made out in the village of Laide. Kim linked her arm in with Taylor's and held on as the wind picked up and threatened to take her off her feet. Clouds were now rushing in and had already concealed all chance of moonlight. A storm brewed and the dark outlines of rolling waves looked set to mount a battle-plan against Gruinard Island.

The rain started with small occasional pellets as they linked in close walking briskly back to the tent. Within a few yards they were running full pelt back up the beach, hands held tight, faces feeling each stinging bullet-like droplet.

They scrambled back inside the tent thankful that it was holding out and started to dry themselves and get comfortable. There was simply no way they could make it back to the mainland tonight.

FIFTY SEVEN

THE CALEDONIAN Hotel in Quay Street, Ullapool lay a mere ten miles as the crow flies from Gruinard Island. No crow would be bird brained enough to undertake such a journey though. Especially at ten o'clock on a black windswept March night in the teeth of a howling gale.

Mike Nelson's journey from London had started first thing on that Friday morning. He had set off with nothing more than a fingers-crossed hope that the behind-the-scenes research he'd arranged would eventually provide him with a more accurate destination than merely Ullapool. The numerous delays due to road works, speed restrictions and bad weather, coupled with petrol and rest stops made the drive tedious and slow. A one hundred and eighty miles detour formed the first leg of the trip and was included in the plan to collect another team member. The entire excursion took over twelve hours and covered a full six hundred and fifty-three miles. A telephoned pre-booking at the hotel had been an essential forethought.

The Minch View state room with lounge and en-suite remained as the hotel's *best* and would be a good overnight base. The sumptuous American sized "King" bed at over six feet wide gave ample space for one person. Nelson would not be sleeping alone though.

His mobile phone lay on the table. It was not an MI5 phone, but an anonymous, unlisted one. His official works phone had been unceremoniously flung from his car window as he'd driven into the Dartford Tunnel at the start of the journey. Within seconds it had been pancaked by the HGV following behind. Nelson knew that his time with MI5 was now at an end and he certainly didn't want anyone tracking him.

His British Military issue Browning 9 mm pistol and shoulder holster also lay on the table. He was not sentimental over firearms.

Most British and American everyday pistols were as good as the next. The Browning served as a good killing weapon and he'd become used to it over the years.

A comprehensive map of the area made up the trio of items on the table. Folded open at the relevant page, a blue penned oval had been impressed deeply into the paper of the map. Evidently this had been drawn with some satisfaction and intensity. It surrounded that landmass which showed half a mile out into the Atlantic Ocean from a place named Mungasdale – Gruinard Island. An unnecessary, but under the circumstances understandable exclamation mark, also appeared alongside the oval. It had been scored with such force as to almost penetrate the fabric of the page.

Nelson's phone had remained silent throughout the latter parts of his journey. Only vibrating back into life again as his car entered the outer reaches of the two base station masts covering Ullapool. The researcher who had spent an entire day at the British Newspaper Archives before discovering the vital pointer had made dozens of attempts to contact Nelson. His eventual success caused the double agent to pull up sharply alongside the A832's name-sign for Ullapool and make those forceful additions to the map.

The hissing of the en suite shower gave a clue to the location of his co-conspirator. Nelson took the opportunity to check out the weather from the room's elegant curved bay window. A sea view had been part and parcel of the booking. The waves which slammed into the harbour wall down below underlined the impossibility of a sea journey at least until tomorrow.

There had been plenty of time for the pair to discuss the situation during the journey. They'd worked out that Harding and Taylor may already have landed and retrieved the documents. It might even be possible that they could already be heading back to London with the file. Nelson didn't think so though, and neither did his partner. None of the timing fitted that picture. It was more likely that the two detectives were hoping for better weather to make the crossing to

Gruinard or were trapped there waiting to return. Either scenario might play into their hands. Taylor and Harding could even unwittingly do all the dirty work themselves and bring the file back across the Minch. An ambush and a bullet apiece in the head would make the job so much easier. Whether or not they had engaged a third party in their sea crossing was not of concern. It would just be one more body to dispose of – a simple matter at sea. Both of the detectives were on an unauthorised vigilante expedition and not armed. They offered no real threat.

Nelson pulled the curtain back across the window and smiled as he settled into a comfortable chair facing the door of the en suite. He wore nothing other than a pair of black boxers. A gold chain hung around his neck, glinting under the room's central light. The medallion it supported swung side to side before resting back amongst his thick dark chest hair. The shield shaped pendant sported the image of a gold handled sword pierced through a gold five pointed star. Embossed into the centre of the star was the hammer and sickle of the Soviet Union. The red enamelled banner entwining within the design bore Russian wording. It was the KGB 30 year badge of honour. Not Nelson's of course, but his father's.

Dmitry Molodtsove died many years before his son Oleg took on the false identity of Michael William Nelson. It seemed a pity that Major Molodtsove did not live to see his son progress through the Military Academy and the higher school of the KGB in the Michurinsky district of Moscow. Ironically Dmitry's end did not come about as a result of a daring piece of espionage or in a hail of gunfire. He died in rather more pathetic and mundane circumstances in Ward 23 of the N.N Burdenko, Central Military Hospital in Moscow.

Dmitry's death at fifty-five years of age resulted from a liver so pickled in his favourite Hrenovuha strong horseradish vodka that the pathologist compared it to "fossilised dinosaur shit". The young Oleg was the product of one of his father's concluding acts of bullying upon a wife thirty years his junior. The boy never really knew his father. The vodka saw Dmitry off before Oleg reached three years.

Oleg (Michael) was brought up on a diet of tales of adventure and heroism about his father. Most of these were false but they did succeed in engendering a determination to follow in his footsteps. With the help and guidance of the late Dmitry's colleagues the young man excelled at every military and academic problem launched at him.

His additional language skills, in particular, faultless English with that educated Cambridge accent, made Oleg a prime candidate for an unusual and rarely employed post. He was sent into the UK as an illegal – a sleeper, but not into an ordinary job. Michael William Nelson was destined for much higher things – MI5 itself as a security agent.

With a watertight legend backed up by a number of other lesser illegals posing as family and friends he achieved that target within seven years and became a trusted MI5 operative. His remit to lie low and work patriotically in defence of Britain – the country of his birth – was adhered to without question. His orders to remain a sleeper until awoken were observed without question until that awakening came.

Oleg Molodtsove reopened his eyes and put Michael Nelson to one side in December of 1990. This event happened following the discovery of what was undoubtedly Robert Thornberry's body in the air duct at the VSEL ship yard at Barrow-in-Furness. The three months since that discovery were now history.

The Soviet agent held his father's badge between finger and thumb, placing his chin down onto his chest to read its inscription. The smuggling in of the treasured memento served as his sole connection back to his real roots. The act of taking it with him had been his singular disregard of orders. This "crime" could so easily have trashed the entire operation before it began. The cost would have been enormous – millions of Rubles spent on the training of himself and his supporting agents. The security and longevity of those other illegals would also have been heavily compromised. The worldwide discredit and subsequent embarrassment to the Soviet Union would have been a stinging blow. If Oleg's masters had known of his indiscretion it would have spelled a death penalty.

Oleg had retrieved his father's medal from its secure hiding place after leaving the New Eltham area of London the night before. He had not set eyes on it in seven years. Whatever the eventual outcome, Michael Nelson no longer existed.

The woman now showering would be his ticket back home. Although British born and the daughter of a high ranking army officer she had quickly become embroiled in the idealism and adventure which the Soviet Union purported to be. The intelligent but naïve woman was swept off her feet by the dashing Captain Michael Nelson when they first met at Sandhurst Military College. He used his ruthless and callous skills to prepare for the future and engage her as a sleeper. He did from time to time engage her as a sleeper in the more obvious sense of the term – when it suited him.

Nelson kept the charade affair going on and off over the years as their separate careers blossomed. It was on when it suited him and off when it did not. His reincarnation as Oleg with the discovery of the Barrow-in-Furness dead drop caused the liaison to be switched firmly back ON.

The woman's own mobile phone lay on a bedside table. Its plastic back cover was now detached and the battery removed. Alongside this lay her own firearm – not her legal Browning pistol like Nelson's but a slightly larger and heavier weapon. The deadly Stetchkin machine pistol was her choice for this part of the operation. Any use of her own legitimate Browning 9mm would easily have been traced back to her. She needed to retain her cover so that she could use her status to manage Nelson's escape from the UK with Eleanor Thornberry's file of documents. If she kept her own involvement secret long enough it would enable her own exodus from the UK to

Russia. She could then be with the man with whom she was obsessed.

The highly illegal Stetchkin, a gift from Nelson seemed to inspire her loyalty and passion for the Union of Soviet Socialist Republics. Whilst Nelson was not sentimental about firearms it seemed that she was. Or could it have been the vicious streak in her temperament which craved a weapon capable of cutting a man – or woman – in two?

The sound of the shower stopped. A short towelling-dry intermission took place before the en suite door swung slowly open. If it is possible for the slow opening of a door to be a prelude to sex then this door opening achieved exactly that.

The three long legged steps the woman took forward were choreographed almost ballet fashion as the pointing of the red toe-nailed feet left three damp marks upon the carpet. The slender ankles came together and the feet went up onto tip toe before resting down onto the heels in a mocking military attention stance.

She looked down at Nelson with her arms straight down by her sides presenting her nakedness for inspection. Of course Nelson knew her age and her face *did* register most of those forty-three years fairly accurately either with, or without the sultry pout on the lips. The body though, held its shape and form more in keeping with that of a twenty-five year old.

He sat back more into his chair and planted his feet harder into the carpet, aware that his loose boxer shorts had tightened and were morphing in shape. His heart rate increased as his eyes took in the detail – the neck, the fine collar bones, slender wrists. The alabaster white skin showed a tinge of pinkness and a glisten of moisture from the recent shower. The breasts firm, rounded and uplifted shuddered slightly with the enactment of the attention pose. The flat stomach and faintly indented navel showed an outline of a gym toned six-pack of abdominal muscles. A willowy patch of auburn pubic hair sat beneath. Careful trimming perfectly framed the area upon which

Nelson's widening eyes had unashamedly locked.

'Captain Lowell reporting for duty Sir.'

Oleg Molodtsove blinked once before running his eyes again over every part of Jenny Lowell's body currently on display. He made a "firm" decision to ensure that no stone would be left unturned.

He gave one single downwards nod of the head. His fingers gripped hard into the leather arms of the chair. The Special Branch officer knelt between his open legs and eased eager fingers into the sides of his now taut boxers.

Benedict Cappelli was not having anywhere near such a good time. Yes, he now also shared a hotel bedroom with a dynamic and attractive woman. Yes he had also enjoyed a decent meal in the hotel's restaurant. But no doubt had been left in his mind that the pretence given at the Garve's reception desk was anything other than necessary cover. Mr and Mrs Hall would be staying over for one night, two at most.

Mrs Hall took the room's double bed whilst Mr Hall lay on the room's sofa. 'Any funny business Cappelli and you're through that window,' she said.

Cappelli looked over at the hotel window at which Jennings' finger pointed and the thought passed through his mind: *Well it won't be the first time!*

FIFTY EIGHT

MI5 DIRECTOR General, Sir Peter Walker met Home Secretary Walter Baker in the lift of the Home Office at 50 Queen Anne's Gate London SW1. It was something of a rarity for the Home Secretary to visit his official workplace on a Saturday and half past seven in the morning made the meeting unique.

With a five o'clock start at his own office, Walker's day was destined to be even longer. The men did not speak throughout the two-floor journey other than to pass a perfunctory "good morning". Standard security practice barred the holding of confidential conversations other than in spaces with clearance.

Baker hefted his briefcase onto the desk and delivered his rain specked mackintosh to the coat stand. He pressed a button on his intercom. 'Coffee please Janet.' He waved a hand over at the chair opposite his desk and the two men sat to face each other.

Baker viewed Walker with a solemn expression. 'The standard opening line Peter, would normally be "this had better be good", but I get the feeling that the circumstances have far exceeded that introduction already.'

Walker nodded, 'Quite, Home Secretary… quite. My regrettable duty includes informing you that two of my agents who were working closely on the case have both disappeared off the radar.'

Baker blinked and shuffled forward in his chair as he decoded the implications. He then waited as Janet delivered a stainless steel Picquot tray and coffee set along with two large ivory coloured Wedgwood mugs. The door closed behind the secretary before he said: 'You're saying… working for the other side?'

'Seems that way Sir.' He then gave more on the gunfire incident at Taylor's house. 'A man and a woman were seen running away from Taylor's house after Harding fled on the motor bike. The man was bleeding from a minor facial injury and as I mentioned before, we recovered a tiny amount of blood from glass fragments on the lawn. I've pulled some strings in view of the serious implications. All field agents are required to supply blood samples and with the recent progress on DNA research I managed to get tests quickly done. I can confirm that it WAS Nelson. Evidently both Nelson and Jennings were the pair seen there during the shooting. Now that they have both failed to make contact it strongly implies that they are working to their own agenda.'

'As in… for the Soviets,' Baker added.

'Quite,' Walker said, making use of his much loved term.

'So when did you last hear from them?'

'They were both at a meeting with a detective inspector and a Special Branch officer in Exeter on Wednesday afternoon. We've collected data from Nelson's mobile phone since then. He was tracked to the New Eltham area of London on Thursday evening. He visited MI5 HQ at Gower Street at half past nine that evening. He disappeared at half six yesterday morning, when two separate mobile phone base stations tracked him entering the northbound end of the Dartford Tunnel. He never came out the other end. So he's either still in there or he's trashed his phone.'

Baker nodded his understanding as Walker continued. 'As for Jennings, her last assignment tasked her particularly with tracking down Cappelli. She contacted Barclay's Bank head office twice on Thursday. Details were given to her over the illegal use of a stolen credit card Cappelli now has. Her mobile phone last showed up in Bristol on Thursday evening. Since then it was either turned off or it's out of range.'

Baker took a sip at his coffee. 'Why did Nelson visit the Gower Street HQ on Thursday evening?'

'He told the on-duty station chief he had to write up an urgent report, but he left nothing for typing and no report has been filed.'

Baker's expression increased in severity. 'Can you step the operation up any more Peter? Do we have any idea where this is all leading?'

'I was coming on to that Sir. We've had a major breakthrough as a result of the newspaper disclosure on Harding's motor cycle. We not only have an area, but an actual address… west coast… Scottish Highlands.'

Walker enlightened the Home Secretary about the telephone call which had come in at quarter past eight the night before from the holidaying Mr James Boyle.

'Ullapool is the closest settlement to it,' he added.

Baker nodded. 'So what are we doing?'

'A team are researching the area to see what the connection could be to the case. Alex Tremaine is flying up to Inverness with a couple of trusted heavies as we speak. We can't involve the local police at this stage. We simply cannot gamble with the possibility of this leaking out.'

Baker leant back in his chair and clasped his hands across his stomach. 'Anything more on the source of the nerve agent which killed the detective at Exeter?'

Walker extracted some papers from his own briefcase which he rested onto his knee. 'Yes, we knew at a fairly early stage that Miss Hewitt died from the effects of Sarin. It's a lethal nerve agent acting in a similar way to VX but is many times less deadly. What we didn't initially understand is where the Sarin came from. Sarin rapidly evaporates and by the time our experts arrived at the death scene there were no traceable residues anywhere within the room or on Miss Hewitt's clothing. Indeed the only way we proved Sarin to be the cause of death came from the changes created in her blood. Now after meticulous examination of every item from the room we have pinpointed the cause as being a clock.'

Baker looked baffled as Walker explained the intricacies of Geoff Fry's stolen clock.

'The pay-as-you-go mobile phone component allowed it to be both an efficient listening device and a location tracker.' He reached into his briefcase and then laid a two inch long, half inch wide metal capsule down onto the desk between them. His summary of the clock's nerve gas mechanism left Baker shaking his head.

'This is the same type of canister used in the devices, Walker advised. 'As I said, it's from an automatic air freshener. It was pressurised and filled with Sarin liquid which would be released via an aerosol nozzle as an atomised spray. As long as the mobile phone component is able to receive a network signal it requires nothing more than a coded number to be sent via the listening phone. That would then activate the nerve gas spray… or for that matter whatever other weapon the device contained within its casing.'

Baker leaned in across his desk. 'Why Sarin… why not VX?'

'VX is hundreds of times more powerful than Sarin. There's little doubt that if VX had been a viable alternative they'd have used it. The device would have had the potential to kill anything in the building rather than perhaps one person nearby. Normal VX could never work in the atomiser spray system in the clocks… it's too viscous. It's a thick oily substance and would be more likely to block up and do nothing. There's little doubt that the Sarin gas capsule was supplied by our friends at the Kremlin. If they had known Thornberry's altered VX recipe I'm sure they'd have used it. Our experts remain confounded by the recipe. Whilst we know the additional chemicals, the actual procedure is hugely complex and has left everyone baffled. '

Baker flattened his hands down onto the desk as he took in Walker's explanation. 'So Thornberry's VX formula could be even more valuable to our enemies than knowing where the dead drops are to be found.'

Walker's nod included an expressive face – tight lips and widened eyes.

Baker picked up the capsule from his blotter. 'This one's clean?'

'Yes,' said Walker. 'That one still contains its genuine Forest Pine.'

'A deadly piece of kit,' Baker commented as he turned it between finger and thumb. 'Could there be more of these clocks?'

'Yes,' Walker said. 'Due to some good work by an Exeter detective we've recovered a second one from the nursing home room of Dr Prestwich. Both of the mobile phones inside the clocks were purchased from different outlets in the New Eltham area of London. I can't deny the possibility that there could be others but there must also be a listening cell monitoring them.'

Baker continued to roll the metal capsule between his finger and thumb. 'So the two clocks inside Fry's and Prestwich's homes allowed them to listen in to most conversations and almost certainly gave them a head start in all of this.'

'Yes Sir. The Exeter detective also established that the Daily Herald reporter... Cappelli visited Prestwich at his care home in Salisbury on Friday 22nd February.'

The MI5 boss sat back in his chair and explained Cappelli's devious pretence of being a relative. 'Cappelli fell right into the trap. That conversation would have been monitored by the Soviets through the clock. Interestingly we've now established that Cappelli used his own mobile phone to call his newspaper on the same day he visited Prestwich. We can prove that he was at the care home when he made that call. From enquiries with his editor it seems certain that he gave enough away during that conversation for anyone listening in to identify him. He met with his editor the next day and divulged what he'd found out but not how he'd gone about it. His summary suggested a big story involving a suspicious death along with possible malpractices at Porton Down several years ago.'

Walker shook his head. 'Cappelli hadn't got a clue what he was getting into.'

Baker interrupted. 'Obviously he was talking about Thornberry's death though.'

'Exactly,' Walker said. 'But we've also learned that Prestwich's room was burgled not long after Cappelli's visit. Without doubt that burglary came about as a result of Cappelli's bugged conversation with Prestwich. Prestwich's address book went missing but it seems that happened before the break-in. I'm certain that the burglars were after it but I think Cappelli had already snitched it. There is little doubt that is why someone attempted to abduct him from the hotel.'

Baker had made a few notes during Walker's explanation. 'When and how were the clocks installed?' he said.

'Cleverly,' Walker replied. 'Sent through the post with documentation suggesting they were competition prizes. It was then down to the unwitting prize winners… Mr Fry and Mr Prestwich to plug them in, and that's what they both did. The phone records for the two mobiles inside the clocks show they both first switched on at lunchtime on Wednesday 9th January. They successfully ran on their batteries then until they were plugged in… probably the same day that they arrived.'

Walker had been rummaging through his paperwork as he explained the story. 'Once again, when the phones first came to life they both connected to a mobile phone base station in the New Eltham area. That would have been before they were parcelled up and posted. The staff at Dr Prestwich's nursing home worked out that the clock arrived via Royal Mail sometime around the second weekend in January. That fits with normal postage. All the packaging and any details of postage have been destroyed.'

Baker flipped a few pages of his desk diary back and forth, landing on January. 'So they started listening in from sometime around the 12th January. That's a month after the Cumbria body was found.'

'That's right sir, but the Cumbrian Forensic lab didn't discover what was in the canisters until 2nd January. Porton Down were immediately involved on that same day and unwittingly informed Nelson who, possibly with Jennings, then got his own clandestine operation off the ground.'

Baker came straight to the point. 'Who's been listening in?'

Walker smoothed a crisp piece of A4 onto the desk. It contained typed details. 'Two separate mobile phones regularly called both Fry's and Prestwich's clock phones to listen in,' he started. 'The main one operated from the New Eltham area. This will have been a monitoring station and almost certainly where the clocks were parcelled up. The other phone is switched off for long periods. It only comes on to listen occasionally, probably after receiving information from the monitoring station. Interestingly Dr Fry's clock phone was also listened to throughout its time at the murder victim Lenny Gill's house. The earwigging peaked during its stay in Exeter CID office. We are now satisfied that the second phone which had been listening in is another pay-as-you-go mobile being used by Nelson. We know this due to locations which tie up with some of his known whereabouts.'

Walker gave several innocent examples of where Nelson was known to be which also coincided with the tracking of the listening phone. He then outlined other more suspicious times and places where the phone had been tracked. 'It shows up in the same base station area as The Kingsland Hotel in Exeter at 5 a.m. on Monday 18th March during the abduction attempt of reporter Cappelli. Hours later that morning it's connected to a mast at Little Stoneleigh in Staffordshire. The time coincides exactly with the gunfire incident at Inspector Taylor's house which was within range.'

Baker's expression reached its most serious. 'What about the incident which killed detective Hewitt?'

Walker nodded. 'Yes, it was back down in Exeter centre throughout the morning of Tuesday 19th March. It made a call to the phone in Dr Fry's clock whilst it was in the Exeter CID office at 11.30 a.m. It listened for an hour and ten minutes. At 12.40 p.m. the coded number was dialled into that phone which initiated the Sarin spray in the clock killing Detective Hewitt. That phone then switched off.'

Baker gritted his teeth. The small gesture he made of lightly bumping the side of his clenched fist down onto the desktop portrayed his controlled anger over the affair.

Walker ploughed on. 'As I've said, Nelson's legit phone went dead when he entered the Dartford Tunnel at 6.30 a.m. yesterday heading north. His other, *killer* phone came back onto the network within a couple of minutes… exiting the tunnel. It was intermittently tracked heading north as it passed in and out of large areas without cover. It eventually pinged a base station at Ullapool in the Scottish Highlands at 7.05 p.m. last night and immediately took a two minute call. We tracked that call as being made from a payphone in Longfield Road New Eltham. It was switched off after that call and that's the last time we've heard from it. Ten other unanswered call attempts were made from public payphones in London from 5 p.m. up until the answered call at 7.05 p.m. It seems someone was desperate to relay information to Nelson.'

Walker delved into his briefcase, selecting a road map of the highlands and tracing a finger along a route. 'Ullapool is a road journey of around thirty-five miles from the property owned by the witness Mr Boyle where Alex Tremaine is heading. '

'What about the monitoring station.'

Walker's expression showed his dismay on this subject. 'This mobile phone tracking is very much in its infancy. It relies largely on how many base stations the phone is within range of, along with the movement of the phone. Vodafone have put everything into helping us but have already admitted that their system has been compromised many times by hacking. We got as far as pinpointing twenty-four possible houses and businesses in and around the Longfield Road area of New Eltham. Any one of these could have been the position of the monitoring station. With the help of local police and Special Branch all the properties were raided last night. We identified a rented semi in Longfield Road as having been the site of the monitoring station.'

Baker shook his head at the mention of the phrase: "having been". 'The bird had flown then?'

'Fraid so Sir. We've recovered remnants of trashed mobile phones and evidence of a great deal of burnt documentation in the garden. We're still interviewing neighbours but I'm not holding my breath. The one phone which was a major player in all of the listening episodes and was the mainstay of the monitoring station has not been used since Tuesday morning. It was switched off not long after the call from Nelson's clandestine phone killed WDC Hewitt. I don't think we'll hear from it again.'

FIFTY NINE

TAYLOR and Harding spent a restless night. The bad weather had threatened on several occasions to uproot the tent. It still flapped crazily but the real sting had gone from the storm and they'd stayed warm and dry. By seven o'clock they were eating bacon and beans.

An hour later they were bending into the wind dressed in quilted anoraks looking out across the water towards Mungasdale. Their eyes drifted over to the more distant area of First Coast from where their sea crossing had started. Although the storm had subsided The Minch still rolled heavily between them and the mainland. The dark grey swell lifted and fell exhibiting a warning not to challenge it, asserting itself as the Atlantic Ocean rather than a minor sea channel. It looked daunting.

Michael Nelson held his treasured *Komz* 8x30 binoculars to his eyes. He stood legs apart against the battering wind and gazed out to sea. The rare 1970s Soviet military eyeglasses had been found by him a few years earlier at Camden Antiques Market and since then he had shown them to many of his MI5 colleagues. The binoculars always created a good talking point and a few laughs. Had those colleagues known the real reason behind his attachment they would not have found it so funny.

The two black specks now visible in the eyepiece lenses remained stationary and so they may after all have been innocent bushes.

Nelson decided to scan further around the rocky shoreline of Gruinard Island when something made him reposition back on the two specks. He adjusted the focus wheel sharpening the distant image and locked on again. One of the bushes had now moved.

He handed the binoculars over to Lowell. 'Take a look, it can't be anyone else.'

Lowell adjusted the image for her own eyesight; she exhaled and held her breath in the manner that a sniper will do when readying to pull the trigger. The smaller of the two outlines particularly held her interest. It incited a strong wish that she really did hold a rifle rather than binoculars. 'We need to take them on,' she said almost with a snarl. 'We need to get over there while the sea is manageable. Perhaps onto the other end of the island and catch them unawares.'

Nelson's gloved hand stroked his chin. The sea still looked pretty *unmanageable* as far as he could tell, but a definite improvement on last night. 'Let's not be impetuous. We need to work this through.'

They climbed back into the grey Range Rover parked on the lay-by behind them. A new looking, five metre Novamarine inflatable RIB with Yamaha 90 outboard rested on the attached trailer. Nelson pointed a thumb back over his shoulder as he started up the Range Rover. He was indicating to a boxed parcel lying on the rear seat. 'I'll have to get that little present posted as soon as we're through this part.'

He pulled his door closed. 'I agree that going in from the other end of the island is the best bet.' He unfolded a large map out on top of the dashboard so that it draped over the central console. He had done his homework. 'We can journey back along the A832 and branch off onto this track back alongside Little Loch Broom.' His finger traced the route. We should be able to get down near to the old ferry jetty here.' The finger landed upon Badluarach. 'If we can launch from there we'll have a steadier journey along the loch and then out into the open sea. I think they're waiting for better weather or cover of darkness. Their boat must be somewhere near to where we saw them so there's little chance of them seeing us if we can land somewhere on the far end.'

Lowell absorbed the suggestions. 'Okay, how far and how long.'

'The launching site is about six miles all told from here but nothing more than a farm track when we're off the main road, so perhaps twenty-five minutes. It's two miles down the loch and maybe another two across to the island. If we can get the boat on the water okay we could be there within perhaps two hours.'

At half past eight Jennings and Cappelli retraced yesterday's journey back along the A832 towards Mungasdale. They knew they were close to the action, but with no fresh leads they were searching in the dark. Other traffic didn't seem to exist and so the sight of a distant, oncoming Range Rover and trailer served as a notable event. Cappelli grasped the logic behind Sheila Jennings' unclipping of her seat belt and slithering down below dashboard level.

Cappelli's altered appearance had been shaped to some degree by events. Shaving a battered face was neither comfortable nor practicable. The resulting minor growth of beard helped to hide both facial features and injuries. The flat cap which Jennings had borrowed from a coat stand at the Garve Hotel was a useful addition. She'd plonked it on his head before they started off. He'd raised his eyes upward as though examining the style of the addition but then shrugged and carried on. She was after all the Boss.

Cappelli's head kept rigidly to the front as he trundled along at the elderly-gent's pace that he thought was in keeping with the cap. His eyes however, chanced a darting glance at the two Range Rover occupants when the vehicles necessarily slowed to a snail's pace to pass each other by.

A stare and a craning of the neck from the driver bothered Cappelli. His vision went onto the rear view mirror as the vehicles separated. The lack of noticeable body language from the two outlines gave him some confidence that he had not been recognised. Not one shred of doubt survived in his mind though that the face of the driver was the same face seen through his hotel door spyhole and then outside Exeter Police Station.

His corner-of-the-mouth observation on the situation seemed unnecessarily secretive. The Range Rover had long gone. 'It was himmm,' he said, almost singing the sentence, mouth closed and head still locked forward. 'It was definitely fucking himmm.'

'Did he see you?' came Jennings' voice as she repositioned back into her seat.

'Don't think so. He'd got a woman passenger though.'

Nelson turned the Range Rover off the A832 onto the narrow pot-holed lane that ran parallel to Little Loch Broom and back to the Badluarach Ferry point. His suspicious stare at the driver of a car a few moments before was to be expected in these circumstances. He trusted no one.

Almost three miles of narrow rough terrain lay ahead of Nelson and Lowell before they would reach the spot. The term *ferry* had long since become a misnomer. There would be no queues of people or lines of cars. The service which once operated between Badluarach and Scoraig on the North Shore had ceased to exist years before. The old concrete jetty running down to the water's edge was still useable though.

As the three miles was covered a weathered black and white fingerpost came into view. It pointed to the now defunct Badluarach Ferry. A slightly narrower, slightly rougher track took them over a cattle grid and down an incline towards the water's edge of the sea loch, Little Loch Broom. It was deserted. A couple of tatty rowing boats lay upturned nearby and a patch of turf served as a parking space for the vehicle and trailer.

Nelson's watch showed the time as ten minutes past nine as he switched off the engine and fumbled in a pocket for his mobile phone. 'Damn, no bloody signal,' he said. 'I hoped the thing would work from here. I thought I'd be able to hook up with the masts in Ullapool.'

'Who do you need to phone anyway? Sounds a bad move even though it's an anonymous phone.'

'Don't worry yourself. It's a little job I have to do. I've got a score to settle and it should turn into a useful diversion.'

They successfully launched the Novamarine from the old concrete jetty onto Little Loch Broom. Being a sea loch it did suffer from the effects of the tide and so was choppy and blustery, but by comparison to the rough beach launching Taylor and Harding had endured it was a piece of cake. There were no witnesses to the event – a good thing as they weren't in the mood for small talk.

The launch site meant that they would have to take the boat almost two miles up the loch before meeting the open sea. It was a similar distance of almost two miles before they'd meet the northern tip of Gruinard Island. They both took a long look through their binoculars at the rolling grey Minch. Clearly that part of the trip would be different from the relative peace of the loch.

Lowell puzzled when Nelson set off and instead of heading westwards to the sea he started to make for the loch's north shore. 'What are you doing,' she screeched over the engine noise.

Nelson one-handedly checked his phone screen as the boat cruised on. 'Told you… I have a phone call to make. I need to get a signal and the only masts to link up to are in Ullapool.' He shook his head in desperation. 'Still no bloody signal… must be these hills.'

He continued to steer one-handed, upping the speed to a steady twenty knots and occasionally looking up from his phone. They almost covered the one mile breadth of the loch before he tugged at the wheel and made a sharp right turn.

Lowell pulled a confused face. The new direction was now sending them eastwards back down the loch and away from the sea. 'This is wasting time she shouted. We're going to miss our chance. They could be gone.' Nelson ignored her and upped the speed more.

An additional fifteen minute journey in the wrong direction put them almost seven miles from the loch's sea mouth. Lowell hollered over at Nelson through cupped hands. 'This could cost us the entire mission.'

Nelson discounted the opinion with a wave of the hand. A smile came to his face. He held the mobile phone aloft staring at the signal bars. 'Got it,' he said. He quickly reached down to the dashboard and turned off the engine.

The sudden silence was broken only by the slap of waves against the boat's hull. Lowell sat back in her seat watching him as the craft wallowed side to side and end to end. He keyed a number into the phone and listened. The call was answered with unnatural speed – not even the chance for a ring tone to begin. Nelson's confident sickly grin increased as he switched the phone onto speaker mode. The sound of a jumble of voices could be heard, but they were not responding to the phone call. This was a private conversation. Nelson's grin broadened even more. He looked over at Lowell. 'Hear that voice?' he said. 'The one talking now.'

Lowell's nod accompanied her bemused expression. 'Yes.'

'That's the Director General of MI5 having a tête-à-tête in his office in London with some of his underlings. My little diversion is going to put so many cats amongst the pigeons that they'll be too busy to bother with us. The immediate threat is going to be on their own doorstep.'

He then pressed four digits on the phone's keypad and followed up with the hash key. The phone went dead.

Nelson made a self-satisfied grin as he started the boat up again and headed off at full throttle back down the loch toward the sea. The vision came into his mind of the devastation now engulfing the Gower Street London HQ of MI5. The almost certain death of the Director General, Sir Peter Walker would create mayhem in the country's intelligence and security service. The additional deaths or serious injuries to other important staff members would, in Nelson's mind, serve as a bonus. It would be a massive triumph for the Soviet Union but with no provable connection to the Kremlin. More importantly, it would divert attention from the current action in Scotland. His decision to use an explosive rather than the Sarin gas spray had been made out of necessity. Maximum effect was needed along with a certainty of Walker's death.

SIXTY

DIRECTOR GENERAL Sir Peter Walker lived on. No damage had been caused to his office or other parts of the building. Walker, along with a gathering of white-coated lab technicians had interestedly watched the device at close quarters as it sat in the centre of his desk and exploded. Except that it didn't actually explode!

Walker had initiated a full scale search of the building as soon as he discovered Nelson's treachery along with that late night visit to the HQ. The newly arrived compact paper shredder which sat boxed and awaiting installation outside his office door drew the attentions of his secretary Audrey immediately. One had been ordered but not this particular model or colour. Audrey pointed the search team in the right direction as soon as they arrived. The explosive segment of the contraption, comprising a quantity of Semtex and a micro detonator were easily and quickly removed. The coded message sending application on Nelson's phone had also been disabled by Vodafone as a first step. The resulting side show ended up being nothing more than the sudden flashing of a harmless red LED. It did however, evidence Nelson's attempt to murder Sir Peter Walker. It also fleetingly showed his phone's connection to the Vodafone network via a mast in Ullapool. It all went towards proving that Nelson remained at the forefront of the race for Thornberry's file.

Taylor and Harding decided to make a move, or at least prepare to. The sea still looked less than inviting but at least they'd be ready when the right time came. Now that they had the file they weren't too bothered about being spotted by locals making a daylight journey back across The Minch. The most important matter was to get off that island and deliver the documents into the hands of someone they could implicitly trust. If they were to take Kim's father's advice that person would be the Director General of MI5 himself.

The return sea crossing would be made with only the bare essentials. The tent and camping equipment were to be left behind. The boat was a lot more manageable without that extra weight, but the launching would still be a nightmare without the trailer. There seemed no immediate rush though, and they both held an unspoken hope that the weather would improve.

After preparing the boat they wandered back along the eastern shore in the direction of the northern end of the island. They covered a quarter of a mile before venturing over for a glimpse through the gorse bushes at the distant mainland. The site gave a more open view of the wide expanse of ocean back toward Ullapool. It also brought home the real dangers of the sea crossing. The conditions were worse than when they'd made their night time journey. The wind lashed the wave tops and lifted a spray of white foam into the air.

'Looks fearsome,' Taylor said.

Kim linked her arm in against him and used her other hand to shield her eyes from the gusting breeze. 'Yes,' she said and then turned her head over to face north eastward. She kept the hand against her forehead as she squinted against the wind. This wasn't a casual look out to sea. She was trying to focus on the regular pattern of sea spray she'd caught sight of.

'A boat,' she muttered.

The small but powerful craft had rounded the shark's tooth shaped rocky outcrop where the mouth of Little Loch Broom meets the open sea. She watched in silence for a moment. The speck looked to be a full two miles distant from where they stood and hardly visible. Of course there would occasionally be small boats even in harsh weather. But the uniformly spaced flurries of white spray as the hull slammed into the sea swell showed this boat was being driven hard. Recklessly might be a better description. It was heading for Gruinard Island.

Taylor saw it too but kept quiet as he calculated from its path what its destination might be. For a fleeting moment he considered that it might be an innocent outing. Thrill seekers, or a journey out to a fishing spot. Perhaps the intention was to hug in close along the coast between Gruinard and the mainland.

The speck grew in size with each methodical slam into the waves and soon there was no doubting its heading. Taylor crouched to his knees, rested both elbow points onto a remnant of dry stone wall and aimed the binoculars. The stable platform gave a better view. A little tweaking of focus kept in sync with a measured and gradual rotation to the left as he followed the craft's progress.

The figures of a man and a woman could now be made out sitting firmly in the two seats with the man at the wheel. No features could be discerned through the constant veil of spray, other than the two lifejacket clad outlines. A glimpse of tousled windblown hair and a perception of aggressive determination became more apparent with each closing yard.

'Come on, let's get going.' Taylor got back to his feet, binoculars dangling from neck strap. The pair broke into a jog as he gave another sentence 'There's only one conclusion we can come to: those two are our enemies. If they are part of the band you met at my place they're going to be armed.'

Kim kept a steady pace alongside Taylor. They both adopted a runner's posture: looking straight ahead, elbows bent at right angles, hands in an unclenched fist. Their condensing breath trailed from their lips in the cold air.

'We need to time this.' Taylor's words came out readily despite the exertion. 'If we can get our boat on the water and ready to go, but delay setting off until they've landed, it could give us a head start.'

'Understood,' Kim panted. 'The further from their boat we can let them go the better, but we can't let them get too close to us if they are armed.'

They arrived back at the boat and started dragging it down across the sand to the water's edge. The relentless procession of curling crashing waves made a successful launching seem either impossible or lucky. They dumped the boat down on the sand right at the limit of the water's rush up the beach. Taylor unravelled the bow line and tied it off to one of the warning signs. They trotted back up the beach and onto the other side of the spit of sand to catch a look at their enemy's progress. The same wide expanse of ocean was not available to them from this point but they would still be able to see the oncoming boat.

The sea was empty – no sign at all, nothing other than the bleak windswept waters of The Minch. They had misjudged the speed of the boat. It had already disappeared in behind the rocky outcrops and might be attempting a landing at that very moment. It could already be ashore with the two crew members out hunting for their prey.

'We must get off here, and quick,' Taylor shouted over the roar of a retreating wave. He untied the boat's bow line. 'We need to get on the water and make a run for it. We're trapped here and they have guns.'

The launching was an amateurish, rushed and risky piece of work. The relentless rolling waves showed no mercy and the Angry Boyle ended up meeting the water sideways on. Taylor was waist deep in the icy surge with his feet jammed hard into the constantly shifting sand. He was quivering with exhaustion and cold as he called on his last reserves of energy to ease the vessel further seaward. Kim was necessarily in the boat but her weight added even more difficulty to his part of the job. His instinctive shoulder checks over at the beach were made as his mind subconsciously counted off each wasted minute. The expectation of two gun-toting figures emerging from behind rocks and dashing across the sand kept playing out. He wrestled stubbornly against each wave to push the boat deep enough for Kim to use the trim lever. She needed to drop the propeller to get the boat under power. She was fighting for stability as one wave after another slammed into the boat pitching it violently one way and then the other. Her frozen fingers inside waterlogged gloves fumbled the kill cord tag into its slot. She pulled on the choke, turned the ignition key and banged her numbed palm down onto the start button.

The motor exploded into life and within seconds she dropped the prop down and used the power of the outboard in reverse against the waves. Taylor felt the pressure of the surge against the boat decrease and stumbled forward into deeper water desperately attempting to fling his chilled, sodden body over the top tube. Kim lunged over and made a grab for the big man's anorak collar. That extra bit of muscle did the trick and in a second he was sprawled half in the passenger seat and half over the top tube. Kim thumped back down into her seat as the boat rode up high on an incoming wave. She gunned the still cold, spluttering engine hard in reverse as Taylor scrambled down properly into his seat gasping for breath. He still had the presence of mind for a worried glance over at the beach. He was sure that he would see the two figures running full pelt, gun hands outstretched.

SIXTY ONE

THE HEAVY seas and treacherous rocks around the northern end of Gruinard Island had stopped Lowell's and Nelson's plan to land there. They'd been forced to motor along the western coastline, but the rolling Atlantic swell and jagged outline provided not one single place for an even half-safe landing. As their boat slammed on into wave after wave, the southern tip of the island with its banana shaped spit of sand started to appear. Nelson gritted his teeth hoping that Taylor and Harding were somewhere inland still, and that the element of surprise was not yet lost.

He opened up the engine for more power as the sand spit started to give away its detail through the spray. What they saw was unexpected. Three hundred yards away and just off the beach floundered a dirty red RIB with a big Mercury outboard. The lolling craft was in the process of getting underway, reversing from the shore, searching for deeper water. The two figures on board were soaked through and dishevelled. They were working hard and not expecting company from behind.

Lowell dragged a gloved hand across her forehead scraping wet hair from her narrowing eyes. A vicious snarl took over her face as she fixed her attention onto the head and shoulders of the woman at the wheel – Kim Harding. She zipped her wind cheater part way down and reached inside with her right hand.

Nelson rammed the throttle lever forward and an extra kick of power lifted the bows from the waves pushing the pair back into their seats.

Kim was readying to swing the Angry Boyle around but the scream of the other boat's Yamaha 90 penetrated through the weather conditions. They spun around, jaws dropping at the high-speed collision course Nelson had set. The reckless manoeuvre virtually put the boat into flight, skimming across the waves with less than one hundred yards to go.

Kim opened up the throttle of the 115 horsepower Mercury but her eyes widened in disbelief as the boat only chugged forward – puffs of black smoke wafting from the exhaust. Taylor turned back to Kim, apprehension spreading across his face.

'SHIT,' Kim swore through gritted teeth. 'Too much choke…' Her frozen fingers scrabbled at the choke pull, trying to tease it back in. Not too much, not too little – the engine was still cool. Taylor reached over and one-handedly took the wheel as Kim balanced the throttle with one hand against the amount of choke with the other.

Without warning the optimum petrol/air mix for the Mercury reached the engine's cylinder tops. The rugged power source delivered the hoped-for muscle with an almighty kick up the backside. The bow lifted, white foam churned and the black smoke altered into a blue tinge. The Angry Boyle might have looked tatty but it was a beast and was living up to its name.

Kim took the steering wheel back and hared off in the direction of the mainland. As she pushed the choke right in against the dashboard she found still more power waiting under the throttle lever. That tuned up Mercury 115 was ready.

Taylor gripped the side rail, his soaking hair plastered against his head. He looked over at Kim, a frown creased his forehead as he watched her throttle back a fraction and then turn the boat hard on its end. They were now pointing back at the island, facing the Novamarine and charging toward each other head on.

Taylor reached behind his seat with his outstretched right arm and took a solid grip onto the heavy red life ring. If he could inject a little of his own no-nonsense temperament into the mix he would.

A sudden reverberating burst of automatic gun fire made him duck. Half a dozen, two feet high sticks of water spat from the wave tops in front. The sound crashed through, many decibels above both the weather and the screaming outboard engines. The pulsating tongue of orange flame which sizzled from Lowell's gun barrel identified the cause. The idea that the woman might achieve an accurate aim in these circumstances seemed less than impossible. One lucky shot though, would mean certain death.

Taylor wedged his feet hard against the bulkhead and gripped tightly onto the side rail with his left hand as the gap closed. His right arm was held back behind Kim, fingers keeping a vice-like grip onto the life ring. He momentarily turned to face Kim. Was she mad? Was she going to ram the boat?

Kim pulled back hard on the throttle at the last moment and dipped the bow down into the water. A quick left and then right spin of the wheel followed. The boats were nearly upon each other. Nelson dithered with his decisions, steering wildly one way then the other. Taylor readied himself as the two craft rapidly closed together. He leapt to his feet with the life ring held back behind him like a javelin thrower and launched it, letting out a bellicose roar to send it on its way. The thirty inch wide red circle flew through the air like a giant Frisbee. It crashed through the Novamarine's Perspex windshield as the two boats shot past each other with inches to spare.

Taylor and Harding gawped wide-eyed as the event played out like a slow motion car crash. A shower of shattered Perspex, a lash of sea spray, streaks of colour and fearful expressions. It was nothing more than a blurred moment but seemed to last for minutes.

Unlike Kim, Taylor had yet to meet Michael Nelson, but after the previous attempt on Kim's life the identity of the boat's pilot was an easy guess. What shocked Taylor to the core was the identity of the gun-toting woman passenger. The vicious look of hatred in Jenny Lowell's eyes as the two craft flashed past each other and her additional two crazy gunshots added to his disbelief.

Kim swung the boat in toward the western coast of the island, bouncing off the wave tops as she hiked up the power and zig-zagged. The Novamarine and hopefully its occupants had suffered some damage but she was not going to take chances on a lucky shot striking home. It was time to make a break for it and use those jagged contours as a shield. Every yard counted and they needed to employ the Angry Boyle's greater power to put distance between them. The boat was flying as they reached the northern tip of Gruinard Island.

Nelson had taken some cuts to the face when the life ring smashed through the windshield. The steering wheel bore the brunt of the attack though, and was badly buckled, leaving the vessel awkward to control. The boat's best efforts had become pathetic, and by the time Nelson forced it into an attempted pursuit the Angry Boyle had already rounded the Northern tip of the island.

Taylor looked back over his shoulder squinting through stinging eyes and wiping away the salt water with a coat sleeve as the Angry Boyle slammed onwards across the Minch. He pushed in closer to Kim and yelled above the engine noise. 'We could do with making use of this head start by getting the hell out of here. I need some dry gear first or I won't last the day.'

Kim was equally soaked and chilled through to the bone. Her initial head nod as she pressed the throttle to maximum quickly changed to an anxious shake as the engine note lowered its tone and misfired. They were slowing and her repeated attempts to coax power started to fail. The Mercury spluttered to a stop and silence engulfed them. They were over a mile from the shore and wallowing end to end on the heavy swell. A tell-tail meandering rainbow of fuel patterned out onto the grey surface behind them. The outboard had taken a hit from one of Lowell's shots. Kim turned to face Taylor. 'Now we're in trouble.'

During the ten minutes it took for Nelson and Lowell to close the gap several crazy schemes were discussed. None of these inspired much confidence.

There had been an additional few words over the identities of the other two. 'I recognised Nelson, and I've met Jennings before but that wasn't her,' Kim said.

'No,' Taylor announced, taking his first opportunity to break the news. 'I recognised her though, it was Jenny Lowell.'

SIXTY TWO

LOWELL held the Stetchkin out at arm's length as Nelson edged the Novamarine within a few yards of the wallowing Angry Boyle. After her manic display at Taylor's house another guns-blazing performance was possible.

Taylor's own arm's-length posture deterred her. They only had one decent card to play in their pack. He now held the Vaultzsafe out over the water.

'Any shooting and this goes to the bottom.' There was no doubting his honesty.

Nelson put the engine in neutral and let it tick over. His suggestion that they should hand the document container over drew laughter from Taylor. It was their only protection, but even that would run out as soon as they landed.

Taylor looked over at Lowell. 'Why Jenny,' he shouted. 'Why the hell are you doing this?'

Lowell's peevish expression came strongly through in spite of the rough conditions. 'You had your chance to convert me Doug, but you didn't take it. It wouldn't have worked mind you. I've been on this side of the fence for years. You've been too busy spending all your time with Miss Goody Two Shoes to be interested in me.' The grin changed to a gritted-teeth snarl as the gun jabbed out with a straight arm at Kim. The jabs came from metres away, but may as well have been with the barrel shoved against Kim's forehead.

The sea continued to pitch both boats on a one metre swell. Kim's eyes fixed on Lowell's gun hand and the finger which was curled in around the trigger. One sudden jolt could fire the gun.

Kim had no option but to fling the Angry Boyle's bow line over to Nelson and a slow floundering haul back toward the mouth of Little Loch Broom then began. Lowell soon tired of holding out her gun, she figured the time to use it would come soon enough. She took a second hateful glance over at Harding and made up her mind where the first bullets would go.

Taylor also settled back into his seat with the Vaultzsafe on his lap as the slow journey commenced. It seemed unlikely that a compromise would be reached. A violent end to the trip looked like the only possible outcome, but they would not go down without a fight. Kim's quick examination of the damage to the engine suggested a simple fix if only she had the right equipment. A flexible fuel line had been severed, but there were no tools.

The Angry Boyle had taken on a lot of water during the events and as the boat heaved with the swell it took on more. Taylor and Harding struggled over into the rear seat and grabbed a bucket each to bail out. Lowell watched, suspiciously at first, but then accepted it as necessary.

The Angry Boyle slumped low in the water with the added weight causing the tow rope to stretch and then sag between waves. The Novamarine's engine droned as it laboured onwards. The noise successfully drowned out the sound of the Mercury engine being turned over by its starter motor. Kim knew that the outboard would never start without a fuel supply but she kept it turning over for as long as the battery let her. They stopped bailing as they reached the calmer conditions of the loch.

A Range Rover and trailer parked near to the old ferry jetty gave Taylor the clue that this would be the mooring spot. He held his arm out over the side of the boat again. Nothing more than a finger and thumb stopped the Vaultzsafe from dropping down into the depths. The water was still deep enough to lose the item forever and even a quick soaking might ruin the documents.

The two couples faced each other off for a few seconds as Nelson decided on his next move. The tow rope slackened. The two craft drifted within a few metres of each other. The slow tick-over of the Novamarine and the bump-bumping of the Angry Boyle nudging at the concrete jetty were the only sounds.

'Time to hand over Doug,' Lowell said. She stared at Taylor but the gun pointed at Harding.

A snatch of movement in Lowell's peripheral vision served as her only warning. It was never enough for her mind to calculate the danger and take some action. Her over-confident words had not even finished before Kim had leaped to her feet and launched the contents of her bucket. The two gallons of yellow liquid hurtled across the three metre gap between the boats, morphing in shape under its own heavy fluidity. It hit Lowell full in the face like a wet blanket almost toppling her. The gun spun from her hand and landed with a thud down onto the fibreglass hull.

She gasped as the liquid drenched her. A prickling sensation to her skin joined the fizzing taste on her lips and the stinging in her eyes. Fear and incomprehension inspired screams only usually heard in a lunatic asylum as she realised that it was not sea water.

Nelson scrabbled at his shoulder holster for his own gun, but didn't even manage to unclip the press stud before Taylor's own bucket of petrol hit him even harder. It had been a simple matter to direct the severed fuel line into the two buckets during the journey. With the engine turning over against the starter motor it soon filled them. The charade of bailing out had worked well.

Taylor and Harding hopped over the side of the Angry Boyle, their feet searching for the seabed. Swimming was impossible in the lifejackets and heavy clothing. Taylor somehow still held the document container up above the water in one hand as his toes touched down onto unseen rocks. His feet scrabbled for purchase. He made a lunge for Kim's sleeve with his free hand as she wallowed helplessly. He put the power of his legs and stomach muscles to work struggling against the buoyancy of the lifejacket and the treacle effects of the water. It was like the repeating theme from a bad dream as he heaved onwards – split seconds seeming like hours. He snatched a backward glance as Lowell's vicious hysteria overcame any common sense. She was on hands and knees fumbling half blinded by the petrol for the Stetchkin whilst Nelson, equally sightless groped at his shoulder holster.

Taylor, gasping on hands and knees, dragged his wide eyed sodden partner out onto the bankside one-handed. He stumbled up to his feet and instinctively swivelled around to face the boat.

Lowell now stood, gun in hand, petrol-wetted strands of hair plastered against her cheeks. Brown trickling rivulets of dissolved hair dye ran freely down her throat. The same solvent effect attacked the traces of lipstick, mascara and makeup that had survived the sea trip, melting it all into a boiling purple melange.

The two watched, chests heaving, searching for breath but transfixed onto the horror. Lowell had lost all reason and sense. She blindly pointed the gun out at nothing in particular and squeezed at the trigger.

Taylor, Harding and even Nelson all screamed in unison… 'NO'.

The Stetchkin obeyed with a full burst releasing all of its remaining twelve rounds. The Russian made gun was truly inhuman but had several drawbacks. It was wildly inaccurate and almost impossible to control in automatic mode. Each bullet fired would jar the gun wrist upwards another two inches. Lowell's aim ended skywards by the time the clip had emptied.

The worst failing of the gun however, was one which made it a particularly unwelcome sidearm during night time manoeuvres. Its eagerness to produce that long tongue of orange flame along with each bullet fired was a downside which readily attracted the attention of sniper's bullets.

In automatic mode it resembled a flame thrower.

The deep WHOOMPH came as the joint cry of 'NO…' tailed off and the boat and its two crew members ignited.

Flames differ in colour and intensity. These flames, in keeping with their petrol source were a dark orange tinged with a deep red. A cauldron of thick boiling black smoke was instantly generated as the screams of the two flailing banshee figures within intensified.

Nelson's will to live triggered both his plunge into the water and the mechanical thrashing toward the bank which followed. The twitching convulsions given off by his smoking body as it lay on the shingle were not an indication of recovery. He was dead – horribly burned. The inferno that was Lowell's corpse did not even warrant as much as a second thought as the two boats drifted slowly from the bank.

Taylor and Harding looked around at the smouldering devastation feeling sickened by it all. It was not an outcome they had wished for, but had been the unfortunate cost of their own survival. Taylor's shake of the head attended a long and despairing sigh. Kim's reaction might have been considered an imitation. The tears streaming down her cheeks were the only deviation.

The activity, the smoke and flames had attracted some interest. A number of small dots had now gathered by cars on a grey ribbon of tarmac a mile away across the loch.

Taylor hugged Kim in tightly with his right arm. 'There's nothing we can do here. The biggest priority is getting this to the Director General.' He held up the Vaultzsafe with his other hand. That hand shook with cold. The condition affected them both in equal shivering measures. The fight or flight response of adrenalin was now wearing off and their physical condition had entered a serious stage. They could not approach anyone for help, even if anyone were to be found. Word would be getting around now though and although the closest local police were over thirty miles away in Ullapool the balloon would soon be going up. Two bodies and a burning boat would take some explaining.

As police officers themselves they knew that an encounter with the law would lead to arrest and a long stay in the cells before the truth was believed. All these things would jeopardise the security of the file. Geoff Fry's suggestions that no one could be trusted still held fast. They needed to see this through to the end themselves to ensure his shrewd demands were fully met.

They had a journey of almost nine miles before they would be back at The Lodge. That would take hours on foot and almost certainly be thwarted by exposure before a short distance had been covered. They both now visibly shook uncontrollably with cold.

Taylor fumbled his frozen, maladroit fingers against the Range Rover's door handle and managed a clumsy tug. It was locked. He looked down at Nelson's smouldering corpse and shook his head with distaste as he took on a gruesome but necessary task. He knelt down alongside the body, turned it onto its back and rummaged tentatively inside the ragged pockets. He looked up at Kim with more than a hint of shame on his face as he pulled out a set of keys. If he could have crossed two of his ice numbed fingers before he pressed the button on the remote door opener he would have done so.

The Range Rover's locks jolted upward with a satisfying *clunk*. Urged on by his triumph, his practically paralysed, shaking hands were able to unhook the trailer and push it to one side.

SIXTY THREE

THE RANGE Rover's heavy duty heater quickly got to work thawing the pair out as they began the journey back to The Lodge. The neatly boxed parcel on the back seat grabbed Kim's attention as soon as her senses started to return. Anything inside the vehicle could be of interest and relevant to Nelson's treacherous deeds. She reached over for the box placing it onto her lap for a closer look.

Cheddar's explanation of what he'd found out about the clocks was at the forefront of Taylor's mind. He kept one eye on the road and the other on Kim's examination. A part label showed through additional bands of sellotape, giving away enough wording to decode the contents. It added sufficient anxiety to generate Kim's single hushed word. 'God…'

Sessions Electric Mantel Clock.

'Careful,' Taylor said. 'Remember what happened to Angela.'

Kim nodded, but didn't need a warning. She slowly turned the package over. A printed name complete with a Wilshire address:

Mr V. Pasechnik.

'A potential subject for eavesdropping?' Kim said.

'Either that or someone Nelson wanted eliminating.'

Kim nodded. 'It's too dangerous to throw out.'

'Agreed,' Taylor said. 'Put it carefully back on the seat. It can't possibly be set off out here, we're out of range for mobiles and I'm guessing its battery's dead anyway.' He turned the Range Rover into the driveway of The Lodge and coasted down to the door.

The journey had taken twenty minutes and they were soon inside shedding their sodden clothes onto the kitchen floor. 'Let's get changed and get on the road.' He raised his voice a little as Kim was in the bathroom. 'We don't know who else is on our tail and the local police are likely to be interested by now.'

Kim emerged towelling her hair and flung a fresh towel over at him. Lowell's collaboration with Nelson still hadn't sunk in. 'Jenny Lowell,' she said as she pulled dry clothes from a bag. She shook her head as the scene back in Taylor's garage vividly came into her mind. 'She tried to kill me.'

Taylor accepted a pair of dry jeans from her. 'She tried to kill us both back there. I'm having as much trouble as you are at understanding this, but it does answer a few questions.' He tucked in a fresh T shirt. 'Lowell tipped me off about who Alex Tremaine was. She started all this off. That was no doubt a little bit of bait to get us stirring things up so that she and Nelson could see what floated to the surface.'

Kim struggled into dry jeans and a pullover, but the sodden hiking boots would have to do. She was still towelling her hair. 'Devious cow…' Her words tailed off as a video of how Lowell had died played out in her mind. 'That visit to your house… you must have surprised her. She'd gone there to bug the place. She didn't expect to find you in. I bet she thought it was her birthday.' The added sentence had sarcasm attached to it, but Kim started to cry as soon as she'd said it. Lowell had paid the ultimate price for her treason. The screams now ringing in Kim's ears would stay with her forever.

Taylor put his arms around her and hugged. 'It was horrible and not what we intended, but it was them or us. We need to get the hell out of here now and get that file down to London.'

He finished the sentence as he walked through to the lounge dragging fingers through his wet hair.

A man was sitting in the arm chair near to the window. He faced in toward the room, a pair of large powerful binoculars hung against his chest. He smiled casually at Taylor and then pointed a thumb backwards over his shoulder at the window and the Minch which lay beyond. 'An exciting display out there earlier on. I thought all was lost when your boat stopped. I saw the smoke rising further around the coast and gathered there had been a few other complications. Anyway you seem to have come out on top… so well done.'

'Who the hell are you?' Taylor said.

The man's lived-in craggy face complemented his muscular build. His still-dark hair belied his fifty-one years. He got to his feet and extended his right hand for Taylor to shake. 'Oh sorry…Alex Tremaine. Excuse me for listening to your conversation, but I was as surprised as you obviously were to hear who the woman was. It's taken me a couple of seconds to put a personal record to the name but I do recall that Jennifer Adelle Lowell was at Sandhurst with Nelson. Special Branch now I think, a senior officer with Staffs Police. Obviously you knew her before all this Mr Taylor.' A wink accompanied the man's smile.

Kim stood behind Taylor, her mouth slightly open with astonishment. The day had been filled with surprises and here was another.

'Kim,' Tremaine said. 'Nice to see you again. You'll not remember me I was a good friend of your father. I … worked with him.' Tremaine hesitated with the word. 'Perhaps worked *alongside* him would be more accurate. Some of that stuff he did was beyond me.' Tremaine added a half laugh. 'I visited him at home a few times over the years but you were a little girl back then.'

Kim said nothing but a distant recollection started to wake itself.

Taylor had been forced into a handshake, but his wary expression spoke volumes and caused Tremaine to make a comment. 'Don't worry Mr Taylor I'm on your side.'

'Nelson and Lowell are both dead,' Taylor said.

Tremaine calmly turned and gazed out at the ocean. 'That's an unfortunate turn of events. Still I suppose it will stop the Russians trying to come up with a bartering deal.' He shook his head. 'A swop for some of our agents or some such nonsense would have been on the cards. It was a real shock to discover a bad apple right at the heart of our organisation though.'

His stare kept on the ocean but the question he now posed was somehow directed at them both. 'So you have Dr Thornberry's file?'

Kim answered, but her reply was less than direct. 'My father's instructions are to hand it over in person to the current Director General.'

'Understood,' Tremaine said quickly. 'Always the cautious one, Geoff Fry and it seems he's passed those same genes on to you. I have a plane on standby at Inverness and so you can both come back to London with me.' He pulled up his jacket cuff to check his watch. 'We could be with Peter Walker by tea time.'

Tremaine turned back into the room and faced Taylor and Harding. 'I've seen that you've got your motor cycle outside. I can arrange to get that sent down to you. There'll be no need for you to come back up here.'

Taylor caught Kim's eye. He had reservations and knew she felt the same way. He wondered if the events had made them paranoid. There seemed no reason not to trust Tremaine. What they knew about the story supported the man's loyalty and reliability He'd been an important kingpin within Government security services for years. He'd sent the coded letter to Geoff Fry tipping him off that the Rosa incident had resurfaced.

'Your offer is appreciated,' Taylor added a smile as he looked Tremaine straight in the eyes. He was trying oh-so-hard not to appear distrustful of the man, but something kept stopping him. 'We'd rather get sorted out here… showered and fed and make our way down first thing tomorrow on the bike with the file.'

Tremaine gave a closed-eyes nod of understanding. 'I'm sure that won't be a problem… Doug. There's plenty for me to do here anyway. I'll have to get local Special Branch over to arrange some explanations so that the police and Coroner can deal with those two bodies.'

Taylor kept his smile intact, although some niggles dented its sincerity. 'Incidentally Major… where is your car?'

'I've got two men with me,' Tremaine explained. 'I never expected that you would have accomplished so much on your own. They're parked further up the road, didn't want to frighten anyone off.'

Down at Little Loch Broom the activity had attracted attention. A couple of local fishermen had hauled the charred floating remnants of the Novamarine back in against the jetty along with the still attached and hardly damaged Angry Boyle. The men knew of the Boyles and their boat. The two charred corpses had initiated an overdue 999 call.

Jennings and Cappelli had seen the smoke and suspected it was connected. Jennings' confident demeanour and quick flash of her Security Services ID card to the fishermen backed up her claim of being a police officer. Mr Boyle, or "Mr Angry" as the natives knew him was something of a local celebrity and so the home of his boat was established before the arrival of the real police.

The information had led Jennings and Cappelli to where they now stood – inside the grounds of Boyle's bungalow staring at a discreetly parked Vauxhall Senator.

It was a sickening sight, not just because it WAS "a sickening sight" but more so because of the callous way in which it had been done. The car's two occupants – driving seat and front passenger seat were both big men – muscular, fit, smartly dressed and in their late twenties. The bullet holes through the front windscreen originated from within the car. The blood, brain, hair, skin and skull fragments sprayed onto the inside of the screen corroborated this fact. The damage to the heads of the two corpses, even without a pathologist's keen eye, had been inflicted by a gunman in the rear seat.

Jennings was as hard as nails but the sight made even her stomach turn enough for one small, but fortunately checked, gagging episode. Cappelli, not so disciplined, quickly discarded his full Scottish breakfast onto Mr Boyle's recently tarmacked drive.

Jennings' revulsion had been magnified. 'I know these men,' she said. 'I've worked with them before. They're part of an SAS team assigned to special ops with us.'

SIXTY FOUR

TREMAINE watched as Kim turned and went through into the kitchen. She filled the kettle and soon its muted roar added a background noise. He followed her in, hands clasped behind back. 'Ah cuppa tea,' he said. The best problem solver there is.'

Kim turned to face Tremaine with her own poor attempt at a half smile. There was a minute red fleck present on the man's white shirt collar. An immediate conclusion would have been a shaving cut from earlier that morning, but no corresponding mark existed on his neck. She noticed it.

Tremaine's expression had contorted into an over exaggerated crescent moon grin. 'Where did you say the file is now?' he said.

Kim's attempts at cheeriness stopped. Her eyes bored through Tremaine's deceit. 'I didn't. I might have been a little girl when you last met me but children can be perceptive when it comes to sincerity. That little girl all those years ago didn't like you. This big girl of today feels the same way.'

Taylor came into the kitchen. 'I'm not sure what your agenda is Tremaine but get this straight… we've come this far on our own and we're going to see this through our way.'

Tremaine reached inside his jacket. The Velcro fastener of his shoulder holster gave a tearing sound as he ripped it open. He stood firmly back against the edge of the worktop making his gun aim at either of them easy. 'I don't think we'll be doing it your way at all. Quite the opposite in fact, but before I decide what to do with you let's see if we can reach a deal.'

'That's not going to happen Tremaine,' Taylor said.

Kim's stare stayed fixed on Tremaine, but her expression had now turned to disbelief. She didn't like or trust the man, but hadn't expected this. She blinked twice and her bottom jaw dropped a little. 'You…?' She said the single word as a question, her forehead wrinkling with confusion. 'It was you all along.' It was not a question now, but a statement, a firm statement of fact. 'Dad was right; there *was* a mole… a Soviet agent on the inside.'

Tremaine gave a casual shrug. 'Yes, your father was always a fly in my ointment, but fortunately he never suspected *me*. He was even kind enough to keep me updated on his theories.' Tremaine's eyes darted from Kim and back to Taylor. 'The British Government desperately wants that file so that they can neutralise the sites, but none of that is what this is all about.' Tremaine now cranked his head to one side and gave a patronising smile. 'You see, knowing where the dead drops are will only be of real use to the Russkies if there's a chance of imminent war between them and the UK, and that's unlikely.'

Taylor listened but held his poker face. His real focus stayed on Tremaine's gun hand. The Browning Hi-Power Mark 3 contained thirteen 9mm rounds and could punch right through a car. It still pointed at Taylor but a swivel to target Harding was easy.

'It's Thornberry's formula which is the most important thing.' Tremaine said. 'It's an incredibly complex procedure which no one has been able to reproduce. The United Kingdom has kept rigidly to the policies of The Biological and Toxin Weapons Convention since its introduction back in 1969. Britain has no interest in the formula other than to stop anyone else getting hold of it. The Soviet Union and many other countries who signed the agreement have never stopped secretly working on Biological weapons and stockpiling. Thornberry's VX is the ultimate of all non-explosive Doomsday weapons.'

Tremaine's eyes moved between Harding and Taylor hoping for a glimmer of interest. 'You see, the Soviet Union is by no means the highest bidder in this game and we are not talking in meagre terms of millions. You two could be wealthy beyond your wildest dreams… a new identity, a new country, a place in the sun.'

Taylor and Harding's disgusted shake of the head was so

spontaneous and synchronised that it might have been rehearsed. The proposition sickened them. None of the words held any sincerity anyway. It seemed more likely that Tremaine intended leaving alone with the file whatever happened. Witnesses to his behaviour would not be something he would want, and the suggestion of business partners was clearly a sham.

Outside, Cappelli and Jennings had quickly tracked down The Lodge as being the centre for the current action. The phone box near to the outskirts of Laide enabled contact with London. The carnage in Tremaine's staff car pointed the finger at him as being an unexpected deviator from the straight and narrow. The Director General immediately dispatched a team to assist Jennings and gave her an overriding instruction before he made a dash to board a rooftop helicopter. 'Deal with it… don't let Tremaine out of the country with that file.'

The unlikely Jennings and Cappelli duo covertly made it down the driveway of The Lodge. The raised voices of the kitchen conversation gave them enough to get fully up to speed with the events. Tremaine's ruthless slaughtering of the two SAS men left them in no doubt that a similar fate lay in store for Taylor and Harding. Tremaine only needed the file.

The thought of Tremaine's car came into Jennings' mind again and presented another puzzle. He would not be able to use that car for his getaway and must have planned to take Harding's motorcycle. Without doubt he'd now set his mind on the Range Rover.

Jennings tried the vehicle's doors and the idea of disabling it ran through her mind, but Taylor, through force of habit had locked it. Maybe she could let the tyres down? It would take ages and gave no guarantee of stopping Tremaine. She peered through the windows and spotted the box on the rear seat. But what really grabbed her attention was the metal document container down in the front passenger foot well. The corroded metal container bore a red Dymo tape label. Jennings angled her head for a better look. The name numbed her: *Dr E Thornberry*.

If Tremaine twigged where the file was and managed to get the Range Rover keys he had everything.

Inside The Lodge Tremaine kept the gun on Taylor. At the same time his eyes searched the room for any item not there when he'd first entered. A bag, a folder, a briefcase – anything which might hold the file.

He knew that Kim had only made it as far as the bathroom before going into the lounge. The process of elimination whirred inside the veteran MI5 traitor's mind like an old fashioned mechanical calculator – gears and cogs spinning and slotting into place. The answer, when it came, jolted the entire phenomenon to a crashing halt. The file was in the Range Rover.

Tremaine was wily though and he would not be taking chances. Taylor and Harding were the only people who actually knew where the file was. They would not be killed until he was sure.

His powerful left arm shot out and grabbed Kim by the neck pulling her in against his side like a rag doll. He pressed the gun barrel so hard against her temple she squealed.

'Careful Taylor… no false moves or she'll be the first one to go.'

Taylor's arms rose upwards even though no order had been given. 'Okay, okay… what do you want?'

'It's in the Range Rover… right?'

Taylor nodded.

'KEYS… on the table then stand back.'

Taylor obeyed, dumping the Range Rover keys down.

'Pick them up,' he hissed into Kim's ear and twisted her around towards the table. His left elbow now crooked tightly around her throat.

She obeyed, eyelids flickering from the pain of the gun barrel as her shaking fingers clutched at the keys.

'Okay Taylor, outside.' Tremaine nodded sharply at the back

door.

Taylor opened up, immediately focussing on Jennings. She was half crouched on the other side of the Range Rover, leaning across its bonnet facing him. She held her Browning pistol two-handed with arms out-stretched and pointing directly at him. She winked. Taylor's big frame filled the door opening. There was one step down onto the pebble covered drive. Tremaine had no view other than that of Taylor's back.

Taylor hovered for a moment wondering on the best action. He tried to sum up Jennings' gun skills from the limited data available. He drank in the professional stance, the grip on the gun and the calm determined stare. If he'd been a betting man he would have come down on the side of Jennings being good. He wasn't a betting man though – not with Kim's life at any rate.

'Get a move on Taylor,' Tremaine shouted. Aggression and impatience now joined the mix of emotions. Jennings made a sharp head movement at Taylor directing him to one side. He slowly stepped down and equally slowly stepped to his right. He didn't want to panic Tremaine into sudden careless shots.

Taylor need not have worried, Tremaine's cunning seemed to thrive on surprises; he'd reduced his outline by squeezing in behind Kim. So little of the bulky man's frame offered itself as a target for Jennings' gun, that even a sniper would have baulked at pulling the trigger.

'Join the party Jennings,' Tremaine said. One florid cheek and one wide eye was all that could be seen. His hot breath filled Kim's nostrils, his rough spiky chin scraped like sandpaper into her neck. The gun muzzle pushed in hard enough to almost crack her skull.

'Game's up Tremaine.' The words came from the kitchen. They came from behind Tremaine. They were spoken in the same moment that a hard pressure squeezed in against the traitor's own temple.

Tremaine could never have known that the meddling reporter Benedict Cappelli was the man behind him. Neither did he have any way of knowing that Cappelli's gun was anything other than a TV remote control. It was the only gun-feeling thing available to Cappelli when he'd sprung a bedroom window and climbed in.

Tremaine's clockwork mind spun at full speed as he assimilated all the facts of a worsening situation. Jennings had no official colleague with her. Indeed it had suited Tremaine's own purposes to initially blacken her character as being Nelson's partner in crime.

Whilst he didn't know the identity of the man behind him, certain unprofessional moves gave the game away. The man's legs were wrongly placed. They were too close in against him, and as for that gun, well it wasn't right. Tremaine determined that he could almost certainly twist and disable the man. But the action might expose enough of himself as a target for the necessary head shot that Jennings needed to take. It was now four onto one and Tremaine needed to adjust the odds.

SIXTY FIVE

TREMAINE stamped down hard into the instep of Cappelli's right foot. At the same time he hinged his own gun away from Kim's temple to line up with Jennings' head and shoulder outline. The throat lock around Kim tightened as though Tremaine's arm was hydraulic and he instantaneously twisted his head from Cappelli's fake gun.

Two rapidly fired and deafening shots rang out as Tremaine's military brain mechanically employed the double-tap shooting technique. His aim though, was more of a barrel-pointing exercise, but it served its purpose. Jennings catapulted violently backwards as though she'd been hit by a car. Her body crashed end over end several feet away and her gun flew away into the undergrowth.

Cappelli's inexpert attempt to regain the upper hand was rewarded with a gun butt hard on top of the head. He dropped to the ground, blood spouting from a scalp wound and stars of concussion flitting in front of his eyes. The TV remote clattered onto the tiles.

Tremaine spun to face Taylor and held the gun out toward him with a fully outstretched arm. The face of the dangling ragdoll which hung inertly from his quivering crooked left arm had taken on a deathly pallor. A bubble of saliva grew from Kim's lips.

'You're killing her you bastard, Taylor shouted.

'Sooner or later Taylor… sooner or later.'

A small metallic rattle followed Tremaine's words. It was the sound of metal on floor tiles.

Tremaine flinched, instantly knowing the source of the sound. He looked down to see the Range Rover Keys had dropped from Kim's lifeless fingers.

It was the smallest of diversions but it was the only one Taylor would get. Tremaine let Kim's body drop – dumped it down, half-in, half-out of the doorway. He snatched downwards for the keys as

Kim's head hit the hard floor with a sickening thud. The fingers of his left hand scooped up the keys as he swung the gun back on Taylor.

The broad, flat, white skimming stone would have been close to the maximum size according to Doug Taylor's father's recommendations. At four inches in diameter it might even have been a tad over the limit, but in these circumstances it was ideal. It struck Tremaine edge-on with every ounce of power and accuracy that the six feet four detective could muster. It embedded itself with a stomach churning crunch into his left eye socket.

Tremaine's head jerked backwards in a spray of blood. His gun fired twice in quick succession as his animal instinct took over. One bullet zinged skywards whilst the other slammed through a rear door of the Range Rover visibly rocking the vehicle. He stumbled dazed against the wall of the building half blinded by the streaming blood and overwhelmed with both vengeance and escape. His head pivoted in a one-eyed search for targets, gun-hand waving crazily.

Taylor picked his chance. He dragged Kim inside the kitchen, slamming and locking the door as Tremaine lurched around the back of the Range Rover fumbling with the keys. Cappelli, semi-conscious, sat propped, bleary-eyed and blood smeared against a kitchen unit.

Taylor's hands shook as he lifted Kim into a more comfortable position. He knelt beside her and swiftly went through procedures he had done so many times as a police officer – checking for pulse and breathing. His hands had never shaken on those occasions though.

Kim's eyes flickered open and she blinked to focus on his face. Her puzzled frown implied confusion as she battled for full consciousness. Taylor looked up catching a glimpse of the blue sky through the window. 'Thanks Dad,' he said. Kim's bewilderment increased at the comment but the sudden roar of the Range Rover's engine jarred Taylor back into action – Tremaine was making his getaway.

Kim unsteadily pulled herself up as Taylor made a grab for the door. 'Don't let the bastard take it,' came her breathless words.

The Range Rover's engine screamed as the injured Tremaine demolished Boyle's gateposts in a one-eyed reversing frenzy.

Taylor dashed over to Sheila Jennings. She was slumped against a tree stump, rapidly losing blood from a bullet wound to the shoulder. She gazed up towards the top of the drive, widening her eyes at Tremaine's manic escape attempt – crashing gears, spinning wheels, over-revving. The vehicle had now backed halfway out onto the road and it was a good bet that once he'd selected a forward gear he'd be back in control. Jennings grabbed Taylor's sleeve with her good arm and murmured something as a trickle of blood escaped from the corner of her mouth.

Taylor leaned in to make out her whispered slurred words.

'He's going to get away with it. You must stop him.'

Kim appeared at the door, deathly pale and clutching at the frame for support.

'Look after her,' Taylor yelled back and started a sprint up the driveway.

He reached the tangle of ironwork that had been Boyle's gates as the back end of the Range Rover disappeared over the brow of the hill by Boyle's bungalow. He instinctively started to chase after it. It seemed a futile crazy action but he couldn't stop himself.

He ran on hard until he stopped hands on knees gasping for breath at the top of the hill outside the entrance to the bungalow. From here the road started to dip steeply back down to the coast again. He fully expected to see the tail end of the Range Rover speeding away down towards Laide village and the coast.

What he saw just over the brow of the hill dumbfounded him. The Range Rover stood in the centre of the narrow asphalt road. Its front wheels were pointing in the direction of the sea shore which lay one hundred feet below. Two thick, black tyre skid marks led away from the rear wheels. The engine had stalled.

Taylor tentatively started to approach. He could see Tremaine's bolt upright outline in the driving seat. It didn't take much to work out that MI5 man was still in control as the brake lights were glowing red. His foot must have been pressing down onto the pedal and holding the vehicle on the steep bank.

Taylor stepped back and weighed things up for a moment. This was odd. The engine had stopped, but the brake lights were lit up. It meant the ignition was still turned on. Taylor stayed put for a second and concluded that Tremaine had hit the brake pedal so hard with the car still in gear, that he'd stalled the motor. The vehicle was being held on the steep bank by the pressure of Tremaine's foot on the brake pedal. Kim's mechanical mind would soon have pointed out that this was no mean feat. Without the power-assist of the engine it needed a mighty foot pressure to keep that one and a half tons from rolling away.

Slowly, he edged a little closer as the thoughts of a trap entered his mind. Tremaine may jump out firing at any moment. A little confidence was gained as he moved around to the offside – he could not see the gun.

After another two cautious steps he arrived alongside the driver's door and looked in through the window glass from five feet. His initial thought had been to wrench open the door and drag the man down onto the road but what he saw rooted him to the spot. Both of Tremaine's white knuckled hands gripped the steering wheel with such rigid vibrating force that it seemed he might snap it clean off from the central spokes. The man was shuddering; his whole body seized in a vice-like tension. His one good eye stared blindly straight ahead, so wide and bulging, that it looked likely to explode into a gelatinous blur. The other eye was a bloodied swollen lump from where the stone had smashed into the bone. The man had become a convulsing vibrating uncontrollable mass. The vehicle visibly shook in sync with Tremaine's tremors transmitted through his immense pressure on the brake pedal.

The police officer inside Taylor came into his consciousness and forced him to consider the options. Both he and Kim could justify all of their actions so far, but this might be different. Tremaine appeared to be having some kind of fit.

Should he drag him out and try first-aid? He'd rather let the bastard die, but his training told him that was wrong. His hand gripped at the driver's door handle. He delayed for a second as his eyes briefly landed on the bullet hole in the rear passenger door. It happened during Tremaine's manic battle for freedom – those two random shots fired off as the stone sliced into his skull.

Taylor's hand stayed on the door handle as his senses fought to understand the slow misting up of the Range Rover's windows. He rubbed his other hand over the glass of the passenger door and discovered it was on the inside. He inquisitively pressed his face against the glass.

Tattered furrows in the seat's grey leather showed the route of Tremaine's bullet after it penetrated the metal door skin. Cardboard, wooden splinters and shards of glass had erupted and evidenced the projectile's impact into the boxed electric clock which had lain there. The workings of the evil device had been disgorged and scattered. The shattered clock face and a clump of solid state circuitry from the mobile phone component lay on the rubber mat. Wiring and plastic from the air freshener module, were similarly strewn. The two inch long metal capsule, designed to contain the pressurised Forest Pine liquid – as printed onto its label – had punctured.

Only a pinhole had been made in the capsule and so the contents had taken some time to empty. It would have been a fine, vaporising, pressurised jet in the first few moments, but had died away to intermittent spurts. Forest Pine air freshener is a pungent but pleasing odour. Sarin nerve agent is said to have no smell or taste although from whom this fact was learned seems unknown. Taylor started to take slow backward steps as he wondered how airtight a Range Rover might be. His eyes landed back on Tremaine as his convulsions altered and the vehicle jolted forward an inch – a movement of the foot on the brake pedal perhaps?

The frenzied juddering reached a crescendo as a bar of projectile vomit sprayed against the inside of the windscreen. Oddly, the fingers remained clamped to the steering wheel and his single bulging eye, kept its bloodshot stare riveted forward.

Taylor, unblinking and open mouthed, took more backward steps and watched as Tremaine's shoulders finally slouched. His hands still gripped the wheel, but the convulsions stopped. The pressure of the foot on the brake pedal also stopped. A small creak of springs came as the immense force from the man's right foot released and allowed brake pads to draw away from discs. Gravel crunched under tyres and gravity instigated a downhill journey. A kangaroo style action quickly developed as speed gathered. The vehicle, stuck in third gear and with the ignition still on, was now attempting to start.

Taylor, motionless apart from his slowly turning head, watched as the pace quickly picked up and the vehicle impacted rocks and bushes on the offside verge. The square box shape of the Range Rover looked almost comical as the increasing gradient took it faster and further off the road. Each boulder and gorse covered rut bounced it higher until it hurtled, wheels, doors and panels tearing and separating, flying into the air and spinning away. The silence when it dipped out of sight over the cliff edge lasted a little over two seconds. The sound of the impact onto the beach below was a dull muffled crunch. The smoke which followed broadcast the intensity of the unseen raging fire.

Taylor turned at the sound of footsteps. Kim looked over at the rising smoke and raised her eyebrows. 'Oh,' she said.

'How are the other two?' Taylor asked

'Brice Guaire and his wife are there; they've phoned it in and the air ambulance is on its way. Mrs Guaire used to be a nurse, so fingers crossed. The place will be swarming in a bit.'

The sound of distant klaxons supported Kim's theory and seconds later the *whop, whop, whop* of the air ambulance blades drowned out all conversation. Some expert arm signalling from Mr Guaire guided the helicopter down for a roadway landing close to The Lodge, flattening grass and battering bushes in the process.

Taylor took hold of Kim and hugged her, he yelled in her ear above the din. 'You okay?'

Some colour had returned to her cheeks. She bit down lightly onto her bottom lip. 'I'm okay,' she said, eyes still fixed on the column of smoke. She looked back at Taylor. They said nothing more, but started a slow walk through the gorse bushes and bracken towards the cliff edge. A little used footpath pointed a route to the beach and hand in hand they started down. They needed to be sure.

They arrived on the sand as the clattering rotor blades of the air ambulance helicopter indicated its departure with the two patients.

The remnants of the Range Rover had somehow finished upright. Only one wheel had stayed put. The bonnet, boot lid and two of the four doors had all parted company. These lay strewn over a fifty yard wide area along with countless other bits and pieces. Flames still licked outward through door and window openings feeding on a mixture of carpets, plastic and upholstery. The petrol which started the blaze was now all but gone and the intensity of the fire had dwindled. Tremaine's battered body had been flung forty feet out across the sand to the water's edge. The tide's attempts to capture the corpse resulted in a macabre repetitious wallowing of arms and legs.

Kim averted her gaze from Tremaine's body and wandered across the sand picking her way through pieces of burning debris and smashed car parts. Taylor was head-down, thirty yards away searching along by the base of the cliff at the point where the Range Rover had plummeted over. Kim watched him for a moment, fascinated by his persistence, *ever the detective,* she thought as he started to make his way across to her.

Taylor came to a sudden stop and raised a hand in the air beckoning her over. At his feet half buried in the wet sand was the Vaultzsafe. The lid, damaged in the impact lay half open with yellowed fluttering paperwork on show. Its buckled metalwork had preserved the contents but signs of seawater showed how the tail-end of a wave had purged it of the nerve agent which killed Tremaine. The deadly secrets of Thornberry's formula could without question be recovered by scientists even if the seawater had penetrated.

Kim's eyes met Taylor's in a long, hard stare before blankly looking down at the sand and then back up to him. The lip was between the teeth again. Taylor's input showed as nothing more than a shrug. It had to be her decision. She got to her haunches, tears streaming down her cheeks as she touched the fingertips of her right hand against the edges of the fluttering sheets of paper.

The intensity had gone from the fire inside the shell of the Range Rover although bright red flames still licked out. Kim gingerly positioned the Vaultzsafe in through the car's gaping driver's door opening, blinking at the heat and stepping back. The crisp old documents inside generated some fresh yellow flames for a short while and then died away to leave the metal of the case slowly warping and distorting. It was odd that the Dymo tape label had lasted so long. They watched it fry into a small bubble of celluloid. The name of Dr E Thornberry and her work were now obliterated forever.

The shadow of a British Army Westland Lynx helicopter darkened a patch of the beach. The throb of its engine drowned out all other sound as it slowly touched down. Taylor and Harding watched, hands shielding eyes as sand whipped and slowing rotor blades began to droop. A number of black clad figures climbed out and made their way over.

MI5 Director General Sir Peter Walker and his entourage were soon standing in front of the pair.

It was a disappointment to Walker to discover that the file had gone up in flames inside the Range Rover during Tremaine's attempt to steal it.

He quickly gave out orders to his team and in no time they probed the debris and scoured the beach for signs of loose paperwork which might have escaped. It seemed unlikely.

It was several minutes later when Kim reached into her pocket and withdrew one single crumpled piece of A4. The slight tilt of the head she gave accompanied her resolute expression.

'I picked this one up…' she said with nonchalance. 'It seems to be the only one that survived.'

The MI5 boss braced himself against the sea breeze and pulled his spectacle case from his pocket. He quickly ran his eyes over the smudged words before handing the document to an assistant for careful safekeeping. 'Hmm,' he said as he pushed his hands deeply down into his overcoat pockets and looked back up at Kim. The smile he returned would have fitted the description of *knowing*.

'So at least we have the list of dead drops,' Walker said. 'All the places where the nerve agent may have been stored. It seems that your father has completed his mission to keep the country safe.'

He looked out to sea and blew out in an exaggerated sigh. 'But no one… not even us, will ever get their hands on the formula.' The two whispered words he added were lost on the wind: 'Thank God.'

Epilogue

THE JOB of restoring normality after these events was code-named *Operation Dark Harvest* by the Security Services and a total blanket of secrecy engulfed the entire issue. The need to know rule applied to everyone touched in one way or another by the affair.

None of the stories given by witnesses to various parts of the episode could be corroborated by anything written in public records. The military quickly admitted that they had been involved on training exercises in the area. Their suggestion that some of the exaggerated stories may have evolved from these manoeuvres was the only statement issued.

A worried Mr Boyle returned from holiday to discover a new set of wrought iron gates fitted to refurbished stone gateposts at The Lodge. It hinted at something more severe than the minor prang suggested by the local police chief.

The motorcycling couple who had rented out Boyle's property vanished without trace. Their connection to a Staffordshire shooting incident, as reported in the newspaper was not elaborated on. Oddly even the newspapers seemed disinterested in following up the story.

The usual closing of ranks to which the close-knit locals around Gruinard Bay were so accustomed, played to the advantage of the Security Services. Very quickly the story was treated with the same wall of silence which for so many years had protected the legend of Gruinard Island.

Despite being a local himself Boyle did remain puzzled that his RIB had made it back to the boathouse intact and ready to go. His surprise turned to astonishment at a later sea trial when he described it as "faster than when new". He gathered that the repaired fuel line had all been part of the mystery restoration. He never did get to find out who had so expertly rebuilt the engine, or indeed why it had been done.

Boyle knew which side his bread was buttered and quickly decided not to ask any questions about the mystery bikers. Weeks later he realised that his outside security lights were not working. He soon remedied the problem by simply switching them back on in the boathouse, but he did wonder what exactly had gone on. All in all, Boyle came out of the events well. His only minor gripe related to the awful stain on his tarmac which no amount of jet-washing would remove. "Looks like someone's thrown-up," he said.

Brice Guaire and his wife could have added to the local gossip with tales of gunshots, helicopter landings and burning cars, but they never spoke about the incident again. They later invested a large sum into the caravan park, turning it into a thriving business. They'd never had time for chit-chat and inevitably word went around that perhaps they'd won the pools.

MI5 Agent Sheila Jennings survived her gunshot wound and made it back to active service within eight months.

The situation regarding the cause of death of Dr Geoffrey Fry was not reinvestigated. The toxicology reports on his post mortem samples showed no signs of nerve agent. The laboratory tests on the clock devices also proved that they were designed for once-only use as an assassination weapon. All of the Sarin gas in the tiny capsule would be expelled during the activation and so if it had killed Mr Fry it could not have killed Angela Hewitt. This was a relief to Taylor as he'd already accepted that there would be little to be gained by reopening that part of the case. He didn't want Kim to have to go through such an ordeal.

In September 1991, on the instructions of the Lord Chief Justice a single inquest investigated the accumulated deaths connected to the affair. A Judge of the High Court acting as Coroner presided over the affair. The entire proceedings were held in-camera at an unknown location. The documents and verdicts remain protected from access by members of the public under the Thirty Year Rule.

The Lord Chancellor's Advisory Council added a caveat to the thirty year ruling:

If after the expiration of the thirty years, the release of the documents was deemed likely to cause damage to the country's image, national security or foreign relations then a further time limit should be imposed.

Benedict Cappelli's injuries required stitches to the top of his head. He remained uneasy for months afterwards fearing that he would be prosecuted for his criminal actions involving Lenny Gill and the baker's credit card but he never was.

He tried on several occasions over the years to use the story as a major newspaper exposé. But as no public records could be accessed which substantiated his claims he considered that fiction might be a better outlet. He has not yet published.

Gruinard Island underwent examination for the presence of the anthrax bacterium soon after the matter. Junior defence Minister, Michael Newton, visited the island in December 1991. He formally announced its safety and arranged removal of the warning signs. The Ministry of Defence later allowed the heirs of the original owner to repurchase the island for £500 which was the price paid by the Government in 1942.

The identity of Tremaine's buyer for the long life VX formula was never fully established. The dead man's carefully prepared dual identity had been backed up with an authentic passport recovered from his sodden jacket. A one-way air ticket to Malaga in Spain, also recovered would have taken him on his way that same afternoon from Glasgow's Prestwich airport.

It would be December 1992, before a clue to Alexander Tremaine's paymaster was teased from an informant. The teasing took place at the hands of operatives of the American Central Intelligence Agency. It followed the capture of a number of al Qaeda terrorists at Aden Airport in Yemen as they prepared to launch rockets at US military planes.

One of the terrorists, Hassan Ghul, mentioned Tremaine by name and knew of his connection to biological weapons. It created the possibility of a tenuous link between Tremaine and al Qaeda. The strength of Ghul's inside knowledge and of his connections to the right people were not accepted until many years later. He was to become the chief informant behind the much later assassination of the group's leader – Osama bin Laden.

After the initial close of the case Doug Taylor was promoted to Detective Chief Inspector in the Stafford police division. Kim Harding transferred from Devon and Cornwall Police to start at Little Stoneleigh CID in Staffordshire as a Detective Sergeant. Their return to the investigation of organised crime and murder would be a little mundane after this case – or would it?

The End

Please read on for some more interesting detail on the story.

Endnotes

MANY FACETS of the storyline within Guardian of Lies are based upon true events, real places and people who did exist.

Porton Down

Porton Down near to Salisbury in Wiltshire has been the HQ of Britain's chemical and biological military defence since its first beginnings during WW1. The area surrounding the 7000 acre site is identified on maps as a Danger Area.

The facility has had various different names over the years and is currently known as the Dstl (Defence Science and Technology Laboratory). It is an executive agency of the Ministry of Defence and is one of the United Kingdom's most secret government military research facilities. It now specialises in the fields of chemical, biological, radiological and nuclear defence.

At nearby Winterbourne Gunner lies the chemical-biological-radiological-nuclear (CBRN) training facility.

During WW2, research at Porton Down concentrated on nitrogen mustard, the use of anthrax and botulinum as biological weapons. When the Allied armies penetrated Germany, they discovered operational stockpiles of munitions and weapons containing new chemical warfare agents. These included highly toxic organophosphorus nerve agents which were then unknown to Britain and the Allies. When World War II ended, the advanced state of German technology regarding these nerve agents, including Sarin came as a surprise. The Allies were eager to capitalise on it. Eventually the German nerve agents were used as a starting point and the deadly nerve agent VX was developed at Porton Down in 1952.

In the late 1940s and early 1950s, research and development at Porton Down was aimed at providing Britain with the means to arm itself with a modern nerve agent-based capability and to develop specific means of defence against these agents. In the end these aims came to nothing as an offensive weapon due to the decision to abandon any sort of British chemical warfare capability.

Various conventions and treaties came into effect from 1969 onwards which Britain signed up to. These effectively banned our production and stockpiling of biological and chemical weapons, only allowing for infinitesimal amounts of such substances to be created. Even these can only be used for research.

Many countries are known to have ignored the strict controls banning the mass production of chemical and biological weapons. This feature makes the continuing work at Porton Down hugely important. Much of the work today is confined to antidotes, neutralising agents and protective clothing. The destruction of ancient chemical weapons recovered from earlier battle sites also forms an important part of the work along with research into vaccines and therapeutics.

Many experiments were carried out at Porton Down during the forties, fifties and sixties involving human guinea pigs. Volunteers for this were usually servicemen encouraged to take part with the offer of a small monetary payment and a few days leave. At least one fatality is recorded: In 1953 Leading Aircraftman Ronald Maddison died within minutes of having a tiny bead of Sarin dropped onto his skin.

Dozens of other stories of human guinea pig tests involving LSD, CS gas, Kyasanur Forest Monkey disease, plague, smallpox, anthrax and polio exist and the testimonies of many people are recorded with several claiming to have suffered life shortening illnesses.

Sarin and VX

Sarin is a nerve agent, an organophosphorus liquid used as a chemical weapon. It was discovered in 1938 by German scientists who were trying to create stronger pesticides. The Germans arranged mass production of the substance for wartime use. About ten tons was created and some Sarin nerve agent was incorporated in artillery shells. Fortunately the allied forces overran the Germans before they had the opportunity to use any.

VX or venomous agent X, is another chemical compound of the organophosphorus class. It acts in the same way as sarin but is many, many times more potent.

Under normal circumstances both sarin and VX have a short shelf life of not much more than a few years. Sarin evaporates very quickly following exposure to air leaving no trace. Death from Sarin can often only be proven from changes made to the blood of the victim.

Sarin has been quite widely used over the years both to assassinate individuals and for mass extermination. Chile has used it and Saddam Hussein used it to kill up to 5000 people in the Halabja attack against Kurdish people on March 16th 1988.

In 1994 eight people were killed with Sarin and 200 injured in the Japanese Matsumoto incident. Another twelve died in 1995 during the Tokyo subway attack. At least two attacks have taken place in Syria the most recent being the April 2017, Khan Shaykhun attack where at least seventy-four people were killed and over 500 injured.

VX has very rarely been used to kill. Proven instances are almost unheard of. On February 13 2017 Kim Jong-nam the half-brother of North Korean leader Kim Jong-un died after an assault in Kuala Lumpur airport in Malaysia. Traces of VX were found on the victim's face and one of the attackers suffered VX type symptoms.

Government Sponsored Assassinations

Over the years bizarre government sponsored assassinations have taken place, often using the most audacious and horrific methods. Devices contrived for this purpose make the antics of a James Bond movie seem tame.

In 1978 Bulgarian dissident writer Georgi Markov died in a London hospital. Markov had defected to Britain and was working as a broadcaster and journalist for the BBC. He was taken ill after an incident at a bus stop near to Waterloo Bridge where he later recalled being jabbed by a passer-by with the point of an umbrella. The incident was initially dismissed by him as being unconnected to his illness.

He died four days later. The minute injury to his leg which was nothing more than a pin prick was examined and it was found that a miniscule, well-engineered metal sphere had been injected into his right thigh. The object contained the deadly poison Ricin. It was later established beyond doubt that the murder had been carried out by the Bulgarian Secret Police assisted by the Soviet KGB.

Another notable and similar incident also occurred on British soil in November 2006. The victim on this occasion was former Russian FSB secret service officer Alexander Litvinenko. Litvinenko had fled to the UK and had been granted asylum after several fall-outs with his Russian masters.

He was taken ill on November 1st 2006 and hospitalised in London. As his condition deteriorated MI6 officers and police were called to his bedside. Although sinking fast from his then undiagnosed illness, he started to go over his recent movements and contacts. He died four days later but not before it was discovered that he had been poisoned by a deadly radioactive substance – Polonium 210.

A comprehensive police investigation followed which involved nuclear scientists and assistance from MI5 and MI6. In short it was established without any doubt that Litvinenko had been murdered by two named Russian FSB officers. A cup of tea which he drank in a London hotel had been laced by the men with the deadly substance.

At a public enquiry in January 2015 it was also concluded that the order to carry out the murder had been personally given by Vladimir Putin.

Gruinard Island

Gruinard Island is a real place with a real history. Its location is, as described in the story, at a latitude/longitude coordinate of *57° 53 N by 5° 28 W*. It sits off the western coast of Scotland and is an island of the Inner Hebrides.

During WW2 following information that the Germans were developing anthrax bombs to use against Britain, the remote island was used as a test bed for research into a similar weapon. The 1942 tests did not result in such an armament being used, but so contaminated the island with the deadly disease that it was declared dangerous to all mammal forms of life for many years.

The eventual project to decontaminate the island did not take place until 48 years later. That action was code named *Operation Dark Harvest* and used 280 tonnes of the chemical, formaldehyde mixed with 2000 tonnes of seawater. It was a success and the island was then sold back to the heirs of the original owners for £500 which was the original price paid in 1942 by the government.

MI5 & MI6

Britain's Security Service has been known publicly as MI5 for many years although in tighter circles the label, *Box 500* is used. This name stems from a previous, now defunct, Post Office box number which used to apply to its headquarters. MI5 comes under the authority of the Home Secretary.

The actual title MI5 originates from the fact that the organisation was originally Section 5 of the Government's Military Intelligence Department. There were many "Military Intelligence" (MI) sections from 1 upwards. MI1 was responsible during WW1 for codebreaking whilst MI2 and 3 had responsibility for different countries. MI4 looked after photographic development and aerial reconnaissance whilst MI5 had, and still does have responsibility for domestic intelligence and security.

Many of the MI sections have since become obsolete but the two which still remain operational and are familiar to us are MI5 and MI6. Whilst MI5 deals with domestic problems MI6 is concerned with foreign intelligence and security (these are our spies).

Special Branch

Special Branch is a label customarily used to identify units responsible for matters of national security and intelligence in British police forces. The people employed in these units are police officers, usually detectives and each of Britain's police forces will have a Special Branch department. Special Branch comes under the wing of the Criminal Investigation Department (CID). A police force's Special Branch acquires and develops intelligence of a political or sensitive nature. It conducts investigations to protect the state from perceived threats of subversion, particularly terrorism and other extremist political activity. Police Special Branch liaise and work regularly with MI5.

Book Codes

Book codes or book ciphers like the one used in Guardian of lies (The Island of Adventure) have been used for many years to protect secret messages. More complex versions were extensively used by both sides particularly during WW2.

The first edition hardback copy of Enid Blyton's "The Island of Adventure" (1944) from my own collection was used to formulate the code details as featured in Guardian of Lies.

Mobile Telephones

The first mobile phone call was made in 1985 when comedian Ernie Wise called from London to Vodafone's offices in Newbury Berkshire. Things moved rapidly along as the individual devices became smaller and more reliable. The network coverage slowly grew and became more extensive. It was many years before some of the outlying areas of the UK were included and even now large holes still remain where there is no cover.

The tracking of mobile phones has been something that police and security services were quick to identify as a useful tool. Security agencies of other countries also quickly got to grips with this feature. The use of mobile phone technology is recognised by police and security services throughout the world as the most fundamental and reliable method of bugging and tracking. It is also made use of regularly by terrorists as a reliable remote detonation trigger for explosives.

Russian/Soviet Agents and Scientists

On 25th December 1991 the last Soviet leader, Mikhail Gorbachev resigned and the remaining twelve constituent republics emerged from the dissolution of the Soviet Union as independent post-Soviet states. Although the Soviet Union had then become "Russia" it seemed that in relation to murder and espionage, spying and double agents, little was to alter.

Alexander Kouzminov, a former KGB top operative now lives in New Zealand. He discloses in his fascinating book, *Biological Espionage*, and also in his interview with the Californian Literary Review some of the clandestine activities involving the Soviet (now Russian) government concerning the use of chemical and biological weapons.

He explains the use of Soviet (now Russian) Illegals and Sleeper Agents living for many years in target countries in high powered important roles, often as husband and wife teams. Indeed he specifically gives the code names of a husband and wife team (Illegals) ROSA and ROMAN. Rosa was actually employed as a research Microbiologist and worked in a government scientific research institute not far from London specialising in dangerous pathogens.

Kouzminov also discloses that covert sabotage operatives prepared secret sites where phials of deadly substances would be left, (dead drops) ready to poison western Military establishments (Ben Fenton The Telegraph 12 Feb 2005).

Vladimir Pashnick is mentioned in Guardian of Lies. Pashnick was a senior Soviet biologist and bioweaponeer who defected to the UK in 1989 and alerted Western Intelligence to Moscow's huge clandestine biological warfare programme. He went on to work for the British at Porton Down for many years and died in Wiltshire in 2001. He is believed to have died from natural causes although there is little doubt that the Soviets (Russians) would have preferred an alternative.

Ossie Dennis

Ossie (Oswald Dennis) inspired the character of that name in Guardian of Lies. He was a homeless man who I became acquainted with during my early years as a police officer in Stoke on Trent.

Ossie was not a knight of the road in the truest sense of the phrase as he spent most of his time in and around Stoke on Trent. He was a pleasant, humorous and intelligent man with a military background and a surprisingly diverse wealth of knowledge He was a chronic alcoholic, but a joy to speak with during his infrequent sober moments.

oOo

Now that you have read Guardian of Lies why not look into the stories behind the story. Go to the author's website www.cathedraloflies.com and enter the code given below. It will open secret pages and enhance the experience of reading the book with details and photographs of the places, the buildings, the vehicles and the real events which took place and which inspired the author's imagination. It will also reveal some of the truth behind this fictional story and give details of my other books.

CODE: germ-warfare

Remember the code is both case and character sensitive, so don't forget the mid-word dash.

If you have enjoyed Guardian of Lies or any of my books can I ask you to spare a little time by adding a review to the amazon website. Those good reviews are the lifeblood of books and without them little known authors would fail. The positive feedback makes the months and sometimes years of research and writing worth the effort.

40465945R00240

Printed in Poland
by Amazon Fulfillment
Poland Sp. z o.o., Wrocław